A dedicated reader and scribbler all her life, **ROSIE JAMES** completed her first novel (sadly unpublished) before reaching her teens. Significant success came much later, and over the last twelve years newspaper and magazine articles, short stories and romantic novels followed under her other pen name Susanne James. Rosie's four family sagas were the next stage, the plots reflecting her fascination with the human condition – how different, yet how alike we all are. And in every story one thing is guaranteed – a happy ending.

The War Girls

ROSIE JAMES

ONE PLACE. MANY STORIES

HQ
An imprint of HarperCollins*Publishers* Ltd
1 London Bridge Street
London SE1 9GF

www.harpercollins.co.uk

HarperCollins*Publishers*
1st Floor, Watermarque Building, Ringsend Road
Dublin 4, Ireland

This paperback edition 2021

4
First published in Great Britain by
HQ, an imprint of HarperCollins*Publishers* Ltd 2021

ISBN: 978-0-00-838695-5

MIX
Paper from
responsible sources
FSC www.fsc.org **FSC™ C007454**

This book is produced from independently certified FSC™ paper
to ensure responsible forest management.

For more information visit: www.harpercollins.co.uk/green

Printed and Bound in the UK using 100% Renewable Electricity at
CPI Group (UK) Ltd

For my loyal readers who get in touch with a word of praise - the essential oxygen for writers.

Chapter 1

June 1939

Abigail lay perfectly still, not wanting to disturb her daughter who was fast asleep beside her. It was not yet five o'clock, but pale sunlight was already getting stronger, infiltrating a gap between the flimsy, partly drawn curtains.

Now that her plan was about to happen, Abigail felt a sense of strange weightlessness, as if she might float away with nothing to hang on to. But she had no doubts. She was nineteen years old. It was time to go.

But first, she must inform her aunt of her plans and Abigail knew that the reaction would be scathing and critical. Because that was Aunt Edna's way. It always had been.

Their isolated cottage, named 'Coopers', was one of the most remote in the vicinity. Nestling deep in the Somerset valley, for many years the place had been run as a small holding, and after the death of their parents the young Edna and Arnold Wilson had carried on rearing the chickens and goats, growing the long field of vegetables and tending all the trees in their orchard. The soil was rich and provided a reasonable living so long as they worked from dawn to dusk and the same had been expected of

Abigail. Long before she'd started school she'd washed the dishes – standing on a little stool to reach the sink – she'd fed the chickens, milked the goats, picked all the raspberries and strawberries, her aunt always criticising, never praising her.

They had no near neighbours, no one ever came to visit, and their only form of transport was the pony and trap which Edna drove to take their produce to the village on market day. When Abigail started school, and for all the years that followed, she'd always walked the two-mile journey alone, and was never given a lift in the trap, even when it was cold and wet.

Arnold had had a mild nature and had found it hard to stand up to his domineering sister, and although Abigail couldn't remember her mother, she'd had a doting father for the few years fate had allowed. Sadly, owing to the effects of mustard gas while he'd served in the Great War, his lungs never recovered and in 1930, he'd passed away. Abigail had been ten years old.

But she'd always known that Dada had loved her dearly, and with any money he'd managed to earn, and the little he'd saved, he'd bought her books and games. Each night before she went to sleep, they'd play cards or do a jigsaw and always told each other their secrets. And however late it was, Dada loved to hear her read, so that before she'd started at the village school, Abigail was almost fluent.

And as well as all that, he'd taught her how to draw and paint, and she'd soon learned how to make just a few lines on a page turn into a picture you could recognise and bring to life. 'Pictures tell stories, Abigail,' he'd once said. 'And practice makes perfect, so keep practising because you will find it gives you solace.' Then he'd gone on to tell her that sometimes in the trenches during the war, he'd sit and draw things that he could see because it gave him peace. Other soldiers would make up poetry, or write long letters home, but he only wanted to draw. And, somehow, he'd been able to bring those pictures back with him and the little wad in the wax packet was among Abigail's most treasured possessions.

Now, very gently, she turned to gaze down at her daughter's

face, at the mass of dark ringlets tumbling on the pillow, at the long lashes resting on her cheeks, at the cherubic mouth, lips slightly parted as she breathed.

Emily Grace, Abigail's pride and joy, was just two and a half years old and thanks to Edna's constant demands and expectations was already another member of Coopers' hardworking team.

And that was the reason they would soon be leaving.

At last, Emily was about to be introduced to the world. She was not going to be hidden away like something to be ashamed of, as Edna had demanded when sixteen-year-old Abigail had confessed her state of health to her aunt. There had barely been a moment's silence before the torrent of abuse had begun.

'You vile, dirty creature,' Edna had spat out. 'How dare you bring shame on the house! Well, no one is ever going to know about this, do you hear me! It must be a secret, and eventually, when it gets older we'll just say we found the child wandering and gave it a home . . . that's what we'll do! But before that, it must be kept hidden away from respectable eyes and ears! You are a sinner! You have committed a grave sin, and God will not forgive you – and neither will I! Shame on you, and shame on the father of your bastard child!'

And the following year on a cold February day, it was Edna who'd delivered the baby in the downstairs room on a rug in front of the fire with no one else there to witness the event. It had been an uncomplicated birth, and true to type, from the very first, Edna refused to show any interest in the child.

The memory of that awful time caused the familiar lump to form in Abigail's throat. With no one to turn to she'd been forced to obey her aunt, but things were about to change. She lowered her head to gently place her lips on Emily's soft cheek.

How could anyone not love her precious daughter, and how could a beautiful child's existence be a shameful thing?

July 1934

It was Abigail's very last day at school and although she would have loved to stay on longer, her aunt would have none of it. 'You'll learn far more working on the land than wasting any more time with books, and drawing stupid, pointless pictures like your father did,' Edna had declared.

But Abigail had had a very special reason for wanting to delay leaving school and that was because of Luke.

Luke Jordan was the most handsome boy for miles around, and they'd sat next to each other in class for the last eighteen months.

About two years earlier, the Jordan family had come to live at the auspicious Mulberry Court, an elegant house on the outskirts of the village. The couple who owned it decided to rent the place out while they went travelling, and it was not very long before Mr and Mrs Jordan and their son Luke took up temporary residence.

And that was when Luke – a little older than Abigail – had started at the school and had been told to sit at the desk next to hers.

So on that warm, sultry afternoon in late July when the school year had finally come to an end, Abigail checked her desk for the very last time, making sure that she'd packed all her own precious books in her bag, leaving nothing behind for the next person who would sit there in her place. She sighed, trying hard not to cry.

Luke was standing there waiting for her, and as she came towards him, he automatically took her bag, slinging it over his shoulder, and together they left the building and began strolling away from the village.

He knew she was upset, and he glanced down. 'I'm going to walk you all the way back home this time, and you're not going to stop me,' he said softly.

She shook her head briefly but didn't reply, knowing that, as usual, they would part company at their own special, secret place down there by the river, tucked away from prying eyes, and a full mile from Coopers where strangers rarely set foot.

As soon as they were alone he took her hand. 'I know you're fed up about leaving,' he said, 'and I'm really going to miss you, Abigail. But look, it won't be that long before it'll be my time to clear off, too, and I expect we'll be going back to London to live. My college place awaits me, and after that, who knows?' He shrugged. 'University, I suppose. My father wants me to follow him into the Law, and I quite like the idea . . . if I'm clever enough. It might even be fun if I have to deal with thieves and murderers and horrible stuff!'

Abigail clutched his hand more tightly. 'Of course you'll be clever enough, Luke,' she said quietly. 'From the moment you arrived you always did better than the rest of us, coming top in all the tests.' She didn't want to go on, knowing that today really was the parting of their ways. Sadly, before very long, handsome, dark-eyed, dark-haired Luke would be in London doing brilliant things and meeting interesting people – interesting, beautiful *girls* – and she would still be at Coopers, obeying Aunt Edna.

Just then, as they crossed the small road which would lead them further into the countryside, a man on a bicycle appeared. It was a Wall's 'Stop me and buy one' ice-cream man, and he got off the bike, waving his hand and grinning cheerfully.

'Cornets? Wafers or tubs?' he said. 'Good job I saw you two a'fore I reach the village because this lot will soon be snapped up!' He blew out his cheeks. 'Hot today, in'it?'

Abigail shook her head. 'Sorry – I haven't got any money.' But Luke stepped forward.

'Two wafers, please,' he said, reaching into his pocket for some change. Wafers were their favourite.

The sudden distraction helped to break the downbeat feeling, and soon the pair were enjoying the deliciously cold ice cream as they strolled on.

'Thanks, Luke, for this,' Abigail said. 'Sorry I didn't have the cash to pay for myself.' But she needn't have apologised because he knew very well that she never had any money with her. She'd told him often enough that her aunt held the purse strings.

Luke paused for a moment. 'D'you know what I wish, Abigail?' he said. 'I wish that your chair could stay empty next year, rather than that anyone else should be sitting by me. Because we've got on really, really well. We've never fallen out, and we've always found something or other to laugh about. Well, we make each other laugh, don't we?

'I never expected to find anyone like you . . . a friend at school that I liked, I mean,' he went on. 'Of course, I knew I wasn't going to be there for very long in any case, but it is nice to have someone who you really enjoy being with, isn't it? Who you look forward to seeing each day.'

Abigail nodded, but didn't reply immediately. Everything he was saying was true. 'I've never had a friend, Luke. I didn't have any friends at all until you came.'

He looked down at her, frowning. 'Why do you say that?'

'Because it's a fact. Even when I was in the Infants I always seemed to be by myself and was never asked to join in the games at playtime. And it got worse in the upper classes when the others could be really spiteful.' She made a face. 'It's probably because of my aunt who everyone thinks is really a witch. And, to be fair, she does look a bit odd, always in her long black skirt, and that awful old apron she made out of a sack . . . and with her long hair tied back in a bow! I mean, honestly! Doesn't she realise how silly that makes her look? When she comes on market day, yelling out all the stuff she's got on the trap, everyone laughs at her. I've heard them enough times from the classroom – and when we're in the playground. And some of the kids shout out and call her names.'

Luke looked down at Abigail, slipping his arm around her waist. 'Poor you,' he said. 'You've been fighting a lone battle, and I wish I'd been with you all the time. I wouldn't have laughed at your aunt and I don't know why anyone should be unkind to you just because of her.'

'They probably think she's taught me how to cast spells and turn people into spiders and frogs,' Abigail said. Then she paused. 'The thing is, it's made me afraid that I will *never* have friends, that I don't know how to make friends, or that no one will *want* to be friends with me,' she added slowly.

Luke pulled her in closer to him. 'Of course, one day you will have friends, true friends, Abigail,' he said softly. 'Trust me – you will.'

Neither spoke for a few moments after that as they walked on slowly, their steps taking them across the field and down to the river. To their special place, the spot they always stopped before Luke retraced his steps and Abigail walked the last mile home alone. They sat down on the soft turf and Luke lay right back, stretching his arms above his head.

'I know you're never allowed to come back to the village after school,' he said, 'but surely your aunt would allow it just this once . . . It is your last day, after all, and they're showing *Treasure Island* at the WI hut tonight and tomorrow.' He turned to look up at Abigail who was sitting with her head resting on her bent knees. 'We've covered some of that book in English, haven't we?' he went on. 'And it would be great to see it at the cinema.'

Abigail didn't look up. 'It's no good, Luke,' she said, her voice muffled. 'You don't know what she's like. She'd make a terrible fuss if I even mentioned it.'

Luke frowned, irritated. 'Is this how it's going to be for the rest of your life, Abigail?' he said. 'Are you going to be stuck down at that place when you're fifty or a hundred? Aren't you ever going to make a run for it?'

Now she did raise her head and look down at him. 'I will escape one day, Luke,' she said firmly. 'When I'm grown up – when I'm no longer a child, I mean – the time will come when I will leave Coopers and never go there again.'

He pulled her slowly down towards him and they stayed close together in silence for a few moments. Then he leaned over and placed his lips on hers, gently at first, then with increasing longing.

And Abigail felt her whole body shiver with pleasure. Of course, they'd kissed many times as they'd walked home from school together, but it hadn't been like this. This was something different and she liked it. She turned to face him properly and he stroked her hair, twisting a curl gently between his fingers.

'You are beautiful, Abigail,' he said quietly. 'I am never going to meet anyone else who's got your sweet green eyes . . . and hair that looks like a splash of sunshine around your shoulders.'

'But you will, Luke,' Abigail said quietly. 'When you leave and go back to London and to college, beautiful girls will be falling at your feet. And you won't ever think of me again.'

She didn't want to go on because she knew she was going to sob. Her own words were like knife wounds, hurting and stinging. Because it was terrible to think that they were never going to meet again and even more terrible that someone else would be special to Luke Jordan. Someone he would want to kiss like he'd just kissed her.

In the languid summer heat, with just the occasional drone of a honey bee and the sound of the shallow river trickling at their feet, they lay in each other's arms, neither wanting to say anything else to disturb the enchantment of these special moments. Moments that were slipping away from them and which they knew would never return.

Then Luke raised himself on his elbow and gazed down into Abigail's eyes which he could see were wet with tears. 'I will *never* meet – or want – anyone but you, Abigail,' he whispered. 'And I will never love anyone else but you. I would never *want* to love anyone else. I give you my word.'

The time was passing all too quickly, and after a few moments Abigail disentangled herself from Luke's arms and got to her feet. 'I'll have to go,' she said reluctantly. 'My aunt will be waiting with a hundred and one jobs for me to do. And she'll be looking at the clock, wondering why I'm late.'

He stood and put his arm around her waist, pulling her towards him again. But Abigail moved away. 'Goodbye, Luke,' she said quietly. 'I am going to miss you . . . so much.'

His expression was dark as he gazed down at her. 'This is *not* goodbye,' he said, his tone unusually terse. 'Not if you don't want it to be, Abigail.'

What had he meant by that? Abigail asked herself as she trod swiftly across the fields towards the cottage. Had he meant that however hard it might be, it was up to her to free herself from the stranglehold of life at Coopers? So that they could be together again sometimes, if only for a few hours?

That thought put a spring in Abigail's step as she hurried home. Luke's words filled her with determination.

Now it was up to her.

Chapter 2

Early October that same year

Standing at the sink as she washed their breakfast porridge bowls, Abigail glanced back at her aunt.

'Aunt – why don't you let me take the trap to market today?' Abigail asked tentatively. 'It's very hot, isn't it, and you might like to stay home for a change.'

Edna glanced at her sharply. 'Why *ever* should I want to do that!' she said. 'You've never taken our stuff to market in your life and wouldn't have a clue as to how to get the best sales! Besides, the plums are nearly falling off the branches and are just right for harvesting . . . it's going to take some time to pick them and box them all up so that's what *you'll* be doing today!'

Abigail hadn't been to the village since the day she'd left school because Edna made sure there was never the time nor the need. The couple of occasions on which Abigail had ventured that she might like to go to the village had met with the usual objections. 'What for?' Edna always demanded. 'There's nothing for you up there anymore, and there isn't time for you to go skiving off when you're needed here.'

So, as usual, Abigail did what she'd always done: obeyed her aunt's wishes.

But today was going to be different Abigail assured herself as she put their dishes away, because she desperately wanted to see Luke! She couldn't wait a day longer! It had been ten whole weeks since they'd been together, ten whole weeks for her to go over and over that first, really passionate kiss they'd had, the kiss that had said so much.

And remembering Luke's last words to her, 'This is not goodbye. Not if you don't want it to be', Abigail had made her plans.

She would leave the cottage as soon as Edna left to go to market, and then take a roundabout route to the village. Once there, it would be easy enough to avoid her aunt noticing her, and anyway, once Edna had begun shouting her wares, she wouldn't have eyes or ears for anyone or anything else.

Even so, as Abigail watched the trap disappear around the bend, she felt her heart begin to race. She had to get to the village, see Luke and return to Coopers before her aunt came back. It should be easy enough, shouldn't it? But Abigail wasn't used to subterfuge and the first thing her aunt would do was to inspect what her niece had been doing, and the quantity of plums which had been piled into the huge boxes. Abigail made a face to herself. It was going to be a tight operation – but it would be worth it, just to see Luke again. And the thought that she would soon be gazing up into his black eyes, and hearing his calm, reassuring voice, gave Abigail the determination she needed.

Wearing a simple blue dress, and with her light cotton shawl around her shoulders, Abigail left the cottage and made her way swiftly along the hilly route she'd used many times before. The shawl was partly to cover her head and face in case she was recognised by anyone when she got to the village – anyone who might mention to her aunt that they'd seen her.

11

Within a very short time Abigail found herself among the large crowd gathered around all the stalls and, keeping her head well down, she skirted the edge of the market and almost ran towards the school. Of course, lessons would still be going on, but she knew that Luke usually went home for his lunch on Thursdays and the church clock had just struck twelve. Moving quickly now, she rounded the corner out of sight of the school and kept walking along the dusty road towards Mulberry Court knowing that soon she would see Luke making his way home, his easy stride swallowing up the comparatively short distance.

With her heart racing in anticipation, Abigail wondered whether to hide and jump out and surprise him . . . but no, she didn't want to do that. All she wanted to do was to see him and feel his arms around her again. The dreams that she dreamed every night were not enough. She needed to feel him close, to feel his heart against hers.

And suddenly there he was, walking towards her, his bag slung over his shoulder as usual. He seemed to be looking up at something in the sky, but then his gaze turned towards her and he saw her. Dropping his bag, he was beside her in an instant, throwing his arms around her, almost lifting her off her feet.

'Hey,' he said slowly, softly, 'how have you managed this? You haven't killed her, have you?'

Abigail laughed shakily. 'No – I've managed to escape but I haven't got long because I've got to get back to Coopers before my aunt returns from the market. I just had to see you, Luke. The last couple of months have seemed endless.'

'For me, too,' Luke murmured. 'I've walked down to Coopers twice hoping to catch you alone but your aunt was there right in the front and I didn't want to get you into trouble.' With his arm now tightly around Abigail's waist as they walked along, he looked down at her, the look in his eyes almost making her melt. 'Luckily, there's no one at home this afternoon,' he said, 'but my sandwiches will have been left for me – so we can share them in private – if you've got long enough.'

'I've got long enough,' Abigail said.

She had never been inside the house before, and Abigail felt as if she was entering another world. As they went through the richly carpeted hall into the kitchen, she was immediately aware of the rows of bright copper pans hanging above the Aga cooker, of rows and rows of expensive crockery on the tall dresser, of the huge jug of wild flowers placed on one wide window sill, everything shining with fragrant cleanliness. On the opposite side of the room were three full-length windows looking out onto a rolling lawn that seemed to go on for ever.

'What a beautiful garden, Luke,' Abigail said, and he nodded.

'Yes, there's a lot of it, which keeps the gardener busy,' he said. 'And just out of sight there's a summer house. Not that I've sat in it much,' he added, 'but my mother seems to like it.'

Abigail turned away, glancing at the scrubbed wooden table on which there was a tray covered with a white cloth, together with a crystal water jug and matching tumbler.

It seemed rude to go on staring, but Abigail couldn't help it – while thinking what a good job it was that Luke had never been to Coopers, and never would. What ever would he make of their primitive abode, their earthy surroundings?

He pulled out two chairs for them to sit side by side. Then he removed the white cloth to reveal a plate of neatly cut sandwiches which had leaves of moist watercress tucked between the layers, a china dish of chocolate biscuits and a bowl of fruit – apples, bananas and grapes. He grinned down at her.

'Our lunch,' he said. 'I think the sandwiches are ham, so get started while I fetch another tumbler and fill the jug.' He glanced back at her as he went over to the sink. 'The housekeeper has taken the day off to visit a cousin who's not very well,' he said, 'but she'll be back in time to make dinner for when my parents return from London.'

13

If she had been invited to eat at Buckingham Palace, Abigail couldn't have felt more honoured to be having her lunch here with Luke. Everything was so special. He was so special.

For the next ten minutes between mouthfuls, they exchanged news of what they'd been doing – though Abigail didn't have that much to reveal. But Luke kept making her laugh about things that had gone on at school: that there'd been a real fight in the playground, that the usual culprits regularly got the cane for talking in class and that Miss Jones who taught the Infants was leaving next year to get married.

But there was something more important that Abigail wanted to know.

'And . . . who is sitting next to you in class now, Luke?' she asked, and he shrugged.

'Derek – you remember Derek – but I hardly know him because he doesn't say anything. Not anything interesting or funny, anyway,' Luke replied. 'It's not the same at school without you, Abigail . . . I mean, it's just work and routine now, slightly boring to be honest.'

After a moment, Abigail said, 'I wish I was coming back there with you, now, this afternoon, Luke,' and he took her hand in his and looked down at her.

'You don't know how much I hate you not being there,' he said quietly. 'But at least you've found a way to get to the village incognito! That's a start, isn't it? When I saw you standing there as I turned the corner, I thought I was dreaming!' He bent slightly to brush his lips across her cheek. 'Do you think you'll be able to escape again? Soon?'

'I'll try,' Abigail murmured, loving the feel of his face against hers, 'but it can only be on a Thursday when my aunt is here at the market. And I'll always have to get back before she does.'

'True love never did run smooth,' Luke quoted softly. Then he moved their lunch things right away and pulled her in close to him. Then he kissed her and she kissed him back, properly . . .

Presently, like Cinderella hearing the midnight chime, Abigail heard the clock on the kitchen wall strike one, and she moved away, standing up quickly.

'I'll have to go,' she said. 'It'll take me half an hour to get back and I've got all those baskets to fill.'

He stood as well, reluctant to let her go. 'But – you will come here again, soon, won't you?' he said.

'I will do my very best, I promise,' Abigail said.

Chapter 3

Almost as if she knew something was going on, for the next few weeks Edna announced that she would be returning early from the market on Thursdays. 'This is always a busy time,' she'd said. 'As you know very well, Abigail, all the ground has to be cleared and dug and made ready for spring planting, so I'll cut it short in the village while there's still enough light for us to work by.'

So apart from two brief visits to the village just before Christmas, it wasn't until the following year that Abigail began a routine of seeing Luke for their treasured time together, when Edna stayed all afternoon at the market.

'I know it's difficult for you, but I wish you didn't always have to go back so soon,' Luke said regretfully. 'I mean, I could always find some excuse about being late for the afternoon session at school . . . and I'd love a bit longer for us to be together so that we could, you know, just talk about everything, like we used to.'

He was so right, Abigail had thought. Not only that, but he always held her in the way that only Luke Jordan knew how. Caressing her possessively as if to hold the rest of the world at bay and to tell everyone that she was his, and he was hers. And that nothing would ever change it.

*   *   *

It was one day in early April the following year that Edna imparted the news of the moment – Lillian, the vicar's sister, was gravely ill.

'Dear me,' Edna said as she and Abigail trudged down to the back field with their hoes and buckets. 'I do hope she recovers soon because she and the vicar have lived together all their lives and it would be so hard for him to do everything without her help and support.'

Abigail nodded. She remembered the vicar's sister who occasionally came to the school with him when he took morning prayers every Monday. 'I always thought she looked a very kind lady,' Abigail said.

'Hmm,' Edna said, 'I'm afraid that's a false hope – from what I've heard. Anyway,' Edna went on as she started hoeing her row, 'I shall go to the funeral, of course – which is sure to be a big affair, what with the two of them being so well known in the area.'

'But she's not gone yet, Aunt,' Abigail said. 'Her brother's prayers might save her.'

'Praying does not always do as you want it to,' Edna retorted. 'Or, rather, the word "No" is often the answer. Anyway, nothing we can do about it,' she went on as she continued with what she was doing. 'But at least I've got my black outfit ready to wear – the stuff I had to buy for your father's funeral, if you remember.'

But of course Abigail remembered Dada's funeral, and seeing Edna in her long black skirt and top, with a tiny little skull cap on her head . . . Goodness knows where she'd managed to find that, Abigail had thought at the time.

Two Thursdays later, Abigail repeated the heart-tightening operation of getting to and from the village unseen, but this time she had news for Luke.

Next Friday, the 1st of May at 4.30 p.m., Lillian's funeral was to take place and there would be a large gathering of faithful parishioners attending, invited to take tea and cake in the church hall afterwards. Edna was going to be there and did not expect to return to Coopers until perhaps seven o'clock.

'*No* one goes to a funeral by pony and trap!' she'd said, when Abigail had posed the question.

So on that Thursday when Abigail saw Luke coming towards her, she almost threw herself into his arms with the news. 'I can't believe it, Luke,' she said breathlessly. 'I have never known my aunt to be away from Coopers for that length of time! We shall have at least two hours . . . two whole hours . . . just to be together.'

Luke put his arm around Abigail's waist. 'And guess what?' he said. 'Not only is the housekeeper also going to the funeral, but my parents are in London that evening and won't be home until next morning!' He held her to him tightly. 'We shall have Mulberry Court to ourselves without interruption!'

When that special Friday in 1936 dawned, the weather was surprisingly warm for so early in May. And although the passing of the vicar's sister had little to do with them, Edna went about her usual duties with a very solemn look on her face, barely saying a word to Abigail but every now and then repeating, 'Dear, dear. God rest her soul.'

And despite feeling genuinely sorry about Lilian's death, Abigail could barely stop smiling. In just a few hours, she and Luke were going to be together. And this time with no urgent rush for her to get home – though she'd have to make sure she reached Coopers well before her aunt returned from the funeral tea.

Just after three o'clock, Edna came down the stairs in her mourning attire, and Abigail glanced up in surprise. Her aunt looked quite respectable out of her working clothes. She also seemed to have taken some trouble doing her hair, and the little skull cap perched on top looked quite nice . . . nicer than Abigail remembered it the last time it had been worn.

'You look very smart, Aunt,' Abigail said, and Edna pursed her lips.

'How I look is hardly the point of today,' she said, but Abigail knew the remark had pleased her aunt. 'One thing I am grateful for is that it's not raining,' Edna went on, 'because it's unpleasant walking to and from the village when it's wet.'

Abigail would love to have retorted – 'Don't you think *I* know that?' But she resisted the temptation. Her aunt was in a good mood, and obviously looking forward to her unusual afternoon out.

Keeping an anxious eye on the little clock on the shelf, Abigail saw that it was quarter to four. Enough time had passed since her aunt had left, and Abigail knew she could get to the village in twenty minutes. By that time all the mourners would be safely in church and out of the way. The coast would be clear.

Wearing the only pretty, flowery cotton skirt she possessed, and the pale blue top that went with it, plus her shawl loosely around her shoulders as usual, Abigail left Coopers and walked to the village. When she arrived it was eerily quiet and practically deserted. The curtains of any dwelling she passed were drawn tightly shut, the sultry warmth of the afternoon seeming to add to the sombre atmosphere.

But Abigail wasn't sombre – she was almost deliriously happy – and when she saw Luke waiting for her by the gate of Mulberry Court, his face wreathed in smiles, she automatically broke into a run to meet him. He ran forward, drawing her into his arms and closing his lips over hers.

'You look lovely,' he murmured.

She smiled up at him. Well, she had taken trouble to do her hair which was floating loose around her shoulders.

Then, with their arms around each other's waists, they walked slowly up the drive and into the house.

Luke nodded towards a plate of fancy cakes on the kitchen table. 'The housekeeper didn't want me to starve before she got back,' he said, 'and as you can see, there are plenty for the two of us.' He pulled out the two chairs. 'Shall I make us a pot of tea – or would you prefer something cold? There's a bottle of pop waiting to be opened.'

Abigail took the chair offered and gazed up at him. He was

wearing light, casual trousers and an open-necked, dark brown shirt, and his hair – with its usual wayward lock falling carelessly across his forehead – glinted and shone like polished ebony.

'I'd like a glass of pop, please, Luke,' she said.

He grinned. 'Yeah. Me too.'

Abigail half-smiled as she watched him. When they were together on those precious Thursdays, they always had so much to say in such a short time that their words would often tumble over each other, but now, today, they weren't saying much at all. Just revelling in being together, with no anxiety that she would be found out.

Abigail broke the silence. 'My aunt made a real effort to look the part for the funeral . . . she was a perfect vision dressed in black!'

'Good for her,' Luke said. 'Keeping up appearances, then.'

'It was quite something for her to get scrubbed up like that,' Abigail admitted, 'so perhaps she harbours a secret wish to be someone else, after all.' Abigail paused. 'We all have secret wishes, don't we, Luke?'

There was silence for a few moments, then he said, 'By the way, all the formal papers came yesterday about my college course – and, unusually, it's not going to start until November this year, which is rather late.' He glanced across. 'But until then at least I'll be home here for us to see each other – if and when we get the chance,' he added.

Abigail didn't say anything for a moment. The thought of Luke – her Luke – moving right away was something she didn't want to think about. No more occasional Thursdays to look forward to. No more anything to look forward to. 'Will you be in London?' she asked, and he nodded.

'I think the course starts there, but they apparently send students all over the place to other colleges from time to time during the whole procedure,' he said. 'A sort of movable feast, by the sound of it, which I hope I'm going to enjoy but I probably won't.' He glanced down and saw that her eyes had filled with tears.

'Come on,' he said lightly. 'Don't be sad, because that last cake is yours.' But Abigail shook her head.

'No thanks – you have it, Luke,' she said, cross with herself at feeling so terrible that he would be going away at the end of the year. After all, she'd always known that he would be furthering his education far, far away from this inauspicious village. But to be reminded that the time was fast approaching was painful. She stood up suddenly, picking up the empty plate and their glasses.

'It's such a perfect afternoon, Luke,' she said, trying to sound upbeat. 'I would love to look around the garden.' She glanced out of the window at the vast rolling lawn. 'We don't go in for much decorative planting at Coopers. There is never any room for things which do not produce food to sell,' she added ruefully.

They cleared up the tea things, then, hand in hand, they left the kitchen and began wandering along the grassy paths of the garden which seemed to go in every direction, Abigail stopping every now and then to inspect something which particularly took her fancy.

Out of sight of the house, they took a left turn and Luke said, 'Behold – the rose walk! My mother's particular interest.'

Abigail stared. It was like something out of a fairy tale. Numerous arches stood at regular intervals down the long path, all festooned with trailing foliage. Most of the flowers were still in tight bud but one or two were already opening their fragrant faces to the sunshine.

'How absolutely beautiful,' Abigail said, and Luke looked down.

'I was thinking the same thing,' he said, gazing at her.

Abigail blushed, and still holding hands they wandered past the rose trail and almost immediately came to the summer house Luke had mentioned the other day. Without saying another word, Luke reached into his pocket for his bunch of keys. Then he moved forward and opened the door.

'Come on, it's been all aired and freshened up for the summer,' he said, 'so we might as well have a sit down for a few minutes and admire the view from inside.'

Going in first, Luke immediately went over to the canvas garden chairs which were stacked neatly against one wall. Setting two of them up, he pushed one towards Abigail before sitting down on the one next to her.

Putting her head back and half-closing her eyes, Abigail said, 'I may fall asleep in a minute – so I hope you won't mind.'

'You're hardly likely to fall asleep sitting up like that,' Luke said. 'Oh, I know.' Then he got up and went over to the other side of the room, bringing back a striped sun lounger which he opened up in front of her. 'Here, try this for size,' he said. 'It's actually quite comfortable.'

Abigail did as he suggested, then lay back outstretched, and sighed contentedly as she felt the gentle breeze from the open door begin to fan her face. 'This is heavenly,' she murmured, turning to look at him, 'but I feel really mean having the only bed.'

Without any hesitation he got up. 'Move over a bit, then,' he said.

Then he stretched out beside her, and soon they were entwined in each other's arms.

'This seems the perfect moment for me to make something absolutely clear to you, Abigail Wilson,' Luke said softly. 'Because I promise you now, that when I am earning enough money to support you, I shall arrive at Coopers and snatch you away from your aunt for ever.'

Abigail turned to gaze into his eyes. If only that could be true. But the chances of Luke Jordan being able to escape the charms of other women were slight because he was simply irresistible. And he was going to be away, he'd said, for three or four years. What hope did *she* have when she wouldn't even be there to compete with the attractive women he was bound to spend time with?

He raised himself on one elbow and gazed down at her. 'You do believe me, don't you?' he said, and she smiled up at him, her eyes moist.

'I believe you, Luke,' she said, though she was really thinking, *I want to believe you, Luke.*

Then his lips closed over hers, more urgently this time, and Abigail responded readily as his hands began to trace her soft curves beneath her clothes. And then, without any sense of shame, she helped him undress her. It sent her pulse racing and her heart soaring.

'I love you, Abigail,' he whispered, 'and I will never love anyone else, ever. I give you my word.'

Cruelly, fate decreed that for the rest of that month Abigail could only get to the village once to see Luke. But it had been worth it because, without either of them putting it into words, their relationship had changed. Now, the sense that they really belonged to each other filled them with a warmth which was different from anything they'd felt before.

But it wasn't until the middle of July that Abigail realised the plight she was in.

Getting out of bed, she drew back the curtains and stared out at the familiar scene. The scene that never changed. But something else *had* changed. Something had changed in her.

Standing back, she placed her hands lightly over her tummy, feeling for something, anything. How did you feel the tiny beginnings of a baby? Having seen the goats giving birth to their kids many times, and from everything she'd read in her books, Abigail had a good idea about reproduction, and she knew that it took nine months for a human baby to emerge into the world. But how did you look – and what did you *feel* – during those months?

Well, how was she to know? All she did know was that she'd missed last month and was late for this one – the first time ever. And the realisation filled Abigail with absolute terror. Because when her aunt was told, Abigail would be thrown out of Coopers and she'd have nowhere to live and nowhere to go.

And that was why she would have to tell Luke, soon. She would go tomorrow, Thursday, and break the news. He would find ways to look after her and their baby because he would never leave her to face this by herself, she knew he wouldn't.

'Can I help you?' A man's gruff voice from behind the hedge at Mulberry Court made Abigail look up, startled.

'Oh no – thank you,' she replied quickly. 'I'm just waiting for someone – waiting for Luke Jordan. He should be home in a minute.'

Coming into full view, the man stared at her over the gate. 'Well, you're going to be disappointed, luvver,' he said. 'The Jordans don't live here anymore.'

Abigail's mouth dropped in surprise. 'What . . . what do you mean?' she said. 'Where are they living now?'

He shrugged. 'I'm only the gardener keeping the place tidy until the owners take up residence,' he said, 'but what I was told was that the Jordans had gone back to London and then someone said the lady and the young lad have gone to France for a few months – where they've got a place in the south, so I believe.' The man made a face. 'A'wight for some, innit – but the lady hadn't been too well, so I heard.'

Feeling as if the ground beneath her was going to melt away and suck her down and down, Abigail just stood for a moment trying to take in this terrible news.

'Well, thank you,' she said faintly, turning to go.

As she retraced her steps along the road and past the school, keeping well away from the market, Abigail tried desperately to let the news she'd just been given sink in. Luke had obviously left school a couple of weeks before the end of term to accompany his mother – so now he was further away from Abigail than he'd ever been. He was never to know that they were to have a baby . . . and they would never see each other again.

Stopping for a moment to regain her breath, Abigail paused in her thoughts. Her first impulse, her first instinct, had been to tell Luke – but now she wasn't so sure. Would he *mind* that she was pregnant? Anyway, how could he be a proper father to their baby when he was away at college – and what on earth would his parents think when they found out? They would surely be angry at the situation and the last thing Abigail wanted was to do anything to harm Luke – to harm his chances of graduating and fulfilling the career which had been decided for him.

Abigail put her hand to her mouth, tormented by sudden guilt. Why hadn't she stopped to think what this news would undoubtedly mean to Luke? She knew that he loved her – he'd said so over and over again – but he was in no position to provide a home for her . . . not yet! It wasn't the right time for them. It was too soon!

Abigail straightened her shoulders defiantly, even though her heart was at breaking point. She was going to have this baby – she was going to *love* this baby – and conquer whatever troubles lay ahead.

And telling her aunt was going to be the first hurdle.

That thought made Abigail pause, holding her sides for a second. Well, hadn't Luke told her that she was bright and clever and funny and that if she really wanted something, it was up to her? That if she was determined enough, she could change her life to however she wanted it to be?

Well, one day, Abigail would prove his words.

But she would never see the long letter he had addressed to her because it had slipped from the postal tray on the hall table and had become trapped, right out of sight, under a corner of the sturdy cabinet alongside.

Chapter 4

June 1939

'Come on, Emily, it's time to wake up,' Abigail said softly. 'The chickens want their breakfast, and there will be lots of eggs for you to collect.'

Emily sat up, rubbing her eyes and yawning, and Abigail hugged her tightly, the endearing scent of her little girl's warm body filling her with the usual enchantment.

It was six o'clock, and Abigail quickly got herself dressed, then helped Emily button up her liberty bodice and put on her frock. Presently they went downstairs where Edna was stirring the porridge. She barely looked up as they entered, merely nodding a greeting, and soon they were all sitting at the table to begin their breakfast.

Abigail was about to drop her bombshell. It was not going to be easy to break the news to her aunt, but it had to be today, Wednesday, because tomorrow was market day and Edna would have the best chance of acquiring extra help. And then it would be Friday – the very last one in which Abigail and her daughter would wake up at Coopers. And the first one of their new lives.

They ate in comparative silence until Edna said, without

looking up, 'The back field must be cleared this morning because all the vegetables are just right for market – you can pack them in those new boxes I managed to buy cheap last week.'

It was the peremptory tone, the familiar, terse instruction that gave Abigail the courage to speak out. She turned to look down at Emily who had finished the last of her porridge and was sitting quietly swinging her legs. Young as she was, she'd learned how to read the situation, whether it was better to keep quiet rather than chatter endlessly to her mother as she usually did.

Abigail smiled down at her. 'You go and collect the eggs, now, darling,' she said, 'because I want to talk to Aunt Edna for a moment.'

'Goody goody,' Emily said, jumping down from her chair. She loved putting her hands into the warm straw to find the eggs. It was her favourite job.

'And mind you don't break any,' Edna said to Emily's departing back, 'like you did last week.'

That was all that Abigail needed; she turned to look straight at her aunt.

'I have something very important to say to you, Aunt,' she said firmly, as Edna stood up to collect their three dishes.

'Oh? Well, hurry up about it because there's a lot to do this morning.'

Abigail didn't beat about the bush. 'You need to know that Emily and I are leaving Coopers on Friday,' she said quietly, 'and we won't be coming back.'

That stopped Edna in her tracks, and she stared at Abigail. After a long silence, she said, 'What ever are you talking about? And where on earth do you think you're going?'

'We are going to seek a new life, Aunt, where I can show my daughter that there is something other than this. Where we can be happy. Where she can grow up among other people and find out about things, do things. And where she will have friends . . . friends to play with.'

'Oh, really?' Edna said sarcastically. 'And how are you going to

27

achieve all that? You have no money, no experience of the outside world that you seem so anxious to be part of. You'll never make anything of yourself out there because what have you got to offer? And your daughter will be nothing but a millstone around your neck, I can promise you that! And I should know – personal experience taught me a hard lesson!'

Abigail bit back the retort that was forming on her lips, but said patiently, 'Emily and I will make our way together, come what may, Aunt. And I do have a little money – enough to see us through until I find myself work.'

Leaning forward with both fists on the table, Edna's eyes narrowed. 'Oh? And where did you get that money from?'

'It was what Dada gave me on each of my birthdays,' Abigail said calmly. 'And he impressed on me that I should save it because I was sure to need it one day.'

For a moment, Edna said nothing. 'And I suppose you're going to seek your fortune in one of the towns along the way?'

'No – I thought we might try our luck somewhere bigger . . . perhaps Bristol,' Abigail said, 'where there are more opportunities.'

'*Bristol?* But what *work* do you intend looking for? What experience have you had other than what you've learned here?'

'I don't care what it turns out to be,' Abigail said quickly, 'but it will be one for which I shall be paid money. And you're right, Aunt, I've learned many things which will be of use to someone who will *pay* me to do them.' Abigail swallowed. 'I have worked hard at Coopers, all my life, long days, long hours, and you have never given me a single penny to call my own.'

'Ha!' Edna said. 'Well, I have given you a roof over your head and food in your belly and clothes on your back – and now the same for the child! That is surely payment enough, isn't it?'

Abigail let a moment pass. 'And I will always be grateful, Aunt, but you have trapped me like a bird in a cage. And every bird eventually wants freedom . . . even if it's far worse outside. Birds have to fly, *need* to fly . . . I have to fly! And I'm going to make sure that Emily, too, will escape to spread her wings.' Abigail pressed her lips together before going on. 'My daughter is going to live her life without shame. Everyone is going to know that there are just the two of us, that there have always been just the two of us. And I am going to teach my little girl to hold her head up and face the world with courage.'

Edna stood back. 'Well, I think you're absolutely mad and you're turning out just like your father!' She folded her arms. 'My brother was always a dreamer, and he only volunteered to serve in that war because he thought it would be more exciting than staying here, and what did it do for him? It killed him! Oh, he came home, eventually, but not the strong, healthy lad he'd always been. If he'd listened to me, he'd be here now, today, instead of lying up there in the churchyard, no use to anybody.'

Those bitter words hit Abigail like a hammer blow, and she stood up defiantly. 'Whatever Dada did, he would have done it because he thought it was right,' she said. 'You can think of it differently, but Dada and I talked to each other, and he told me the things he believed in.' Abigail choked back her tears. 'He told me that by volunteering he'd thought he could help. That it had been his duty.'

'Well then, let's talk about duty!' Edna spat out. 'Your duty to *me* and the fact that you have always had a home here and enough of everything and—'

'But it was also Dada's home, wasn't it,' Abigail interrupted, 'and he would have expected me to live here for as long as I needed to.'

Edna pursed her lips. She could see that Abigail had made up her mind. 'And have you given *any* thought as to how I am going to manage here on my own?' she said coldly.

'Yes, I have, Aunt,' Abigail said, 'Tomorrow is market day, the perfect opportunity for you to find anyone looking for work, and there will be plenty of choice.' That was true. Thursdays always drew people to the village in large numbers, selling or buying produce, or those seeking temporary or permanent employment in the fields or on the farms. 'Of course, you will have to pay them,' Abigail went on, 'but perhaps you could employ two youngsters, instead of an adult. That would be cheaper because children will agree to work hard for very little.' Abigail had often heard older boys in the playground talking of work they'd done at the weekends for which they were never paid more than a few pennies or a shilling.

Edna shook her head in silent disbelief. Then, slowly – 'Have you any idea, any idea at all,' she said, 'as to what is going to face the pair of you? You are going to be *homeless*! And at a time when the country will soon be at war again! *War*, Abigail! Nothing is going to stop it now! Did you consider *that* when you decided to go and live in an industrial city?'

Abigail shrugged briefly. How could she have considered something she was ignorant of? Very little news of any kind found its way to Coopers. 'I am sure that Emily and I are going to be all right, Aunt,' she said. 'And whatever happens, we'll find a way to look after ourselves.'

Just then, Emily trotted back in and went straight over to her mother. 'I've put all the eggs into the little boxes and the chickens were very pleased to see me.' She smiled up at Abigail. 'Can we give them their breakfast now?'

'That's exactly what we're going to do,' Abigail said, 'and then there are all those vegetables to be dug up, so there's no time to waste.' She looked across at Edna who remained stony-faced. 'Just give me a list, Aunt, of anything more you need us to do, and of course, Emily and I will be here tomorrow as well, to do everything as usual. I wouldn't want to leave too much for the new helper, or helpers to tackle. It will take them a little time to get used to everything.' *To get used to you*, Abigail would like to have said.

Early on Friday morning Abigail woke with a start. She hadn't slept well, her mind going over and over her plans, trying to reassure herself that the massive step she was taking was the right one for them. She'd nearly gone mad asking herself that question, but how did anyone know if a huge change in their life was taking place at the right time? Surely, in the end it had to be a matter of trusting your instincts?

Yet with every doubt that crept into her mind, Abigail could hear her father's reassuring voice telling her to always have faith in herself. 'In the end, we must all stand up for what we believe in,' he'd said gently, 'With determination – and a little bit of luck thrown in – you can change things in your life if you really want to. Remember that, Abigail.'

Thinking about those words now, Abigail realised that it must surely have been his wish that one day she should strike out on her own. And that thought made her heart soar with optimism. She *knew* she had the determination.

All she and her tiny daughter needed was the little bit of luck . . .

At that moment, Emily sat up, immediately wide awake. 'We're going on a big puffer train today, Mummy, aren't we?' she said eagerly. 'And we're taking dolly with us, aren't we?'

'Of course we are!' Abigail exclaimed. 'I've packed all our clothes, and there are bags to carry. They're not very heavy.'

And how could the bags be heavy when they had so few possessions? They had just two basic sets of clothes each – most of which Abigail had made herself with various pieces of material or wool which Edna would only bring back from the market when Abigail had insisted that either she, or Emily, really had to have another cardigan or skirt, or to replace some underwear that wouldn't survive another wash. As for shoes, Emily had always worn little canvas daps easily available at the market stall, while Abigail, after her school shoes had finally become too small, wore the same steel-tipped clogs as Edna and many others who worked on the land did. Reasonably comfortable, clogs were strong and reliable and never wore out.

Emily clambered out of bed and started getting herself dressed.

She'd already reached the point when she refused to have any help. 'Is Aunt coming with us, Mummy?'

'No – no, of course not,' Abigail said. 'This is just our adventure – yours and mine. I told you that yesterday, didn't I?' She pulled back the curtains. 'Look, it's another lovely day, and after breakfast we're going on quite a long walk across the fields.'

'But I can collect the eggs first, can't I?' Emily said, sitting down on the floor to pull on her daps. 'There'll be time for me to do that, won't there?'

Abigail smiled quickly. 'Yes, and after we've had our wash in the scullery, I shall tidy up the kitchen, and milk the goats,' she said. 'One last time.'

Downstairs Edna was nowhere to be seen, but, as usual, the porridge in the large saucepan on the range was ready to eat, and Abigail went over to fill their two bowls. 'Perhaps we should have a second helping today, Emily,' she said, 'so that we won't feel hungry on our journey.'

'Can I have some honey on mine?' Emily whispered, darting a glance at the door in case Aunt suddenly appeared. Edna didn't see the need for sweet stuff and rarely bought any sugar, insisting that the honey from their own bees was sufficient. 'I don't really like porridge without honey,' Emily said.

'No, and neither do I,' Abigail agreed, reaching into the cupboard for a jar. And just then Edna came in from outside and looked down at them.

'So, you're enjoying your "Last Supper" are you? Well, I hope wherever you're going that they feed you properly. And with the same good food you've enjoyed all your lives.' Then, to Abigail's surprise, her aunt took a spoon to put some honey into Emily's porridge.

'Thank you, Aunt,' Abigail said quietly. 'And Emily would like to collect the eggs before we go – and shall I milk the goats?'

'No need,' Edna said shortly. 'I've done both, so you can run along whenever you're ready to go. I've got two young lads taking over from you, starting this morning at eleven. I've taken them on for the next two weeks to start with, and if they turn out to be suitable, I've said they'd be able to stay longer. I'll have to see whether they know what hard work really means. Their hours will be seven in the morning until seven at night when they will go home. Of course, they'll have to stay longer when it's fruit picking – I've told them that.'

After breakfast, Abigail collected their things from upstairs, then went down to find Emily sitting on the doorstep, waiting. She stood up, patting the front of her dress. 'Look – dolly always likes sitting in my pocket!'

Abigail smiled. The small doll had been one of the first things, perhaps the very first thing, that Dada had given her all those years ago. 'Well, she is a very tiny dolly, isn't she, and she does look very comfy there.'

Just then, Edna came through, carrying a small string bag. 'Goodness knows when and where you're going to find anything to eat,' she said, 'so there are sandwiches and a bottle of my elderflower cordial in this. I hope it's not too heavy.' She handed the bag to Abigail. 'Now, you'd better be off because those lads are due in a few minutes.'

Abigail was almost dumbstruck. That was the first time she could remember her aunt showing any concern, for her niece or her great-niece. For a second, Abigail wanted to put her arms around Edna's neck and hug her, but thought better of it. Edna would not have appreciated it. Instead, Abigail said, 'Thank you so much, Aunt.'

Edna merely nodded before going back outside.

Then Abigail, holding Emily's hand in hers, walked down the front path and away from Coopers for the last time. And with her heart full of hope and anxiety, Abigail whispered under her breath, '*I promised you I would escape one day, Luke, but I wish you were here with me. And I wish you knew about your daughter. Our little girl . . .*'

*   *   *

Abigail decided to skirt the village rather than go through it, in case they were recognised. She didn't want to be stopped by any locals and questioned about who Emily was. This wasn't the time for explanations.

After half an hour walking, they stopped under the shade of a sycamore tree and Emily said, 'Can I have a drink now, Mummy?'

Abigail opened the string bag and unscrewed the lid of the bottle of elderflower. 'Here you are, but don't drink it all. Save a bit for later – until I can buy us something else.'

'But where are we going now?' Emily said. 'Aren't we going to get on a puffer train?'

'We are,' Abigail said patiently, 'and we've seen those huge clouds of steam in the distance already, haven't we? But there's just a little further to walk before we reach the station.' She smiled down. Emily's sturdy little legs seemed to be having no difficulty in making the journey across the fields. She'd refused Abigail's offer that she should be carried for a few minutes.

Abigail had decided that they wouldn't get on the train in the village, but would walk to the Halt a short way up the line, then take the smaller train going to the main branch. Then, finally, they'd be on their way to Bristol.

Lying back with her eyes half-closed, Abigail let her memory take her to all the times she'd spent with Luke . . . especially those magic Thursday afternoons she'd managed to get to the village to be with him, more often taking their sandwiches to one of the more isolated corners he'd discovered rather than to Mulberry Court, because the housekeeper was usually there. And, held closely in each other's arms, they'd talk about anything and everything. Well, there was nothing Luke didn't know because he and his family had travelled all over the place, and it was Luke who'd explained how the trains worked, and that from here the biggest cities were London in one direction and Bristol in the other.

'London is much bigger than Bristol,' he'd informed her. 'In fact, it's huge. I know London well because we've lived there most of my life, but I've only been to Bristol a few times. My father was at university there – perhaps that's where I'll end up,' he'd added.

Now, they heard a train whistle and Emily clapped her hands excitedly.

'Is that our puffer?' she said. 'Are we nearly there?'

'I think so,' Abigail replied, and almost at once they could see the railway line, like a long brown snake, appearing in the distance, the noise of the approaching engine getting louder. Hurrying their steps now, she glanced down, remembering that her little daughter had never been anywhere near a station, nor had she seen many people. The only visitors who'd come to the cottage had been the gypsies, the vicar or the occasional itinerant salesman – who was soon seen off by Edna. Abigail bit her lip. Emily had such a lot ahead of her.

'I've told you that trains make a terrible noise, haven't I, Emily?' she said. 'So when we get to the station you won't be afraid, will you?'

'I'm not afraid!' Emily replied. 'I'm *not*, Mummy!'

Presently, they stood on the platform watching the train pull in at the Halt. There were few other passengers around, and as they alighted they found a compartment all to themselves. As Emily clambered up on to her seat, Abigail said, 'Well, I think this might be the time to eat our picnic now, Emily.' She unwrapped the honey and cheese sandwiches, and, with Emily sitting beside her looking at one of her books, Abigail tried to relax, tried not to let any nagging worries spoil the day. They'd taken the first huge step, but was the money she had going to be enough? Exactly how much was she going to need when they got to Bristol – and was it going to be as easy as she'd thought to find work to support them both? Not to mention the fact that she had no idea where they might be sleeping tonight.

Resting her head against the soft back of the seat, Abigail checked that the small, secret leather purse she'd stitched securely into the lining of her bolero was there resting against her heart. And that everything in the strong canvas holdall – her pens and paper, and especially Dada's war drawings in the wax packet – was protected. His pictures had come through so much already, she was going to look after them until the day she died. Abigail's heart swelled with love as she thought of her gentle dada and all that he'd gone through.

Abigail allowed herself a small pat on the back that, so far, this momentous day seemed to be going well. They had escaped and they were on their way.

Arriving at the branch line, they got off the small train and went across to the ticket office. 'One and a half to Bristol, please,' she said, holding out her money. The desk clerk glanced up.

'Single or return?'

'Oh . . . oh single, please,' she said quickly. Then, as the man took her coins – 'We are not coming back, you see. We are never coming back,' she added.

He looked up curiously at the beautiful young woman standing there in front of him, with the tiny youngster beside her.

'Well, good luck,' he said cheerfully.

'Thank you,' Abigail said, putting the tickets into her purse. 'I expect we are going to need it.'

Chapter 5

It had been a long journey, the train stopping at every station before finally pulling in at Bristol. Abigail stood up and went into the corridor to stare out of the window.

'Bristol Temple Meads!' the guard called out, then the doors were thrust open, all the passengers spilling out onto the platform and making for the exits.

For much of the time, Emily had been fast asleep in her corner of the carriage, and Abigail went back to wake her up.

'Come on, Emily,' she said gently. 'We have to get off the train now.'

Emily stirred, blinking her eyes, but immediately got down from her seat. 'Have I been asleep a long time?'

'Quite a long time,' Abigail replied, 'so you will be nice and fresh to set off on the next step of our adventure! We must find somewhere to stay tonight, mustn't we? But first we will have something to eat.' Abigail had seen the restaurant sign on the platform as they'd pulled in, and now she was suddenly dying for a cup of tea. 'Are you hungry, Emily?'

'Yes – and can I have some chips?'

Abigail retrieved their belongings from the rack above their heads, then helped Emily get off the train. And as they stepped onto the platform, the noise, the shouting, the hissing from the engine, the guard's whistle, the hubbub with everyone rushing about was frightening. Abigail pulled Emily towards her.

'Don't be afraid,' Abigail said. 'We'll soon be getting away from here.'

'I'm not afraid,' Emily said, 'but can we have chips soon? I'm hungry, and so is dolly.'

The restaurant was a huge room and it was fairly busy, but there were several vacant tables and Abigail led Emily over to one in the corner. 'You sit here and look after the bags, Emily, and I will go to the counter and order our food,' she said. 'I won't be long. You can see where I am.'

The queue of people waiting to be served was not long, and soon it was Abigail's turn. The woman behind the counter looked down, a half-smile on her lips. She'd seen these two come in a few minutes ago and admitted to being curious. Well, the little child was quite cute, and the woman very beautiful – but who would wear *clog*s in this weather! Those things clattering along the floor had made everyone look up. 'What can I get you?' she said pleasantly.

'A pot of tea and a glass of milk, and some chips? Two plates please,' Abigail said, already opening her purse.

'Oh no chips left, I'm afraid,' the woman said, 'and we won't be frying any more tonight. But we've got sandwiches, and beans on toast or eggs on toast – and, oh yes, there are some sausages left.'

Abigail's heart sank. Emily was an easy child to please, but she'd specially asked for chips, her favourite food, and she'd been so good all day. Abigail, too, had imagined the pleasure of dipping a few chips into some salt . . . sometimes potato chips were the only things that would immediately satisfy the pangs of hunger.

She shrugged. 'Oh, well, four sausages, please, and some bread – and two packets of those biscuits?'

The woman began preparing their order, and without looking up she said, 'Your little sister is very much like you, isn't she?'

And it was true. Apart from the difference in the colour of their hair, they both had the same heart-shaped face, the same tip-tilted nose, the same appealing expression in their wide green eyes.

Without a beat, Abigail said, 'Oh – Emily is not my sister – she's my daughter.' Well, Abigail had been determined that from the outset everyone was going to know the situation. That was how it was going to be from now on.

The woman's brief smile disappeared, and, tight-lipped, she almost slapped the order down on the counter. Her *daughter*, had she said? Huh! And no ring, so obviously not married! Disgusting! Young girls like her were no better than sluts!

Abigail paid the bill – which she'd noted from the list above the counter that she had enough money for, then took their tray of food across to Emily. 'Sorry, darling – they didn't have any chips,' she said.

Emily's face fell. 'No chips? Oh but – I *wanted* chips! I'm so *hungry*!' And to Abigail's surprise, her little daughter burst into a flood of tears.

'Shhh, Emily,' Abigail said, glancing around. 'Don't make a fuss, there's a good girl. I promise we'll get some chips tomorrow.'

'But I want some now!' Emily wailed. 'Why can't we have them?'

'Because they're all gone,' Abigail said, drawing Emily onto her lap.

'Well then, I wish we were back at Coopers where you would cook me some chips,' Emily said, pushing the plate of sausages away so crossly it nearly fell on the floor. She buried her head into Abigail's shoulder. 'You would have made me some chips. I'm hungry and I'm tired and I wish we were going to be sleeping in our own bed tonight.'

To her own consternation, Abigail realised that without much trouble she could have shed a tear of her own. It had been a long day and a long journey, and she had no idea where they would be sleeping tonight.

What had she done, jumping into the unknown like this? She'd been so certain that it was the right thing, the thing she'd wanted to do for so long. Yet it had taken a silly little incident to make her feel unsettled and unsafe.

She took out her handkerchief to dab briefly at her eyes which had begun to mist, and Emily looked up. 'Are you crying, too? Do you wish we were back home?'

Abigail shook her head. 'No, I do not, Emily,' she said firmly. 'We shall soon find another home where we will be just as comfy, I promise you.'

From her seat a few tables along, Eileen Matthews couldn't help being aware of the small drama taking place over there in the corner. Earlier, she had seen them enter the restaurant – the young woman and the very small child – and it had been hard not to stare because there was something about them that made you look twice. The woman was attractive – no, beautiful – and the little girl was picture-perfect. They only had bags with them, not cases, so perhaps they hadn't got off the train but were waiting here for someone.

Eileen was about to get up and ask if she could help when, just then, two men came over and each pulled up a chair to sit down next to the young woman and the child. And it seemed obvious that these must be the men who'd been expected because the young woman looked up, raising her eyes, and they all began talking. Then one of the men got up, said something to the woman, and went over to the counter, ruffling the child's hair as he went past.

Eileen turned away, glancing at her watch. Carrie – her closest and best friend since school days – would be here any minute, then they would go to The Royal Hotel for their supper. They sometimes did this on a Friday evening, even if Mark, Carrie's boyfriend, was on leave. Mark, a dedicated soldier, having joined up as soon as he'd been old enough, was already working his way up the ranks. Tall, with tousled fair hair and a generous, warm-hearted smile, he'd always been aware of the close friendship between Carrie and Eileen, and sometimes, when he was home, he would join them for their Friday supper.

Eileen smiled as she thought about tonight, knowing that Carrie would be sure to order the same thing – crisp whitebait followed by fillet of pork with mushrooms, while Eileen's preference was prawn cocktail and steak, medium rare.

Now, stifling a yawn, she glanced at the door again. Carrie had been seeing Mark off on another platform – he'd had a forty-eight-hour leave – and it had been agreed that Eileen would wait for her here in the station restaurant.

Carrie Waters hurried along the platform, threading her way through all the passengers waiting for their train. She pushed open the door to the restaurant and, upon seeing her, Eileen immediately stood up and came over to join her.

'Hello Carrie,' she said. 'Did Mark catch his train OK?'

'It was ten minutes late,' Carrie said as they left the restaurant, 'but he got a good seat. Sorry to have kept you waiting.'

Carrie was quite short and on the plump side, her bronze hair cut into a neat bob framing a sweet face, while Eileen was tall and slender, with long, dark hair, her open face dominated by thoughtful grey eyes.

'Oh, I didn't mind waiting,' Eileen said at once. 'I've been people-watching and a really attractive young woman and small child were sitting a few tables along. They were rather unusual, and I thought they were on their own and seemed to be a bit . . . well, upset . . . and I was going to go over and speak to them, but then a couple of lads arrived who obviously knew them.'

'Oh well, that was all right, then,' Carrie said, linking her arm with Eileen's as they walked along. 'No need for Eileen Matthews to do another of her good deeds for the day.'

'What you really mean,' Eileen said, 'is that there was no need for Eileen Matthews to be her usual bossy self.'

'If you say so,' Carrie said, 'but everyone loves you, Eileen, especially when you're bossy.' She smiled. 'Talking of love – has that bloke at work made any more advances?'

Eileen snorted. 'If you can call leaving me a note and a large eating apple on my desk an "advance", then yes. But I thought apples were treats for horses! I'd rather he'd left me a bar of Cadbury's.'

Carrie couldn't help laughing. 'But you're the problem, Eileen. You're too hard to please! I suppose someone will arrive eventually and steal your heart.'

'Let's hope so,' Eileen said airily. 'Or perhaps my lot in life will be to help you look after all the children you and Mark are going to have.'

'And you would be my first choice as super nanny, Eileen,' Carrie said. 'But all that is a very long way off. I think it's going to be ages before you walk behind me to the altar as a bridesmaid.'

In the restaurant, the man who'd remained at the table leaned forward and grinned at Abigail. 'So, you say you don't know Bristol very well,' he said.

Abigail looked at him uncertainly, disliking the smell of cigarette smoke on his breath. 'No, this is our first time here,' she said, 'but we hope to make it our home . . . we've always lived in Somerset. Of course, we don't know anyone at all yet, so it's going to be exciting finding our way around a big city by ourselves.' The man seemed friendly enough, Abigail thought, which was cheering.

The man nodded, glancing at Emily. 'And who's this? Your sister? She's very pretty.'

'No – Emily is my daughter,' Abigail said firmly. 'And I'm hoping she isn't going to find our new venture too daunting. But it'll be fine once we've found ourselves accommodation.'

The man's gaze dropped to Abigail's left hand . . . No wedding ring, eh?

'Look – my name's Don,' he said, 'and my mate over there is Reg. We work together on the line.' He paused. 'Perhaps we can help you find your way around the town – we've both lived here all our lives.'

Something in his suggestion made Abigail falter . . . after all, this was a complete stranger. She smiled quickly. 'Oh, it's all right, thanks,' she said, helping Emily unwrap one of the packets of biscuits. 'We're used to fending for ourselves – aren't we, Emily?'

Emily didn't say a word, just stared at the man curiously.

Just then Reg reappeared, holding two pints of beer which he put down on the table.

''Yer you are, mate,' he said to the other man jovially. 'Get this down yer neck – it's been a long day.'

Then he sat down, and without a moment's pause they both gulped at the beer noisily, Don pausing briefly to wipe his mouth with the back of his hand before continuing to swallow until his glass was empty.

'Blimey, Reg,' he said. 'I needed that! Me stomach thought me throat had been cut!'

Suddenly, Abigail wanted to remove herself and Emily from this present company. They were making her feel uncomfortable. But then, Don said, 'D'you know what, Reg? This little lady and her *daughter* have just arrived and they're going to make their home in Bristol. And they don't know anyone and haven't got anywhere to stay yet, either.'

'Go on,' Reg said slowly. He gazed at Abigail. 'And – no husband here to take care of you both? What sort of a man is that to leave you high and dry!'

'I am not married,' Abigail said stoutly, wishing that these two had never sat with them. Everything about them was offensive. 'And I can assure you that we can take good care of ourselves.' She began to clear their things from the table and stood up. 'I think it's time we went to the rest room for a wash and brush up.' She smiled quickly. 'It's nice to have met you,' she said.

''Ang on a minute,' Don said. 'I told you just now – Reg and me know Bristol like the back of our 'ands. Why don't you let us show you around? Bristol can be a whole lot of fun on a Friday night, and I'm sure my mum would look after the little one for a couple of hours.'

Abigail had had enough, feeling her mouth go dry with unexpected apprehension. 'No, *thank* you,' she said, helping Emily from the chair, and barely looking at them as she turned to go. 'Goodbye.'

After she'd left, Reg said, 'Nice try, mate. But she's obviously the frigid type. Not your sort at all.'

'Well, she can't always have been frigid,' Don said.

As they walked quickly towards the sign which read 'Rest Room', Abigail glanced down at Emily.

'I'm glad you managed to eat a sausage and one of the biscuits, Emily, and you drank most of your milk, didn't you?'

Emily nodded. 'Yes, but we can have chips tomorrow, can't we, Mummy?'

'I promise,' Abigail said, automatically glancing back over her shoulder in case those men were following them. *Why* had they had to come in and spoil everything, their intentions being obvious, even to Abigail's untrained senses.

And she had to admit that the last hour had been a learning experience she hadn't expected. The expression on the face of the woman who'd served their food had been positively hostile when she'd learned that Abigail wasn't married, and Abigail had distinctly heard her whisper that horrible word – 'slut' – to the other woman serving. And then they'd both looked back, tight-lipped, their opinions written all over their faces. So was Edna right after all? Abigail asked herself. Was it so disgraceful for a single woman to produce a child? Was she going to be spurned, judged and condemned in this big city?

And even worse – was she going to be subjected to unwelcome attentions from *men*? Men she didn't know and wouldn't *want* to know!

Abigail shuddered at her own thoughts, feeling vulnerable and suddenly unsure of herself. She'd seen no reason not to tell the truth that she was Emily's mother, despite not being married. It was her business, so why should anyone else care? Yet there were already signs that it may be better to avoid any trouble if she could, so perhaps she should not be so open in future. She bit her lip in frustration. This was something she had not thought about, and for Emily's sake, and for her own protection, it seemed that she was going to have to be evasive in future. She could almost hear Edna's voice.

'Well, what did you expect? What you did was a sin and a disgrace which you will bear for the rest of your life! Serves you right!'

Abigail pressed her lips together. One thing she would not be evasive about was that Emily was her little girl. It would be a secret no longer. But there may be something that might help . . . if she could find a way to bring it about.

The rest room was large and quite inviting as they went inside, with only a young couple already there, talking together quietly. There was a long, padded bench all along one side of the room, and on the other were several comfy chairs and a few small tables. The toilet was clearly indicated at the far end.

'I think we should have a wash and brush up before we do anything else,' Abigail said, glancing down at Emily. 'It's quite a long time since we used that toilet on the train, isn't it?'

'It was funny going wee wee when it was moving, wasn't it!' Emily said as Abigail pushed her gently in front of her.

'It was,' Abigail agreed, realising again just how many new experiences were to confront both of them. *I was right, Dada, wasn't I, to bring us away from Coopers?*

The three cubicles were all vacant, and just as they were about to enter one of them, something in a dusty corner caught Abigail's eye, and she automatically bent and picked it up, glancing at it quickly. It was an ancient curtain ring, and she slipped it into her pocket. Emily, distracted by working out how to lock the door behind them, had noticed nothing.

By now it was almost eight o'clock and Abigail realised that it was far too late to try to find accommodation in Bristol for the night. But the rest room, empty of others now, was quiet and it seemed quite a good idea to stay here until morning. Although feeling slightly apprehensive, she led Emily over to the long, upholstered bench and, taking her own light woollen shawl from one of their bags and a comfy cardigan which she rolled up into a ball, she made a little nest in the corner for Emily.

'Look – we're both tired,' Abigail said, 'so we'll just have a little nap here and set off on our big adventure in the morning.'

Emily, yawning, immediately climbed up and obediently curled herself inside the shawl.

'This is a funny bed,' she said, pausing to open one of their bags, 'but dolly won't mind. I shall cuddle her all night.'

And within two or three minutes, Emily was fast asleep.

As the night wore on, the noise of the trains became less as fewer of them appeared to be running, and it was almost midnight before Abigail even began to close her eyes, constantly glancing over at the door in case those men should come in. And a couple of times, when she did drift off, she woke with a start, imagining that that awful man's face was close to hers again, leering at her.

Then, suddenly remembering, she put her hand into her pocket and took out the curtain ring. It was a pathetic object, bent along one side, but after carefully wiping it over and over again with her hanky, Abigail put it on the third finger of her left hand and stared at it. It actually shone a bit, and fitted her perfectly. She allowed herself a little smile.

Not quite as wonderful as the one which Luke would have given her, but it was going to serve its purpose, her first mode of defence.

To outside judgemental eyes she was now a married woman,

a respectable mother of children – or of a child. And should Emily notice it – as she surely would – Abigail would merely tell her that she'd had it for ages but that she always forgot to put it on.

Chapter 6

The next morning, Emily was first to wake up and she shook Abigail's arm gently.

'Mummy – I need to go somewhere,' she said. 'And so does dolly.'

Abigail roused at once, surprised that she'd been able to sleep at all under the circumstances. But she had managed to snatch a few hours' fitful rest, and now, waking up properly, she kissed Emily's cheek.

'Yes, we'll have a little wash, and then go and find a taxi to take us somewhere nice for breakfast,' she said. Abigail was determined never to set foot inside the station restaurant again. She shuddered as she remembered yesterday evening.

It was only seven o'clock, and glancing out of the window it was obvious that it was going to be another warm day. There was no one else in the rest room – perhaps she and Emily had been there alone all night, Abigail thought as they went into the toilets. Well, if so, that suited her perfectly. She didn't want to speak to anyone who might undermine her confidence, even though she felt more than ready to face the world again. And today, she'd be more prepared.

Brushing Emily's hair out gently – those dark ringlets did tend to tangle, exactly like Luke's did – Abigail's mind immediately went back to all those magical times she and Luke had spent together. He'd told her so much about life outside in the proper world, including the hustle and bustle of London's sights, and what Bristol looked like with all its historic buildings and churches and green parks, and the docks where huge ships brought exciting things from overseas. And he'd said that there were always cafés and restaurants where you could get nice food. And that outside Temple Meads Railway Station a long taxi rank stood waiting to take departing passengers on to their next destination.

That was exactly what was going to happen to them today, Abigail thought as, presently, she replaced their wash things into the toilet bag. She didn't exactly know what a taxi ride would cost, but she hoped she had enough in her purse to take them to the nearest café for their breakfast. And anyway, she always had that other little bag tucked safely inside her bolero, her safety net.

As they left the rest room, an early train had already hissed its way into the station and people were getting on and off hurriedly. Abigail felt a pang of envy as she passed by. They all knew where they were going, their day planned, familiar, safe. While hers and Emily's was like stepping into the abyss.

But, as Luke had once said, there was the taxi rank outside and Abigail led Emily over to the first one in the row. The driver immediately got out and opened the back passenger door for them to get in.

'Morning,' he said affably as they climbed in. Then he got into the driver's seat and glanced back. 'Now, where can I take you young ladies to today?'

Abigail swallowed. She had no idea where they were going. But she answered him brightly. 'Perhaps you could take us to a restaurant where we might get some breakfast?'

He started the car and they made their way down the wide approach into the town. 'Just got off the early train, have you?' he said. 'Where've you come from?'

Abigail stared out of the window as he spoke. Everywhere seemed so huge and so busy! The buildings tall and awesome! Automatically, she pulled Emily in closer to her.

'Oh – deepest Somerset,' Abigail said casually in answer to his question, not bothering to say that that had been yesterday. 'It was a very long train ride,' she added, 'but we're here, and hoping to make our home in the city eventually, even if we don't have anywhere to stay yet. And first we do need a good breakfast . . . could you possibly tell us the best café you know?'

The driver glanced at them curiously in the rear-view mirror. A beautiful woman and her sweet little girl, here alone in Bristol and not knowing anyone? He cleared his throat. 'You have a very pretty daughter, madam,' he said. 'Reminds me of my little granddaughter.'

Yes! Abigail felt triumphant. The curtain ring had worked.

'What's your name, and how old are you, luvver?' the man enquired as the car wound its way along the streets.

'I am called Emily Grace,' Emily said, unperturbed. 'And I will be three next birthday.'

He chuckled. 'You are going to break a man's heart one day, Emily Grace,' he said. 'Now, I am going to drive you to Robertson's in Denmark Street, just off the Centre. The lady who owns the place is called Janet, and her food is famed throughout the city! I sometimes stop there if I'm not busy.' He smiled back. 'Janet does smashing bacon and eggs and toast and marmalade – and afternoon tea and homemade cakes as well. You'll like Janet.'

Abigail felt her spirits surge. This was a pleasant man, eager to help.

The journey to the café was only a five- or six-minute drive, and after carefully counting out the coins to pay their fare, Abigail led Emily into Robertson's. Even at this early hour of the day the place was crowded with city workers grabbing a coffee, or others enjoying a full plate of bacon and eggs and sausages as they chatted among themselves. There didn't seem to be many tables vacant, but as Abigail looked around, a woman approached them, smiling. She was tall, and had a mass of fair hair, slightly greying. She was wearing a full, printed cotton overall.

'Hello there,' she said. 'Look, I know we are a bit busy this morning but there's a nice little table for two over here.' She led Abigail and Emily across the room and pulled out two chairs.

'Oh – thank you so much,' Abigail said, warming at once to their surroundings. The taxi driver had been right; this was a lovely, welcoming place, and the smell of frying food and hot coffee made her mouth water. She hesitated. 'Are you Janet?' she asked diffidently. 'Our taxi driver recommended your café as the place to enjoy our breakfast.'

Janet smiled down at them. 'Yes, I'm Janet,' she said, 'and it's always nice to welcome new customers to Robertson's.'

Having seen them come in, she now studied them with polite interest, the dear little girl and her beautiful young mother, whose unusual footwear – a pair of solid country clogs – had made Janet look up. Those clogs had certainly announced their arrival.

'What can I get you?' she asked. 'There's always a full English breakfast, or something simpler if you prefer . . . boiled eggs, toast and marmalade? Shall I go away for a minute while you make up your minds?'

Emily, who'd been taking in their surroundings with her usual intense curiosity, spoke up.

'Please can I have chips?' she said. 'With salt to dip in?'

Abigail touched her arm. 'No, Emily – chips aren't usually served for breakfast. Why don't you have an egg and some fried bread instead?'

Emily's face crumpled. 'But you promised I could have chips today, Mummy,' she said. '*Please*, Mummy. You promised!'

Janet spoke up. 'I don't think there'd be any problem in making a few chips,' she said brightly, 'because my two helpers, Pat and Fay, who are doing all the cooking out at the back are used to unusual requests. So – Emily – is it just chips you want, or an egg as well?'

Emily immediately cheered up. 'Just chips, please . . . with salt?'

'And what would Mummy like?' Janet said.

'A poached egg on toast and a pot of tea, please,' Abigail said, 'and a glass of milk for Emily?'

Janet did a mock salute. 'Order coming up in five or six minutes,' she said, pausing briefly as she paused to ruffle Emily's hair and whisper, 'Don't tell anyone about the chips or they will all want some!'

The food was absolutely wonderful, and as Abigail sipped at her tea, she sat back feeling at peace with the world, even though she still had so much to do before she could start to relax.

Janet, with her own cup of tea in her hands, returned to their table and pulled up another chair to sit with them. By this time, most of the customers were beginning to leave, and Janet Robertson admitted to being curious about the newcomers. 'Do you live in the town?' she said. 'Or are you from outside?'

'My name is Abigail Wilson, and we only arrived yesterday,' Abigail said. 'You see, we are hoping to make our home in Bristol . . . we've been told what a nice place it is. But we've only ever lived in the country – deepest, darkest Somerset! – so we have a lot to learn. Don't we, Emily?'

Emily had been watching the two young employees putting things away and cleaning the counter, and she looked at Janet. 'Can I go and help?' she said.

'Emily is used to doing things around the house,' Abigail explained, 'and is never happier than when she is occupied.'

Janet smiled broadly, moving aside for Emily to leave the table. 'Pat and Fay will be delighted to let you share their duties,' Janet said, 'and so will I! You can drop by at any time and help. I'm sure we can find you a little apron, Emily!'

Abigail looked at Janet gratefully. 'Emily can't sit still for very long,' she said.

There was a moment's pause before Janet asked tentatively, 'So . . . you are here alone, Abigail? Just the two of you, I mean?'

'Yes,' Abigail said carefully, 'because my . . . husband . . . has had to go away and I'm not sure how long for.' Her own words made Abigail colour up because she was not used to telling lies, and that pathetic curtain ring on her finger had been the first one, the first deception. How many more was she going to have to tell now that she'd started? But it was all for her protection, she reassured herself, hers and Emily's. She'd never dreamed that she was going to have to resort to this. All she'd ever wanted was for her and Emily to be free, and to live lives of their own choosing.

Janet nodded sympathetically, obviously assuming that the war was the reason for this young woman's husband being absent.

'Who ever would have thought that we were going to be at war again, so soon after the last hideous one,' Janet said. 'It beggars belief – and of course conscription is in full swing, all young men having to go and do their duty.' She pursed her lips. 'One of my best friends is in a similar position to you, though he was already a serving officer in the Somerset Light Infantry so he would obviously have been one of the first to go. He's always being sent off somewhere for yet more and more training, and never knows when he's going to have leave.'

Abigail looked away for a second, ashamed at pretending to be married. So, Aunt Edna had been right about the possibility of war, though she, Abigail, hadn't known much about the facts – which was why she'd shrugged off Edna's warning.

'How lovely to have a best friend,' Abigail said, wanting to switch the conversation on to more comfortable waters.

'Yes – and I have two,' Janet said happily. 'Eileen and Carrie. Carrie is the one with the soldier boyfriend who she doesn't see so much of now.' Janet finished her cup of tea before adding, 'Eileen and Carrie both work here in the town and they often pop in for a coffee or a quick meal – or just for a bit of a gossip, which we are all very good at!'

Two best friends, Abigail thought briefly. Well, hadn't Luke said that *she* would have friends, real friends, one day? Perhaps Bristol was the place to be to have that sort of luck . . .

Just then, Emily returned all smiles. 'I finished wiping the cups and saucers,' she said triumphantly, 'and Pat said I did it very well!'

'Well, maybe next time you come in we can find you even more things to do,' Janet said, 'because we're often short of help at busy times.'

Abigail looked at Janet quickly, instinctively feeling that the owner of this café was someone she could talk to with confidence. 'As a matter of fact,' Abigail said, 'I shall be looking for work myself in a week or so . . . after I've found us somewhere to live. And I would be happy to help you out – I can turn my hand to almost anything on the domestic front,' she added.

Janet raised her eyes. 'You mean you've nowhere to stay?' she said, unable to hide her surprise. Who came to a strange city with a tiny child and nowhere to stay?

'Not yet,' Abigail replied, 'but there shouldn't be too much difficulty, should there? We only need one nice room, and I have . . . I have the money to pay for it,' she added.

Janet stood up. 'Well, there's a very reliable estate agency a short walk away from here at the end of Clare Street – just off the Centre over there,' she said. 'They might have something which could be suitable.'

Abigail stood as well, taking out her purse. 'Breakfast was lovely, Janet – how much do I owe you?'

After the bill had been paid, Janet saw them to the door and suddenly Abigail hesitated. She turned to Janet.

'You will think me very naive,' she said, 'but I need a little advice.'

Janet smiled. 'Of course. What can I do to help?'

'It's just that . . . most of the money I own is actually in sovereigns,' she said, 'and I realise that shops don't accept them . . . do they?'

'Lucky you to have sovereigns!' Janet said, 'I have just one which I keep with my other little treasures. But there won't be any problem if you take them to the General Post Office, which is a ten-minute walk away from here. I'm sure they will exchange them for pounds, shillings and pence. And then away you go to spend the lot!'

Abigail nodded, smiling. 'Yes – and I think we are going to need to, because we didn't bring many clothes with us. But of course, as I don't know Bristol, I have no idea about where the suitable shops are,' she added.

Janet folded her arms. 'I can tell you exactly where you will find everything you need – for both of you,' she said firmly. 'Baker Baker at the bottom of Park Street – just round the corner – they cater for every age group so you wouldn't need to go traipsing all over the place and tiring yourselves out. Everything you might need is all there under one roof.' She paused for a moment, glancing at Emily. 'They also sell prams and small pushchairs,' she added, 'and I think that if you are going to be doing a lot of walking in the next few days, Emily might be glad of a lift.'

Abigail nodded quickly. At Coopers, Emily had only ever been pushed around in the hand cart which years ago Arnold had made to bring up the vegetables from the field. A proper pushchair for Emily would be a real treat.

Emily, who'd been taking all this in, said, 'I shan't want a lift. But dolly might.'

'I love your little dolly,' Janet said, 'and she looks so sweet sitting in the pocket of your dress, Emily.'

'That's where she lives,' Emily said.

They turned to leave, and Abigail said, 'Thank you so much. I can't tell you how good it's been to meet you and to enjoy your lovely food – and your wise words.'

'The pleasure has been mine, Abigail,' Janet said, 'and I hope we see you again here as soon as you're ready to help me out here. I'll make absolutely sure we have a little apron all ready for Emily!'

Chapter 7

Leaving Robertson's and following Janet's instructions, Abigail and Emily began to make their way up the hill towards Baker Baker.

'I *like* Janet,' Emily said, skipping happily alongside Abigail. 'And I like Pat and Fay. They said they wished they had a dolly like mine.'

'Yes, we're lucky to have gone to Janet's café, aren't we?' Abigail said. 'Were the chips nice?' But she needn't have asked because Emily hadn't left a single one on her plate.

It really was a lovely warm day and Abigail was filled with a huge sense of optimism. How different she had felt last night! But today it seemed that luck was on their side, and soon she was going to buy herself and Emily a new dress and cardigan, and new shoes. New shoes at last! But she'd have to be careful to study the price of everything first . . . though Abigail felt sure she had enough of Dada's money until she was able to swap those sovereigns.

Presently, carrying a bag holding the few items they'd bought, and with both of them wearing new shoes – Abigail's being a pair of sling-back, cream, open-toe sandals, and Emily's white canvas daps with tiny silver buckles at each side – they made their way back down the hill towards the estate agent's office that Janet had told them about.

They had also bought a small pushchair which Emily refused to sit in, but which she had soon found out how to manoeuvre along the pavements and over kerbs.

'Wouldn't you like to have a ride, Emily?' Abigail asked, wishing they could walk a little faster. 'I'm sure dolly would love to have one.'

That made all the difference, and Emily immediately climbed in to the pushchair and leaned her head back. Abigail thought what a piece of luck they'd had in meeting Janet Robertson. The pushchair had been her idea and it was obvious that it was going to be put to full use in the coming days as they walked about discovering Bristol, their new home. Their new home! It was hard to believe that they were actually here in this busy city, the streets noisy with Saturday morning traffic weaving its way in every direction, and with crowds of people all walking or strolling along, free to come and go as they pleased. Abigail couldn't help a smile forming on her lips because they were free, too. She and Emily were no longer trapped and could do exactly as they liked without Aunt Edna's demanding voice constantly in their ears. This was what Abigail had dreamed about for so long, and now it was reality, and with childlike trust, Emily had accepted everything without complaint.

And what would Luke think of her great escape? Abigail wondered. Well, he probably wouldn't be all that surprised because she had promised him that one day, she would leave Coopers, and never go back. But what he would be surprised about was the presence of a little daughter he knew nothing of. Tears immediately sprang to Abigail's eyes. It would be wonderful if things were different and he was with them now, together, as a family.

Abigail lifted her head, annoyed with herself. She hadn't seen Luke, nor heard a thing about him, since that afternoon in the summer house, and it was known that the Jordans no longer lived at Mulberry Court. So by now he would be well on with his studies, achieving everything expected of him and would probably have had no time to give a single thought to her.

Now, they arrived at the estate agent's office and stopped to look in the window. There were lots of advertisements displaying properties to buy or to rent, and Abigail bit her lip as she stared. The prices quoted seemed rather high to her. And exactly how much money were they going to eventually exchange for those sovereigns? Was it going to be enough?

Just then, a man emerged from the agent's office and looked down at Abigail. He'd seen her looking in. He smiled. 'Good morning – or should I say good afternoon because it's past noon now! Can I help you with anything today?'

Abigail smiled back. 'Well, um, I am . . . my name is . . . is Mrs Wilson . . . and my daughter and I have only just arrived in Bristol and have nowhere to stay. I've no idea where to start looking for accommodation.'

'Well,' the man said, 'come inside and let's see if anything on our books appeals to you.' He paused. 'Is it a house, or a flat that you have in mind? Are there, um . . . are there just the two of you . . . Mrs Wilson?' He raised one eyebrow quizzically as he gazed at Abigail.

'Yes,' Abigail said firmly, 'it's just Emily and me. Our needs are few and we would only want one bedroom . . . with suitable facilities as well, of course.'

The tone of her voice implied that she had a mind of her own, and the man immediately began thumbing through his large book.

'I gather there was nothing in the window that appealed to you,' he said, 'but we do have one or two that might be suit-able . . . ah, yes . . . this one in Stapleton Road is a one-bed. It's on the ground floor of a terraced block but . . .' He glanced at Emily who was sitting quietly staring at everything around her. 'But it is on the main road and would be rather noisy, especially during busy times of the day . . . and night. But it does have the one bedroom you require, and you would share bathroom and kitchen with the tenants upstairs.'

'And where is Stapleton Road?' Abigail asked, feeling that she should show some interest even though she didn't like the sound of that noisy place. They'd never even heard one car hoot outside Coopers. Still, she and Emily were going to have to be prepared for changes of all sorts, that was obvious.

'Oh, some way from here . . . a bus ride or so,' the man said.

Abigail let a moment pass. 'I would really prefer something central if possible,' she said.

The man pursed his lips as he turned the pages. He had to be honest, they didn't have much to offer this unusual customer and the only other one-bedroom places were in St. Philip's and Horfield. Hardly the central locations the lady had requested. Then suddenly he remembered! There was the one that only came in yesterday. It wasn't even in the book yet. He turned to Abigail.

'Well, I might have something after all,' he said, beginning to check up. For some reason he hadn't held out much hope with this customer and it was past his lunch time. 'It may be just what you're looking for,' he went on. 'One bedroom with shared facilities at number fourteen Redcliffe Way which is as central as you're ever going to get. And right next to Queen Square – or nearly so – which is a lovely open space. And the property is easy walking distance from the Centre,' he added triumphantly. 'From here, you could get there in ten minutes.'

This sounded more like it, but Abigail needed to know a little more. 'So – who would we be sharing with?' she asked tentatively.

'Oh, it's a very simple arrangement,' the man said. 'The owner of the house is a Miss Grant who lives there alone. You would be sharing her facilities, obviously.' He paused for a second. 'The only thing is the room is on a rather short lease . . . three months, actually . . . but you never know I'm sure that could be extended. If all went well.'

Abigail thought quickly. A three-month arrangement might be perfect because if she and Emily weren't happy there, they wouldn't have to put up with it for long. 'When could we go and meet Miss Grant?' Abigail said. 'It is a matter of urgency because, as I've already said, we have nowhere to stay tonight.'

The man nodded. 'Miss Grant informed us that she will be available for viewing every day – apart from tomorrow – from two o'clock to six,' he said. He glanced at his watch. 'I would happily have taken you there myself and introduced you to the lady, but we close at three today – my afternoon off – so there's hardly time, I'm afraid.'

'Oh that doesn't matter,' Abigail said, 'Emily and I will be able to find our own way without any problem. Going there by ourselves will be a wonderful opportunity to start getting to know Bristol.'

The man bent to scribble something on a piece of paper. 'Look, here's a note showing how to get there, but anyone can direct you to Redcliffe Way.' He began ushering them to the door. 'And of course I will follow this up with Miss Grant first thing on Monday morning.'

Abigail turned back. 'We haven't discussed rent, or what it would cost,' she began, and he waved his hand.

'Oh – I assure you it's usually very little,' he said airily. 'Miss Grant didn't actually say on this occasion, but we've had dealings with the lady before and I'm sure what she's asking this time would not be too much. Anyway,' he added brightly, 'you can discuss the financial terms with her and come to a decision that suits you both. You might even try a little bartering!' He held out his hand to shake Abigail's. 'It's nice to have met you, Mrs Wilson, and I have a feeling that you are going to like number fourteen Redcliffe Way.' He patted Emily's head briefly, wondering whether Miss Grant would be happy to accept a child in the arrangement, though he had to admit this one hadn't made a single sound.

* * *

'Gosh, it's good to sit down,' Eileen said as she and Carrie took their seats in the restaurant of Jones's department store. 'Wandering from floor to floor can be very wearing.'

The large store in Broadmead Shopping Centre was always very popular with residents and visitors alike, and today it was crowded.

Carrie nodded. 'Yes, especially as neither of us have bought anything to show for our efforts. Though I'm still thinking about that red dress. After we've had lunch I might go back and try it on again.'

'It did suit you, Carrie,' Eileen said, 'as I told you at the time. But you are never very good at making up your mind, are you?'

'No,' Carrie agreed cheerfully. 'Before I part with my money I need to think several times, and then think again.' She looked pensive for a second. 'The thing is, I wonder if Mark would like me in that particular colour? It was a bit hot and bothersome, wasn't it?'

Eileen made a face. 'Does it *matter* whether Mark likes it or not?' she said. 'You're the one who'd be wearing it, and if you like it, then surely that's all that matters.'

'You're probably right,' Carrie said, 'but I'm always extra happy when I know he really admires something I'm wearing.' She smiled. 'At the moment, you haven't got a man in your life, Eileen, so you're fun and fancy free.'

'Yes, and that state of affairs is likely to remain for some time to come,' Eileen retorted. 'Life's too short to be worrying about what someone else wants me to wear, say or do.'

Carrie smiled across at her friend fondly. What Eileen had just said didn't really ring true because she always went out of her way to help others and put herself last – and had devoted her life to her handicapped mother who'd been widowed for many years. Although Mrs Matthews had always been a dominant character, she'd met her match in her daughter because Eileen was determined that her mother should live as happy a life as possible, despite her infirmities. After the death of her husband,

Gladys Matthews, retired head of a junior school, would have been quite happy to sit in her chair and shut the world out. But Eileen would have none of that, taking her mother to church most Sundays, and to the municipal park at the end of their road to sit watching the children playing on the swings, and to the Theatre Royal now and again. It was hard going because Mrs Matthews was often depressed. But she had certainly become used to the sound of hilarity in the house when Carrie, and Eileen's other friends, came in for a cup of tea and a game of cards or Monopoly. Though Mrs Matthews could never understand what they found so much to giggle and laugh about all the time.

Just then, the waitress came to take their order for lunch, and as so often the case, both girls chose the same. Fish and chips with bread and butter and a pot of tea.

'Right,' the waitress said, marking up her pad, 'and pudding?'

'Ice cream, please,' they chorused. 'One strawberry, one vanilla.'

Presently, as they sat enjoying their meal, Carrie said, 'How is your mother today, Eileen? You said she hasn't been sleeping well.'

'She hasn't slept well for ages,' Eileen said, 'so nothing new there. But I wish she would eat a bit more. I've left her some soup I made earlier – leek and potato, which she used to enjoy so I'm hoping she'll have had some when we get back. Though I don't suppose she'll have touched the fresh roll I buttered for her.'

Carrie didn't answer for a moment, thinking how lucky her own life was in comparison. Her father was the vicar of All Saints in Knowle, and he and her mother were both in good health, and happy in the lives they had chosen. Jonathan Waters' church always had a full congregation, and Mrs Waters was a faithful partner to him, presiding over the Mothers' Union, and always ready with tea and sympathy for needy parishioners. But best of all, Carrie knew that they approved of her relationship with Mark and they always welcomed him into their home when he was on leave. Even though Mrs Waters had once said she thought he had chosen a very dangerous career.

'I'll give you a penny for them,' Eileen said now, glancing across. 'What's on your mind?'

Carrie smiled quickly. 'I was just thinking of Mark and . . . and how glad I am that my parents like him. And how glad I am that you, Eileen, like him as well,' she added. 'That you like each other. Wouldn't it be awful if you two didn't hit it off! I would probably have to chuck him!'

'No you wouldn't,' Eileen said. She finished her meal and put down her knife and fork. 'You'd be an idiot to chuck someone like handsome Mark Anderson. Mark with his sense of humour and that infectious laugh is someone special. If I thought I was in with a chance, I'd try my hand at stealing him from you.'

Carrie laughed out loud, knowing that Eileen would never do such a thing. They had always been great and loyal friends, and nothing would change that. Carrie's eyes clouded briefly. She wished that Eileen could find someone like Mark, even though Eileen always said she wasn't interested in having a man in her life. There had been one or two flirtations in the office at the Royal Insurance Company where Eileen had worked since leaving school, but Eileen was always the one to end a relationship.

'It's funny when you think how you and Mark met,' Eileen said, and Carrie nodded.

'You mean how we collided!' she said. 'I didn't think it was funny at the time, but looking back on it, it certainly was funny. I mean, I had only popped down from Accounts to buy everyone a cake to go with our afternoon cuppa, and Mark was there with his back to me at the counter and turned suddenly, and knocked me right off my feet! There I was, full-length on the floor and covered in crumbs!' Carrie giggled happily at the memory. 'But he was so gallant as he picked me up and brushed me down and insisted on paying for all the lost cakes.'

'I should think so too,' Eileen said. 'And he made sure that that was not the last time he came into The Berkeley Hotel and

Restaurant, either. He haunted the place after that in the hope of seeing you, didn't he . . . and that is how the affair of the century began,' she added.

'Lucky me,' Carrie said simply.

'Lucky him,' Eileen said firmly.

With Emily in the pushchair in charge of all their bags and shopping, Abigail began walking away from the estate agent's office in the direction she'd been given. He'd said it would only take them ten minutes and it was now two-thirty so they would be in plenty of time to arrive at the property to meet Miss Grant during the time specified.

Abigail hummed a little tune under her breath. She had a good feeling about number fourteen, and as long as she could afford the terms, they could be installed straightaway, then think of something nice for an early tea. The breakfast at Robertson's had been very sustaining, but presently something on toast would go down very well. But the first and most important thing was to know where they were going to be sleeping tonight.

Her expression darkened as she remembered what Aunt Edna had said. *You must be mad, how on earth do you think you will manage . . . you have no experience outside here . . . and you won't even have a roof over your heads . . .*

Well of course, part of that was true, Abigail thought, but she and Emily had managed so far, they'd arrived and survived, and it seemed likely that very soon they would have a roof over their heads. Luke was right – you could change things if you were determined.

Abigail was about to cross the road at the end of Baldwin Street in order to follow the instructions she'd been given, when suddenly a car, with its horn blasting, careered around the corner in front of her making her stop and pull back abruptly. And as she did so, Emily, together with all their belongings, was jerked right out of the pushchair. She was thrown to the ground, taking her weight on both her knees. And after a second . . .

'*Ow!* Mummy! Look, look . . . my knees are bleeding! Oh, Mummy, you made me fall out of the pushchair! Ow, *Ow!*'

Unable to stop herself, Emily let out a scream of pain and horror as she watched blood begin to trickle down her legs.

Equally horrified, Abigail pulled Emily towards her, annoyed with herself that she hadn't thought to strap Emily into the chair. But before this disaster, there hadn't seemed to be any need.

'I'm so *sorry*, darling,' Abigail said, 'but I had to stop quickly or we might have got run over. That car was so close to us!'

Still sobbing quietly, Emily continued examining her wounds while Abigail gathered up their belongings and wondered what to do next. They couldn't arrive at number fourteen like this – at least not until she'd cleaned Emily up.

'Oh *no!* Oh my goodness me! Let us help you! You poor little thing!'

Eileen and Carrie, having strolled to the Centre from Broadmead after their lunch, arrived just in time to see what had happened, and both sprang forward, arms outstretched.

'I *saw* that!' Eileen exclaimed, gathering Emily up into her arms but being careful to avoid her knees. 'That taxi must have been going ninety miles an hour!'

Abigail, still crouching to collect their things, looked up gratefully. 'Oh – thanks . . . thank you,' she said. 'I didn't realise I was so close to the kerb.' She swallowed. 'We could have been killed!'

Carrie bent to pick up the remaining bag on the ground and smiled at Abigail. 'Well,' she said, 'you stopped just in time, and a miss is as good as a mile, isn't it? And your brave little girl has already stopped crying.'

Suddenly, the penny dropped as Eileen realised she recognised these two. Still holding Emily to her, she gazed at Abigail. 'I think I've seen you before,' she said slowly. 'Weren't you waiting for someone last night at Temple Meads? In the restaurant?'

Of course she'd seen them before! How could she ever forget those two beautiful people!

Taken aback for a moment, Abigail hesitated. 'Well, we weren't actually waiting for someone,' she said. 'My name is Abigail Wilson and this is my daughter, Emily, and you see, we'd been on a long journey from Somerset and were having a bit of a breather before we . . . before we had to leave to find ourselves somewhere to stay.' She paused. She was not going to admit that they'd spent the night in the rest room. 'We've left our old home,' she went on, 'and intend starting a new life here in Bristol even though we don't know anyone yet. As a matter of fact, we were actually on our way to view an address which might be suitable for the two of us.' She paused again, knowing she'd been gabbling. 'But first I need to make Emily more comfortable.' She glanced down. 'Is it still stinging, darling?' she murmured.

Still in Eileen's arms, Emily nodded, but had stopped whimpering as she took in this new situation.

'Well, I know *exactly* where we can make Emily more comfortable,' Eileen said firmly, 'don't you, Carrie?'

'Of course,' Carrie said at once. 'Come on, we are going to introduce you to our favourite watering hole, Mrs Wilson! Robertson's café just over the road there! Janet will have everything necessary to make Emily forget she ever fell down! Janet's cakes are always the talk of the town,' Carrie went on, 'and she sells lovely ice cream, too!'

That put a faint smile on Emily's face. 'Can I have an ice cream, Mummy?' she said.

'You can have whatever you like, Emily,' Abigail said, relieved that things were not as bad as they could have been if she'd not stopped in time to let that car go past – and even more relieved that these two young women had arrived to help them at just the moment they were needed.

As if reading her thoughts, Eileen said, 'Look – I am Eileen Matthews, and this is my best and most-trusted friend Carrie Waters. So – a few minutes ago you might not have known anyone, Mrs Wilson, but now you know us. You do have friends in Bristol, after all.'

Abigail, swallowing over the lump in her throat, looked up gratefully. 'Please call me Abigail,' she said. 'And I am *so* glad to have met you, Eileen and Carrie, just at the moment I needed someone,' she added.

But as they crossed the road towards the café, Eileen couldn't help being curious about Mrs Abigail Wilson and her small daughter. Why would anyone come to a strange city knowing no one, and with nowhere to live? And as far as Eileen could tell – not having many belongings either. She'd noticed last night that they'd had no luggage with them, no cases for their clothes. Though they now had a pushchair and a Baker Baker carrier bag with them, so it seemed they'd done some shopping . . .

Which was more than could be said for Carrie who'd decided against that red dress after all.

Chapter 8

They arrived at the café, and as soon as Janet Robertson saw them enter she came forward immediately, all smiles.

'Well – hello again!' she said to Abigail. 'I'm so glad you've popped back for some tea!'

'Oh – you've been here already, Abigail?' Carrie began, and Abigail interrupted quickly.

'Yes, I'm sorry I didn't mention that Emily and I did have our breakfast here earlier. But I do feel at sixes and sevens at the moment,' she added apologetically.

'There's nothing for you to be sorry about,' Carrie said, 'and in view of everything I'm not surprised that you feel a bit bewildered.' She turned to Janet. 'We were on our way here when we noticed this little girl had fallen out of her pushchair – and look, Emily has hurt herself. She needs a little tender loving care, Janet.'

Within a very few minutes, out in the kitchen and with Emily sitting up on a small table, Janet had provided soap, warm water, a clean towel and some gentle ointment to put on Emily's knees.

'I don't think we'll put a plaster on these little grazes,' Janet said, 'because they will heal better in the fresh air.'

With the others all observing the proceedings, Abigail said,

'Thank you *very* much, Janet – my goodness, we are meeting so many Good Samaritans today!'

By now it was gone three o'clock and the café was getting crowded with customers as Janet found a table for Abigail, Eileen and Carrie. Emily, having sat back in the pushchair, looked up at Janet.

'Can I go and help Pat and Fay?' she said. 'After I've had my ice cream?'

'You certainly can,' Janet said, turning to go. 'We are going to be very busy presently, so what a good thing you turned up.'

The others exchanged glances at this, and Eileen said, 'Janet has such a way with everyone – young, and the not so young. No wonder this place is always full of her friends.'

Abigail agreed at once, going on to explain what had happened earlier. 'Janet was so kind and she told me about Baker Baker where we bought the pushchair and one or two other things this morning.' She paused. 'Because . . . we brought very little with us.'

'Well, what a lovely opportunity to begin all over again,' Carrie said. 'A fresh start for you both!'

'That's certainly what I'm hoping,' Abigail said.

Janet arrived then with their tea and cakes and scones, and an ice-cream cornet for Emily. She glanced at Abigail. 'Have you had the chance to go to Clarks estate agency yet?'

Abigail nodded. 'Yes, thank you . . . and we were just on our way to visit a place they recommended when poor Emily fell from the pushchair.'

The others immediately looked interested, and Eileen said – 'Where is this place? Do you know how to get there?'

'Well, I was given instructions,' Abigail said, 'and the agent said it was a ten-minute walk away from the Centre. It's number fourteen Redcliffe Way.'

'Oh, that's very close to St Mary Redcliffe church,' Carrie said at once. 'Not far away at all.' She smiled at Abigail. 'My father is a vicar, and he has preached there a number of times. It's a beautiful building, inside and out,' she went on, 'and apparently when Elizabeth I came here, she declared it "the fairest and most beautiful church in all England!"'

'Not a woman to mince her words, obviously,' Eileen said dryly. 'And who would dare to disagree with the queen of England.'

As soon as Emily had finished her ice cream, she jumped from the pushchair, went over to the counter and reached up to help put out cups and saucers. Eileen smiled.

'I think your little girl has forgotten her tumble already, Abigail.'

'She needs to be busy,' Abigail explained. 'Well, she has always been expected to do her share of everything.' Abigail didn't go on. Now was not the time to unwrap their lives to these new friends. Perhaps, one day she would, if she ever saw either of them again.

Presently, she looked at her watch and stood up. 'I'm afraid we shall have to go,' she said, 'because the owner of the house – a Miss Grant – won't allow viewings after six o'clock. It's hardly that, I know, but I haven't found the place yet – though Emily is not going to like being dragged away from helping wipe down the tables.'

Eileen stood as well. 'Would you like us to come with you?' she said eagerly. 'To make sure you find it OK?'

Abigail shook her head quickly. 'No, honestly . . . I'm sure we'll be all right by ourselves, and the agent said anyone could direct us.'

'It would be no problem,' Eileen persisted, but Carrie interrupted.

'I expect Abigail would like a few minutes on her own to collect her thoughts, Eileen. And besides – I did promise Mum I wouldn't be too late home this afternoon.' Carrie shot her friend a warning glance as she spoke. Eileen had a heart of gold, everyone knew that, but sometimes she could be a bit over helpful, and Carrie thought that Abigail Wilson might prefer to deal with this particular matter on her own.

'Oh, all right,' Eileen said, catching on at once. She took a small notebook from her handbag and scribbled something then tore out a page and handed it to Abigail. 'Look – this is my home telephone number if you're desperate. So, if you need us, don't be afraid to ring, will you?'

'I promise,' Abigail said, putting the note in her pocket.

Finally, with Emily in the pushchair, strapped safely in, Abigail set off towards her destination, passing through Queen Square where small knots of sunbathers were lying stretched out, relaxing on the grass. And with her thoughts keeping time with her steps, Abigail went over and over everything which had happened since they'd left Coopers.

What an eventful first day in Bristol they'd had. They were already getting the feel of being in a big city, they'd been introduced to the best café in town, they'd been shopping for clothes – and for *shoes*! And now they were on their way to meet Miss Grant and possibly find their first home.

Abigail frowned briefly as she walked on. She would never forget how they'd almost been knocked off their feet by that speeding taxi. Poor Emily. She hadn't been able to save herself from falling to the ground but she'd been very good about it, not making too much fuss.

But out of the blue, she had met kind people . . . so different from the hateful experience she'd had last night in the station restaurant.

She'd met two people who'd said she could call them her friends.

Number fourteen was a neat, red brick, terrace house at the end of the row, and for a moment Abigail stood back to view it. The place looked quite nice, with white net curtains billowing slightly at the open downstairs window.

She knocked on the front door which was opened by a short, middle-aged woman with greying dark hair tied back from her face. She was wearing a black dress and a frilly apron around her waist and, frowning slightly, she stared down at Abigail.

'Have you come about the room?'

Abigail stepped forward. 'Yes,' she said, 'I went to the agency this morning and you . . . your house was highly recommended. My name is Mrs Wilson, Mrs Abigail Wilson. And this is my daughter Emily. There are just the two of us,' she added.

Abigail was amazed at how easily she was uttering that lie . . . '*My name is Mrs Wilson.*' *Perhaps that is how it is with telling lies,* she thought. *It gets easier if you keep doing it.*

The woman nodded, standing aside for them to enter. 'I am Miss Grant,' she said, 'and the room I am offering is upstairs, if you'd like to follow me.'

Leaving the pushchair and all their bags outside by the front door, Abigail and Emily did as they were asked, and stood just inside the accommodation they'd come to see.

The room was very clean and tidy, and fairly spacious, with two single beds covered with blue cotton eiderdowns, the material matching the curtains. There was a dressing table with a mirror, a cabinet and a small chest of drawers. On the floor just inside the door there was a well-worn mat on the lino. Abigail stared around her. Although the room was unexciting, this would be like sleeping in a palace compared with where they'd been last night.

'The bathroom and lavatory are there along the passage,' Miss Grant said, 'and the outside scullery is where you can swill your clothes.' She sucked in her cheeks for a moment as she stared down at Emily. 'She doesn't wet the bed, does she? These mattresses are quite new.'

'Emily has not wet her bed for a very long time,' Abigail said shortly, 'so there will be no problem there, I assure you.'

The woman nodded, apparently satisfied with that. 'Well, anyway,' she said, 'the kitchen is downstairs, obviously, and you can use it at certain times. I charge seven shillings and sixpence a week plus a three-pound deposit – returnable when you leave. As long as there's been no damage,' she added, glancing at Emily.

Abigail's early optimism began to fade. This was hardly an

encouraging interview and she couldn't help wondering whether Miss Grant really wanted to let the room at all.

Leaning against the door jamb and with her arms folded, Miss Grant said, 'This bedroom is normally my brother's, but he's working away for three months so I thought I might as well let it while he's not here.' She paused. 'As you can see, it is fully furnished so I hope you don't intend to bring much with you. I wouldn't want the place cluttered up.'

Abigail shook her head briefly. 'We have very few possessions so it would only be clothes and a few books and Emily's little games.'

Miss Grant was clearly intrigued by this young woman with such a small child. 'So – this is your daughter?'

'Yes, and she is two and a half years old, going on three, and very well behaved. She will be no trouble, I assure you,' Abigail said, beginning to get irritated at the woman's unfriendly attitude. Was this how landladies treated prospective tenants?

Her eyes narrowing, Miss Grant looked Abigail up and down. 'By the way,' she said, 'I do not allow gentlemen to visit – under any circumstances. I hope that's understood.'

For a moment, Abigail felt like taking Emily's hand and marching back down the stairs and out of number fourteen. But this room was good enough, and there was very little time left today to find anything else. And at least they wouldn't be here for long.

'We have recently come up from the country and are new to Bristol. And we know no one,' Abigail said stiffly. 'So I would not be inviting anyone here, Miss Grant. Anyone at all.'

Softening her tone slightly, Miss Grant said, 'Well, as you will have noticed, we are in a very convenient position, being near the Centre where all the buses leave from, and Queen Square is just around the corner. Nice open place for the little one to run about. And that church over there is the famous St Mary Redcliffe. You'll hear the bells tomorrow morning.'

Miss Grant glanced at her watch. Time was going on, and

she always went to the whist drive at St Mary's hall on Saturday evenings. She hoped Mrs Wilson would make up her mind one way or the other.

'Well,' Abigail said, coming to the only decision she felt she was left with, 'I think I should like to accept your terms, Miss Grant – so may we move in straightaway?' She opened her bag. 'I have the deposit here, together with the rent for the first month of our stay.' As she counted out the cash, Abigail realised that first thing Monday morning she *must* go to the post office to change some of her sovereigns. But she was all right for now. And she must also think about finding work because her money was not going to last very long. She sighed briefly. She couldn't do anything about it until Monday.

Cheering up as she saw the money, Miss Grant accepted it graciously. It was going to be nice to have a few extra bob in her purse. 'What about your things, your cases?' she enquired. 'Have you left them for safekeeping in the office at the Tramways?'

'We have no cases, Miss Grant,' Abigail said firmly. 'Our belongings are outside with the pushchair. So – as you will appreciate – we shall not be cluttering up our bedroom,' she added.

Mystified that they appeared to be complete strangers to the town and owned nothing, the landlady shrugged to herself. It was their business, not hers, and on the face of it, it looked as though these two would be no trouble. Not like the couple of students she'd let the room to last year.

'Right, I'll show you the kitchen and then leave you to settle in,' she said, going in front of them down the stairs. 'And by the way, the shops are a short walk up the hill at the other end of this row because you will need a few groceries, won't you? Milk and bread.' She led them to a door at the end of the hall. 'Here's the kitchen, and the pantry is there by the window, where you can store your food. That gauze keeps out the flies,' she added.

Turning, she pointed to a basket of cutlery. 'You can use those knives and forks, and the pots are on that shelf there.' She hesitated. 'Any breakages will have to be paid for, of course.'

'Of course, Miss Grant,' Abigail said, glancing around her. As with everywhere else, the place was immaculate.

Coming straight to the point, Miss Grant continued, 'Now, I have my breakfast at seven o'clock and I finish by eight. And I have my dinner at twelve and my tea at five. So you can use the kitchen either side of those times – I'm sure we won't get in each other's way.' She actually smiled for the first time that afternoon. 'Just as well to know where we stand, isn't it?'

'Yes, of course,' Abigail began, but the landlady hadn't finished.

'And here's a spare front door key so that you can come and go as you please. But the house is always bolted for the night by ten o'clock so if you come in after that you won't be able to gain entry. Oh, and another thing – I don't allow smoking on the premises. I can't stand the smell of cigarettes.'

Half an hour later, with their clothes – old and new – put safely in the chest of drawers, and with Abigail's precious drawing materials and Emily's toys and books in the cabinet, Abigail went across to the window and looked out at the small back garden. Very neat, with pots of geraniums placed at strategic intervals. She glanced down at Emily who was lying on her tummy drawing in her little notebook.

'Well, do you like our new room, Emily? Do you think we are going to be comfy here?' Abigail said.

'No,' Emily said, without looking up.

'Oh – why don't you like it?'

'Because there isn't a bed for us.'

'But there are two, Emily – two beds,' Abigail began, and Emily interrupted.

'We don't need two beds,' she said. 'We only ever have one, don't we, Mummy? We sleep together in the same bed, don't we?'

That was true. They had always shared the double bed at

Coopers because there was no alternative. 'Of course we do,' Abigail said at once. 'So we shall sleep in one of these and cuddle up together. Which one would you prefer?'

Emily pointed. 'That one,' she said.

Abigail's eyes softened. Emily was – always had been – such a compliant little thing, and she'd gone along with everything that Abigail had dragged them both into over the last couple of days. And she hadn't mentioned her grazed knees since.

Emily turned to a clean page. 'I don't like Miss Grant,' she said, 'because she thinks I will wet the bed. Only babies do that, and I'm not a baby, am I Mummy?'

'You certainly are not – and Miss Grant was only asking.'

There was a pause. 'I don't like her shoes,' Emily went on. 'They're horrible – not like the ones you've bought, Mummy.'

Abigail smiled. As usual, Emily had been taking everything in, missing nothing. Even though she'd not uttered a word while the landlady had been there.

'Well, perhaps Miss Grant has sore feet,' Abigail said, 'and needs to wear those sorts of shoes. Black, strong and reliable ones.'

'I still don't like her,' Emily said matter-of-factly, 'but I like Janet and Pat and Fay, and I like Eileen and Carrie as well.'

'Yes, I like them, too,' Abigail said. 'They were all very kind to us, weren't they?'

Emily looked up eagerly. 'Can we go back to Janet's now?'

Abigail shook her head. 'No, not tonight. Besides, Eileen and Carrie will have gone home, and perhaps Janet will soon be closing for the day. But we will go there again soon.'

Presently, with Emily in her pushchair, Abigail made her way up the street towards the rank of shops the landlady had told her about. They were only going to need milk, sugar, cornflakes, tea, bread and butter, and some biscuits. And perhaps half a dozen eggs. Just enough to be going on with. Besides, Abigail didn't want to upset Miss Grant by putting too much of everything on the one shelf in the pantry that had been allocated as Abigail's.

They arrived at Dawson's the grocer's, and the owner immediately came forward to serve them. 'Oooh, you're in luck because we're nearly closing!' he said. 'But we are always open for special people!' He tickled Emily beneath her chin.

Abigail looked away quickly. She wasn't used to this sort of reaction from anyone. 'Thank you for staying open,' she said as she itemised the things she'd come for, adding, 'Oh, and perhaps a bottle of orange squash and a jar of Marmite? Thank you.'

As he put their order into a strong brown paper bag, Mr Dawson looked at Abigail quizzically. 'I haven't seen you around here before, luvver,' he said. 'Are you just visiting?'

'No, we hope to be staying for a while,' Abigail said, 'and for the moment we shall be living at number fourteen down the road.'

'Ah – Miss Grant's place,' the grocer said. 'Well, I'm sure we'll be seeing a lot more of you. I hope so, anyway!' He winked. 'Everyone knows everyone else around here you d'know! And that's the way we like it!'

They left the shop, next to which was a small sub-post office, and on a whim Abigail went inside, thinking that it was just possible they might stock the other essentials that she and Emily were running short of. And yes – there right in front of them were drawing materials, paints, paper, pencils, colouring crayons! And all very cheaply priced. Immediately interested, Emily got out of the pushchair and began to help Abigail choose what they wanted, putting everything into one of the bags which were obviously there for the purpose.

'There, I think that must do for today,' Abigail said firmly, noting that Emily was about to add more things to the contents of their bag. The man behind the counter smiled as he took the money from Abigail.

'All that'll keep the little one quiet for a bit,' he said cheerfully.

Later, appearing to have the house to themselves, Abigail and Emily sat in the kitchen eating their supper. Emily had asked for a boiled egg with soldiers to dip, while Abigail needed nothing more than a strong cup of tea and a couple of Marmite sandwiches. She still felt full after the food they'd had at Robertson's.

And now she admitted to feeling worn out after the first day of their new lives and couldn't wait to get to bed – even though it was hardly dark.

Fortunately, it seemed that Emily was tired too, because she couldn't stop yawning, and after everything had been cleared up and the kitchen left exactly as they'd found it, the two made their way upstairs.

Fetching their toilet bag from the bedroom, they went into the bathroom, and Abigail bit her lip as she glanced around her. They could hardly use Miss Grant's towels, all so beautifully folded over the bath, and they had only brought two small towels with them from Coopers because they just couldn't carry anything else. But those would have to do for now.

Presently, with all these thoughts churning in her mind, Abigail slipped into bed beside Emily who had already snuggled down.

And lying there close together, they both slept soundly all night – though it being mid-summer, the eiderdown soon ended up on the floor.

Much later that evening, Eileen went into her mother's sitting room carrying a tray holding their night-time drinks and a small plate of bourbon biscuits. This was a normal ritual – to enjoy a chat together at the end of the day.

Mrs Matthews was sitting in her armchair, her book and a copy of the *Bristol Evening Post* on her lap. She looked up as Eileen went in.

'Is it that time already?' she asked. 'There was a lot to read in the paper today, and I'm trying to finish this book before it's due back in the library.'

Eileen put the tray down on the small table beside her mother. 'It's not even ten o'clock yet, Mother, but I wanted to tell you about someone Carrie and I met today when we were in town. Well, there were two of them, actually.'

And Eileen proceeded to tell her mother all about Abigail and Emily.

Mrs Matthews had been listening intently, and now she said, 'And what did you think of this young woman? Did you consider her a responsible mother, a responsible adult capable of having the care of a small child? In their present circumstances, I mean?'

'Oh there was no doubt about her being a responsible mother,' Eileen said at once. 'The close relationship between her and her daughter was there for all to see. And Mrs Wilson knows exactly how to express her point of view. Both of us – Carrie and I – took to her immediately. You couldn't help it, Mother, apart from the fact that she is very, very attractive. But what was just as attractive was her personality, because despite her obvious courage and determination, she has a certain naivety about her which is very appealing.'

'So,' Gladys Matthews said, picking up her drink, 'what happened after that?'

'Well, we all said goodbye and Abigail thanked us and everything, and then she and Emily went off to view somewhere to stay tonight. Apparently, Clark's had recommended number fourteen Redcliffe Way.' Eileen made a face. 'I hope they did find it, and that it came up to their expectations.'

'Try not to worry too much about them, Eileen,' Mrs Matthews said. 'It sounds to me as if this young woman has a head on her shoulders. And you can't take everyone's worries on yours, my dear,' she added.

Eileen nodded. 'I know – but you would have liked them, Mother. And Emily is about the sweetest little thing you can imagine and seemed unbelievably grown up. She hardly mentioned her poor knees and was trotting around helping clear the cups and saucers – and spoke beautifully to us all. Not a bit shy.' Eileen patted her mother's knee. 'You would have loved her, Mother.'

'I'm sure I would,' Gladys Matthews said. 'You never know, you might bump into them again, and if you do, you could invite them here for a meal or a cup of tea, Eileen. I mean, as they have no friends they might be glad of a little hospitality.'

Eileen nodded. 'I thought of that,' she said, 'so I gave Abigail our telephone number and told her to get in touch if she needed us.'

Chapter 9

Next morning, with Emily still fast asleep, Abigail slipped out of bed and went across to the window. Quietly drawing the curtains aside, she gazed out at another perfect day with not a cloud in sight. She drew in a long, deep breath. This really was the first day of their new lives. You could hardly count yesterday which now seemed a kaleidoscope of strange things – new places, new people, a whole new world. And – maybe – new friends.

Now she and Emily were away from Coopers, away from everything they'd ever known and just then, as if to welcome them to their new lives, bells from the church nearby began to ring out, welcoming worshippers to the Sunday morning services.

The strident clanging certainly encouraged Emily to wake up, and she jumped out of bed and went over to stand by Abigail. 'What are we going to do today, Mummy?' she asked. 'Are we going to see Janet?'

Abigail shook her head. 'Not today, Emily – because we need to really look around Bristol and find out where everything is. But we will go to the café soon,' she added.

'And see Eileen and Carrie?' Emily said eagerly. 'Will they be there?'

'Oh, maybe,' Abigail said. 'But first of all, after we've had our breakfast, we will just wander around and get our bearings.' She hugged Emily to her. 'We are going to be in Bristol for a long time, so we must try and remember the names of streets, and how to get around – and where all the buses go.'

Emily's face lit up. 'I've never been on a bus,' she said.

'Nor me,' Abigail said cheerfully. 'This is going to be fun, Emily.' She paused. 'And that bed *was* comfy last night, wasn't it? We were like two bugs in a rug!'

There was no sound in the house as they crept along to the bathroom. After getting dressed, they went downstairs to the kitchen which was deserted. It was eight o'clock so Miss Grant would already have had her breakfast, Abigail thought, as she shook some cornflakes into their bowls and fetched milk and sugar from the pantry. After they'd cleared up, they were going out into the sunshine, into Queen Square where she had seen those people sunbathing yesterday afternoon. In fact, they might as well take a few sandwiches and biscuits and some orange squash with them and have a picnic there on the green. Emily would love that.

Abigail glanced down at her daughter who was scooping up the last of her cornflakes. 'You look lovely in your new dress, Emily. What a good job we could buy one which had a pocket for dolly.'

Emily nodded. 'I promised her we would,' she said. 'Do you think Aunt has collected the eggs yet, Mummy? And given the chickens their breakfast?'

Abigail shrugged briefly. 'Probably,' she said, 'but Aunt Edna has others to help her do everything now, so she doesn't need us, and we don't need her, do we?'

'No – but the chickens might need me, because they did love me,' Emily said. 'They used to run up calling and clucking as soon as they saw me coming.'

'Never mind those chickens,' Abigail said firmly. 'Now, help me make our picnic. We are going out for the day!'

* * *

The following morning, the first thing Abigail knew she must do was to change her sovereigns. Not that she would change all of them – perhaps ten to start with. The ready money she'd brought with her seemed to be going a bit too quickly, and the thought that she might be faced with a bill she couldn't pay filled Abigail with horror.

It proved to be quite a long walk to the General Post Office, but the building was easy enough to find, and when they emerged – with Abigail feeling like a millionaire as she clutched her purse now comfortably full of notes and coins – she gave a sigh of relief. This was going to keep them going until she found a job, and until then she needed no instructions in how to be thrifty.

For the next few days it seemed to Abigail that she and Emily were here on holiday enjoying themselves instead of trying to establish a foothold on the city. Part of this was thanks to Miss Grant who directed them to the children's play parks nearby where there were swings and seesaws. She also told them that you could stroll along beside the river at Bristol Bridge and watch the little boats. And she also gave them the number of the bus that would take them to Clifton Downs. The landlady much preferred it when her tenants were out of the house for the day.

'Lovely place for a picnic, the Downs,' Miss Grant had declared. 'There'll be crowds of other people up there, and if you walk along and look over the wall you can see right over to the Suspension Bridge.' She'd paused for a second before adding smugly, 'I don't suppose you'll have ever heard of the Clifton Suspension Bridge?'

'Of course I have, Miss Grant,' Abigail had replied at once. 'It was designed by Isambard Kingdom Brunel, who was famous for many other buildings, too, including Temple Meads Railway Station.' Abigail remembered all those history lessons she'd loved, drinking in every detail. Her education, though not extensive, had been sound and well taught, and she would always be grateful for that.

Miss Grant had looked quite disappointed that she'd not been able to impress this newcomer up from the country. The landlady had eyed Abigail suspiciously for a moment. This Mrs Wilson was a strange one, you couldn't make her out really. And why wasn't her husband with her?

So, as far as Abigail was concerned, July was turning out to be a month of interest and relaxation as she enjoyed watching Emily having time out to play with one or two other children in the parks, or throwing bread into the river for the ducks. And once, they'd gone to the Central Library where Emily had soon become engrossed in the children's section where there were hundreds of books for her to look at.

The time had gone so quickly that despite Emily's entreaties that they go to see Janet and Eileen and Carrie, they had only visited Robertson's twice, and the first time, as it happened, neither Janet, nor Eileen and Carrie, had been there at the time.

The second time, the following Wednesday afternoon, the place had been packed as Abigail and Emily looked in at the door. But Janet had spotted them and had hurried across at once.

'Hello!' she'd said. 'We've missed you! And tell me quickly – are you living at number fourteen? Was it a nice place? Eileen, Carrie and I have been thinking about you – and worrying about you!'

Abigail had nodded. 'Yes, we took the room,' she'd said, 'and it's perfectly adequate – but we're not allowed any visitors, or I would invite you all over to come and see it.'

Emily – who hadn't said a word – had spoken up. 'Can I come and help Pat and Fay now, please? We can stay, can't we, Mummy?' she'd added eagerly.

Abigail had shaken her head regretfully. She'd only come in to buy an ice cream for Emily. 'No we can't, Emily, because we need to get a few supplies from Dawson's and he closes early today.'

Janet had given Emily a quick hug. 'Never mind, Emily – you come whenever Mummy says you can –because I can always do with your help. And I've found a little apron all ready for you!'

Then Janet had smiled apologetically at Abigail. 'I'll have to fly, it's always frantic on Wednesdays. But just you wait until I tell Eileen and Carrie that I've seen you and that you accepted number fourteen! They will be *so* relieved when they know where you are – but I'll warn them that they're not allowed inside the door!'

After they'd had breakfast the following Monday, Abigail and Emily left number fourteen, preparing to go into town. As usual, they'd seen nothing of Miss Grant who seldom put in an appearance until later in the day – unless she could find something to complain about. Last week it had been that she'd been certain she'd had three eggs left on her shelf, but that now there were only two. Had Mrs Wilson taken one by mistake? (Afterwards the landlady did admit she'd forgotten she'd used one to make a Yorkshire pudding.) And one of the major things that seemed to rattle her was when the mat in the hall by the front door wasn't left neat and exactly straight, but at an angle. 'It makes the place look so untidy,' Miss Grant would declare.

Now, as they walked along, Abigail's eyes clouded briefly. After having found them a roof over their heads – obviously the most vital thing of all – her next hurdle was to find work . . . And she didn't really know how to start. As Aunt Edna had said – what did Abigail have to offer, with no experience outside Coopers?

Even so, Abigail thought, the new amount of money she now had in her purse would soon dwindle if it wasn't replaced.

Then her eyes softened as she thought of Dada – her lovely, gentle dada – who'd made sure that she was going to be safe, at least for the time being, in a savage world where money was so essential. And Abigail knew that he would have loved his little granddaughter as much as he'd loved her, his beloved daughter.

With Emily now in charge of the pushchair, they went into the Centre and began to walk up Park Street. As they passed Baker Baker, Abigail stopped to gaze in at the window thoughtfully. The assistant who had served them recently had been so pleasant and helpful, but she'd also mentioned that they were short-staffed at the moment. Did Abigail dare?

She glanced down at Emily. 'Come on, I need to go in here again for a moment.' Emily interrupted.

'Are we going to buy another dress for us, Mummy? And more shoes?'

'No, not today,' Abigail replied, pushing open the heavy door and leading Emily inside. Almost at once an assistant – not the same one as before – came over.

'Can I help you?' the woman said pleasantly, and Abigail smiled hopefully.

'Yes – I would like to speak to the manager, please,' she said.

'Well, you have come at just the right time,' the woman said, 'because I am duty manager today. Now, how can I be of assistance?'

Abigail swallowed. 'Well, the thing is, my name is Mrs Wilson, and my daughter and I are new to the city having recently moved up from the country, and we came to your shop recently and bought a few things, and—'

'Yes,' the woman said, 'I recognise the pushchair and the pretty dress!' She paused. 'Was there a problem with any of your purchases?'

'Oh no, not at all,' Abigail said at once. 'Everything suited us perfectly, but . . . what I am really looking for is a job.'

'A job?' the woman repeated. 'Um – what sort of job?'

'Well, to help in any way I could, and to serve the customers,' Abigail said. 'I thought it would be lovely to work here, and the assistant who dealt with us mentioned that you were short-staffed.'

'Have you had any experience in the retail trade, Mrs Wilson?'

'No, I haven't. But I'm quick to learn new things,' Abigail said, 'and Emily would be no trouble.'

The manager glanced down at Emily who was standing quietly by her pushchair. 'Oh, are you saying that you would expect to bring the little girl with you to work each day?'

'Oh yes,' Abigail said, 'I'm afraid I have no option, because we know nobody here with whom I could leave her – and besides, I wouldn't want her to be without me all day. Not yet. She is far too young.'

The manager smiled kindly. 'I think you have hit the nail on the head, Mrs Wilson,' she said, 'but I'm afraid it would be totally impossible for me to take anyone on who is in your position.' She paused. 'I'm sorry, but I think you are going to have great difficulty finding any employment under your particular circumstances.'

Abigail stepped back, automatically taking Emily's hand in hers, and turning to leave. 'Oh well, never mind. I shall have to go on looking.'

The manager went forward to open the door for them. 'What I might suggest is that you visit the Labour Exchange across the road over there, Mrs Wilson. They will tell you of any vacancies they have on their books, and you never know, there might be *something* they could offer you.'

Abigail had never heard of the Labour Exchange, but it wasn't difficult to work out what the words meant.

'Thank you, anyway,' she murmured as they left, and the manager nodded.

'Good luck,' she said.

As they made their way slowly across the road to the Council House, Abigail couldn't help feeling dejected. Although she hadn't imagined she'd find a job straightaway, she had not expected such a flat refusal – together with a warning that finding work was not going to be easy if you had a small child in tow.

She bit her lip, hard. So Edna had been right all along. What had she said Emily would be? A millstone around the neck?

Emily had chosen to sit in the pushchair, and Abigail leaned down to gently caress that precious head of hair. Her little daughter could never be described as anything other than a gift from God, a treasure – whatever Aunt had said, and however many more times she, Abigail Wilson, was going to be shown the door by a prospective employer.

The Labour Exchange turned out to be a small room on the ground floor of the building. There were three chairs for people to sit and wait, and three booths allowing some privacy for hopeful employees to be interviewed. All the booths were occupied, the candidates speaking quietly to someone sitting on the opposite side of the desk.

Abigail and Emily sat down in the waiting area, and Emily looked up. 'What is this place, Mummy?' she whispered. 'What have we come here for?'

'To see if they have a job for me, Emily,' Abigail whispered back. 'I've told you that I must find work, haven't I, so that we have enough money to pay for whatever we need.'

Emily nodded slowly. She'd picked up something of what had been said at Baker Baker, but hadn't fully understood it. 'Will you get a job here?' she said softly.

'Maybe,' Abigail replied, smiling. 'But don't worry. I will make sure we're going to be all right.'

They had to wait for half an hour before being called over, and, taking Emily's hand, Abigail went across to sit at the empty booth, lifting Emily onto her lap. The man facing her was not young, but he had a kind face.

'Now then, who have we here, where do you live, and what are you looking for today?' he said.

Trying to be as precise as he was, Abigail gave him the details he'd asked for. 'So you see, I am hoping to find something – well, anything, really – which would allow me to take my daughter with me.'

The man sat back, shaking his head slowly. 'Oh dear,' he said, 'that is going to be very difficult, I'm afraid, because casual work – which I assume is what you want – would not be suitable with a very young child involved.' He glanced down at his lists. 'There is something here, but I imagine that cleaning schools and offices in the early hours of the morning, or later in the evening, would be hard for you – and of course you'd have to find your way there on your own.' He sighed. 'And the money is not very good,' he added.

Abigail looked away for a moment. She'd imagined that a big city would have plenty of opportunities for someone willing to work. But she had to admit that what he'd suggested just wouldn't be suitable.

'So – there's nothing else that you could suggest?' she said.

He sat back. 'Yes, there is, my dear young lady,' he said. 'Why don't you think about applying for the little one to attend a nursery school? She would be looked after all day, and you would know that she'd be perfectly safe there.'

Abigail's first instinct was to turn the suggestion down straight-away, but it seemed only polite to show a little interest. 'Would you, um, give me a few details?'

'Yes, of course. Now then, there is a very good nursery school in Milk Street. A bit of a walk from here – but it's very well run. And it is a council-run school, so would cost nothing.'

'I see, and how many children attend?'

'Oh, I think that altogether there are about forty youngsters there, separated in three classes,' the man said, 'aged between two and five years old.' He glanced at Emily. 'How old is the little one?'

By now, Emily had picked all this up, and she immediately spoke. 'I will be three next birthday,' she said. She turned to Abigail. 'Won't I, Mummy?'

'Just right, then,' the man said. He glanced at Abigail. 'Some of the children are eighteen months old or so, and little more than babies of course, but they'll be accepted as long as they can walk, and are not in nappies.'

Abigail frowned briefly. Tiny babies, going to *school*?

The man warmed to his subject. 'Now, when they arrive each day, they are given a light breakfast, and at mid-morning they have a mug of milk and a rusk. A very good, hot dinner is provided – freshly cooked on the premises – after which they are expected to lie down for a little rest. The canvas beds are quite comfortable,' he added. 'Then, just before their mothers come to fetch them at three-thirty, they are given a mug of orange juice.' He paused. 'And of course, during the day the older ones receive a basic education as well.'

Listening to all this made Abigail feel uneasy. This was never what she'd intended for Emily – who, although advanced for her years – was still too young to be holding her own with a crowd of strange children in a city she was only just beginning to know. And the oldest ones, the five-year-olds, would have already learned how to demonstrate their superiority – about which Abigail herself knew only too well.

The man turned to Emily. 'So – do you think you would like to go to this nice school?' he enquired. 'I know that you would have your own peg to hang your coat on, and your own apron to put on at dinner time when you wait in line for your meal to be given you . . . and of course there are lots of other children there as well. I believe the playground can be quite a noisy place which means everyone is having fun, doesn't it?'

Emily considered this for a moment. 'Mummy will be there as well, won't she?'

The man chuckled. 'Oh no, my dear, mummies are not allowed to stay! Mummy's got to go to work, hasn't she, but she will take you to school first, and then hand you over to your teacher who will show you where to sit and what you must do.'

In the silence that followed, the man glanced over at his waiting area where all the chairs were now occupied. 'So,' he said, 'do you think you would like to go to this school?'

'No,' Emily said. 'No thank you.'

The man looked quite disappointed. He thought he'd given that nursery school a very good recommendation and he knew it was well thought of. He glanced at Abigail.

'What do *you* think, Mummy?' he said. 'Don't you feel that this would be a very good solution to your little problem?'

Abigail lifted Emily from her lap and stood to leave. 'It was kind of you to try and do your best for us,' she said, 'but I'm afraid my answer is the same as Emily's.' Abigail smiled sweetly. 'No, thank you,' she said.

With Emily in charge of the pushchair, they left the building, Abigail admitting to feeling quite queasy at the slightest thought of Emily being deposited in a strange place, a strange situation, and knowing no one – and for an entire day. And so soon after she'd been brought away from the safety and security of Coopers.

Abigail tightened her lips. Well, it was unthinkable, and it was never going to happen. She would go on looking for a job until *someone* gave her one.

And it was going to be a very long time before Emily was thrown to the lions in the playground.

Chapter 10

Taking their time, and with Emily agreeing to have a lift in the pushchair, the two made their way slowly all the way up Park Street, glancing in the shop windows as they went. They hadn't been this far before, and it was a long walk. And just then, the chimes of Great George rang out, the big clock on Bristol University tower which Luke had spoken about.

And there it was. The university that his father had attended, and to which Luke himself had said he might go.

Luke. Oh Luke. If only you knew what has happened to us.

Admitting to herself that she was feeling insecure and vulnerable, Abigail stopped to catch her breath for a moment. Pausing, she allowed her imagination to run away with her, to believe that they *might* see each other again one day – and here in Bristol. Perhaps that's why she'd chosen the city? What a miracle it would be if she and Luke were to come face to face! They would have so much to catch up with, and she would have so much to tell him!

And he would hold her close, tenderly, lovingly, as only Luke Jordan knew how . . .

Then she shook herself angrily. That was never going to happen now, and Abigail felt annoyed that she'd allowed her thoughts to drift back to that other life, the life they'd left behind them. That was then, and this was now – their present, and their future. Hers and Emily's. There were just the two of them, and that was always as it was going to be. The past was the past.

'Can we go across the road, Mummy?' Emily asked eagerly, looking up from her pushchair. 'That shop over there has got cakes in the window!'

Abigail followed her daughter's gaze. They were looking at The Berkeley Hotel and Restaurant, and it did look inviting. Abigail sighed briefly. She was going to push all her negative thoughts to one side, and she was sure she could afford to treat them both to a nice lunch for now.

They had to wait quite a few moments to cross the busy road, and as they entered The Berkeley a waitress approached them.

'Good afternoon,' she said. 'Are you here for coffee today – or for lunch?'

'We would like lunch, please,' Abigail said.

'Then follow me,' the waitress said, beginning to lead them further inside, and just then Emily cried out. 'Look, Mummy there's Carrie!' And without waiting for a response from her mother, Emily sprang out of the pushchair and ran across the entrance hall, flinging her arms right around the waist of the young woman who was just about to enter a door which stated 'Staff Only'.

'Oh – *hello*!' Carrie exclaimed, turning to pick Emily up and hug her. 'How *lovely* to see you again!'

Her eyes lighting up, Abigail came to join them. It was so good to see that smiley face!

'Hello, Carrie,' she said. 'Yes, we've had one or two things to do this morning, but as soon as Emily saw this restaurant, she insisted we come in and have some lunch,' Abigail added. 'For a treat.'

'Oh, I'm so pleased you did!' Carrie exclaimed. 'Because Eileen and I have been wondering about you – though Janet did say you'd called in briefly and told her you'd accepted number fourteen. Is it any good – are you happy there?'

Abigail nodded. 'Yes, it's a suitable room, and the arrangements are fairly simple to follow. And we have slept very well – haven't we, Emily?' Abigail glanced around her for a second. 'So – this is where you work, Carrie?'

Carrie nodded, setting Emily down gently. 'Yes, upstairs in the Accounts department,' she said, 'where I've been since leaving school.' She paused. 'Look. I've got time to sit and have a coffee with you, if you would like me to – while you have lunch. We can have a bit of a chat – the details of which I shall have to recount to Eileen when I see her, of course! We've thought about you both so much.'

'We'd love you to sit and talk to us – wouldn't we, Emily?' Abigail said as all three made their way towards the restaurant area.

'And have your little knees fully recovered now, Emily?' Carrie asked, automatically holding Emily's hand. Emily nodded.

'They're fine,' she said airily.

Presently, seated at a corner table by the window enjoying their lunch, Abigail looked across at Carrie.

'So, you and Eileen have been friends for a very long time?'

Carrie nodded as she sipped at her coffee. 'Yes – ever since we met at secondary school. And when we left – that was four years ago when we were sixteen – Eileen got a job at the Royal Insurance Company – just off the Centre – and I got this one. So we actually work fairly close to each other and can often meet up – especially at Janet's place.' Carrie shot a glance at Abigail. 'I expect you left school at sixteen, too, didn't you, Abigail? Most of us did, didn't we? Which probably means that we three are all about the same age.'

'Yes – I shall be twenty next birthday,' Abigail said. 'Do you and Eileen live near each other?'

'Yes – as I think I mentioned, my father is a priest, and our church is All Saints in Knowle. I live in the vicarage with my parents. It's less than a mile away from where Eileen lives with her mother in West Road, near Broad Walk, so it's a short distance for us to meet up when we want to get together.'

Abigail glanced at Carrie for a second. As a vicar's daughter, was she expected to attend church every Sunday, and did the family always say Grace before meals? Abigail bit her lip, remembering her aunt's strict religious views even though her behaviour had often been less than Christian. After all, shouldn't Edna have wanted her great-niece to be baptised in the name of Jesus rather than insisting the innocent baby should be nameless and hidden away in disgrace? It hadn't made any sense to Abigail then, and it still didn't now.

As if reading her thoughts, Carrie said, 'Did you go to your village church, Abigail?'

'I did go to Sunday school,' Abigail said carefully, 'but the aunt who I lived with was the religious one in the family. I know she used to kneel down every night to say her prayers and she used to enjoy the vicar coming to give her Holy Communion every so often. He used to arrive on his big black horse and he always looked so solemn, but after their little service he would stay for tea and homemade cake which used to cheer him up.'

Carrie giggled. 'Sometimes, when he's done his parish rounds, my father has been given so many cups of tea he says he could nearly swim home! But people are very kind, and they mean well,' she added.

Carrie watched Emily scrape up the last of her lamb casserole before going on. 'You see, luckily, Eileen and I have always enjoyed the same things. In the summer we sometimes play tennis on Saturday mornings if neither of us have to go to work – we use the local court near Eileen's place. And we both *love* going to the cinema. When a new film comes out, we're always first in the queue.' Carrie smiled happily. 'My boyfriend, Mark – he's in the army – seems really fond of Eileen, and I know she likes him. They're always teasing each other when he's home on leave.'

After a few moments, Carrie went on, 'And do you know, Eileen and I have never fallen out. Not once. Because, as friends, we enjoy just getting along together. And not looking for arguments!'

Abigail smiled slowly. 'I had a friend like that once,' she said.

Carrie looked at her quickly. 'And you don't now?'

'No,' Abigail replied. 'It was a long time ago, and we don't see each other anymore.'

'That's a shame,' Carrie said lightly. 'A good friend is better than money in the bank.' She didn't go on but couldn't help being curious about Abigail and her little daughter. Why were they really here, and what made them choose Bristol of all places? Didn't she realise that when war came – and it was going to be soon – Hitler's bombers would aim for the city's factories, the aeroplane company, the docks? The obvious, vulnerable targets in any warfare?

And surely Abigail must be missing Emily's father – who, Janet had said, Abigail had briefly implied was away on war work of some kind. Carrie looked away for a moment. If she was missing Mark, how much more must Abigail be missing her husband? But, it was Abigail's business, no one else's, and perhaps one day she would tell them a little more.

Emily suddenly chirped up. 'We've been looking for a job for Mummy today,' she announced, 'because we must have enough money to pay for everything.'

Carrie immediately looked interested. 'Oh?' She turned to Abigail. 'And did Mummy find a job?'

'Not yet,' Abigail said lightly, 'but it's early days. I expect something will come up.'

'And the man wanted me to go to school,' Emily went on conversationally, 'but I didn't want to and Mummy didn't want me to, either.'

Carrie raised her eyes and Abigail said, 'Oh, it was the chap in the Labour Exchange, that's all. He thought it would free me up but I said I wasn't interested.'

After a moment's pause, Carrie said, 'Well, I suppose I had better go back upstairs or they'll give me the sack.' She smiled down at Emily. 'I hope we see you in Janet's place again soon,' she said.

'We're going there this afternoon,' Emily announced, 'aren't we, Mummy?'

Later, Abigail and Emily began wandering back down the street, and suddenly Abigail's eyes lit up. She stopped abruptly. A book-shop! A bookshop with rows of beautiful volumes set out there in the window. And the auspicious sign above read 'Blackwell's'

How she would *love* to work in a bookshop! From a very young age, she'd read all her books over and over again – when she'd been allowed. But would she – could she – find the courage to go inside this important-looking building and ask if they would take her on? Abigail shook her head quickly. Asking herself that question made her realise just how easily her self-belief had lessened. After all, so far she'd only been turned down once, but it was her experience at the Labour Exchange that had turned the screw.

Well, tomorrow was another day, and it would be tomorrow that she'd find the courage to return to this spot and go into Blackwell's.

Looking up from the pushchair, Emily yawned. 'Can we go to Janet's now? Eileen might be there.'

'No, she won't,' Abigail said, 'because Eileen works in an office and that's where she'll be now.'

'And when *you* go to work, I'm coming too, aren't I, Mummy?' Emily said.

'I'm not sure where I'll be working but of course you will come too,' Abigail said. 'I wouldn't leave you by yourself, would I? But anyway, here we are at Janet's! Have you got room for anything else to eat after our lunch – you finished everything on your plate, didn't you?'

'I've got room for an ice cream,' Emily said.

It was almost three o'clock and the café was quite crowded with customers coming in for tea. As before, Janet spotted them at once and came across.

'Oh – what luck that you turned up!' she exclaimed hurriedly. 'Poor Fay has gone home with a terrible headache, and Pat seems to be developing a really bad cold so I've sent her home, too. I can't risk infecting all my customers!' Janet made a face. 'Those two are *never* ill – certainly not at the same time! So, I would be *really* glad if you could stay and help me, just for an hour, Abigail?' She hesitated, obviously feeling awkward. 'You did mention – some time ago – that you might be looking for work – and it seems that this might be the day! If you have the time, of course,' she added quickly. 'You might be on your way to something else.'

Warming at once to this new situation, Abigail shook her head. 'No, we're not,' she said. She drew the pushchair and their belongings into a far corner out of the way, before following Janet into the kitchen.

'There's a fresh tray of cakes just ready to come out of the oven,' Janet said, sounding unusually harassed, 'and I was just about to rub up another batch of pastry.' She glanced anxiously out towards the door where more customers were coming in, and Abigail immediately turned to wash her hands in the deep sink.

'Leave the pastry to me, Janet,' she said briskly, 'then I'll add jam onto those scones over there, shall I?'

Obviously relieved, Janet touched Abigail briefly on the arm. 'You are a visiting angel,' she said. 'And just look at your daughter. What a little treasure.'

Having stood there listening to everything that was being said, Emily had caught on at once, and without being asked, was setting out rows of cups and putting teaspoons into every saucer. She called out to Janet. 'Some of the sugar bowls are nearly empty, Janet, and there's no milk in this big jug. Where can I get some more?'

Working there in Janet's neat and inviting kitchen, Abigail

hummed a little tune under her breath. Only a few minutes earlier she'd felt so low about trying to find work, and here it was! Without even asking for it! And although this was obviously just for today, Abigail instinctively felt that she was going to be able to earn a little money here from time to time. Which was a start, wasn't it? She could bake bread and cakes, she could bottle fruit, make jam – and the best bit was that Emily was welcome here, too.

Before rolling out the pastry, Abigail glanced into the café, which was now humming with customers, and she smiled as she watched Emily busily clearing an empty table and reaching up to wipe it down vigorously with a damp cloth, then chatting happily to the people now sitting there as if she'd known them all her life. It was obvious from the expression on their upturned faces that these customers were enjoying the attention of this new little waitress.

It was almost six o'clock before the last customer left, and as she began emptying the till and putting the day's takings into a large bag, Janet looked across at Abigail and Emily who were setting out the chairs and tables neatly for tomorrow.

'I do not know *how* I would have managed this afternoon without you two,' Janet said. 'I've never known it to be this busy on a Monday.'

'We've enjoyed helping you out, Janet,' Abigail said, 'haven't we, Emily? It's been fun!'

Emily nodded. 'Can we come again tomorrow, Janet?'

'Well, let me give you your wages for today, first,' Janet said, coming across towards them, and Abigail stepped back uncertainly.

'Oh . . . really . . . are you sure, Janet? We've been only too happy to help out. But . . . thank you very, very much.'

Janet smiled gratefully. 'I could not have managed here without both of you today!'

Stopping to take her apron off, Abigail said, 'Look, Janet, as you said, you remembered me mentioning on the first day we met that I shall soon be looking for regular work and if I could really be of use to you, perhaps we could arrange something? Say, a few hours now and again? At times which might suit both of us?'

'That would be fantastic,' Janet said at once. 'How about next week – Wednesday and Thursday? From three o'clock to five? Wednesdays are Pat's afternoon off, and Fay takes hers on Thursdays.' Janet paused, before adding, 'I usually employ standby help on those days,' she said, 'but people are not always reliable.' She smiled. 'But I feel I could really count on you, Abigail.'

'And me!' Emily had been listening to all this with great interest. 'I can count up to a hundred, Janet!'

'Well, I will never forget how you welcomed us to Bristol, Janet,' Abigail said. 'You were our first friend in the city and you gave me such good advice. So, Emily and I will be here on duty next week. Wednesday at 3 p.m. sharp, though I am quite sure we shall be here before that. Emily will make sure of it!'

'And Eileen and Carrie will be really pleased to hear that they will be seeing lots of you from now on,' Janet said, 'because they were terribly worried that you and Emily were here by yourselves.'

Chapter 11

The following afternoon, Abigail stood for several moments outside Blackwell's bookshop. She was going in now – and she would ask for a job. After all, they could only say no, and she'd made sure that she and Emily were both looking their best. Deciding not to put it off any longer and, with Emily in her pushchair, she went inside. An elderly lady approached.

'Good afternoon,' she said. 'Can I help you? What are you looking for?'

Fortunately, there were no customers present, and clearing her throat, Abigail decided to come straight to the point. 'I am looking for a job,' she said, 'and I was wondering if you had any vacancies. My name is Abigail Wilson,' she added politely.

The woman was clearly surprised. 'What sort of vacancies are you referring to?' said.

'Anything at all,' Abigail replied promptly. 'Serving behind the counter or cleaning shelves or making tea.' Barely pausing for breath, she went on, 'You see, my daughter and I are new to Bristol and have recently arrived here from the country. And I need to find work. Unfortunately, my husband has been called away,' she added quickly. 'But to spend my days in a bookshop would be my ultimate dream because I have always loved books, they have been a massive part of my life. I was always in charge of our school library,' she added, hoping that didn't sound too pathetic.

The woman waited before replying. Of course, they seldom had any vacancies, especially at this quiet time of year when the university was on its summer break. During termtime the shop was always crowded with undergraduates waiting for the books they'd ordered. But there was something about this young woman's straightforward way of speaking, of her obvious sincerity, that held the shop owner's attention. She smiled at Abigail and glanced down.

'You have a very pretty little daughter, Mrs Wilson,' she said.

'Thank you,' Abigail replied, 'and if you were able to offer me anything, Emily would be no trouble. She is used to entertaining herself while I am otherwise engaged.'

The woman shook her head quickly. 'Oh, I'm afraid that does put a rather different complex on the matter.'

Just then, a man who'd been hovering behind one of the tall units, put his head around. 'What is it, Mother – can I help?'

'This young lady – Mrs Abigail Wilson – is looking for employment, Martin, but I don't think we have anything, do we? Especially as she has to bring her little girl with her.'

He came forward and gazed at Abigail with unashamed interest. An attractive young female like this behind the counter at Blackwell's would not be bad for business – especially when the students returned! But his mother was right, they had nothing at the moment.

'I'm really sorry, Mrs Wilson,' he began – then he paused. 'But wait a minute, we begin stocktaking next week after the shop has closed for the day.' He looked at his mother. 'We really could do with some help, couldn't we, especially as Dennis doesn't feel up to staying late this time. He's not getting any younger.' He turned to Abigail. 'Does the tedious task of sorting, cataloguing and indexing appeal to you, Mrs Wilson?'

Abigail's eyes shone. 'That would *certainly* appeal to me,' she said at once. 'It is what I am quite used to, though not in quite so auspicious surroundings as this,' she added.

The man looked pleased at that. 'Well then, would six o'clock until about eight each evening suit you?' He paused. 'Though that would be very late for your daughter's bedtime, wouldn't it?'

'Not at all,' Abigail said. 'The busy life we led in the country always meant getting up very early and going to bed rather late. Emily is quite used to unusual hours.'

'That's all right, then,' Martin said. 'Stocktaking usually takes two or three weeks, so it would hardly be long enough for you to get sick of!'

For a full ten seconds Abigail was speechless. She'd done it! She'd got herself a job – *another* job! Even if it was only going to be for a few hours. And this one in a bookshop!

'That would suit me perfectly,' Abigail said. 'Thank you so much. And I promise you I would never find the job tedious – and Emily will be happy enough reading and doing her drawing and colouring. She will be no intrusion at all and you'll hardly know she's here.'

The two looked down at Emily who hadn't made a single sound. 'Good, then that's settled,' the man said, smiling. 'Of course, you will be given an overall to protect your lovely clothes – stocktaking is a dusty old business. Let me have your details, Mrs Wilson, where you're living and so forth, and we'll look forward to seeing you straight after the shop has closed next Monday.'

The early days of August were turning out to be humid, with frequent claps of thunder echoing around the city, often accompanied by sudden gusts of rain. Abigail gazed out of the window for a moment. It was obviously going to be another wet day and they hadn't brought their mackintoshes with them when they'd left Coopers all those weeks ago. They couldn't possibly have carried anything else.

Looking briefly into her own eyes in the dressing-table mirror, Abigail couldn't help wondering about Aunt Edna and hoping she was all right, even though she knew her aunt would not care tuppence about what may have happened to her niece and great-niece. If you were no more use to her, she'd wipe you out of existence. How cruelly indifferent Edna had been to her own ailing brother when he'd no longer been able to work at Coopers.

Abigail turned away decisively. Today, Monday, she was going to buy them both a pair of Wellington boots. Emily loved splashing in puddles.

As usual, Emily was engrossed in her books, lying flat on the floor on her tummy. She looked up at Abigail. 'Can we go to the café today, Mummy?' she asked. 'Because we haven't seen Eileen and Carrie for a long time, have we? They don't seem to come in when we're helping Janet, but they may come in today.'

Abigail smiled down. 'Oh, we *have* seen them, Emily . . . even though it's usually been for just a few minutes, because we're so busy. But we did all go for a lovely walk on the Downs the other Saturday, didn't we, and took a picnic.' She paused. 'Anyway, you and I are going shopping today – for new macs and wellies!'

That put a smile on Emily's face and she immediately got up to put her books neatly on the side of the cabinet which had become her desk.

Abigail finished making the bed and tidying up their room, realising how content she was feeling. She'd loved the little job at Blackwell's. Stocktaking had been tiring but very straightforward, and it had been the end of July before it was completed. Then, totally unexpectedly, she'd been offered the chance to serve at the counter from twelve o'clock to two-thirty each day so that Martin's mother could have a proper dinner time. Martin was always there too, in case Abigail got confused, but she'd proved so quick to learn and to remember where everything was, he'd once said he thought she was after his job.

But those two and a half hours of employment turned out

to suit Abigail perfectly because afterwards, on Wednesdays and Thursdays, she and Emily would go straight down to Robertson's where they were given something to eat before starting to help Janet. So from three o'clock to five, as well as often working behind the scenes in the kitchen, Abigail served tea and coffee, buttered scones and fancy cakes to their regular customers, with Emily clearing up the used dishes and wiping down the tables. People seemed to like chatting to the new employee and her little daughter, often insisting on buying them tea and ice cream, so that in the end, Abigail felt that she and Emily were part of Janet's family of friends.

Not only that, but – despite Emily's complaints – Eileen and Carrie did manage to pop in from time to time to catch up with all the news, and to perhaps make plans to go out together. They'd mentioned several times that Emily would love going to the swimming baths or to Weston-super-Mare where you could have donkey rides on the sands.

So how much more could she want from life? Abigail asked herself as she and Emily left the house that morning. From a very shaky start in those first few weeks, things seemed to have settled in her favour – even though part of that was due to the fact that she was living a lie, pretending that she was married. And it did weigh heavily on her heart. Again and again, Aunt Edna's words tormented her – '*Be sure your sins will find you out!*' But she'd been *forced* to lie, to pretend, hadn't she? To ensure that she and Emily were accepted as decent and respectable human beings. Abigail would do anything to protect her little girl from vicious tongues.

'What the 'ell are you doing home, Ronald?'

Miss Grant stared unbelievingly at the man who'd just let himself in at the front door.

'Well, that's a nice way to treat your brother, Iris!' He slung his bag down on the floor. 'It's just that the contract ended early, 'that's all.' He tutted. 'And who forgot to slip the bolt on the door last night, eh? I didn't know whether I could get in without ringing the bell!'

Miss Grant ignored the reprimand, though she knew she did forget to lock up properly now and then.

'Anyway,' he went on, 'I'm home for a bit of a holiday before things get back to normal in September.' He grinned. 'I'll be able to stay in bed until dinner time if I d'feel like it!'

The man was tall and broad-shouldered, with a full head of red hair and a moustache to match, and now he went across to give his sister a kiss on the cheek. 'I know it's early, but I hope you've got some breakfast for me, Iris.'

Miss Grant, her arms folded, looked anything but happy to see the newcomer. She came straight to the point.

'You'll have to sleep in the box room, Ronald,' she said, 'because we've got visitors and they're using your bedroom.'

Ronald took a step back. 'What d'you mean? What visitors?'

'Shh, keep your voice down. They're not up yet.'

It was only five-thirty and the landlady had come down for some aspirin – which she kept in the kitchen cupboard – because she'd woken with a headache. 'You'd better let me make you something,' she said reluctantly, 'before they come down for their breakfast at eight.'

Presently, enjoying his plate of bacon and eggs, sausages and black pudding, Ronald Grant looked up at his sister. She wasn't eating anything, just looking at him stony-faced. 'So what's this all about?' he asked between mouthfuls. 'New friends I don't know?'

'No, they are my tenants,' Miss Grant said flatly, and before he could interrupt, she went on. 'I thought it's such a waste having that lovely bedroom with no one in it, so I decided to make myself a bit of extra money while you weren't here.' (She wasn't going to admit that she'd done this once before.) 'I don't charge that much, but it's nice to have more money in my purse.' She watched as her brother mopped up the grease on his plate with the last of his fried bread. 'And I must say, they're quite nice – a young woman and her little girl. They've caused no trouble at all. They're out quite a lot and keep themselves to themselves,' she added.

Ronald finished his meal and reached for his mug of tea. 'Well, I'll look forward to meeting them,' he said easily. 'What's the young woman look like?'

Iris Grant glared at her brother. He'd never married, but he'd always been one for the ladies. 'It doesn't matter to you *what* she looks like!' she snapped. 'So keep your eyes off. Anyway, she's married, though I haven't seen anything of her husband.'

'Gets better and better,' Ronald Grant said. 'While the cat's away the mice can play! And you're only young once! I could take her to the Landogger with me – you'd look after the kid for a couple of hours while we're gone, wouldn't you, Iris?'

Miss Grant almost threw the dirty dishes into the sink. 'I would *not*, Ronald!' she snapped. 'You keep me out of this – and another thing,' she added, 'they're here for another three weeks until the beginning of September, which is when I thought you'd be back. They've paid in advance, so I don't want you upsetting things.'

Stirring restlessly, Abigail turned over, pulling the pillow closer beneath her chin. Then she glanced at the small clock beside her. It was only six so there was plenty of time before they needed to get up. Emily had hardly moved a muscle since going to bed last night, and was still deeply asleep.

Abigail frowned briefly. Something had woken her just now; it had sounded like subdued voices, but to Abigail's knowledge Miss Grant never had visitors in the house – and if she ever did, it would not be at this time of the day. But all seemed quiet now and Abigail closed her eyes again.

Now that she'd started letting her thoughts wander, Abigail knew she'd never get back to sleep. The main thing on her mind was that their agreement with Miss Grant was a very temporary one and then they'd have to start looking for somewhere else to live. And although the landlady had given them a rather cold welcome, things were working out well on the whole. Abigail had made sure that every demand had been met, and Emily had never once given Miss Grant a thing to complain about. Perhaps ... perhaps, Abigail thought now, the lease might be extended – because this room had become their home and they were comfortable enough here. It would be unsettling for Emily if they had to pack up and go on somewhere else.

Abigail yawned. Anyway, as far as today was concerned, she'd promised Emily that they'd walk to Woolworths to buy sweets and perhaps a little toy or book before going on to Blackwell's. Emily was so good at amusing herself at the shop while Abigail was busy at the counter. In fact, Martin often stopped what he was doing to talk to the little girl and watch what she was doing. And a couple of times he'd let her help him unpack one of the huge boxes of new books which were regularly delivered to the shop.

A couple of hours later, washed and dressed, Abigail and Emily left the bedroom to go downstairs to the kitchen. It was eight o'clock, so Miss Grant would be nowhere around. She always stuck to the rules. But while they were still on the landing, a man's deep voice made them turn and look up, startled.

'Oh, good *morning*!' he said, going forward to stand beside them. 'I am Ronald Grant and I'm very pleased to meet you.' He smiled at them both in turn, not bothering to hide his admiration. 'Well, you are certainly a very picturesque pair to enhance the place, I must say,' he said smoothly.

Abigail stared at him for a moment. His shock of red hair, brushed upwards, made it look as if he was on fire, and he had the strangest blue eyes Abigail had ever seen on anyone. His parted, rubbery lips made him look like a hungry fish about to leap for its next meal. He held out his hand to Abigail – who coloured up at once as she extended her own.

'Oh, good morning, Mr Grant,' she said, 'I am Abigail Wilson

– Mrs Abigail Wilson – and Emily is my little girl.' She paused awkwardly. 'We have been staying with Miss Grant for a couple of months, and as I understood it, she let us rent your room while you were away.'

He nodded, not taking his eyes from Abigail. 'Yes, I was told that this morning,' he said, unperturbed, 'but it's no problem, because we do have somewhere else for me to rest my head.' He nodded towards the room at the far end. 'The box room will be sufficient for me, for the time being,' he added.

Feeling thoroughly embarrassed, Abigail took Emily's hand and began leading her down the stairs. The landlady, who'd heard all that had been said, was standing by the kitchen door looking unusually flustered.

'I'm sorry, Mrs Wilson,' she said, 'I had no idea my brother would be returning home so early. But don't take any notice of him,' she added quickly, 'because, as we agreed, that room is yours until the end of the month. Now, go in and have your breakfast. I expect you're longing for a cup of tea.'

Well, that was a surprise, Abigail thought later as she buttered some slices of toast. But – she shrugged inwardly – it didn't matter to her whether he'd turned up or not because Miss Grant had said the room would still be theirs until the date agreed, though it did mean that they would definitely have to leave then, and find somewhere else.

On Wednesday afternoon during an unusually quiet few moments at the café, Abigail told Janet about Ronald Grant having turned up at number fourteen.

'It did take me by surprise,' Abigail admitted, 'but when he introduced himself he seemed quite, well, friendly. And Miss Grant assured me that, as agreed, the room is still ours until our arrangement comes to an end.'

'What's he look like?' Janet asked curiously as she poured Abigail and herself a cup of tea and passed Emily a cornet.

Abigail thought for a moment. 'Rather odd,' she said. 'Not a bit like Miss Grant.'

Janet sipped from her cup. 'Oh well, never mind,' she said. 'You won't have to look at him for ever.'

Abigail nodded. 'No, but now I must start thinking about other accommodation,' she said. 'And I hate the thought of unsettling Emily.'

On Saturday morning, Abigail, Eileen, Carrie and Emily took the bus to Jubilee Road swimming baths in Knowle. The venue had been Eileen's idea because Abigail had once mentioned that neither she nor Emily had ever been near deep water – certainly not water deep enough to swim in – though they'd sometimes paddled in their shallow river. Today's outing was quite a treat, because Eileen and Carrie sometimes had to work on a Saturday morning, but for once they were both free.

'We'll see whether Emily Wilson is a little water baby or not,' Eileen teased as the bus reached their stop, 'or whether her mother is, for that matter!'

Retrieving the pushchair from the conductor's hatch, they began walking up towards Jubilee Road and Abigail admitted to feeling excited at the thought of experiencing something entirely new. She'd bought herself and Emily bathing costumes and swimming caps – which had proved very uncomfortable when they'd tried them on at home.

'This is *horrible*!' Emily had declared, staring at herself in the mirror. 'It's squashing my face! Look, Mummy! I look silly!'

'We'll have to get used to them,' Abigail had said, 'because Eileen says everyone must wear a cap when they go into the water at the baths.'

As it turned out, Emily loved being in the water – which was quite nice and warm – and loved even more being passed to each of the others as they swam around, holding her up. Eileen and Carrie both tried to demonstrate what you did with

110

your arms and legs in order to stay afloat, and Abigail did try taking her feet off the ground once or twice, but ended up staying fairly close to the side. This needed practice, and she hadn't had any.

Eileen swam towards her. 'You'd soon get used to the feel of the water taking your weight,' she said, trying to catch her breath. She'd just swum two lengths of the baths.

'What I'm pleased about is that Emily doesn't seem at all afraid of being in water when she knows her feet can't reach the bottom,' Abigail said, nodding over to where Emily, holding on to the side, was splashing Carrie. 'She's loving it and is going to want to come here again!'

Eileen nodded as she turned around and prepared to swim back to the deep end. 'She'll be worn out after this,' she said. 'Just look at her! But it wouldn't take long for her to gain the confidence to swim, I'm sure of it.'

They spent a whole hour in the water before getting dressed and leaving the baths. It was a really warm and pleasant day, and although they were quite near West Road, Eileen did not suggest that they call in at number six because she felt her mother was not yet well enough to receive new visitors. Especially damp visitors smelling of chlorine. So, after buying buns and fruit and soft drinks from the shops in Broad Walk, and with Emily happy to have a ride in the pushchair, they waited for the bus which would take them to the Downs to have their picnic, where their wet bathing things would soon dry spread out on the warm grass.

At Emily's insistence, they all went up to the top deck of the bus, and as all four of them sat together in the very front two seats with the aisle between them, Abigail hugged herself with happiness. She *did* have friends, friends who seemed to like being with her, as Luke had said they would.

Then Eileen said, looking across, 'Didn't we have a lovely time in the water this morning – you loved it, didn't you Emily? And everyone seemed to be enjoying themselves with not a care in the world.'

An elderly man sitting right behind them leaned forward. 'Well, we'd better make the most of it, my luvvers,' he said, 'because we might not be enjoying ourselves for much longer.' He shook his head. 'See, I ain't got no faith in our prime minister who d'seem a spineless sort of bloke to me. Neville ain't no match for Adolf, in my opinion!' The man leaned forward even further to make his point. 'The papers d'say that the German armies are already being amassed in great numbers! So what does that tell you? Eh? What does that tell you! Well, let's hope our blokes are ready for 'em, that's all I can say.'

Eileen glanced quickly at Carrie, whose eyes had suddenly become bright with tears. Even though Mark always brushed off Carrie's anxieties, Eileen knew her friend never stopped worrying about him, his future – about their future. When this war came, would they *have* a future together?

Eileen half-turned to speak to the man behind them. 'Let's not spoil this lovely day,' she said cheerfully. 'It hasn't happened yet, and you never know . . .'

The man stood up to get off at his stop. 'I'm afraid we do know, luvver,' he said. 'Nothing's gonna stop it now.'

Abigail decided not to add to this conversation because she'd be ashamed to admit that she didn't know too much about the war, or what it might mean to them, to her and Emily. Aunt Edna had been the first to mention it the day they were leaving Coopers and Abigail had thought her aunt was just trying to scare them into staying. But war, any war, did sound terrible. Dada had told her a little about the one he'd fought in, that many of his comrades had lost their lives. But mostly he would tell her how, when things went quiet, his sketching and colouring helped him to gather his courage. Of course, Abigail thought, at school, they'd learned something of that war and what it had meant to both sides – but wasn't that supposed to have been the war that ended all wars? And if so, why would there be another one?

Abigail gazed out of the window at the passing scene of people going freely about their normal business. Why couldn't it always be like this?

Chapter 12

'Come on, I think it's time you got out now,' Abigail said, holding out one of the new large towels they'd bought when they'd gone shopping for Wellingtons. Emily clambered out of the bath and Abigail smiled. 'I think you are smelling so much nicer this evening than you did this morning!'

Emily wrinkled her nose as she snuggled into her mother's outstretched arms. 'What *was* that smell?' Emily said, 'I thought it was horrid!'

'It was a sort of disinfectant to make sure no one caught any germs,' Abigail said as they left the bathroom. 'But our Pears soap has done the trick, hasn't it? Now you are smelling just perfect again.'

Back in their bedroom, it didn't take long for Emily to climb into her clean pyjamas, and Abigail said, 'I think you wore Eileen and Carrie out this afternoon on the Downs, Emily. That game of leapfrog went on for ages! I gave up after half an hour!'

'I love playing leapfrog,' Emily said, 'and Eileen said she does, too.'

'Well, the only leaping you're going to do now,' Abigail said as she finished towelling Emily's hair dry, 'is into bed for a good long night's sleep.'

'But I'm not tired!' Emily said. Abigail thought, when did her daughter ever admit to feeling tired? But it was obvious that Emily must be fairly exhausted after an hour in the water at the baths, and a whole afternoon running around on the Downs. And that warm bath just now would put the final touch to an eventful day, Abigail thought as she finally tucked Emily beneath the covers.

'Can't I do just a teeny bit of colouring before I go to sleep?' Emily said, yawning. 'Please, Mummy.'

'No, not tonight, darling. There's another day tomorrow.'

And almost before her words were out, Abigail saw Emily's eyelids begin to droop, and within two minutes she was fast asleep.

After going back along to the bathroom to wash and brush her teeth, and to make sure everything had been left spotless, Abigail returned to their bedroom, admitting to feeling quite tired herself. It was only nine o'clock, but it wouldn't take much persuasion for her to climb in beside Emily and have an early night.

She got undressed and slipped into her nightdress and cotton dressing gown, which she'd had for so long it was almost threadbare. Then she paused to look out of the window. It would soon be September, and already the nights were beginning to draw in. September, the beginning of autumn. The time of year when they'd always been so busy at Coopers, harvesting the hundreds of pounds of apples and pears, plums, gooseberries, raspberries. Abigail remembered how rough and raw her hands always became. And as soon as she could walk, Emily had been given the task of picking up all the fallers and putting them into the wheelbarrow. Those fallers would have to be checked over carefully to see that they were undamaged and fit for market. Nothing was wasted at Coopers. Abigail shook her head briefly. What a different life they had left behind them, she and Emily.

And how different that life had been from that of their new friends. Eileen had told Abigail that she'd been caring for her disabled mother for many years, while Carrie, living in a vicarage with her parents, seemed to enjoy supporting them in all that went with being part of a busy parish. Both girls had been born into loving homes and were now happy to repay that love with some of their own.

Abigail turned away from the window, suddenly feeling so tired she couldn't wait to get to bed. But just then, there were two short gentle raps on the door. She paused a moment, confused, then went over to open it. Miss Grant must have come home early from her whist drive, though it was unusual for the landlady to want to speak to Abigail at this time of the day.

But it was not Miss Grant, it was Miss Grant's brother, and it was obvious that he had been drinking heavily. Leaning against the door jamb to support himself, he stood there with an insolent smile on his face.

'Shorry to dissturb you, Mrs Wilson,' he said, his words slurred, 'but it is Saturday night and I thought we could go out for a bit of a tipple. Jush you an' me, eh?'

Frightened beyond words at this intrusion, Abigail desperately tried to close the door and shut him out, but he wasn't having it, coming right into the room, closing the door and standing with his back against it.

He wagged a finger. 'Now, don't be like that, Mrs Wilson. It's only a bit of fun, you d'know. All the girls like a bit of fun, don't they? I bet *you* d'like a bit of fun!'

Trembling all over, Abigail found her voice. 'Get out,' she said quietly, trying to keep her voice calm, and glancing anxiously over at Emily. 'My little girl is asleep. How dare you come into my bedroom, Mr Grant! How *dare* you!'

'This is *my* bedroom, remember,' he said, leering at her. 'I got every right to come in 'ere.'

'Well, you can have it back. As soon as you like!' Abigail said, knowing that her flaming cheeks must look as red as his hair. 'And I will certainly *not* be coming out with you tonight, or any night!'

Although she was managing to put some strength into her

words, Abigail was afraid that in a minute she was going to fall to the floor in a dead faint. This was abhorrent, *he* was abhorrent! And if Emily should suddenly wake and see this huge, drunken man standing there it would terrify her.

But Ronald Grant hadn't finished. It hadn't taken him long to notice that Abigail was only wearing a flimsy nightdress and a dressing gown, untied at the waist, which did nothing to hide her curves. Now he stepped forward and put his hands on both her hips, drawing her roughly in towards him and trying to reach her lips with his.

Now, almost terrified out of her mind as she felt his hands begin to reach up past her waist, Abigail let his mouth get closer. Then, as hard as she could manage, she bit into that rubbery lower lip with such force that he stopped what he was doing and, yelling with pain, he stumbled backwards, almost falling over while trying to stop the blood from pouring down his chin.

Knowing that she now had the upper hand, Abigail edged him towards the door and pushed him outside with all the strength she had left in her body. And just then –praise be – Miss Grant's voice reached them from the hall.

'Ronald? Ronald? Is that you? Are you home already?'

Standing there holding his bloodied handkerchief to his mouth, Ronald Grant's shoulders slumped.

'Bloody 'ell,' he mumbled. 'That's all I d'need.'

Going over to the other bed, Abigail collapsed onto it and covered her face with her hands. That was the last thing she might have expected in Miss Grant's respectable household, and for several minutes Abigail could not stop herself from shaking.

Her first thought was to quickly get dressed, wake Emily and leave number fourteen, now, tonight. How could she bear to be in the same house as that man for another second!

But presently, regaining her composure, Abigail knew that there was nothing she could do about it tonight. She and Emily could not end up on the street with nowhere to go. But tomorrow – tomorrow they would leave Miss Grant's house and never set foot in it again. Though it was going to be very embarrassing to explain to the landlady why they were leaving sooner than arranged.

Abigail clasped and unclasped her hands as her thought ran on – because there would be little chance of finding somewhere else tomorrow. The estate agent's would surely be closed on a Sunday. How was she going to get out of this!

Then, suddenly, Abigail remembered the little note that Eileen had given her all those weeks ago. The note with Eileen's telephone number on it. Eileen and Carrie would help her out of this mess, Abigail thought, because they knew Bristol and where she might find help.

Her mind now clearer as she assembled her thoughts, Abigail went over to pick up her handbag. She had put that note safely right at the back of her purse, though she hadn't looked at it since. But as she fumbled, there it was, the figures of that telephone number boldly written.

Abigail breathed a huge sigh of relief. As soon as she and Emily left the house in the morning, she would ring Eileen. There was a telephone kiosk just up the road, and it shouldn't be difficult to work out how to use it even though Abigail had never done so before.

She gazed at that little piece of paper with the magic number on it. Thank heaven for a friend! Thank heaven for *friends*!

Chapter 13

As soon as they'd had breakfast the following morning, Abigail and Emily quietly left the house and made their way towards the telephone kiosk. There had been no sight nor sound from the landlady nor her brother, for which Abigail was extremely thankful. What on earth could she have found to say to either of them?

'Where are we going?' Emily asked as she guided the pushchair up the hill. 'Can we see Eileen and Carrie today and go to the Downs again?'

Abigail half-smiled, wishing she had the same energy as her daughter who showed no sign of being tired after their day yesterday. Abigail herself had managed to eventually get some sleep after her encounter with Ronald Grant, but it had been an uneasy rest and she'd been relieved to get up this morning. And she'd be even more relieved after she'd spoken to Eileen and Carrie. They would give her sound advice as to what to do next.

They arrived at the kiosk and Abigail opened the door for them to go inside. There was just room for the two of them and the pushchair. 'What *is* this place?' Emily asked curiously.

'It's where I can make a telephone call to Eileen, that's all.'

Although Emily was obviously puzzled, she said no more as she watched Abigail read the instructions in front of her and then put two pennies into a slot before pressing a large silver button. And after a few seconds and some clinking of coins, they both heard Eileen's familiar voice coming through the wires.

'Hello? 6495?'

Speaking carefully so as not to alarm Emily, Abigail said, 'Hello, Eileen. It's me, Abigail . . .'

Frowning, Eileen stared at the receiver for a second. Abigail had never rung their number before so there must be something wrong. 'Oh – Abigail,' Eileen said. 'Is . . . is everything all right?'

Abigail was so relieved to hear her friend's voice, she couldn't answer for a moment. 'Not exactly.' Abigail glanced down at Emily who had noticed the telephone directory and was idly turning the pages. 'But I need to talk to you – I need your advice about something.' Abigail hesitated. 'It's rather difficult to explain – but Emily and I need to see you today. Could we meet somewhere? After you've taken your mother to church, I mean. Or whenever you're free?'

Without a second's hesitation, Eileen said, 'Of course! And as a matter of fact, my mother doesn't feel up to going to church this morning so I can meet you wherever you like.' She paused. 'Um, how about College Green right by the cathedral? I can be there in half an hour, and there are plenty of seats for us to sit down. It's a lovely morning and we can watch Emily go on practising her cartwheels on the grass!'

An hour later, sitting side by side on one of the park benches, Abigail said, 'So you see, we *have* to get out of number fourteen today, Eileen. I've already put our belongings into bags, ready to make our escape, but I'm not sure how I should go looking for somewhere else. The estate agency won't be open today, so should I just see if there are "Room to let" notices in windows, or even knock on doors?' Abigail sat back for a moment. 'Even if we have to end up sleeping under a *hedge*, that would be preferable to being anywhere near that – that man ever again.'

Eileen gritted her teeth at what Abigail had just told her. The revolting Ronald Grant had taken advantage of an unsophisticated young woman and it was obvious that it had really frightened Abigail. Thank goodness Emily had apparently slept through all of it.

Eileen put her arm around Abigail's shoulder. 'Don't worry, you won't be sleeping under any hedges tonight, Abigail,' she said firmly. 'You will be staying at our house until we can find something permanent for you.' As Abigail started to protest, Eileen went on quickly, 'Don't worry. We've plenty of room, and as a matter of fact I happen to know that my mother would like to meet you both because when I explained to her weeks ago that you and your little girl had come to live in Bristol, and knew no one, she suggested that if I ever saw you again you might like to have a meal with us one day.' Eileen smiled. 'So there you are, Abigail – a Sunday roast, and a bed for the night are all yours!'

Emily ran up to them then, and Eileen picked her up, swinging her around and around. 'Come on, we must go and collect all your things – then we are going to *my* house, Emily! Do you like roast lamb and roast potatoes for dinner?'

Although mystified at this unusual turn of events, Emily's eyes lit up. 'And will there be pudding as well?' she said.

'Of *course* there will be pudding!' Eileen exclaimed. 'And on the menu today is rice pudding and ice cream!'

Emily clapped her hands. 'I *love* rice pudding – but I've never had it with ice cream before.'

By now it was eleven o'clock, and at last all the bells had stopped ringing as the city's church services began. And with Emily in the pushchair, Eileen and Abigail walked quickly towards Redcliffe Way.

'I think Miss Grant will probably be at church,' Abigail said, 'but if she hasn't gone today and is at the house, I don't know what I'm going to say to her.'

'Just say you've found a more suitable address and that you won't be coming back,' Eileen said firmly. 'She's got her money for the rest of the month so she can't complain. And if she isn't there, we'll just leave a note thanking her for renting you the room for the last three months – and wishing her good health.'

'But what if he – Ronald – is there?' Abigail began, and Eileen interrupted.

'You leave Ronald to me,' she said. 'He'll have a piece of my mind he won't forget in a hurry!'

Fortunately, when they arrived the house was empty, and after making sure that their room was left exactly as the landlady would have expected – with a polite little letter of thanks on the dressing table – Abigail collected the last of their belongings to take downstairs where the others were waiting.

'Why are we taking all our things with us?' Emily enquired, looking up from the pushchair where she was in charge of all the bags.

'Because we shall not be coming back to Miss Grant's house,' Abigail explained. 'We are going to find somewhere a bit nicer to stay. But just for tonight, Emily, we are going to be sleeping at Eileen's house. What do you think of that?'

Emily's eyes shone. 'I would *like* to stay in Eileen's house! And will Carrie be there, too?'

'She may be – after she's had dinner with her parents,' Eileen said, 'because Carrie's just finished knitting a jumper for my mother and she said she might bring it over later.'

They arrived at the Centre and Eileen said, 'I think with all these bags and belongings with us we should take a taxi this morning and go home in style. Don't you, Emily?'

Emily nodded. 'I've been in a taxi before,' she said. 'Haven't I, Mummy?'

Abigail nodded. 'That was our very first morning in Bristol, wasn't it?'

Eileen hailed a taxi, and soon they were making their way from the centre of the city, up Totterdown Hill and all along the Wells Road, until finally a turning off to the right brought them to a rank of large, imposing terrace houses. They had arrived at number six West Road, Knowle.

After paying the fare, they got out of the taxi, Emily already full of curious interest as they walked up the short path to the front door. Eileen opened it with her key before ushering Abigail and Emily inside.

Eileen tapped gently on the door of the first room they came to. 'Mother, we have visitors,' she called out. 'Dinner will be a little bit later today, so I am going to put the kettle on for a cup of coffee. Will you join us in a few minutes?'

There was a muffled response from inside, and Eileen looked back at Abigail as they made their way through the long hall. 'As you know, my mother is rather handicapped,' Eileen said, 'but I know she wants to meet you.'

The kitchen was a large, homely room, its square table set against the two windows, and with six chairs alongside. There were full-length cupboards built in against the walls, a huge Indian rug covered most of the floor, and three wicker chairs were placed in the corners. And the tantalising smell coming from the oven made Emily tug her mother's arm.

'Is it dinner time now?' she asked eagerly.

'Not quite,' Eileen said, 'because there's time for us to have a cup of coffee before I put the potatoes in to roast.' She smiled at Emily. 'Why don't you help Mummy put all your bags over there in the corner so that no one falls over them.'

Emily did as she was told, then the door opened and Mrs Matthews appeared, leaning heavily on her two sticks. Eileen immediately pulled a chair out at the table for her mother to sit down next to Abigail who had already been offered a seat.

'Mother, these are our new friends – the ones I told you about who've just moved to Bristol,' Eileen said. 'Abigail – Mrs Wilson –

is Emily's mummy. And you will be pleased to know that Emily is always a very, very good girl!'

Mrs Matthews was a heavily built lady with strong features and shrewd blue eyes, her greying hair pulled back and held securely on top with a tortoiseshell clip. She was wearing a formal, navy-blue cotton two-piece, and sensible low-heeled shoes. She turned to greet Abigail graciously.

'I am always happy to meet yet more friends of my daughter's,' she said, her voice gentle. Then her gaze switched to Emily. 'And how old is little Emily?'

'I will be three on my next birthday,' Emily announced promptly. 'So I am nearly grown up.'

Everyone smiled at that, and Mrs Matthews said, 'And when will that be, Emily?'

Abigail spoke first. 'Emily was born on the 1st of February,' she said. 'And she has already said that she would like pink icing on her next birthday cake.'

'I should think so too,' Mrs Matthews said, 'because everyone should have icing on their birthday cake.'

Eileen looked across at them both, her eyes misting slightly. She'd known that the little girl would steal her mother's heart because she'd loved her career teaching small children, and Eileen had also known that her parents had planned to have a much larger family, but it was not to be.

Presently, as they were enjoying their coffee, and with Emily sipping at a glass of cordial, Mrs Matthews turned to Abigail. 'So – Eileen tells me that you have recently moved up from the country and have decided to make Bristol your home?'

Abigail nodded quickly. 'Yes. It was always an ambition of mine, of ours, to move to where there would be more opportunities for Emily to experience a less rural life. We used to live on a small holding, and I wanted her to be spared the long days of everlasting toil working the land and to live somewhere that might allow her to *make* something of herself.' Then, after a moment, desperately trying to avoid saying anything that might incriminate her, Abigail said, 'It's unfortunate that my husband can't be with us yet – he was called away with hardly any notice – but we hope we'll all be together again before too long.' She smiled brightly. 'Bristol had been his idea. I mean, he told me all about the place and thought that we could be happy here.'

Her hands trembling, Abigail picked up her coffee cup and held it to her lips, trying to hide her flaming cheeks. This lie, these *lies*, were having to go on and on! But what else could she do? Although it had never been her intention, she'd *have* to go on saying she was a married woman with a pretend husband.

Well, now there was no stopping it. Her dishonesty was like a snowball, getting bigger and bigger all the time, and Abigail felt almost sick with unhappiness at the situation she'd got herself into. But not all of it was a lie, she told herself desperately – because it *had* been Luke who'd told her about Bristol, and had impressed on her that she owed it to herself to break the stranglehold of life at Coopers. And she'd done it, she and Emily were *here*, but Abigail couldn't bear having to tell lies to her new friends. Whatever would they think of her if they knew the truth?

Thinking about Luke for those few seconds made Abigail's eyes well up and she quickly reached for her hanky, just as Emily came up holding a little picture book and a packet of wax crayons which she'd taken from one of the bags.

'Can I do some colouring now, Mummy?' Emily asked.

'Perhaps after we've laid the table for dinner,' Abigail said, thankful to stand up to clear away the coffee cups. 'Look at those beautiful roast potatoes Eileen has just turned in the pan!'

Mrs Matthews looked over at Emily. 'Am I allowed to see what you've got there, Emily?' she said, and Emily immediately went over to stand next to Eileen's mother.

'I've got two more of these books,' Emily said proudly. 'But they've got different pictures – and I haven't even *started* them yet! *And* I've got more crayons, and a box of paints because

Mummy bought us both new drawing things the other day, didn't you, Mummy?'

Mrs Matthews studied the book she was holding. 'I love doing colouring,' she said quietly, 'because it is such a peaceful thing to do, isn't it?'

Emily nodded thoughtfully, then, after a moment said, 'You can do some with me later if you like,' she said.

'Thank you, Emily,' Eileen's mother said.

Watching the little scene unfold in front of her, Abigail smiled inwardly. This was typical Emily. Ever since they'd arrived at the house, she'd been taking everything in and sizing up Eileen's mother. Abigail instinctively knew that her daughter had taken to Mrs Matthews.

Eileen came over. 'Now, we're nearly done, and the greens won't take long, then dinner will be ready,' she said. 'Will you stir the mint sauce for me, Emily – it's over there in that little jug.'

Always delighted to be given things to do, Emily did as she'd been asked and Mrs Matthews said, 'Do you like greens, Emily? Cabbage and broccoli and peas?'

'Oh, Emily has always enjoyed her greens – haven't you, Emily? Especially when she has helped to pick them from the garden herself.' Abigail added.

'Well, it has obviously done her the world of good,' Eileen's mother said, 'because Emily looks the picture of good health to me.'

'Yes, she is rarely unwell,' Abigail said.

There was silence as Eileen's mother, looking thoughtful for a moment, said, 'Well, I do hope you are going to be happy – and safe – here in Bristol, Abigail.' Mrs Matthews threw Abigail a quick glance before adding, 'If only the country – and the world – would have some sense and refuse to enter yet another war. But' – she touched Abigail's hand – 'in the end, I am sure your little family will be complete again one day.'

With the table laid, Eileen placed the bowls of vegetables in front of everyone and put the sliced lamb onto their plates. Then she glanced at her mother.

'Oh, by the way, Mother, Abigail and Emily have had to leave their present address in rather a hurry and have nowhere to sleep tonight.' She passed Mrs Matthews the gravy jug before adding, 'So they are staying here with us instead. That's all right, isn't it?'

'It is more than all right,' Eileen's mother said, picking up her knife and fork. 'It will be an absolute delight to have them stay.' She smiled at Abigail. 'This house is far too big for just the two of us.'

Chapter 14

After the delicious Sunday roast had been eaten and everything cleared away, Emily got down from the table and went to fetch her books and crayons.

Just then, the front doorbell rang and Eileen immediately went into the hall to answer it. It was Carrie, holding a prettily wrapped parcel, and she immediately followed Eileen into the kitchen – expressing amazement when she saw Abigail and Emily there.

'Well, how *lovely* to see you both so soon again!' Carrie said, going over to kiss the top of Emily's head. 'You've obviously heard about the delicious Sunday roasts they provide at number six!' She turned to Eileen's mother. 'Anyway, I have brought your new jumper at last, Mrs Matthews – sorry it's taken me a bit long to finish.'

Eileen's mother looked up and smiled as she was handed the parcel. 'It's good of you to make it for me, Carrie,' she said. 'Now, shall we ask Emily to unwrap it so that we can all admire it?'

Emily immediately turned to undo the ribbon around the parcel, then took off the tissue paper. And with everyone now standing up to view the garment – a long-sleeved, intricately patterned jumper in a dainty green colour – there was general admiration of Carrie's handiwork. Eileen bent over to see it more closely.

'You were always better than me at this sort of thing,' she said. 'I don't seem to have the patience. But this is gorgeous, Carrie.'

'It most certainly is,' Mrs Matthews said. 'Thank you so much, my dear. Now, you must let me have the bill. I haven't paid you for the wool yet.'

Carrie waved a hand. 'Oh – take it as a little thank you for all the meals you give me,' she said. She turned to Abigail. 'I'm always being fed here,' she said. 'As soon as I set foot in the door, the kettle's on and food appears on the table!'

'Oh, go on with you,' Eileen said. 'I often eat at your place, you know that. The vicarage has an ever-open door for visitors.' Though it was true that the girls were more often at number six because Eileen worried that her mother might need her.

Abigail looked at them both for a moment. It must be wonderful to be so close to someone that their home was like being in your own.

By now, Emily had returned to her colouring, and Mrs Matthews left the table to go to her room. 'I won't be long, Emily, but I must try on this lovely jumper,' she said.

After she'd gone, in carefully selected words that Emily wouldn't catch on to, Eileen briefly explained to Carrie what had happened at number fourteen last night. As expected, Carrie was appalled, shaking her head and mouthing silent words of disgust.

'So,' Eileen said, 'Abigail and Emily are going to be staying with us tonight, Carrie. Aren't we lucky!'

Hearing her name, Emily glanced up briefly as she selected another colour from her packet of crayons. 'Will there be a proper bed for us?' she asked. 'When Mummy said we had to leave that other house, I thought well – next time, I hope we will have a proper bed.'

'I can assure you, Miss Wilson,' Eileen said, ruffling Emily's hair, 'that there will certainly be a proper bed for you tonight.'

Presently, Mrs Matthews returned, wearing the new jumper, and Eileen said, 'Mother – that colour *really* suits you! It makes you look ten years younger!'

'Well, thank heaven for small mercies,' Eileen's mother said. 'And thank heaven for our very kind and clever Carrie. Now then . . .' Mrs Matthews sat down again. 'Where was I, Emily?'

'You haven't finished the engine yet,' Emily said.

'And I think it's time for a cup of tea,' Eileen announced, going across to put the kettle on.

Without looking at Abigail, Mrs Matthews said, 'Eileen told me that you have been taken on by Blackwell's, Abigail. A very nice place to work I should think. That shop has been there for many years, and is indispensable to the university students.'

Abigail nodded. 'I'm really enjoying my hours there, Mrs Matthews – and you probably know that I also work at Robertson's a couple of afternoons.' Abigail smiled. 'As soon as I left home, I knew that it was vital for me to earn money as soon as possible after our arrival, so I consider myself very lucky. Of course, I had enough money to keep Emily and me going for a time – but I knew I must top it up as soon as I could and I've been careful to keep some of my sovereigns in case we hit hard times.'

'Your *sovereigns*?' Eileen asked as she poured boiling water into the teapot. 'I didn't think those existed anymore. How many have you got?'

'Quite a lot,' Abigail said, 'though I did exchange a few at the post office the other day.'

'I have never even seen a sovereign,' Carrie said, 'so I've no idea what they look like.'

'I'll show you,' Abigail said, going over to their bags and rummaging around until she came to the bolero that held the precious purse in its secret pocket. Then she went back and emptied the sovereigns onto the table for the others to see. They gazed in quiet amazement. There were about thirty gold coins lying there in front of them.

'Goodness me,' Eileen said slowly, 'where did these come from? Because this is obviously rather a lot of money, Abigail.'

Thinking that her hosts deserved some explanation, Abigail

said quietly, 'A year or so before he died – when I was about eight or nine – my father gave me these coins and told me to take great care of them because he was sure that one day I was going to need them. He said that he'd always wanted me to have them.'

Abigail paused, unable to go on. The very mention of her darling dada made her want to weep.

Still concentrating on what she was doing, Gladys Matthews said, 'You mentioned, Abigail, that you lived in a very isolated part of the country. What's the cottage called?'

'Coopers, and apparently it was owned by two brothers who were barrel makers,' Abigail said. 'That's what my father was told.'

Gladys Matthews nodded. 'A cooper means barrel maker, of course.'

'Does it?' Eileen said as she handed around cups of tea. 'I didn't realise that. A perfect name for the cottage, then.'

'My father said it was to be our secret – the money, I mean – and I was to tell no one, not even his sister, my aunt, who lived there too. She still does,' Abigail added.

Emily, who had been completely engrossed in what she was doing, looked up at Mrs Matthews. 'Can I borrow the red for a minute, please? I won't be long with it and then you can have it back.'

'Of course you can, Emily. And I love the green and blue of your umbrellas. You are being so careful not to go outside the lines. Well done.'

'But why was the money – the sovereigns your father gave you – kept from your aunt?' Eileen wanted to know.

'Because she is very controlling,' Abigail explained. 'She always held the purse strings – and Coopers made good money which I never saw anything of, despite working from dawn to dusk. And all my father ever had was what he managed to earn doing casual work elsewhere – he loved building dry stone walls and he was good at it And perhaps he had some army back pay,' Abigail said. 'He always gave me money on each of my birthdays, but I never dared ask my aunt for any because I was afraid of her – and I think my father was, too.' Abigail shrugged sadly. 'And she never forgave him for joining up to fight in the Great War – during which he was invalided out because of the effects of mustard gas, which he never recovered from,' Abigail added quietly.

She looked away, knowing she had to watch what she was telling them – because she knew they would obviously want to know more. Carrie broke the following silence.

'But then – then – you met your husband, Abigail?' she said gently. 'And everything changed for you?'

'Yes,' Abigail said carefully. 'Luke and I had known each other from school, and after I left, I found excuses to go to the village and we were able to meet up, because we both knew that we were always meant to be together.' Abigail swallowed hard before going on. 'Luke is the kindest, most thoughtful, most loving person in the world. And whatever happens – you know, for any of us in the future – I will love him with all my heart until the day I die. And I know he will always feel the same about me – wherever he is and whatever he's having to do – because he gave me his word.'

No one spoke for a moment after that. 'Well, I hope there is a Luke somewhere out there for me, one day,' Eileen said soberly.

'So, he – Luke – was your escape from your aunt at last?' Carrie suggested.

'Yes – my escape to happiness, and I – we – had Emily very soon afterwards,' Abigail said, 'which made me feel the luckiest girl alive.'

'Where did you live – after you were married?' Carrie said. 'Surely not at Coopers?'

Abigail had to think quickly before she answered. 'Oh no – Luke's family have a lovely house in the village.'

Abigail felt her tongue almost stick to the roof of her mouth as she tried not to be caught out by saying the wrong thing, giving herself away. *And please,* please *don't ask me about the wedding that never was*, she implored silently. She could not answer that because it would be a lie too far.

Abigail felt her shoulders slump as she realised what a web she had woven around herself, without ever meaning to. Had she made a terrible decision in pretending to be married? Wouldn't it have been better to have braved it out and face up to the consequences of hostility – even hatred – from others? Yes, and to the possible danger to herself and Emily? And as bad as all that might be, could Abigail bear to lose the respect of her new friends? Whatever would Mrs Matthews think when she found out that she had a 'slut' and an illegitimate child under her roof?

Then Abigail sat forward. She had entered this new world and she would deal with it, and if to keep Emily safe, and to be accepted as a decent human being meant wearing a battered old curtain ring on her finger – then she would do the same again.

And even though that lie would always be there, looming large, by being evasive to her friends' questions just now, she'd just about managed to avoid telling any more actual untruths. Hadn't she?

But one day – *one day* – she would tell them everything. Because she would *want* them to know everything.

When the time was right.

Carrie broke the silence. 'Your aunt sounds a very miserable person, Abigail.'

'Yes, she was miserable,' Abigail said, 'but she'd had a hard life, working all hours and then having to bring me up as well.' Abigail paused. 'I never knew my mother. She died not long after I was born.'

The emotional atmosphere in the room was tangible as Eileen's mother said quietly, 'Well, you are here now, Abigail, and you are among friends.'

'Thank you, Mrs Matthews,' Abigail said, trying to stop her voice from breaking. 'I really believe I am.'

Emily, who had been completely detached from all that was

going on, suddenly looked up at Eileen's mother. 'You didn't have any mint sauce with your dinner, did you? Don't you like it?'

'Not very much, Emily, because it makes my tongue tingle,' Mrs Matthews said.

Emily nodded. 'I don't like it very much either,' she said. 'What's your name – your real name, I mean, like mine is Emily?'

'It's Gladys,' Mrs Matthews said promptly. 'My real name is Gladys, Emily.'

Emily considered this for a moment. 'I *like* that name,' she declared, 'because it's got "glad" in it!' She leaned in closer and giggled. 'I'm *glad* you're called *Gladys*!'

'Emily,' Abigail began reproachfully, 'I don't think you should—'

Eileen's mother intervened. 'It's perfectly all right, Abigail,' she said, 'and I'm really pleased that Emily likes my name. That's something to be *glad* about, isn't it?'

Chapter 15

Much later, after they'd had tea – to which it was insisted that Carrie should stay and enjoy with them – Eileen said, 'I think your dolly is ready for bed, don't you, Emily? She must be tired sitting there in your pocket all this time. Shall we go upstairs now?' Eileen smiled across at her mother. 'And I think someone else is nearly ready for a rest too,' she added, noting that Mrs Matthews was getting up to return to her room.

With Emily excitedly following Eileen, and with Abigail and Carrie behind, holding all the bags and belongings, they went up the long, richly carpeted staircase, together, Abigail conscious of how spacious everything was. Coopers could fit into this house about fifty times.

'My mother doesn't have a room up here anymore,' Eileen said, glancing back at Abigail, 'because she finds the stairs too difficult to manage. So you and Emily will be sleeping in what used to be her bedroom – the largest one with the largest bed, Emily will be pleased to know. Mine is right next door, the box room is there at the end, and the bathroom is there at the other end – see?'

They opened the door and Carrie said, 'I can vouch for the comfort of this bed, Abigail, because I've slept here once or twice myself. You won't want to get up in the morning!'

Abigail stared around at the room they would be sleeping in tonight. The massive bed was furnished with several soft white pillows, and there was a huge pink eiderdown covering it from head to foot. The dressing table in the window had a velvet stool in front, and three mirrors to see yourself in. Three! Coopers had only ever owned one yellowing mirror above the kitchen sink. At each side of the bed there was a small table each holding a reading lamp, and at either side of the window there were two comfy bedroom chairs.

Realising that she hadn't said a single word for several moments, Abigail turned to Eileen. 'I don't know how to thank you for letting us stay here tonight.'

Eileen squeezed her arm. 'It's our pleasure – and look – Emily has already chosen her chair.'

Emily was sitting there sucking her thumb, and Abigail went over to her.

'Come on, I think it's time for a wash before we get into this beautiful bed, Emily.'

As the others turned to leave, Eileen said, 'Use whatever you like in the bathroom, Abigail. There are always fresh towels and plenty of soap in the bath and basin.'

In bed later, and staring up at the high ceiling, Abigail wished that she could quell her teeming thoughts. So much had happened since they'd left Coopers that the world seemed to be spinning at twice its normal pace. How had they got from there to here in so short a time?

Turning her head, she gazed at Emily who was so cocooned in the luxurious blankets and pillows it was hard to find her. And she was so far away on her side of the bed Abigail had to stretch out her arm to touch her.

Abigail allowed herself a little smile when she remembered how she'd worried that Emily might find it hard to suddenly be among other people, among strangers. She had met so few others in her short life. Still, Abigail thought as her thoughts ran on,

136

apart from the fact that her daughter had always been a naturally happy child – even when in the company of Aunt Edna at her most sullen, Emily had never known anything other than an untroubled life at Coopers. And not yet old enough for school, she hadn't been subjected to the spitefulness of other children.

Abigail bit her lip. Memory would not loosen its grip on that relentless, often subtle, cruel bullying she had suffered, and she was dreading the day when she would eventually have to send Emily into the hurly burly of school life.

But – that was not yet, and until then Emily seemed more than happy in the company of all their new friends and appeared totally at ease with Mrs Matthews as the two of them had sat together at the table colouring in their pictures.

In her sitting room immediately below the one the young visitors were sleeping in, Gladys Matthews shifted restlessly in her chair, trying to ease the discomfort in her back. The little table by her side held a glass of water and her tablets, and she reached over to take the next dose, making a face at the bitterness on her tongue as she swallowed. Eileen always made sure that no tablet was ever missed.

Dear Eileen, Gladys thought, always so attentive, so cheerful, and who, it had to be admitted, was now in full control of their lives. In control of her life. How times change.

But Gladys had no reason to complain. She had everything she needed – if not quite what she might have wanted. This big, light and airy room downstairs which looked out onto the small front garden was where she spent most days, while what used to be the dining room next door had been turned into her bedroom. All making her life as convenient as possible. She could still make her way slowly to the kitchen at the end of the hall where they took their meals, and where, she, Gladys, could prepare herself something if she was on her own. The toilet and utility room beyond had been adapted to her needs.

Just then, as she sat there deep in her thoughts, she heard the little girl who would be lying in the bed above, call out to her mother. A childish cry of fear from a bad dream? Then, that faint, familiar squeak of the bed springs, and the soft, inaudible words of comfort.

Then, complete silence as before.

Gladys gazed into the far distance. So very often as a teacher she'd had that same experience, consoling an anxious child, to make it feel safe after a quarrel or a tumble in the playground. And here, in this house, she'd frequently had to hurry along the landing to reassure her own daughter who'd always been a restless sleeper. A sleepwalker, in fact, sometimes making her way to the front door before being gently guided back to bed.

Was it all these memories, stored so tightly in her mind, that sometimes made her feel such emptiness? Gladys asked herself. Within its own limits her life was full enough, yet full of emptiness. How was that possible? How could something full, be empty? She closed her eyes and breathed in deeply. Perhaps it was an emptiness of the soul, something deep, deep inside, that no one could touch or help.

But she had to admit that today had certainly ended on a different note. To her best recollection they had never before entertained a young mother and her tiny daughter – a lovely little thing, so ready to talk and communicate without being forward or seeking attention.

And Abigail – Mrs Wilson – what of her? Deciding to come to Bristol without the support of her husband, and knowing no one when she got here, had been a huge risk, especially with such a young child. Yet she was clearly not a foolish woman, determined to make her own way, whatever it took. Gladys Matthews narrowed her eyes briefly. To her, there seemed no doubt that Abigail was without any guile, but there was a curious naivety about her which was difficult to define.

It was late now. Eileen had already come in to kiss her mother goodnight, and to explain the predicament which Abigail had found herself in at the landlady's house – to which Gladys Matthews had reacted with disgust.

'So I really did have to offer them both a bed for the night, didn't I, Mother?' Eileen had said, and her mother had replied straightaway.

'Of *course* you did! And as far as I am concerned, Eileen, they can stay as long as they like,' Gladys Matthews had said. 'I see no reason for them to rush off and find somewhere else.'

'So – you really liked them, didn't you, Mother?' Eileen said.

'I think they are both perfectly charming,' Gladys Matthews had replied. 'How could anyone think otherwise?'

Now, Gladys picked up her sticks and moved over to open the door. The few steps along to her bedroom were easy enough and the tablets were having their effect, so perhaps she'd get to sleep without too much trouble.

Easing herself into bed, she pulled the covers up more closely and prepared to settle down – if she could only stop her thoughts from keeping her awake as she went over and over all that had gone on that day.

And one of the things which she remembered was what Eileen had briefly said after she'd heard Abigail describe her loyal husband's love and devotion.

It had been that Eileen hoped there was someone like him out there for her one day.

Gladys Matthews felt just a tiny surge of unusual optimism. That was the first time her daughter had ever made such a remark or expressed any kind of wish for a man in her life. Eileen was always finding a reason to turn down a date.

And Gladys knew only too well the reason for that. She knew that Eileen had marked out her own future as being responsible for her mother's health, happiness and wellbeing until the end of her life.

But that was not what Gladys wanted! Even though she valued

every second of her daughter's love and attention, all she'd ever wanted was Eileen to have freedom, and the same chance as she herself had had – to find a loving partner and to have children of her own, a *life* of her own.

Still, it was going to be difficult to ever convince Eileen of this, Gladys thought as her eye lids at last began to droop. But you never know, perhaps Abigail and little Emily unexpectedly entering their lives might change Eileen's view of her own. And convince her that, when necessary, there was always more than one way to deal with any situation which presented itself.

Chapter 16

1st September 1939

Gladys Matthews stood by her window, gazing out at the familiar scene in front of her. Theirs was a quiet road, with just enough movement of pedestrians, together with local traffic – the occasional small car, a milk float or a bread delivery van – to give the comforting feel of simple, kindly normality.

But what was to become of that simple normality in the days that lay ahead?

On the wireless afternoon bulletin, the BBC had just announced the most dreadful news. Germany had that day invaded Poland, bombing its people in the streets without warning and attacking the Polish fleet at harbour – and now it was the hideous reality that Nazi jackboots were marching over ground where they had no right to be.

Gladys Matthews rarely shed tears, in fact it was a long time since she had done, but now she gave in to her pent-up feelings of horror, lowering her head in a kind of shame. Shame to be part of a human race that could allow such atrocious things to happen to their own kind.

It was Friday and the weather was fine and warm – which, to

her mind, made it worse, somehow. If there'd been a howling gale, or even an earthquake, it would have seemed more acceptable than the hateful of news of war. Because what was happening to Poland would surely be the fate of France and Belgium – and England, too. Although England had still not declared war, the signs of approaching and immediate disaster were everywhere. Now, everyone had been told that they must black out all their windows so that not even a chink of light could be seen by enemy bombers above, and only yesterday two huge barrage balloons – strange, bulbous things – had appeared floating above the rooftops. Even worse, small children, labelled, and with gas masks hung around their necks were boarding trains at Temple Meads Railway Station to be evacuated to places of safety.

Gladys Matthews bit her lip in quiet desperation at all her anxieties. How very strange, she thought, that Abigail had chosen to leave the countryside at just the wrong time, because she and Emily would clearly have been out of harm's way had they still been living at Coopers.

Eileen's mother shrugged helplessly. Well, come what may, there was one thing she had no doubt about. Abigail would never be parted from her daughter, whatever the circumstances. There would be no evacuation for Emily. If Gladys Matthews was any judge, no war was going to separate that devoted mother from her child.

3rd September 1939

Jonathan Waters made his way slowly up the steps of his pulpit and gazed down at the congregation. He tried not to catch the eye of any of his flock in case his extreme disquiet should be recognised. His calling was always to encourage, console and inspire, and that is what he must do this morning, even though his heart was heavy. He cleared his throat.

'My dear friends,' he said solemnly, 'what I am about to tell you will not come as a surprise because we have been expecting this news for many weeks and months.' He paused before going on. 'While we were worshipping here in church today, our prime minister, Mr Neville Chamberlain, gave a speech to the nation in which he said that despite all his efforts to avoid it, we are, once again, at war with Germany.'

There was complete silence as everyone took in the news they'd been waiting for. Then a stifled sob from the back of the church sent a ripple of collective consternation through the sacred building. This was it, then. The die was cast.

Jonathan Waters spoke again. 'I am going to ask you to kneel once more so that we may offer our prayers to Almighty God for the safety of our brave men who will be fighting on our behalf. To pray for the safety of the citizens of this city and cities all over the country.' He waited before going on. 'And for the safety and wellbeing, too, of the civilian German population – people just like us – who must be feeling as we are today.' The vicar swallowed, hoping that what he'd just said wouldn't incur any dissension from the more hot-headed of his flock. He stared down once again before adding, 'The conflict to come will be no more a wish of theirs, than it is of ours.'

It was fortunate that Jonathan Waters did not hear the comment of one of his sidesmen who whispered to his neighbour, 'Oh yeah? In my opinion, the only good German is a dead German!'

Later, sitting at the table finishing their roast beef dinner, Carrie tried to think of something to lift the sombre mood. 'That was a jolly good sermon you gave today, Dad,' she said. 'I admit that I was about to take Mark's letter from my handbag and read it again – even though I know it by heart already! But everything you were saying kept me hooked, and when I looked around at the congregation not a single person was asleep!'

'That's very good news,' Jonathan said. 'And I'm glad I have my daughter's approval.'

Carrie got up to start clearing the dinner dishes, dropping a kiss on the top of her father's head. 'You know you've always got that, Dad,' she said.

Joan Waters got up and went into the kitchen to bring in the pudding. 'It's apple tart and custard – your favourite, Jonathan,' she said lightly. 'The Bramleys are wonderful this year, and there are masses still to come. These are just the fallers.'

'It's good to know that we have at least some food in our own garden, isn't it,' Jonathan said, 'because we are going to have to be thrifty with everything from now on. Food rationing is no longer a rumour, it's a fact, and we shall have our own ration books next year.'

'And not just ration books,' Carrie said, 'because we are all going to be carrying identity cards around with us in case we forget who we are!' She giggled. 'So, if you have a vacant moment, Mum, someone will bring you safely back home!'

'This is no laughing matter, Carrie,' her mother said, trying not to smile. Carrie always seemed to see the funny side of things, and when she and Eileen – and Mark – were all together there was never a dull moment.

Jonathan finished his pudding and reached for his glass of water. Then he stood up. 'I think it's about time for my forty winks.' He glanced at Carrie. 'If you're going to number six later, I take it you won't be at Evensong tonight?' he said, winking.

'Dad, honestly!' Carrie exclaimed. 'You can't expect me to listen to another of your sermons in one day! That terrific one this morning will keep me going until next week – or even the week after!'

* * *

Despite the dreadful, long-awaited announcement that the country was at war, September passed in a kind of strange dream.

The days, still fine and warm, held nothing special to terrify the waiting population. War – what war?

And for Carrie – who hadn't heard from Mark for a while – it was a stomach-churning time of fear and anxiety. It was taking Eileen unusual difficulty in convincing her friend that nothing bad would ever happen to Mark Anderson.

'No news is always good news, Carrie,' Eileen would regularly repeat. 'Mark could take on the whole German army single-handed and charm his way out of danger. You'll soon hear something, stop worrying.'

In fairness to her, Carrie did manage to cheer up, and this was partly due to the diversion of seeing the newcomers at number six on a regular basis. Although Abigail had never meant to stay more than a night or two, Eileen and her mother had persuaded Abigail that not only were they very welcome to live there for as long as they wanted to, but that it was a sensible and safe arrangement in view of all that they might have to face in the coming months. And Eileen knew very well that having Emily around was the reason for her mother's improvement in spirits. If something worked well, why change it? And Abigail was so sweet – insisting on paying their way despite Gladys Matthews' protest that it really wasn't necessary.

October and November were wet and dismal months, though the rumblings of war were still far away from home with nothing at all to upset the worthy residents of the city.

One day, downstairs in the kitchen, Eileen was just starting to scramble eggs for breakfast when Abigail came in and joined her at the stove.

'While you're doing that, let me make the sandwiches for our lunches,' Abigail said, and Eileen nodded.

'Thanks. The ham is over there on the side.'

Eileen always took her sandwich lunch to eat at the office, and ever since Abigail and Emily had moved in, they ate theirs with Mrs Matthews before leaving to go to Blackwell's. Supper, the main meal, was eaten together at about six-thirty.

Abigail hummed under her breath as she started buttering the bread. Their domestic arrangements had worked seamlessly straightaway and seemed to suit everyone, especially Eileen's mother who had actually put on a pound or two in weight.

As for Emily, she was brimming with happiness, especially as she'd become used to having Mrs Matthews' undivided attention. Not just colouring and drawing together, but doing sums and writing sentences and learning poetry.

So far, as expected, Abigail had taken Emily to work with her, but now that the days were getting colder and darker, Eileen's mother thought the little girl should stay at home with her until Abigail and Eileen returned from work at about six o'clock.

Now, Abigail reached for a jar on the shelf, then spread some pickle on to the ham. They all liked a bit of Branston's in their sandwiches. She glanced at the clock on the wall. They'd be here for their breakfast in a minute – Emily always insisted on calling for Mrs Matthews, so every morning they'd come in together and sit side by side at the table, usually giggling about something like two naughty children.

18th December 1939

Thanks to Mrs Matthews, helped by Emily, the roomy kitchen at number six had been turned into fairyland. The paper chains they'd made hung all around the room, there was holly and mistletoe elegantly arranged on both the deep window sills, and in the corner of the room was a five-foot Christmas tree Eileen had brought home, now bedecked with fairy lights, tinsel and coloured baubles.

That Sunday as they sat around the table having their lunch, Eileen glanced out of the window. She made a face.

'They warned us we were going to have snow, didn't they,' she said, 'and I think they might be right. Just look at that sky!'

'Well, if it is going to snow, I hope it doesn't come in time to stop us from going to the carol service,' Abigail said. 'Emily and I have been practising "Away in a Manger" and "Once in Royal David's City" for weeks, haven't we, Emily?'

'I know you have,' Mrs Matthews said as she added a little more gravy to her roast pork, 'because Emily has been making me practise them too.' She smiled across. 'We've just about managed some of "God Rest Ye Merry Gentlemen" haven't we, Emily? But you are so much quicker at remembering the words than I am. And I'm still getting them muddled up.'

Carrie had told them that the service of Nine Lessons and Carols at their church was always lovely, and Eileen had promised that she would bring Abigail, Emily and Mrs Matthews to All Saints so that they could join the choir singing the carols, and to stay behind in the hall afterwards for mulled wine and mince pies.

'The church is always packed to the rafters,' Carrie had enthused, 'and there is a big Christmas tree in the corner, with fairy lights.' She'd smiled at Abigail. 'I would love you to meet my parents because I've been telling them all about our new country friends. The service starts at six o'clock, so make sure you're there early enough to get a good seat. In fact, I'm going to put a "reserved" notice on the front pew just for you. I hope I'll be able to join you before it all starts, but I have to help my mother with the refreshments in the hall first.'

By four o'clock, the sky was so heavy and leaden that it seemed snow was inevitable. In fact, one or two large flakes were already floating past the kitchen window, and as they were enjoying a cup of tea and slice of cake, Mrs Matthews said:

'I'm sorry to be a wet blanket, but I don't think I'll come to church with you this evening. By the look of it, we are about to see a lot more of this white stuff before morning and I worry that we might not be able to get back home afterwards.'

'But I've ordered a taxi both ways, Mother,' Eileen said patiently, 'and All Saints is not very far away as you know. I'm sure we'll be all right.'

'Yes, but what if the taxi can't get up Totterdown Hill?' Mrs Matthews said. 'You know what it can be like. I mean, we may get to the church, but if we have heavy snow and it lays, the taxi may not be able to arrive to take us home afterwards.'

'Well then, Mother, if you feel that concerned it would be better if you stayed here in the warm,' Eileen said. 'But there's always next year. And I'm sure Emily will tell you all about it when we come back.'

Mrs Matthews was obviously relieved. 'What I'm thinking,' she said, 'is if the road is too bad for the traffic, you young people could trudge back on foot – and I would only be a terrible hindrance on my sticks, wouldn't I? In fact, of course, we would never reach home!'

'Well, never mind,' Eileen said, passing her mother another cup of tea. 'Better safe than sorry. Though Carrie will be sorry you aren't there.'

Emily, who'd been listening as she'd nibbled one of the mince pies Abigail had made yesterday, jumped down from her chair and leaned against Mrs Matthews. 'I will take my writing book and pencil and Mummy will help me make a list of all the carols we sing,' she said. 'Then we can go over it all again when we come back.'

'Thank you, Emily, that would be very kind,' Eileen's mother replied.

Presently, dressed warmly, and with their scarves wound tightly around their necks, the three left number six where the taxi was waiting for them. Mrs Matthews waved them off at the door.

'I hope you have a lovely evening, my dears,' she said, 'and I expect to hear your little voice all the way from there to here, Emily!'

After they'd left, Mrs Matthews went into her room and closed the door. It was such a delight having the little family living with them. And Emily, that dear little soul – knowing beyond her years – was a total treasure.

* * *

All Saints was a beautiful Victorian church, made to look even more lovely by the fine layer of snow which had already gathered on its roof and window ledges. Eileen and Abigail, with Emily between them holding their hands tightly, walked carefully towards the open church door from which mellow light flooded the area around it. Plenty of other people were making their way along the winding path which was already a couple of inches deep in snow. Eileen glanced across at Abigail.

'Well, it hasn't taken long for it to settle, has it?' she said. 'My mother was right – as usual. Even the taxi driver said he wondered how long he'd be able to work tonight.'

They went into the porch and Eileen ushered Abigail and Emily in front of her. 'Come on – let's see if Carrie Waters has reserved our places,' Eileen said.

Presently, sitting together in the front pew, Abigail gazed around her, full of awe at their surroundings. The glorious notes from the organ reached every corner of the building as the congregation waited patiently for the service to begin, and Abigail cast her mind back to the carol services at their little church in the village. But this was something different. All Saints was so beautifully decorated with Christmas roses and holly, and ivy wreathed around flickering altar candles, and the tall Christmas tree in the far corner was aglow with hundreds of coloured lights.

She glanced down at Emily who was sitting quietly, her hands in her lap, her eyes wide with interest. She nudged her mother.

'When are we going to start singing the carols, Mummy?' Emily whispered.

And just then, all the lights dimmed, and a lone treble voice sang the first verse of 'Once in Royal David's City' before the choir began processing down the long aisle and everyone stood up to join in.

Eileen immediately lifted Emily to stand up on the seat so that she could see everything better, and at that moment Carrie slipped into the pew beside them, glancing up and smiling.

Abigail had to take a deep breath to hold herself together because she could never ask for a better Christmas than this. The first Christmas away from their old life. And to have friends – friends who had so easily become trusted friends – standing either side of her and her daughter, as if drawing them together in a gentle, human chain.

Abigail reached into her pocket for her handkerchief. Luke had been right. She *could* make friends . . . she'd proved it.

It was quite a long service but Emily was enchanted as she joined in all the singing, and during each lesson, with Abigail's help, she carefully printed in her notebook the name of the carol they'd just sung.

Abigail gazed at Carrie's father as he stepped up into the pulpit to read the last lesson. He was very tall, and had such a lovely, gentle voice which seemed to go with the kindness in his face. He was so obviously Carrie's father with a twinkle in his blue eyes – just like hers. He must be a wonderful dad to love, just as Abigail's had been . . .

When it was all over, everyone went next door into the hall which soon resounded with chatter and laughter as mince pies and mulled wine were handed around. Carrie, who had hurried ahead of them as they'd left the church, suddenly appeared with a plate of refreshments.

'That was a lovely service, as usual, Carrie,' Eileen said, helping herself to a mince pie, and Carrie nodded.

'Yes, it never fails,' she said, 'and I'm so glad that Abigail and Emily are here with us as well. But it's understandable that Mrs Matthews preferred to stay at home.' She looked down at Emily. 'Did you enjoy all the singing, Emily?'

Emily nodded. 'Yes, but I didn't know all the carols,' she said.

'Never mind,' Carrie said, 'the ones you did know you sang at the top of your voice, didn't you? I heard you!'

Just then, Carrie's parents came up to join them. 'Dad, Mum – come and meet our new friends,' Carrie said, 'the ones I've been telling you about. This is Abigail – Mrs Wilson – and her little girl Emily.'

Smiling, Carrie's mother bent down to say something to Emily, and Jonathan Waters took Abigail's hand and held it gently.

'We've been hearing all about you, my dear,' he said, looking straight into Abigail's eyes, 'and I do hope you are managing to settle into your new life in Bristol – in spite of the dreadful situation the world is in once again.'

Abigail didn't hesitate. 'My daughter and I could not be happier,' she said, before swallowing and continuing, 'in spite of the fact that my husband cannot be with us yet. But we have been so lucky, so blessed to have met Eileen and Carrie and Mrs Matthews. In fact, it has been something of a miracle.'

Reverend Waters, who had not let go of Abigail's hand, smiled his twinkly smile.

'Well, miracles do sometimes happen,' he said gently. 'After all, we've been celebrating that this evening, haven't we?'

Gladys Matthews had been right. Heavy snowfall prevented any traffic from going anywhere, and after their visit to All Saints, Eileen, Abigail and Emily slipped and slithered all the way home. It did take them some time, but Emily, who didn't seem at all tired, enjoyed every minute, singing all the carols she knew as they made their way back.

But now in bed much later with Emily fast asleep beside her, Abigail remembered what Carrie's father had said.

'I hope you will come and see us again very soon, Abigail, because we would love you and your dear little girl to be our regular visitors. Any time you like,' he'd added.

But what would he have thought if he'd known she was an unmarried mother? Abigail asked herself. Would he have been quite so generous minded?

Yes, I think he would, Abigail thought, answering her own silent question. He would know, instinctively, that she was not a wicked sinner, she was just another human being who wanted to be loved and valued.

Chapter 17

1st February 1940

'*Happy birthday to you, happy birthday to you, happy birthday dear Emily, happy birthday to you!*'

It was only 7 a.m., and despite it still being dark outside, everyone at number six – including Mrs Matthews still in her dressing gown – was already in the kitchen singing the famous verse and waiting for Emily to open her presents. And almost at once there was a rap on the front door and Carrie let herself in, all smiles.

'Luckily for me, the bus came straightaway,' she said breathlessly, going across to hand over her contribution. 'I didn't want to miss the fun!'

It was still bitterly cold, with the snow lying thick on the ground, but the early start to the day had been unavoidable as Eileen and Carrie both had to be at work at nine o'clock. But Emily had been so excited, she'd been awake long before anyone else. And now, in the warm kitchen and with the kettle singing for their first cups of tea, and with a plate of sugary biscuits already on the table, everyone sat around to see Emily open all her prettily wrapped presents.

Eileen and Carrie had been determined that Emily's first

birthday in Bristol would be one she would remember, and it wasn't long before the table was strewn with cards and presents and discarded wrapping paper and ribbon, with Emily hopping around excitedly showing them all what she'd been given.

As Abigail watched her daughter open one thing after another to add to the growing pile, she couldn't help comparing Emily's birthdays before this one. Of course, Abigail herself had made sure there'd always been little gifts, but they never had special days at Coopers, Edna declaring that there was far too much to do to waste time on such things. And Abigail's own birthday, when Dada was there, had been happy but subdued occasions. Aunt Edna never gave presents to anyone, and Emily's two birthdays before this one had been so quiet, they'd passed almost unnoticed. It didn't do to remind Edna Wilson of her great-niece's shameful first day on Earth.

But today was certainly different, and Emily now had yet more colouring books, reading books, crayons and paints, there was a box of beautifully carved little wooden animals, pink satin hair ribbons, two pairs of pretty socks and a dainty pinafore, together with a box full of sweets and chocolates. Mrs Matthews' gift was a large jigsaw, the picture on the box showing all the sights of London.

'I'm sure you will go there one day, Emily,' Eileen's mother said, 'and you will see the Tower of London and Buckingham Palace where the King and Queen live.'

But more was to come when Carrie handed over a card and little present from her parents.

'Mum and Dad were so pleased to meet you both at the carol service, Abigail,' Carrie said, 'and they wanted to give Emily a little present from them, with their love and best wishes.'

And when Emily opened the prettily wrapped gift, Abigail had difficulty in holding back her tears. It was a necklace, a tiny gold cross on a fine chain and it was going to look beautiful on her daughter's smooth neck.

'Look, Emily,' Abigail said huskily, 'you've never had anything as lovely as this before. Let me put it on for you – the first jewellery you've ever been given.'

Emily's delight was infectious as she went around for the others to admire it, and then Abigail read out what was written on the card. In Reverend Waters' handwriting were the words, 'Happy birthday, Emily. May you receive every blessing as you continue on life's journey.'

Seeing that Abigail was visibly moved, Eileen said cheerily, 'Come on, Abigail. Mummies need spoiling sometimes and Carrie and I are dying to watch you open a little present we've bought *you*!'

'But it's not *my* birthday!' Abigail protested.

'Open it!' Eileen demanded.

Doing as she was told, but completely mystified, Abigail took off the coloured wrapping paper before moving aside several layers of fine tissue, to reveal a turquoise cotton dress. She looked up.

'What have you two been up to?' she said quietly.

'For goodness' sake, put us out of our misery!' Carrie said. 'Hold it up against you!'

It was a full-skirted dress with a boat-shaped neckline, nipped-in waist, and it was embellished with fine white lace at the sleeves and hem. Accompanying it was a pair of strappy sandals. Abigail looked up, clearly amazed.

'This is gorgeous,' she said slowly. 'You shouldn't have gone to all this expense.'

''Course we should,' Eileen exclaimed, 'because you deserve it.' She wasn't going to say that she and Carrie had noticed how few clothes Abigail seemed to own or to have brought with her. 'Carrie and I have been plotting this for a while, and we roughly worked out what size you were. And don't worry if it doesn't fit, because we can take everything back and have our money refunded.' She grinned at Abigail's obvious delight. 'You're going to look smashing in that dress, Abigail.'

'What can I ever say to thank you both?' Abigail said. 'I shall feel like Princess Elizabeth or Princess Margaret Rose when I wear this.'

'And you'll look as good as either of them,' Carrie said.

Emily was in her usual place where she and Eileen's mother had started colouring in one of the new books.

'I hope you're going to find room to keep all your presents, Emily,' Gladys Matthews said, and Emily looked up, pursing her lips.

'Well, I can keep some of them in your room, can't I, Mrs Gladys?' she said.

'Of course you can, Emily,' Eileen's mother replied. 'I'll look after it all for you.'

Eileen, pouring out second cups of tea for everyone, was feeling so happy her heart could have burst. To see her darling mother come so alive again, so interested in everything, and not nearly so aware of her health problems. When the weather had been fine in the autumn, she had even taken Emily down to the park once or twice in the afternoons, insisting that holding on to the pushchair with the little girl sitting in it acted as a support for the short distance.

Eileen glanced across at the two of them sitting there at the table, intent on what they were doing, Emily chattering away, as usual. What a beautiful sight it was.

Eileen put down the teapot for a second. How strange it had been last year, she thought, to have met Abigail and her daughter like that. They were such an unusual pair, and from what Abigail had told them, with a somewhat unusual life. And, somehow, they had arrived here and were living in Eileen's family home. It was hard to explain or understand.

Presently, they all sat down together for more tea and toast and marmalade. 'No time for eggs this morning,' Eileen said briskly as she glanced at the clock. 'Or Carrie and I are going to be late for work. We don't want to be given our cards on such a special day, do we!'

Carrie finished clearing the table, while Abigail stood next to

Eileen, wiping up the dishes. 'I hope I'll be able to concentrate at Blackwell's later,' Abigail said happily. 'Emily has never had such a birthday before, and I've never been given a party dress before, either.'

'Oh, it hasn't finished yet,' Eileen said. 'Don't forget the special tea we're going to have later, with an iced cake and candles to blow out.'

Abigail spread the tea towel to dry and hesitated for a moment. 'There's only one thing, Eileen,' she said. 'When am I *ever* going to have the chance to wear my beautiful dress? It's far too good to wear at the shop.'

Eileen squeezed her arm as she went past. 'Don't worry about that,' she said. 'I told you – Carrie and I have been plotting! You'll get used to our wicked ways – Cinderella *shall* go to the ball!'

It was late before Emily was persuaded to go bed, and presently, as she was being tucked up, Abigail said, 'What a wonderful birthday you've had, haven't you, Emily? What was the bit you liked best? Was it having all those presents, or blowing out the candles on the beautiful iced cake, or playing ring-a-ring-a-roses, or the farmer wants a wife, or oranges and lemons, or—'

'I liked all of it,' Emily said promptly. 'I wanted it to go on for ever.'

Abigail smiled. 'And Eileen's mother is lovely, isn't she?'

'Yep,' Abigail said firmly. 'We're best friends.'

'What do *you* know about best friends, Emily?' Abigail said, tickling her daughter under the chin.

'Best friends are people who you like being with all the time, and who like being with you,' Emily replied, 'and who are never nasty.' She glanced up at her mother. 'Mrs Gladys and I read about best friends in Enid Blyton's stories. Don't *you* know what best friends are, Mummy?'

'Yes, I do,' Abigail said quietly. 'I really do, Emily.'

Chapter 18

The early weeks and months of 1940 would be mostly remembered for the atrocious weather which hit England. Heavy snowstorms came, one after another, making travel almost impossible, and an ice storm of freezing rain caused telegraph wires and poles to snap with the weight of the ice. The Thames in London froze over, and people were skating on the Serpentine. Fun for some, not so funny for most.

As she sat reading all the details in *The Times*, Mrs Matthews could only shake her head in disbelief, but had to admit that the fact which made her most unhappy was that the wild birds could no longer fly because of the weight of ice on their wings. Helpless creatures, dropping to certain death.

And yet – still no actual signs of war in their city. No bombs, no air raid warnings, so what they were left with was a deep, hidden anxiety that this was merely a waiting game. And only yesterday, Gladys Matthews had learned from her neighbours that they all wanted to build an air raid shelter in the plot behind the back gardens.

'Would there be room?' she'd asked them doubtfully, but they'd brushed any negatives aside. Their personal shelter was going to be built because they were going to need it. 'Make no mistake,' someone said firmly. 'Hitler has us in his sights and we're going to be ready for him!'

And what about Mark, dear Carrie's young man? Eileen's mother thought now as she folded her newspaper. They all knew that Carrie was deeply worried because she'd only had one letter from him this year where he'd said he could not tell her what was happening, because it was all hush hush.

'I hate not knowing where he is,' Carrie kept saying, 'and I keep having nightmares that he's not coming back and that I shall never see him again.'

Very soon, Carrie's worst fears were to be realised, because at the end of May, the British Expeditionary Force which had been operating across the Channel, fighting to support the French, had been forced to retreat. The German army had advanced at speed and had been about to surround and cut off the British army, which, if captured, would have ended their term of duty in a German prisoner of war camp. The only option had been to get out.

Dunkirk, the tragedy, the ignominy of Dunkirk.

But it would also be known as the miracle of Dunkirk because thousands of fighting soldiers had been rescued from that beach and brought back to safety – much of it thanks to the resilience and bravery of private boat owners and small fishing vessels ready to be alongside the British ships waiting to pick up stranded men.

But for Carrie, the pain of her anxiety at hearing nothing from Mark was made even worse by seeing groups of disheartened soldiers later roaming the streets. 'I cannot believe it,' she would repeat to her parents over and over again. 'I just cannot believe that we have been defeated so soon into this war. It feels like the end of the world. Those poor men – they must feel so utterly pointless. And where . . . where . . . is Mark? Why no news?'

And despite every effort to console and reassure her, Carrie was convinced that Mark had obviously been in France and was one of the many who did not make it back home.

* * *

'There! I knew you'd easily pick it up, Abigail!' Eileen exclaimed, going across to change the record on the gramophone. 'Carrie and I told you – there's nothing to ballroom dancing as long as you've got rhythm, and you've certainly got that! Are you sure you've never done any dancing before?'

It was quite late on a Saturday evening. Emily had gone to bed long ago, and the three girls were in the kitchen practising some dance steps. Eileen had suggested this because she'd known that Carrie was becoming almost inconsolable, even though Eileen had kept insisting that 'no news is *good* news!' And true to type, she'd come up with what she hoped would be a cheerful diversion.

'I told you,' Abigail said, 'the only thing we were taught at school was the Polka, and some folk dancing.' She looked away. 'And I – we – never learned ballroom dancing. Certainly nothing like you've been trying to teach me.'

'We've not only tried, we've succeeded,' Carrie said firmly. 'And of course, the polka and the waltz are similar so it's no wonder you could do that straightaway.'

'I think I like the quickstep best,' Abigail said, going over to sit down, 'but it's going to take me longer to get the hang of the foxtrot! It seems a bit devious to me.'

Eileen grinned as she passed around glasses of orange squash. 'We'll have a breather, and then we'll see if you find the palais glide more to your taste.'

Abigail gazed at her friends as she sipped at her drink. She hadn't been as happy as this for so long – despite that deep, personal guilt which was a dead weight in her heart. And despite the fear and dread which everyone was feeling.

But it did no good to sit and imagine what fate might await them all. The only sensible thing was to live one day at a time.

If only Luke were here, too, Abigail thought, trying to stem that longing for him that never went away. Where was he? What was he doing? Was he thinking about her? And what would he think of his darling daughter? Their Emily Grace? Well, what *could* he think – other than with love and pride?

'A penny for them,' Carrie said. 'What are you thinking about to cause that unusual frown?'

Abigail smiled quickly. 'Sorry – why should I look anything but happy when I'm with you two – who are still speaking to me even though I've been treading on your toes for the last couple of hours!'

'Think nothing of it,' Eileen said, pretending to limp as she went to search for another record. She glanced across at Abigail. 'Now, we are going to demonstrate our very favourite dance. You can watch for just a few seconds, then join in with us. It's easy – once you get the idea. The record I've chosen, "Doing the Lambeth Walk", is just perfect for this one.'

As she sat watching the other two, Abigail's momentary disquiet disappeared, the lively music automatically raising her spirits.

'Now, watch!' Eileen commanded. 'We start, side by side, with our arms around each other's waists. Then, on the first down beat, everyone moves first with right foot forward, then brings left foot to join it. Then right foot back, and left goes to join it, with everyone moving all the time to the left. Then the left foot moves forward, right foot joins it, now all moving to the right. See? You sway with the rhythm and move slightly forward all the time, either to the left or to the right so that you're travelling onwards.' She glanced back at Abigail. 'Anyone can join in – you don't need to have come with a partner, just hook in at the end of a row and then the whole room becomes rows and rows of dancers moving forward together in time to the beat. The palais glide can be done with any number of people,' she went on enthusiastically, 'and sometimes at a dance eight or more will do it together. But the three of us as a little team will be perfect. Come and have a go.'

Although slightly doubtful, Abigail could see that this was not going to be particularly difficult, and soon they were moving forward and backward and onward together, and all singing powerfully in time with the record.

Eileen and Carrie seemed to know all the words as they sang along, and soon Abigail began to join in, finishing lustily with the last line, 'doing the Lambeth Walk – hoi!'

Abigail's spirits soared with the music as it went on and on. This was glorious, innocent, happy fun!

The record finished playing, and they all flopped down, laughing. Even Carrie had managed to hide her distress for an hour.

'I told you there was nothing to it,' Eileen said. 'And it's obvious that you're a natural on the dance floor, Abigail.'

Abigail smiled. 'Well, I don't think we're ever going to prove that,' she said lightly.

Just then the door opened and Mrs Matthews came in. 'Ah – the dancing girls! Sorry to spoil the fun,' she said, 'but I fancied a cup of cocoa.'

Eileen immediately got up to heat a saucepan of milk. 'Come in and sit down, Mother,' she said. 'I hope we haven't been making too much noise, but we've been teaching Abigail some dance steps.'

'Yes, I gathered something like that was going on,' Gladys Matthews said, 'and I was joining in with you when you were singing "The Lambeth Walk".'

'Were you, Mother?' Eileen said. 'It's a long time since you've done any singing, isn't it?'

'Yes, but it's impossible not to sing that particular one as I hear it on the wireless all the time,' Gladys Matthews said. She turned to Abigail. 'Do you enjoy dancing, Abigail?'

'As I told the others, Mrs Matthews,' Abigail replied, 'I was only ever taught the polka at school, but Eileen and Carrie have somehow managed to get me doing the waltz and the quickstep. And the last one, the palais glide, which I love best of all, is such fun! And it was surprisingly easy to learn. But I'm afraid there's not likely to be a time when I will ever put my newfound ability to the test.'

Eileen and Carrie exchanged glances.

'Well, that's where you're wrong,' Eileen said, going across to give her mother the mug of cocoa. 'Because you, Abigail Wilson, and Carrie and I are all going on a date!'

Abigail was confused. 'What do you mean?'

'Eileen has decided that we're all going to a Tea Dance at The Berkeley,' Carrie said. 'It does have a lovely dance floor, and it's surrounded by a low balcony where people can sit and relax and have afternoon tea, and then get up and dance to the gramophone music if they feel like it. They're holding one of these affairs next Saturday and Eileen and I thought it would be a perfect opportunity to introduce you to Bristol high life!'

Eileen burst out laughing. 'It's hardly the high life, Abigail, just a very pleasant afternoon occasion to have nice cakes to eat and then get up and jig around a bit.' She smiled. 'Carrie and I have been before and we usually dance together, but sometimes a gentleman might come over and offer a hand to join him. We don't care, one way or the other,' Eileen added, 'because it's quite usual for girls to dance together.'

Abigail sat back, shaking her head. 'So, this is why you've been putting me through my paces this evening,' she said slowly. 'Is it one of your plotting exercises?'

'Exactly,' Eileen said smugly.

Abigail thought for a moment. 'And was it the reason you bought me my beautiful dress?'

'But of course!' the others exclaimed. 'Because we knew that in it, you would be belle of the ball!'

Mrs Matthews broke in. 'It certainly did suit you, Abigail, when you tried it on for us to admire,' she said. 'And the Berkeley Tea Dance will be a lovely opportunity for you to let your hair down and just go and enjoy yourselves. Emily and I will be very happy here because we're never short of interesting things to do.'

Abigail was suddenly excited at the thought of going somewhere special, doing something special that she'd never done before. The prospect was making her feel free as a bird and young again! Young *again*? But after all, she *was* only twenty. Shouldn't she be allowed to be free and young?

She stood up, holding out her hands to Eileen and Carrie. 'Come on – if I'm not to make a complete fool of myself next week, I'd better go on practising! And can we start with the palais glide?'

The day arrived, and Abigail woke early, feeling ridiculously excited to be going dancing. Such a thing had never entered her head and, luckily, Emily had accepted the fact that she would not be going too, especially as they were all having a fish and chip supper together later.

At two o'clock with Emily in close attendance, Abigail began to get ready. The event was to start at 3 p.m. and Jonathan Waters had very kindly offered to take the three girls to The Berkeley in his car.

The dress, freshly pressed, was hanging up on the wardrobe door, and Emily went over to gently hold out the skirt to its full width. 'You are going to look like a princess, Mummy,' she said. 'And in a minute, I shall do your hair and brush it out until it shines.'

Abigail smiled, slipping her arm around Emily's waist. 'One day, Emily, you will be the one going dancing,' she said. 'And I will have to brush out your hair – if I can possibly untangle all those curls.'

Finally, after smoothing a little Pond's Cold Cream on to her cheeks and adding a touch of Tangee lipstick to her mouth – additions which the others had recommended she try a little while ago – Abigail led Emily downstairs and into the kitchen where Eileen and her mother were waiting.

'Well,' Gladys Matthews said, 'that dress seems to have been made for you, Abigail! It's such a perfect fit, isn't it?'

'Well, I should hope it is,' Eileen said, smiling all over her face.

'Carrie and I spent a long time searching for the right thing, and you know what she's like . . . it had to be absolutely what she wanted in every way or we weren't buying it. She is such a pernickety shopper!'

Just then the sound of two gentle hoots from the car outside made them all leave the house, and there was Jonathan Waters standing with the passenger doors open for Eileen and Abigail to get in beside Carrie.

'Have a wonderful afternoon, my dears,' Gladys Matthews said. 'Emily and I will be expecting to hear full details when you get back.'

They arrived at The Berkeley, but instead of going in at the restaurant entrance as usual they turned left into Berkeley Square and were dropped off at the back, which was where resident guests and those attending special functions entered the hotel. As they went into the foyer Abigail gazed around her. Everywhere was richly carpeted, a huge display of fresh flowers stood on a small table in the centre, and huge, glittering chandeliers hung from the ceiling. Almost at once a uniformed attendant approached them, and Carrie spoke up. 'We have a table booked for three in the name of Waters for the Tea Dance,' she said, and he nodded, smiling.

'Follow me,' he said.

The room into which they were shown would stay in Abigail's memory for ever. As Carrie had already described, the large, circular dance floor was in the centre, and from it, at intervals, three or four shallow, carpeted steps led to the low balcony above. Set discreetly apart were the tea tables all the way around, and as the girls took their places it seemed to Abigail that she was living in a dream. The balcony rails were covered in gold plush matching the seats and backs of the ornate elegant chairs, the subdued lighting just perfect to make out what was going on around them. On every small, round tea table in the room there was glistening silver tableware, dainty china cups and saucers and plates. Gentle background music was already playing on the gramophone.

After Carrie had spoken to a waitress standing near, the three girls were shown to their table. 'I will bring your tea in a few minutes,' the waitress said, smiling down. 'Proceedings are about to start and I expect you would like to dance for a while before you begin eating?'

'That sounds perfect, thank you,' Eileen said, returning the smile.

The waitress left, and Carrie said, 'Look – apart from one table over in that corner, the others are all occupied, so it's just nicely full, isn't it? Room for everyone to dance without bumping into each other!'

'Don't count on that,' Abigail said. 'I'm sure to trip over my feet – despite your best instructions. I'm already beginning to feel nervous because will I remember everything you tried to teach me?'

'Of course you will!' the others said in unison. 'Stop worrying!'

The MC spoke through his microphone. 'Good afternoon, ladies and gentlemen,' he said. 'Welcome to The Berkeley Afternoon Tea Dance! Now, shall we start with the quickstep? Come on – everyone on their feet! It's time to enjoy ourselves!'

And with the music of Victor Sylvester's dance band filling the room, almost everyone left their table and took their places on the floor.

Eileen leaned over and touched Abigail's hand. 'Would you like to have a go, Abigail?' she said. 'Or would you rather sit and watch for a few minutes while Carrie and I make a start?'

'I think that's a very good idea,' Abigail said at once. 'I'll keep a close eye on the pair of you to refresh my memory of all those steps!'

Although the whole atmosphere in the ballroom was disarmingly relaxing, Abigail could feel her knees actually begin to shake in apprehension. In fact, she was even feeling a bit sick. How on earth was she going to join in with the rhythm and steps of the dances after having had so little instruction? It was all very well for Eileen and Carrie . . . Just look at them now, Abigail thought as she picked them out among the crowd. They'd been dancing for years and they made it look so effortless as they tripped along to this very quick quickstep!

Just then the waitress appeared with a tray holding their teapot and water jug which she put down in front of Abigail. 'I thought you might like a cup of tea,' the waitress said kindly. 'I'll bring the cakes a bit later.'

'Oh – thank you so much,' Abigail said. 'You must have realised I was feeling parched!' *Or should I say terrified?*

Filling one of the dainty tea cups, Abigail put it to her lips and sipped. And almost at once, she began to feel a bit better. Perhaps she might actually join in when the others came back, she thought hopefully.

As the quickstep came to an end, the MC spoke again. 'Stay on your feet, ladies and gentlemen,' he said, 'and we will go straight into the waltz.' He turned to change the record. 'Here we go . . . the waltz, the all-time favourite!'

Abigail put down her cup and sank back into her chair. If she was honest, she would almost prefer to stay where she was for the whole afternoon and not dance at all. Just drink in her surroundings. But she could hardly do that, not after her friends had provided her with this party dress and sweet little sandals.

Then, a gentle tap on her shoulder made Abigail turn and look up quickly. A tall, middle-aged man dressed in a smart grey suit stood beside her.

'Excuse me, I was wondering if I might have the pleasure,' he said courteously, 'to partner you in this waltz?'

For a full five seconds Abigail could not find her voice. This was something she had *not* anticipated . . . all she'd expected was to dance with her friends! She cleared her throat nervously. 'Well . . . I don't really know,' she began. 'I don't know if I can, I mean, I'm not sure . . .'

She was sounding pathetic! Would anyone come to a function like this and not dance?

He waited there, half-standing aside to allow her to get up from her chair and Abigail gazed up at him, gazed up into his eyes . . . dark brown eyes, tired-looking eyes, she thought, the expression on his face gentle, unassuming. He spoke again.

'I beg your pardon if you are not dancing this afternoon,' he said. 'I saw you sitting here alone, but I didn't mean to intrude.'

He turned away as if to leave, and Abigail immediately stood up. 'No, don't go – yes – I mean, yes I would like to dance the waltz with you,' she said, amazed at her own words.

Now he smiled, taking her hand and leading her down the steps to the ballroom floor. Without meaning to, Abigail decided to confide in this total stranger with the tired eyes. They stood for a moment and she looked up at him.

'I think I should explain that I don't really dance, and that I have never been to a dance before,' she said. 'And I have only had one or two lessons.' She swallowed. 'I mean, you may wish that you hadn't asked me to partner you . . . and I hope I don't tread on your feet or fall over or do something silly to embarrass you.'

He didn't reply for a moment but slipped his arm around her waist and led her to join the throng. Then he spoke quietly in her ear.

'Just leave everything to me.'

And Abigail could do nothing but relax and accept his words because now, holding her upright and quite close to him, he took the weight of her body in his arms as they began, actually lifting her so that her feet barely touched the floor. Then they were gliding . . . floating . . . the three-step rhythm effortless as he gently nudged against her legs so that Abigail knew exactly what to do as each second passed, with the whole room moving in the same direction. She was not going to fall over, she was not going to embarrass this stranger, or herself. She was loving every moment of this waltz!

It ended far sooner than she'd have liked, but now, once again taking her hand, he led her back up the balcony steps to the table, pulling out her chair for her to sit. But Abigail remained standing and looked up.

'Thank you so much,' she said. 'Thank you so much for trusting yourself with me. And for guiding me in my very first attempt at dancing in public. Your expertise gave me the courage I didn't think I had.'

He smiled down at her, his eyes brighter now. 'You have no idea what courage you have given *me* this afternoon.' He hesitated. 'I have not danced for three years – not since my wife died. You see . . . we met at a dance hall when we were little more than teenagers, and spent many, many happy hours in ballrooms during our thirty years of marriage.' He glanced around him. 'We always enjoyed coming here,' he added, 'and as today happens to be our wedding anniversary, I just wanted to be among dancers. To be part of it and watch the enjoyment of others, though I had absolutely no intention of getting up myself,' he said smiling. 'Not without my lifelong partner with me. But I did, so thank you for giving me the emotional fortitude I needed.'

Feeling tears start behind her eyes, Abigail watched him make his way to the table at the far end by the steps which led to the exit. How strange, she thought, that you could feel you know someone after such a brief meeting. And they didn't even know each other's name.

But she sensed his overwhelming loss. Because she understood it.

Just then Eileen and Carrie came back, all smiles. '*We* saw you being swept off your feet, Abigail Wilson!' Eileen exclaimed. 'You looked absolutely professional dancing with that tall bloke! And your dress looked gorgeous swirling around as you moved.'

'He was the professional,' Abigail replied quietly, 'and he made it very easy for me.'

Just then the waitress arrived with the cakes and fresh tea, and for the next twenty minutes or so the three girls enjoyed the sandwiches and pastries, all displayed on a tiered cake stand. And presently, taking it in turns, Eileen and Carrie led Abigail out on to the dance floor to waltz and quickstep – though she refused to attempt the foxtrot.

At five-thirty the MC announced the final dance. 'You've been a wonderful crowd here this afternoon,' he said through the microphone. 'So everyone on their feet! With or without a partner – it doesn't matter! Hook on to any line which takes your fancy . . . and let's go! Let's enjoy that other all-time favourite . . . let's do the palais glide!'

The girls jumped to their feet to join everyone else already waiting for the music to begin and then they were off. The three of them soon becoming five . . . then seven . . . And Abigail's heart soared. This was the one she'd really been waiting for!

She looked around, searching the lines of dancers for her unexpected partner, half-hoping that he would hook on to their line.

But instead, glancing over to the exit, she saw him leave. Closing the door behind him.

25th June 1940

Gladys Matthews raised her head from her pillow, switched on her bedside lamp and glanced at her clock. It was eleven-forty and she'd only just started to feel sleepy when something made her stir uncomfortably. She sighed. The room was a bit stuffy, even though the window was slightly open. But it had been another warm day and the temperature didn't seem to have dropped very much.

Leaning on one elbow, she reached for her glass of water and took a sip, just as there was a tap on the door and Eileen came in, tying the belt of her cotton dressing gown. She sat on the end of her mother's bed.

'Can't you sleep either, Mother?' Eileen said. 'I came down

170

for a glass of water and saw the light under your door. It's so humid, isn't it?'

Gladys Matthews nodded. 'It's not only that, I feel restless, Eileen. More so than usual, I mean. And it can't be what we had for supper because I hardly had any, did I?'

'No, and that might be the clue,' Eileen said. 'You might be hungry, so I'll make you some warm milk and toast a slice of bread with a little Marmite. That may settle you.'

Before Mrs Matthews could reply, there was a loud rap on the front door, and they looked at each other in alarm. Who on earth could that be at this time of night?

Eileen immediately left the room to go and answer the door. Their next-door neighbour stood there, fully dressed. He spoke quietly, but urgently.

'Get everyone up as quickly as you can,' he said. 'It's just come through that enemy aircraft have been sighted coming across the Channel. It's obviously totally unforeseen so that's why there have been no sirens. But we need to get everyone down to the shelter – now!'

And at that very second the sirens did begin to wail. A loud, ear-splitting, menacing scream which kept coming and going in waves.

Everyone had been told exactly what they should do in such an emergency and over the weeks a considerable amount of practice had taken place in the very recently finished shelter, the children seeming to enjoy the novelty of going up and down the few earth steps into the cavernous hole beneath. But the months of peace and quiet which the country had enjoyed had given a false sense of security and it took Eileen a few seconds to take in the news. But then she sprang into action, returning swiftly to her mother and explaining everything before running up the stairs, two at a time, to wake Abigail.

But being woken by the sirens, Abigail had already clambered out of bed and had started dressing as Eileen thrust open the door.

'We need to get to the shelter as soon as possible,' Eileen said urgently, but before another word was spoken by either of them, Emily woke up, rubbing her eyes and starting to whimper.

'What's happening, Mummy? What's that noise?'

'Nothing for you to worry about, Emily,' Eileen said briskly. 'We're going to be perfectly all right but we must get down to the shelter in a minute – you know – so that we are safe. Can you help Mummy by getting dressed while I go down and help Mrs Gladys? And look, I'm still in my dressing gown so I'd better hurry up, too, hadn't I?' She smiled quickly. 'Mrs Gladys will be waiting for you to call for her, so be as quick as you can, darling.'

Without another word, Emily got out of bed and started getting dressed, putting on her dress and cardigan and pulling her long white socks straight up to her knees. Crouching down to help Emily put on her shoes, Abigail glanced up.

'You're such a good girl, Emily,' she said, 'and now we must get down to that shelter.'

'Yes, Eileen just told us that,' Emily said matter-of-factly. 'But I can take dolly, can't I? I don't want to leave her here by herself.'

'Of course dolly is coming!' Abigail said. 'Mrs Gladys would want us to bring her, wouldn't she?'

'Will Carrie be here in a minute?' Emily said. 'Will she be coming to the shelter with us?'

'No, there'll be no need for that because Carrie and her mother and father will be going to a shelter with their own neighbours. But we'll be seeing her soon.'

Quickly, they left the bedroom and Emily ran down the stairs where Eileen and her mother were waiting. Emily went straight over to hold Mrs Matthews' hand.

'We've all got to go down to the shelter now, Mrs Gladys,' she said conspiratorially, 'but it's just to keep us safe, so don't worry.' Emily smiled up. 'Is that noise giving you a headache?'

Gladys Matthews returned the smile. 'No – but I'll be very glad when it stops, Emily.'

'Now, Emily,' Eileen said briskly, 'your job is to look after our cushions. That's right, cuddle them in to you. They'll help to make those benches we'll be sitting on a bit more comfy. And would you hold Mrs Gladys's little shawl as well? The one she likes to keep around her neck? It's going to be quite a lot colder in the shelter so we'll have to sit nice and close together.'

Despite the complete – and unexpected – shock they all felt, a quiet acceptance of the situation, and the knowledge that they must always act quickly and without undue fuss, meant that in less than ten minutes they were ready to leave the house.

As they went through to the kitchen to let themselves out by the back door, Mrs Matthews turned to Eileen. 'Are you sure we've not forgotten anything – I mean, have we got all our papers, you know, the important, personal stuff we were told not to leave behind?'

'Don't worry, Mother,' Eileen said. 'They're all here safely in this bag: the insurance policies, deeds of the house, bank statements. I'm sure I haven't forgotten anything, including,' she added, 'two large flasks of tea and plenty of biscuits and sweets to keep us going!'

They went out of the back door and made their way down the garden path, and Abigail, with her arm tightly around Emily's waist, found herself wondering whether she was still in bed and having the strangest of dreams. It was almost midnight, the witching hour, and here they were, trudging over damp grass towards the shelter in that huge hole in the ground which had so recently been excavated, and which they hoped may protect them from falling bombs. And now that the sirens had stopped wailing, it was oddly quiet with just a few raised voices from outside calling to each other, and running footsteps in West Road as air raid wardens tried to round up people who didn't know where they were going.

Glancing up at the clear night sky, criss-crossed, now, by the penetrating beam of search lights, it was perhaps the most surreal experience Abigail had ever had in her life.

She might even see Alice's white rabbit run past her in a minute.

The following day, no one in the house woke very early after the night they'd endured. The deafening noise of the explosions above, and the incessant din of the anti-aircraft guns, had caused those in the shelter to cling to each other in fright, and to try to convince the few children present that this would soon be over.

But it was two-thirty before the all-clear had sounded, when everyone made their way to the surface wondering whether their houses were still there. But fortunately for West Road they seemed to have escaped totally undamaged.

Upstairs, with Emily still sound asleep, Abigail got dressed and left the room, closing the door quietly behind her. Today was certainly going to be difficult, because what had happened outside? And should she go to work as usual?

Downstairs in the kitchen, Eileen and her mother were already there having their first cup of tea and listening to the local radio station. Eileen put a cup of tea on the table for Abigail just as the news bulletin ended. Then, orchestral music began and Eileen switched off the wireless.

'Well,' Eileen said flatly, 'apparently that was some raid last night. The details just given were not very expansive – it's obviously better not to go public and release too much. "Listening Ears" and all that,' she added, referring to the street hoardings telling everyone to 'Keep Mum' so as not to give the enemy any advantage, 'but it appears that the bombers were making for Temple Meads.' She made a face. 'If we thought we were going to get away scot-free with this war, we were mistaken, weren't we?'

Abigail sat down by Eileen's mother. 'Did you manage to get any sleep afterwards, Mrs Matthews?' she said. 'It took me a while, but Emily was out for the count in two minutes.'

'I think I had about an hour,' Gladys Matthews said, 'but I am just thankful that we all came out of it alive and that we still have a house to live in.'

'Yes – and I rang the vicarage a few minutes ago,' Eileen said, 'and they're all OK. Carrie said that she and her mother spent the night in the shelter, though her father hadn't joined them because he'd stayed with one of their parishioners who's bedbound.'

Just then, the sound of the milkman leaving the bottles on the step made Eileen go and open the door to speak to him. After a few minutes she came back with the news.

'Well,' she said, 'we can count our lucky chickens! He told me the details he'd heard – we did catch it in Knowle last night – and less than a mile from here! So did Bedminster! So it was a bit close for comfort, wasn't it? He said that St Phillip's and St Paul's have copped it, too.' Eileen bit her lip, clearly upset by what she'd heard. 'There are bound to be many casualties,' she said slowly, 'but, isn't it amazing – the chap said that as far as he could tell the buses seemed to be running, and he'd heard that all the shops have opened, too.' She shook her head slowly. 'What courage in the face of adversity.'

In fact, in Bristol's first air raid, five people had been killed and more than thirty injured, which was terrible enough, but it could have been so much worse. And when the Bristolians viewed the damage that had been caused, they could only shake their heads in wonder that so few lives had been lost.

'Shall we have toast and marmalade this morning?' Eileen said. 'Then I'm going to ring the office and see what's going on.' She glanced at Abigail. 'Shall I ring Blackwell's and see if they're open? I'll fetch the telephone directory in a minute, and you can find their number.'

Despite the shocking awakening to the grim facts of war, by the following Monday, Bristol had picked itself up and got on with the job of living and working. But for the few days after that raid the city held itself in suspense. Did Hitler have them in his sights again? And if so – when?

Chapter 19

On the 10th July, what became known as the Battle of Britain began. Aerial warfare – with Spitfires and Messerschmitts in deadly combat – would continue for more than three months.

As they gazed upwards into the clear blue skies, people watched the flying machines as they ducked and dived and attempted to shoot each other out of existence. For the helpless observers below, it was a macabre, fearful sight as the relentless dog fights went on, the planes attacking and repelling each other, time after time, and it seemed to some that the display might have been put on for their grisly entertainment.

But as it turned out, those few, vital months of aerial skirmish saw Hitler's intention to invade Great Britain completely foiled. Nazi jackboots would not be marching over English soil.

The weeks of July and August continued to be hot and sunny, and despite the country being at war, people went on with their lives as normally as they could, citizens being encouraged to 'do their bit'. It soon became commonplace for housewives to learn civil defence, and how to put out fires with hoses and stirrup pumps.

But one of the things which made people feel they were really helping the war effort was to give away any metal object which might go into the manufacture of spitfires.

One morning, Mrs Matthews, gazing out of her sitting-room window, watched with dismay as the rather graceful chain fencing which linked the fronts of all the houses in West Road was dismantled and thrown into the back of a huge lorry to join the towering pile of other items which had been donated. Pans and kettles, bits of old cars, anything which could be melted down and turned into fighting planes.

Gladys Matthews turned away. West Road had always had that chain-link fencing, and already, the space left by its absence was giving her a feeling of extra vulnerability. But what was that, compared to what others were going through? Absolutely nothing. She had even become accustomed to the claustrophobic sensation she had from the blacked-out blinds at her windows. What had to be done, must be done.

She glanced at the clock. Abigail and Emily would soon be home from their visit to the swimming baths which had become quite a favourite with them once they'd got used to it. Every morning, Abigail tried to take her daughter out somewhere before she went to work – yesterday they'd gone into Woolworths to look around, and afterwards they'd popped into Robertson's to see Janet.

Gladys Matthews' eyes softened. How lucky Emily was to have Abigail for her mother.

Downstairs in the stock room, Abigail stopped what she was doing and took a break for a moment, thankful to rest her back. Despite the disruption of the war, the students' books kept on coming, box after box. And there were still three which she hadn't unpacked.

She half-closed her eyes for a moment, thinking about Emily and Mrs Matthews up there at the play park, Emily being pushed on the swings and being helped to build sandcastles. That little park had proved an absolute boon, because it was close enough to

West Road for Eileen's mother to walk safely with Emily, and today they'd decided to take a picnic with them. Abigail could imagine the two of them now, chatting away like two old friends – which, of course, was what they had become. Her little girl and Eileen's mother enjoyed the sort of relationship which Abigail thought a grandmother would have with a granddaughter, full of love and the wish to make each other happy. Something which she herself had never experienced. Lucky for Emily, and lucky for Abigail too.

Just then, Martin came clattering down the stairs to stand beside Abigail. 'Gosh, it's hot down here,' he said. 'Come on. You can finish this later.' He smiled down. 'I'll make you a cup of tea because I think you deserve one – or would you prefer something cold? I could go over to The Berkeley and get us something special – like one of their milkshakes.'

Abigail returned the smile. 'No thanks, Martin, a cup of tea is fine by me. And I'll come up and make it. You've got other things to do.'

'At least the shop's quiet at the moment,' he said, 'which is just as well since it's my mother's day off.'

He went upstairs and Abigail followed, going straight into the little kitchen to put the kettle on. Glancing out of the window, she could see buses and a few cars making their way up and down Park Street, and she'd noticed on her way here earlier that all the shops were open. She hummed a little tune to herself as she set out their mugs. How did she deserve to be feeling so content with this war going on? But she had to admit it – she was content. She earned enough money to pay her way in the lovely home they were living in, and Emily was safe and enjoying her afternoon outside in the fresh air.

Even so, Abigail paused in her thoughts. It was difficult not to think about – and worry about – all the serving men in the thick of battle. Young men like Mark . . .

Then Abigail suddenly smiled as she remembered something that Eileen and Carrie had decided. Tomorrow, they were all going to Weston-super-Mare on the train! Apart from Mrs Matthews who'd said she'd be happier at home. Because Abigail and Emily had never been to the seaside and when Eileen had described what it was like, Emily had jumped up and down in excitement.

'We'll all take our bathing costumes,' Eileen had said, 'and we'll run in and out of the water and splash each other!'

As Martin had said, the shop was unusually quiet, and presently Abigail took their tea and the finger biscuits they both liked and placed everything on the side counter which was conveniently out of sight from any customers. He stopped what he was doing and turned back to glance at her.

'Ah, good. Thanks, Abigail,' he said, moving over to stand by her side.

And for some reason, for the first time since she'd worked at Blackwell's, Abigail felt a sudden rush of awareness. Awareness that he was a good-looking, well-built, well-dressed male, exuding a whiff of strength. Of superiority. He was standing closer to her than he needed to, so that she could smell the manly scent of him, his toiletries, the shampoo he used on his hair, perhaps the odour of his expensive suit fabric. Moving a step away, she picked up her cup and sipped.

'D'you know, Abigail,' he said, glancing at her, 'my mother and I never thought we really needed anyone to help us in the shop, but since you've been working here, I'm afraid you've made yourself indispensable!' He grinned.

Abigail dropped a slight curtsey. 'Well, I'm glad that I'm giving satisfaction,' she said, 'but honestly, Martin, this is not a job for me, it's a total pleasure. I just love handling books, being with books of any sort, and there are lots here that I could just sit and read right through to the end. Of course, the students' ones are a bit beyond me,' she admitted, 'but I still like looking through them when there's a moment, attempting to follow what they're trying to tell me.' She paused. 'I've always known that I'm a bookworm and think I will be for the rest of my days.'

He nodded. 'We both spotted that within an hour of you working with us, Abigail,' he said. 'You've tackled anything we've asked of you and it's been a huge help.'

There was the briefest pause before he spoke again. 'I don't know if you like the cinema, but they're showing *Gone with the Wind* at The Whiteladies' this week and next. It stars Clark Gable and Vivien Leigh and it's bound to be good.' He hesitated. 'I thought I might give it a try.'

Abigail had never been to the pictures in her life and she looked away for a minute, feeling awkward, because she sensed that Martin was going to ask her to go with him. It was the expression in his eyes as he looked down at her . . . but he *knew* she was married, didn't he, even though she was alone right now?

She shifted away from him, smiling brightly. 'Do you know, going to the pictures is something which my husband and I promised we would do again as soon as he returned home.' She made a face. 'I know I shouldn't grumble because I have so much to be thankful for – but it is a very long time since we were together and Emily and I miss him so much.'

Martin nodded slowly. 'Of course you do, Abigail,' he said. 'And I'm sure he misses you, too.'

Martin finished his cup of tea, then returned to what he'd been doing. Why had fate sent him the most lovely, the most beautiful woman he'd ever met, to work alongside him every day? And why had he thought, for a single moment, that she would agree to go with him to the pictures – or to anywhere else?

A woman who, it was obvious, would be forever out of his reach?

Chapter 20

7th September 1940

In the usual, unhurried peace of a Saturday morning, Abigail sat at the bedside table with her pencils and colours. She'd almost completed this picture – a copy of one of Dada's – and she narrowed her eyes, studying it critically. No, it still wasn't as good as his.

It was early, and she glanced across at Emily who still hadn't woken up, her dark ringlets tumbling around her pillow, framing that cherubic face. Darling Emily, the 'millstone around Abigail's neck', which was what Edna had said she would be.

Abigail half-smiled. She would not change a single thing in her life because she was lucky! She and Luke had produced this little girl who lived in a perpetual world of love and happiness, and if she and Luke were never to meet again, the joy of being Emily's mother would never be taken away from her. It was hers for ever and nothing would change that.

Abigail's expression darkened as she started putting her things away. What about Carrie, sweet-natured Carrie? Would Carrie ever know what it was to have her own child? Mark's child? However much they all tried to reassure her that Mark would have got himself and his men out of danger, Carrie had become convinced that she and her beloved would never see each other again.

'It's just that I keep having this recurring nightmare that Mark is injured and that no one is there to help him,' Carrie had said one day when she was feeling particularly down. 'I even hear him calling my name and I can't do anything about it. And I wake up crying because I know in my heart that hoping for the best is a false hope.'

'You do not *know* that,' Eileen kept saying. 'Just because Mark's name hasn't surfaced yet doesn't mean that *he* won't!'

But despite everyone's encouragement, most were coming to the conclusion that, as the days were passing with still no news, it seemed unlikely that Mark would come home again, or even that his body might ever be found.

One morning at the vicarage as they were clearing up their breakfast dishes, Joan Waters turned to her husband. 'I'm getting really worried about Carrie,' she said. 'She is grieving for Mark all the time, and I know she's not sleeping very well. It's just not knowing that's keeping her awake.'

Jonathan patted his wife's arm. 'Look – I've got a meeting in London next week and I thought I'd go to the War Office and see if I can find out anything.' He smiled. 'Perhaps my dog collar will get me past the door.'

Now, Abigail went over to the bed. It was time Emily got up because last night as they were all playing Monopoly, with Emily there too, Carrie had mentioned that tomorrow there was going to be a garden party on the vicarage lawn and she thought they might all enjoy it.

'Of course, it's a fundraising event, as usual,' she'd said, 'but there are always nice things to buy, plants and books – with a special corner for the kids – and the afternoon teas are a special favourite.' She'd made a face. 'It's been a bit tricky this year because of the food shortages, but my mother has managed to find enough ladies of the parish to come up trumps. And of course we've been saving up things ourselves so that there's enough – my mother is a very thrifty organiser.' Carrie had glanced at Emily. 'But this year, my dad has managed to dig up something extra special for the children. He'd heard of a little roundabout he could hire, just five little cars, but it's not mechanised, so it has to be swung around by a couple of strong men of the parish who are willing to flex their muscles. Stand there in the centre and get the thing rotating. They have to take it in turns, of course, but enough of them have volunteered.'

That had immediately caught Emily's interest because she'd already been on a roundabout on the pier when they'd been to Weston-super-Mare. 'Can we go to the garden party, Mummy?' she'd begged.

'Yes – if Eileen wants to – and if you will agree to go to bed now, Emily,' Abigail had said.

Now, at last, Emily woke, sat up and stretched her arms. Then she jumped out of bed, ran over to the window and looked out. 'It's a lovely day, Mummy, see? The sun's out! And we're going to the garden party later, aren't we? So I can go on the roundabout!'

Presently, they went down to the kitchen where Eileen was putting out the cups and saucers. She smiled.

'What shall we all have for breakfast? The kettle's boiled.'

Just then, Mrs Matthews came through. She'd overslept that morning and hadn't heard Emily's tap on her door and, as had become more normal, she was managing with just one of her sticks. Eileen smiled inwardly. She'd always suspected that part of her mother's fragility had been to do with her losing her earlier inborn love for life. But for a whole year she seemed to have regained quite a lot of it.

'Do you know, I would like my rasher of bacon with an egg today,' Mrs Matthews said as she sat down next to Emily. 'Which book have you got there, Emily?'

After they'd eaten their fried breakfast – which they'd all chosen after smelling it sizzling in the pan, and which Eileen reminded them was the last bacon until their rations were due next week – Eileen said casually, 'Abigail and I are going to the vicarage garden party at All Saints later, Mother. Why don't you come with us? It's going to be another lovely afternoon and the days are already beginning to close in, aren't they, so there are not going to be many more chances to have tea sitting outside.'

Before Eileen's mother could reply, Emily spoke up quickly. 'Oh you must come with us, Mrs Gladys! Because there's going to be a roundabout to ride on. You could come on it and sit next to me.'

Eileen's mother chuckled. 'Well, I probably wouldn't come on the roundabout, Emily, but I think I would like to come to All Saints with you this afternoon, of course. I have been to many of these things in my time and they are always very happy occasions.'

Eileen was thrilled. She hadn't expected such a quick and positive response. 'Oh, good, Mother! So I will order a taxi for two o'clock – the thing opens at two-thirty. And there will be plenty of seats for everyone to sit down, Carrie told me that. She also said that it will be all over by five, so we'll be back home in good time to make supper.'

Abigail stood up to start clearing the dishes and glanced up. 'From what Carrie told us about their afternoon teas, I don't think we'll be feeling like any supper.'

'Oh – not even some chips?' Emily said.

Abigail ruffled Emily's hair as she went past. 'Honestly, Emily Wilson! You're going to turn into a chip one day!'

Abigail had never been to a vicarage tea party – or to any tea party – and as soon as they arrived, she could see there were already groups of people wandering around examining what was for sale on the stalls. And in the far corner, a long trestle table, covered with a white cloth and holding rows and rows of cups and saucers and plates stood prepared to receive all the contributions from the parishioners as they arrived. Standing behind the table, folding paper napkins into neat triangles, was Carrie. She waved as she saw them.

It was a really lovely day, sultry but pleasant, and presently, Mrs Matthews, walking fairly easily with her stick, turned to Eileen.

'Now, you go off by yourselves,' she said, 'because I can see several people I know, so there'll be others for me to talk to.'

'Look, Mrs Gladys,' Emily said, 'there's the roundabout! Shall we go over and see when it's going to start?'

'No, you go, Emily – because there's a lady over there who's beckoning to me,' Eileen's mother said. 'I'll catch up with you all later.'

'So *can* we go over and see when the roundabout is going to start, Mummy?' Emily began, and Abigail shook her head.

'Not yet, because I can see some lovely books over on that stall, Emily, so let's go across and have a look. You may like to buy one.'

'And I'll go over and see if I can help Carrie with anything,' Eileen said, turning away.

Presently, Jonathan Waters formally announced that the event was open for business, and then things really took off. There were plenty of small children present, all running around, chasing each other excitedly and waiting to buy things in the children's corner, and by now the trestle table was laden with cakes and sandwiches, with a queue already beginning to form. But the little roundabout, with its five brightly coloured cars, still hadn't started. Emily looked up at her mother.

'*When* do you think the roundabout will be starting?' she asked.

'You must be patient, Emily,' Abigail said. 'I expect they're waiting for those strong men to arrive to make it work. Now then, let's go and see what cakes you'd like us to have with our tea.'

After a while, people started sitting down at the small tables and almost at once, Eileen, with her mother having re-joined them, found a table for five in a secluded and shady corner of the garden. She came over to speak to Abigail.

'I've bagged that table over there for us,' she said, 'and Carrie will be joining us in a minute. So choose your cakes and I'll bring the tea over for us.' She smiled. 'It's turning out to be quite a busy afternoon, isn't it, and apparently the stalls are all doing well.'

Abigail smiled back. 'Do you know, Eileen, I've never felt so – so completely relaxed,' she said. 'There's such a lovely atmosphere here, and I feel absolutely at ease with the world.' She paused. 'You wouldn't think there was a war on, would you?'

Abigail, Emily and Mrs Matthews went over to their table, and Eileen's mother nodded as she sat down. 'I agree with you, Abigail. This is a different world, isn't it?'

When Carrie joined them, word got around that the roundabout was in business and Emily jumped down from her chair excitedly. 'Can we go over, Mummy? Look, there's a little queue waiting already.'

Gladys Matthews got up. 'Let me come with you, Emily,' she said. She glanced at Abigail. 'You stay and chat with Carrie and Eileen, dear. I'll make sure Emily comes to no harm.'

The others laughed at that and Carrie said, 'I don't think that little contraption is capable of harming anyone! And look – my dad is already taking his turn at making it work! Bless him,' she added fondly, 'he's always the first to volunteer.'

Carrie half-closed her eyes and dropped her head back for a moment. 'Gosh, I'm tired,' she admitted. 'Mum and I were up early to make the scones and finish the butterfly cakes.' She yawned. 'And the phone hasn't stopped ringing with people making last-minute enquiries.'

Presently their attention was alerted to Joan Waters who was sprinting across the lawn, beckoning to Jonathan urgently. He immediately passed his position at the roundabout over to someone else and followed his wife as they both ran back into the vicarage.

'My poor father,' Carrie said as she watched them go. 'Will people never give him any peace! That telephone doesn't leave him alone for five minutes – there's obviously another parish crisis for him to deal with.' Then, after a few moments, shading her eyes from the sun, she pointed at the roundabout. 'Look, it'll soon be Emily's turn – she's been so patient, love her.'

'And I've had to be patient, too,' Abigail said, 'listening to her going on and on about it.'

After a minute or two they saw Jonathan come back outside, and he was almost running towards them, nearly tripping over as he hurried. Frowning, and sensing that something must be wrong, Carrie immediately stood up and went quickly forward to reach his side.

'Dad?' she said anxiously. 'What is it? What's going on?'

And although from where they were sitting the others could not hear what was being said, what they did hear was Carrie's desperate cry, and she clung to her father, burying her face into his neck. Then, horrified, they saw her knees begin to buckle, saw Jonathan Waters try to prevent his daughter from collapsing to the ground.

'Oh no, please no,' Eileen whispered, tears beginning to fill her eyes and Abigail's throat tightened in horror. Because this could only mean one thing.

After a few moments, both girls stood up and slowly walked the few steps towards the heartbreaking scene they were witnessing. Because they knew Carrie would want them to be close.

Then, releasing herself from her father, and with tears still streaming down her cheeks, Carrie looked at Eileen and Abigail.

'It's Mark . . . it's M . . .' The word could barely leave her lips and Eileen grasped Carrie's arm tightly.

'Hold on, Carrie,' Eileen began, but before she could utter another word, Carrie broke in, her voice shaking and tremulous.

'Mark is *alive!*' she said. 'Dad just received the news on the phone! Mark is *alive* and he's all right and he'll soon be coming home! He'll soon be here with all of us again!'

Then, after a few breathless seconds, and as if at a given signal, the three girls clasped each other around the waist and circled around and around and around in a triangular dance of uninhibited joy.

Almost at once Joan Waters arrived to join them all in their excitement. 'What a day!' she exclaimed, hugging her daughter tightly. 'This is the news we've all been praying for, isn't it, and our prayers have been answered!'

Carrie tried to dry the tears which were still streaming down her face. 'What *else* do you know, Dad?' she said. 'Is Mark all right? I mean, it's been such a long time since we've heard a single word. Is he, is he injured?'

Jonathan shook his head. 'I wasn't given much to go on,' he said, 'only that Mark returned to England two days ago and is now being de-briefed. Once that's happened, things will become clearer.'

Drying her own eyes, Joan said, 'Now, all of you go and sit down again because I'm going to make some fresh tea – and there are still plenty of cakes left.' She smiled. 'Of course, I would rather open a bottle of champagne because I think the occasion calls for it, but that will have to wait. And when Mark finally shows up,' she said, 'we'll have a party – a proper party!'

And sitting at the table with the three girls – who were still clutching each other's hands in relief, Jonathan Waters offered a personal prayer of gratitude. Gratitude to the young padre who'd been on the duty desk when Carrie's father had gone to the War Office, and who'd kept his word that, when it came through, any news of Captain Mark Anderson would be relayed to All Saints vicarage at the earliest possible moment.

Chapter 21

The prevailing, peaceful atmosphere of the occasion – disturbed only by the clink of tea cups and the companionable murmuring among those present – suddenly changed into one of abject terror as, without prior warning, the air raid sirens began to scream out their terrifying message making everyone clap their hands over their ears. Straightaway, Jonathan Waters got up and ran among the crowd, urging everyone to leave the garden and run, run to their nearest shelter.

'Quickly!' he called out urgently as he rounded up those who still could not comprehend that they were apparently soon to be in the middle of an air raid. 'Leave everything where it is and just get to your shelters! Take cover! Now!'

Galvanised, Eileen, Abigail and Carrie raced over to the roundabout and grabbed Emily out of the little car she'd just sat in.

'Sorry, darling,' Abigail said breathlessly, 'you won't be having a ride this afternoon after all, I'm afraid. Come on, we must get to the shelter. And Mrs Gladys is coming too,' she added, ushering Eileen's mother in front of them.

Emily looked up. 'Is this another air raid, Mummy?'

'Yes, but we're going to be all right,' Abigail said.

'There might not be enough room for us all in the municipal

shelter across the road,' Carrie said breathlessly, 'so I think we should go straight into the church crypt. Are you all right, Mrs Matthews? Shall I take your other arm?'

'No, I'm managing quite well, thank you, Carrie,' Eileen's mother said. 'My daughter knows how to force me to get moving when the need arises.'

They all hurried, half-walking, half-running out of the gardens, and clutching Emily's hand tightly, Abigail couldn't help feeling that apart from the amazing, wonderful news Carrie had just received, everyone had been dealt an unjust hammer blow that afternoon. It had been such an innocent event, enjoyed by young and old alike, but how could you be sure of anything, anymore? Were they all going to get out of *this* one alive? There had been no mention, no rumour, that this raid was likely, and since the last one in June, the city had known comparative quiet which, once again, had lulled everyone into a sense of passivity.

As they paused briefly at the gate to let Mrs Matthews go first, Emily looked up at her mother.

'I think the Germans are really mean,' she said. 'They *could* have waited until I'd had my turn.'

On Monday two weeks later, the telephone rang in the study at the vicarage, and Jonathan Waters swivelled his chair around to reach the receiver.

'All Saints – good afternoon,' he said pleasantly. Then – a brief silence and Mark's voice.

'Hello, Mr Waters. It's Mark.'

'*Mark*! My dear chap!' Jonathan automatically got to his feet. 'How wonderful to hear you! How are you – and where are you?'

Mark chuckled. 'I'm all right, thanks,' he said. 'Got home an hour ago – to the obvious delight of my parents! But now I have two weeks' leave and I was wondering if I might come up to the vicarage later. I'm going to drop in at The Berkeley first, and see if Carrie's allowed to see me for a few minutes.'

Allowed to see him? Jonathan thought wryly. Any soldier returning from active duty was welcomed with open arms by everyone, and Carrie would most certainly be allowed to see Mark.

'Of course, Mark! Come whenever you like! And I will let my wife know that there will be an extra one at the table tonight. She will be thrilled – and so will Carrie, of course.' Jonathan hesitated. 'We have all been very worried about you, Mark.'

'Yes, I'm sorry that it was impossible for me to get any news through to any of you,' Mark said, 'but it's been, well, rather difficult to say the least.'

'More than just difficult, I imagine,' Jonathan said dryly.

It was afternoon tea time at The Berkeley, and in the Accounts department upstairs Carrie turned to her two colleagues.

'Yes I know, I know . . . it's my turn to fetch the cakes,' she said, standing up. 'Is it to be éclairs or meringues?' But she needn't have asked because they all preferred meringues.

She went downstairs to the main area and stood at the counter waiting to place her order and thinking how glad she was that Monday was nearly over.

Outside, and unnoticed by her, Mark was looking in at the window, and when he saw her there a rush of pure joy ran through him. There she was, no longer a vision in his imagination but his lovely sweet, gorgeous Carrie who he hadn't stopped thinking about all these months.

Keeping a low profile, he went into the main entrance and stood close behind her, desperately wanting to put his arms around her, to hold her tightly to him, here, now. But he resisted the temptation. Then he heard her speak to the counter assistant.

'Can I have the usual, please, Sylvia?'

'Three meringues coming up,' the assistant said, smiling and glancing at the tall, good-looking young man waiting to be served. 'Won't keep you a moment, sir,' she said.

As Carrie reached up to take the plate of meringues and turned to leave, Mark said quietly in her ear, 'Will you marry me?'

'Wha—! Mark! *Oh Mark!*' And in her confused delight Carrie dropped the plate she was holding, and it fell to the floor with a crash, scattering clouds of sugar everywhere.

Then his lips were on hers and they kissed, long and deep, not caring that several others were there witnessing the reunion.

After a few moments he held her away from him and gazed into her eyes. 'So is it yes or no, Carrie? Will you be my wife . . . please?'

She dropped her head against his chest. 'Oh yes, yes, Mark,' she whispered. 'How could you ever doubt it?'

Then her eyes twinkled. 'But not before you pick up all those crumbs you made me drop on the floor,' she said.

It quickly became known to all the others at The Berkeley that Carrie's young man was there after having been away so long, and the manager had no hesitation in giving Carrie the rest of the day off.

'Go home, Carrie,' the man said, smiling broadly. 'I'm sure you and Captain Anderson have a lot to catch up on!'

An hour later the vicarage doorbell rang, and together Joan and Jonathan Waters ran forward to answer it, both wondering how Mark was going to look after all his time away. It had been many, many months since they'd seen him. But at first glance he seemed unharmed, as handsome as ever, his skin bronzed. He was wearing grey slacks, a white, open-neck shirt and black blazer. And they were hardly surprised to see Carrie standing there as well, with Mark's arm around her waist, her face flushed with excitement. Joan spoke first.

'Mark,' she said, 'how marvellous to see you, my dear. The day we were afraid would never arrive!' She glanced at Carrie. 'They've let you come home early, Carrie . . . and I should think so too! Come in – the pair of you. What a wonderful way to start the week!'

Jonathan moved forward and grasped both Mark's forearms in greeting. 'My dear fellow,' he said, his voice almost breaking. 'What words can possibly express our delight that you are home.'

With Mark still holding Carrie closely to him, they all went into the sitting room and Joan Waters said, 'Can I make you some tea, Mark? Or a cold drink?'

Mark shook his head. 'No thanks, Mrs Waters, The Berkeley did the honours earlier – and very generously.'

Joan and Jonathan took their places in the two easy chairs opposite the sofa where Carrie and Mark were already sitting, holding hands. And after they had all exchanged the usual pleasantries Mark came straight to the point. Looking at Carrie's parents, he said, 'You will want to know – and I want you to know – what happened to me during the last three months.' He smiled crookedly. 'It has been an unusual experience.'

'Well, fire away, Mark,' Jonathan said. 'The only information I was able to glean was that your regiment was with the British Expeditionary Force in France.'

Mark nodded. 'That much is true,' he said, 'but when we got there things didn't turn out quite as we'd thought. The German army had already moved into Belgium and the Netherlands, and as we kept advancing, we realised we were soon going to be completely surrounded.'

'Oh Mark,' Carrie whispered. 'I can't bear to think you were there.'

'It didn't take long for it to dawn on us that the only thing open to us was to retreat . . . to get to the beach at Dunkirk and back across the Channel.' Mark's expression was serious as he spoke. 'As a fighting soldier, retreat is not the desired option, but war is war, and one has to face the reality of what is happening at a given time. Our orders were – retreat – get to the beach and get your men home.' Mark waited before going on. 'Retreat does not always mean defeat,' he said. 'Retreat can mean a short intermission or delay – and that is what Dunkirk will be, I'm sure of it.'

Jonathan nodded slowly. Mark Anderson was a soldier, through and through, and although war was not usually on the Christian agenda, sometimes war was unpreventable. Everyone knew what Hitler was up to: he wanted to overrun and command the whole of Europe, and, eventually, England too.

Mark leaned forward. 'Anyway, after what seemed like an endless march back, we got to Dunkirk and then waited in long queues for the shipping which we thought would be there to take us home. And – well, yes, some big vessels did arrive – but not nearly enough because there were now thousands of us waiting on that beach with enemy aeroplanes screaming overhead trying to sink those ships.'

Mark frowned briefly before going on. 'What we couldn't understand was why Hitler didn't command his troops to finish us all off, there and then, because he could have done, easily. Could have mown us down like sitting ducks.'

Carrie dropped her head onto Mark's shoulder, trying not break down at all he was saying.

'But,' Mark went on, 'he chose to let us stew in our own juice. And then . . . and then . . .' Mark swallowed. 'Coming into view, we saw dozens of small boats begin appearing, one after the other, little pleasure boats, fishing boats, small tugs . . . and they began taking on two or three men at a time. Of course, we knew it was going to take days to get us all off that beach and all we could do was to sit there and wait our turn.'

'Mark,' Jonathan said gently, feeling that Mark needed a second to recover himself, because what he was revealing was taking its toll on the young soldier, 'I don't know *how* you all find the courage to do what you do.'

Mark smiled briefly before going on. 'There is an unforeseen end to my story, Mr Waters,' he said, 'because it was suddenly discovered that two of our unit had gone missing and appeared to be unaccounted for. Then someone said that these two had retraced their steps and gone back on the mainland.' Mark shook his head. 'That was completely pointless and counter to orders of course, but war does strange things to people. Anyway, my orderly and I scrambled back away from the beach and started searching for them, and half a mile away we found them – stranded – because one had a broken ankle, and the other was in a state of utter shock. And unfortunately for us,' Mark went on, 'the German troops were there, now, right on our heels.'

'What on earth did you do, what *could* you do?' Jonathan said slowly.

Mark took a long, deep breath. 'Well, the decision was taken out of our hands because there, in that dense part of the forest where we'd found the men, we suddenly heard a voice, a French voice.'

'English . . . you come! Now!'

There was quite a long pause before Mark spoke again. 'I had no choice, really,' he said. 'By this time, I knew we were surrounded by Germans and if we tried to make a run for it back to the beach – carrying a wounded man who couldn't even take his own weight – we'd be picked off with no trouble at all. So we followed this French peasant to his little place, a small farmstead I suppose you'd call it – it took us ages to get there.' Mark smiled for the first time. 'This chap and his very kind wife took us into their humble home, and we were soon given a baguette and a bottle of red wine. I can't tell you how good it was, to taste normality – as well as the wine . . . well, we'd been away from home for a very long time.'

'So,' Jonathan said quietly, 'what happened after that?'

'Not very much,' Mark said. 'By now, the whole area was crawling with Germans, and those good people hid us for more than two months. We slept in their loft by night, and when it was safe enough, we sunbathed in their garden. The lady knew how to deal with the broken ankle, and as soon as I thought we had any chance of getting back we returned to the beach at Dunkirk, which by now, of course, was practically deserted . . . though strewn with all the mess left by a departing army.'

Mark shook his head slowly. 'But we'd never have escaped if it hadn't been that Monsieur and Madame Cariouo found us dark, rural clothing, and provided us with peasants' working gear – which of course included a French beret, which I shall cherish for the rest of my days,' Mark added.

But what Jonathan Waters wanted to know was how Mark had got back to England.

'To complete our huge, amazing good fortune in coming across the Frenchman,' Mark said, 'he'd managed to get hold of a fishing boat – quite a substantial one, actually, to get us home. And it did, taking us all the way back. Thank God the weather was in our favour or we might never have made it, and thank God for the French Underground Movement which is clearly already in full swing.'

By this time, Carrie could hardly utter a word, thinking that all the anxiety and dread she'd experienced over those months had been nothing to what Mark and the men had endured.

After a long moment, Jonathan said, 'I hardly know what to say to you, Mark. Only that seeing you here in front of us, like this, after all you've been through, is the best thing in the world. Against all those odds, you've come back safely.'

Mark nodded. 'Yes, and I am relieved to say that my unit got home too – even without me!' he said. 'Though, as you can imagine, my own debriefing took rather a long time!' He shrugged. 'But the thing is we live to fight another day – and we will, there's no doubt about that. And next time there'll be no running away.'

'And what of the French couple who helped you?' Jonathan asked.

'I shall go back to thank them,' Mark said at once. 'I promised them that they hadn't seen the last of me . . . when this shindig is over.'

Joan Waters spoke for the first time. 'Perhaps it shouldn't be a surprise that you are here, alive and well, Mark, because I have prayed for a miracle every single day. And I believe in miracles,' she said simply.

There was a long silence after that, then Mark cleared his throat.

'The main reason that I wanted to see you both today,' he said, 'is that I have a great favour to ask.'

Jonathan looked up, smiling. 'Ask us anything, Mark,' he said.

'I would like Carrie to be my wife,' Mark said. 'I have already proposed to her, and she has accepted, but I knew I must ask your permission.' He paused. 'You may worry that my chosen way of life is not conducive to a long and happy marriage, but army life does not mean that we are always in a permanent state of warfare, just that we must constantly train to be ready to defend our country.' He smiled briefly. 'I want you to know that thinking about Carrie was what kept me going all those weeks. And made me realise how much I love her . . . need her.' He took a deep breath. 'I just hope that you will allow me to be her husband – for better or for worse. To cherish her for the rest of my life.'

Jonathan passed his wife a handkerchief because he could see her tears. Then – 'Mark – it would be a privilege to have you for our son-in-law.' Jonathan stood up. 'And early in the day though it is, I think it's time to open a bottle of good wine.'

Chapter 22

As the war continued, it was obvious that Hitler's eyes were now largely fixed on the Bristol Aeroplane Company and the docks, and during many days in September and for weeks afterwards, German bombers flew over the city hoping to hit their mark.

The intense bombing which led to the destruction of many parts of the city during those months should have frightened the population to a standstill, but it did not. Despite many of Bristol's famous streets and residential areas being reduced to rubble, within a matter of hours debris was cleared, traffic resumed – albeit in reduced numbers – and many partly demolished shops opened for business, more or less as usual, including Robertson's café in Denmark Street, which thankfully suffered no damage. And spirited people emerging from the shelters to find their homes half-destroyed, lost no time in salvaging what was left of their belongings and transporting them to a safer location.

Fortunately for West Road it received no significant damage. But on one particular night the horrible, unmistakable gnawing throb of enemy aircraft passing directly overhead was so terrifying that Abigail had difficulty in persuading Emily that they would soon be leaving the shelter without a scratch. It wasn't like Emily to sob with fright and even Mrs Matthews' consoling words didn't help much – probably because Emily could sense that Eileen's mother was also very afraid. How much longer would their luck hold out? they asked each other silently. Was this the raid which would end their lives?

Yet amazingly, a few days later after a random bomb had hit the local bakery, bread making resumed. Although most of the building itself had been blown out, the ovens still operated and the staff worked on under tarpaulins by the light of hurricane lamps.

At breakfast one Friday morning towards the end of November, Emily, sitting next to Mrs Matthews as usual, said, 'I'm fed up with this war, because we never know when there's going to be another air raid, do we?'

The others agreed. 'Yes, we are all fed up, Emily,' Eileen said. 'I'm never sure whether my office will open or not, or whether I will have to walk into work, do a couple of hours and then scurry back home again or get to the nearest shelter.' She pinched Emily's nose as she went past. 'War is a tremendous nuisance to one and all, but, you know, Emily, we are all so lucky not to have been hurt, aren't we?'

Emily nodded. 'I know that, Mummy keeps telling me.'

'And there's still enough food in the shops so we aren't going hungry just yet either,' Eileen's mother said. 'Another thing to be glad about, Emily.'

Emily giggled. 'You are a very *glad* person, aren't you, Mrs Gladys! Do you remember me saying that?'

'Of course I do,' Gladys Matthews replied. 'But that was a whole year ago, wasn't it?' she added. 'And the very best thing of all to be glad about is that Carrie's young man came back safely, didn't he – isn't that wonderful? And that when the war is over there's going to be a very special wedding at the vicarage! Carrie and Mark, Mark and Carrie – praise the Lord!'

* * *

Sunday afternoon was cold, damp and miserable, and Eileen had decided that it was not the day for her mother to be taken to All Saints for Evensong.

'I think it would be better if we all stayed in tonight, Mother,' Eileen said. She glanced at Abigail. 'Did you really want to go to church tonight, Abigail?'

Abigail shook her head. 'No – I don't think so, because I think I may have a bit of a cold coming. Martin's been sneezing in the shop lately. So, a cosy night in sounds rather attractive. Anyway,' she added, 'we didn't tell Carrie to expect us, did we?'

Presently, with Emily in Mrs Matthews' room where they'd just started another jigsaw puzzle, Eileen went over to put the kettle on for tea. Abigail, curled up in one of the basket chairs in the corner reading her book, looked up.

'That was a very good idea of yours that we have a lazy afternoon, Eileen,' Abigail said, 'because I think I needed it.' She made a face. 'It's been difficult at work – trying to maintain proper hours and getting to and from the shop in time – as I know it's been for you, too. Disruption of any kind is wearing, isn't it?' She paused before going on. 'But after all, those are trivial worries when you consider what others are suffering. I often think that what I'm doing is hardly helping the war effort – it would be wonderful to do something of real importance.'

Deep in thought and still curled up with her knees under her chin, Abigail remembered what Eileen's mother had said about whether it had been wise for them to have left Coopers in the present circumstances.

Coopers . . .

What was going on there now? Did her aunt still have lads working for her – or had she frightened them, and any others, off her land? Abigail bit her lip. Edna would find it very difficult, if not impossible, to do everything all by herself and the work was hard. Had this war affected those living in the country by now? Surely they wouldn't be bombed? But they would have heard the Nazi planes flying over on their way to Bristol, wouldn't they?

Yet again, Abigail wondered whether her aunt had thought about her young relatives, the only ones she had in the world. But Edna didn't really know where they were, so why would she care, one way or the other?

Then Abigail asked herself a far more serious question. Had she been right to bring Emily away from safety to this large city which was proving such a huge target for the enemy?

She took a deep breath. Yes! And yes! She had been right, and she would do the same thing again despite all the unexpected difficulties. Because she had released the trap that had held her and her little girl, enabling them to live full lives. And not just now, but in all the years to come, they were free to be themselves. Emily Grace was the proof to set her mother's mind at rest. She had got on with every person she met as naturally as if she had done it from birth, as every other child had. Coming here had all been worth it, Abigail thought – even if she couldn't deny the fact that it put them both in extreme danger.

And never, ever again, Abigail thought, would she have to put her hand over her daughter's sweet mouth so that no one would know she was there.

Presently, Abigail stood up and went over to lay the cloth. She opened the door of the pantry and glanced back at Eileen. 'I hope these jam tarts and the fairy cakes I made yesterday will go down OK. There's always something special about Sunday tea, isn't there?' she added. 'Especially on a horrible evening.'

It was just gone six o'clock, and completely dark outside. Eileen moved across to check the blackout curtains and turn on the table lamp. She glanced at Abigail. 'Thank heaven the last few days have gone quiet,' she said. She grinned. 'Tonight, perhaps, Hitler's entire air force is at church!'

Just then, Emily and Gladys Matthews came in, still deep in conversation as usual. Emily went straight over to her mother.

'I managed to finish a really difficult bit of the jigsaw just now,' she said. 'We're nearly halfway through it!'

'That's good,' Abigail said. 'Now then, let's all have tea. Eileen has made some lovely egg and cress sandwiches and there are cakes as well.'

Gladys Matthews sat down next to Emily and glanced over. 'You two always make the table look so appetising,' she said. 'This all looks good enough to gobble up in one go!'

Then, before any of them could begin their tea, the terrifying whistle of a falling bomb, followed by a massive explosion close by, made them all freeze in terror. Emily immediately started to cry, clutching Abigail around the waist.

For a few seconds there was silence outside – soon broken by the sound of running footsteps and voices shouting from the street.

'Take cover! Put that light out! Put that light out!'

And then the sirens. That electrifying, high-pitched sound rising and rising, then falling back, then rising and falling, like turbulent, unstoppable waves in a terrible storm at sea. Then more bombs and the awesome, terrifying din of anti-aircraft guns.

Eileen immediately went out to the scullery and peered through a chink in the blind. Then she came back to the others.

'Come on,' she said hurriedly. 'It's under the stairs for us tonight because we dare not risk going down to the shelter. This raid is all around us, and there just isn't time – we might not get there before the next onslaught. It's absolute mayhem out there,' she added, 'so we must be quick.'

The urgency in her voice had the desired effect, and straight-away, with Abigail half-carrying Emily and Eileen shepherding her mother in front of her, they all hurried out into the hall and opened the little door to the under-stairs cupboard.

This primitive means of safety had been the accepted routine long before shelters were even thought about, and even after their construction many people preferred to stay and chance their luck in their own homes. Eileen, ever practical, had long ago put a small bench in their cupboard, together with a couple of chairs and some cushions and rugs, just in case. The cupboard only had a small light, but it was enough to at least see each other.

Now, as they all crouched down to crawl inside, Eileen said to Emily, 'It's a good job we practised doing this last year, isn't it, Emily? Do you remember? I told you we would be like little rabbits scampering into our hutch, didn't I?'

Emily, who had stopped whimpering, nodded. 'Can I go and get my books?'

'No – I'll grab them for you,' Eileen said, 'and I'm also going to grab our tea and we'll have a picnic! How about that? Good job we hadn't eaten it all! I'll only be about two seconds.'

And within six or seven minutes of that first bomb blast – which was to be followed by more and more in quick succession the little group of four were sitting around in the half-light under the stairs, with Eileen pouring the tea and handing round the cakes and sandwiches as if it was what they always did on a Sunday afternoon.

Abigail looked over at Eileen with admiration. What a wonderful friend, what a wonderful daughter she was, always knowing exactly what to do and when to do it for the good of everyone else. And Eileen's mother seemed perfectly happy – once they'd managed to ease her gently into the cupboard. She was sitting on one of the chairs, well wrapped up in a blanket and sipping from her cup. If she was frightened, she didn't show it, and neither did Emily, who, between mouthfuls of jam tart, had already opened one of her little books.

Abigail, sitting next to Eileen, said quietly, 'I hope Carrie and her parents are all right. And Janet down there in town, too.' She made a face. 'It seems odd that we had no warning about this raid, doesn't it?'

Eileen rolled her eyes. 'Yes – it would certainly help to be informed about such things, but don't worry about the Waters.

They have the crypt, don't forget, so I'm sure they're all right. And the communal shelter Janet uses is right outside the café.' Eileen grinned. 'And the Germans wouldn't *dare* bomb Robertson's, would they?'

The all-clear did not sound until midnight, and after a cramped six hours under the stairs, they all emerged, blinking. Emily and Mrs Matthews had actually managed to have a couple of hours' fitful sleep, but neither Abigail nor Eileen had slept a wink.

Glancing cautiously outside the house, Eileen turned to the others. 'As far as I can see, thank heaven we don't seem to have had any damage,' she said, 'but we'll know more in the morning when it's light.'

Then, suddenly, she threw her arms around the three looking up at her.

'Once again we have survived!' she exclaimed, her voice breaking only slightly. 'We are all in one piece! And look, it's Monday morning. Time for another week to begin!'

Chapter 23

The rest of the night was a strange mixture of dozing, and dreaming and waking with a fright for the adults at number six, though Emily enjoyed a blissful nine hours of sleep before she finally woke up and padded downstairs in her dressing gown to join the others in the kitchen.

'Have I been asleep a long time?' she asked, going over to take her place at the table next to Mrs Matthews.

'Quite a long time,' Abigail said, moving across to give her daughter a hug. 'But that doesn't matter. And you can always have a snooze later – if you're still tired. Now, are you ready for some breakfast?'

'I didn't mind being under the stairs,' Emily said, yawning. 'It was fun. Especially having our picnic in there.' She glanced at Eileen. 'Can we do that again, Eileen?'

'Not for a long time, I hope,' Eileen said, smiling. 'Let's pray that that was a "for one night only" event!'

She picked up the teapot to refill her mother's cup, and Mrs Matthews said, 'I can hardly believe that, once again, we seem to have escaped more or less intact. From the noise all around us, I fully expected that at least some of our windows would have gone, but they haven't, and from what you've said, Eileen, the house doesn't seem to be damaged.'

Eileen nodded slowly. 'Yes, Mother, we have been very lucky because both number one and two at the end obviously caught some of the blast – though no direct hits, thank heavens. And I spoke to next door this morning and apparently everyone's all right.'

Eileen rang the vicarage and was relieved to hear Carrie's voice.

'Yes – we're all fine here, too, Eileen,' Carrie said. 'We're still standing – and so is All Saints!'

'Thank heaven,' Eileen said. 'Look, Carrie, Abigail and I thought we'd walk into town this morning – just to see exactly what happened last night.'

'I'm coming with you,' Carrie said at once. 'We need to see that Janet is all right, what buildings caught it, and whether we've still got jobs! I'll be there in twenty minutes.'

'Can I come too?' Emily asked eagerly when she knew what the others were going to do, but Abigail shook her head.

'I don't think that's wise, Emily,' she said, 'because it might be difficult getting around – we shan't know until we get there.'

'And besides,' Mrs Matthews intervened, 'I need you here with me, Emily, because I've decided that we are going to open our own little school – what do you think of that? We'll take it in turns to be teacher, and you can decide which lesson we should begin with.'

Emily's eyes lit up. 'Oh, I think it should be reading,' she said enthusiastically. 'I will listen to you, Mrs Gladys, and make sure you get the long words right.'

'Yes, Miss,' Eileen's mother said.

Presently, well clad in their warm coats and scarves, and arm in arm, Abigail, Eileen and Carrie made their way out of West Road towards the top of Totterdown Hill, trying to avoid hindering the council workers who were already sweeping up glass and debris from the pavements. The buses didn't seem to be running and there was very little traffic because the main road hadn't been fully cleared. Carrie glanced at the others.

'Isn't it strange?' she said quietly. 'Look, that house over there is practically gone, but the ones either side don't seem to be damaged at all.'

Eileen said soberly, 'Oh look – oh dear! Holy Nativity didn't escape . . . It's smouldering in that far end.' She shuddered. 'I hate the smell of smoke – unless it's part of a lovely fire in the grate.'

They walked on slowly, going over Bath Bridge and past Temple Meads, part of which had been hit.

'Why don't we cut through to Queen Square?' Carrie said. 'I really hope that St Mary Redcliffe wasn't bombed. Not that a church is more valuable than people's homes, of course,' she added quickly, 'but St Mary has always been a sort of symbol of the city, and everyone respects it and loves it, even if they're not churchgoers.'

They walked on, stepping over more and more broken glass and dismantled telegraph wires, but by now the roads had been cleared more fully, and one or two cars and vans were passing slowly by.

There was an unusual, and rather sombre silence between the three as they made their way, then Abigail said, pointing, 'Even at this early stage, don't you feel that people are doing their best to keep going? I mean, look at those road sweepers over there – doing their job as if it was just another Monday morning – and one of them is even whistling the National Anthem.'

The others nodded. 'There'll always be an England,' Carrie said, trying to be philosophical.

They went on past St Mary Redcliffe and stood for a moment to gaze at the building which, even on this dank, miserable November morning, looked as majestic as ever and was mercifully undamaged.

They walked on, finally rounding the corner into Redcliffe Way.

To find that something truly terrible had happened.

The long, hilly street with its neat line of terraced houses, had been badly damaged and number fourteen as well as the house next to it, had been completely demolished.

Miss Grant's well-kept, respectable house now appeared to be just a load of rubble and blackened brick, with the chimney, like a stricken animal in surrender, lying helplessly across the top of the hideous pile.

Abigail paused and clutched Eileen and Carrie in genuine horror. 'Oh *no*,' she whispered. 'Poor Miss Grant! Do you . . . do you think she's all right?'

Eileen went in front of them to take a closer look. 'Well, no one would have got out of that alive,' she said, 'but don't look so worried, Abigail, not yet. I hope Miss Grant had time to make a dash for the shelter.'

Eileen crossed her fingers as she said that, because it was clear that this end of the street had come off worst, and that number fourteen had had a direct hit. And Miss Grant, so obviously very proud of her property, may well have decided to stay there under her stairs, refusing to abandon her pride and joy.

Carrie broke in. 'Well, sadly, there's nothing we can do to help here. So let's go over to check on Janet to make sure she's OK then go on to see if Blackwell's and The Berkeley are still standing.'

They had walked just a short distance when someone shouting made them stop.

'Mrs Wilson! Mrs Wilson! Wait a minute, Mrs Wilson!'

It was Iris Grant, and she came running up to them, her arms wide in greeting. And arriving, she immediately clutched Abigail around the waist and hugged her as tightly as if they were old and trusted friends, which took Abigail and the others completely by surprise.

'Mrs Wilson,' the landlady went on breathlessly, 'I *knew* it was you. I was up at number nine – my neighbour's house – and we were upstairs looking out of the window and I saw you standing outside number fourteen and—'

Abigail could hardly speak for a moment because although she'd had no particular love for the landlady, it would have been dreadful if she'd been killed.

'I could hardly dare to hope, Miss Grant, that you were unhurt,' Abigail said shakily. 'When I saw what had happened to your lovely house, your lovely home—'

Miss Grant stood back, smiling wanly. 'It was lucky that we weren't there, Mrs Wilson,' she said, 'but, would you believe this, my brother came home unexpectedly on Friday night. Never gave me any idea he was coming, of course. But that's like him, only thinks of himself. And yesterday morning, he was just finishing his bacon and eggs – when he said he had a gut feeling that there was going to be a raid. He couldn't explain it – he just felt it in his bones. So' – Iris Grant raised her eyes – 'without even asking me what *I* thought, he decided that we were leaving town and going in his van to Queen Charlton for the night! Hitler won't be wasting any of his bombs out there in the country, that's what my brother said! And he was right! We heard plenty, mind you, and we could see the red glow of flames over the city, but we were out of harm's way in that lovely spot – we used to have picnics there you know, when we were kids. And I was as cosy as anything because there was a rug in the van for me to put round my knees.' She raised her eyes. 'Besides, there's a little pub he knows, so early on we had a drink and it turned out to be a nice little evening after all. Of course, Ronald insisted we stayed there all night, and that meant I had to wee in the hedge a couple of times.'

The three women gazed at Miss Grant as she spoke and could hardly believe what they were hearing. Eileen narrowed her eyes briefly, remembering how her mother had felt before that other raid. That she'd felt uneasy and unusually troubled. Gladys Matthews had said nothing about having a premonition – but Eileen was aware that many people felt they had a second sense, or a special link with another world, and especially during dreadful times, meetings were regularly attended by those who believed they were privy to forthcoming events. Of course, she didn't believe a *word* of it, Eileen thought. But still, looking at

Miss Grant in the peak of good health, and the rubble which was once her home, well . . .

'I think your brother must be a very useful man to know, Miss Grant,' Eileen said, gritting her teeth at her own remark. 'Useful' was not exactly how Eileen would describe the landlady's brother – not after his disgraceful behaviour to poor Abigail.

Miss Grant tutted. ''Course, I feel a bit bad, really, because he's always got on my nerves, my brother has. You never know *where* you are with him and sometimes over the years, I could have killed him. But, it's thanks to him that I'm alive – because I would *not* have gone to the shelter. And when we came back home early this morning – about three o'clock I think it was – and saw the house gone, *gone*, well, I would have gone with it! Because I don't go to any shelters. No, thank you very much. Not my cup of tea at all.'

Abigail touched the landlady's arm. 'I can't *tell* you how glad I am that you didn't stay at home last night, Miss Grant,' she said. 'And what about the shops at the end? Mr Dawson – and the others – are they all right?'

Iris Grant nodded vigorously. 'Yes, thank the good Lord! Not so much as a window gone, so I'm told! In fact, apparently Dawson's opened at nine o'clock this morning as usual – though I haven't gone up there yet because I haven't got round to thinking about groceries.'

Abigail hesitated before she spoke again. 'But I do understand how you must be feeling about your beautiful home, Miss Grant . . . Your cosy, comfortable home. It must be dreadful for you to see what's happened to it.'

Miss Grant looked away, as if collecting her thoughts. 'Do you know, Mrs Wilson,' she said slowly, 'all I feel is relief to be alive. Because things can be replaced, can't they, but once you're dead, that's it. You're dead. And Ronald and I are lucky to be staying with a neighbour for now, until other accommodation can be found for us, and eventually everyone will be re-housed. We've been told that.' She smiled. 'When the time comes, it will be quite exciting to be somewhere different and to have to choose things again . . . it will be like starting out afresh, won't it?'

Then, looking around furtively, as if she didn't want anyone else to hear, she said, 'Anyway, I never really liked that sofa we had in the sitting room. It was as hard as nails. Glad to see the back of it.'

Chapter 24

Mercifully, apart from minor damage to the back of both Blackwell's and The Berkeley, both places were able to carry on trading, as did Robertson's further down the hill. And the last days of November 1940 were free of intense bombing, although the sirens were still regularly heard. The terrifying howl became fairly commonplace – often followed soon afterwards by the all-clear – so that the more philosophical regularly stayed at home rather than seeking shelter elsewhere.

'If your name's on a bomb, it'll find you wherever you are,' tended to become the cynical attitude.

Early December, too, was comparatively peaceful so that the normal Christmas preparations took place, homes were decorated as usual, and fir trees brought in, bedecked with bright baubles and fairy lights. And there was still enough food in the shops for everyone to have their Christmas dinner.

On Christmas Eve, Eileen, Carrie and Abigail stood waiting together at the bus stop. It was lunch time, just after two o'clock, and many places of employment had closed early to give staff a little extra holiday before work began again, the day after Boxing Day. The three girls had just stopped off at Robertson's to have a quick coffee, and to give Janet her Christmas presents.

'Ooh it's such a bitter wind, isn't it?' Carrie said now, huddling closer to the other two. 'I can't wait to get home and put my slippers on!'

Eventually, the bus arrived – standing room only – and as it trundled its way past blackened, half-damaged buildings through Baldwin Street and Victoria Street towards Temple Meads, Eileen nodded at the scene outside as they all stood holding on to the safety strap above their heads.

'What a mess it is out there,' she said. 'The carnage of bomb damage has to be seen to be believed, doesn't it.'

The bus arrived at Eileen and Abigail's stop, and as they got off, Eileen said, 'See you this evening, Carrie.'

As the two made their way briskly towards West Road, Eileen glanced down. 'D'you know, Abigail, I think that, at last, I have finally come to a decision. I've been thinking about this for some time, but it's very important and I'd really like to speak to you and Carrie – and my mother – about it before I take any action.'

Abigail tucked her arm more firmly into Eileen's. 'That sounds terribly mysterious, Eileen,' she said. 'So why don't you unwrap the secret later tonight when Emily is safely asleep and we can talk properly.' Abigail smiled. 'Important secrets will go down very well with a glass of Harvey's Bristol Cream and some mince pies.'

It was gone nine o'clock before Emily was finally persuaded to settle down. As Abigail tucked her in, with Eileen and Carrie standing there as well, Emily said, yawning, 'Do you think Santa Claus has already left with his reindeer? I mean, will he have time to come to every house in the whole world before morning?'

Eileen bent to kiss the top of Emily's head. 'Don't you worry about that, Emily,' she said. 'Because Santa is an extremely clever chap and very hardworking. And of course he's got his little elves to help him. I know he's received your letter, and I expect you'll have nice presents in your stocking when you wake up tomorrow.'

Emily thought about that. 'Did *you* write him a letter, Eileen?' she said. 'Will you be hanging up your stocking?'

'No, of course not. Santa does not have the time to visit adults,' Eileen said. 'He's got enough to do without bringing us presents as well.'

Carrie took her turn to give Emily a goodnight cuddle. 'We were all children once, Emily,' she said, 'and used to have a stocking to open on Christmas morning.'

Emily wound her arms around Carrie's neck. 'Well, don't worry, Carrie,' she whispered, 'because I've got a present for you, and Eileen and Mrs Gladys as well. Mummy and I have been shopping and Mummy has made you all one of her special Christmas cards. They're beautiful! I've seen them!'

'Now, no more talking, Emily,' Abigail said firmly, 'because it really is time for you to go to sleep. And if you get over tired you won't enjoy tomorrow, will you.'

Still holding on to Carrie, Emily whispered, 'Would you like me to tell you what we've got you and Eileen?'

'Emily!' Abigail protested. 'That's a secret, isn't it! Now, no more talking!'

Presently, down in the kitchen which was comfortably warm, and mellow with candle light, the three girls and Mrs Matthews sat around the table wrapping all the small presents to put into Emily's stocking. Abigail glanced up, shaking her head slowly.

'Really, you are all so kind,' she said. 'Emily is going to be absolutely amazed tomorrow morning.'

'It's lovely to have a little one in the house to spoil,' Gladys Matthews said, tying some tinsel around a bag of lollipops. She paused before going on. 'And, you know, after that November raid, I did wonder whether we would ever see another Christmas. I really did. Yet, here we are once again, still alive and determined to put all the horror behind us, just for a few days.' She grimaced. 'Though I do wish we could get rid of the blessed blackout curtains for the festive season, just for tonight and tomorrow. We always drew back the curtains and had candles burning in the windows at Christmas, didn't we, Eileen?'

Eileen nodded. 'We did, Mother. But never mind. It looks as if Hitler's giving us a bit of peace at the moment, doesn't it, which I hope lasts long enough for us to enjoy our Christmas dinner.' She got up to put the kettle on. 'And even though there were no turkeys available this year, we've got that nice piece of silverside, and the chicken is a good plump one. Abigail has gone to a great deal of trouble making the stuffing.'

'My mother actually managed to buy two chickens,' Carrie said, as she carefully pushed another present into Emily's already bulging stocking. 'She had to speak nicely to the butcher, but when it was explained that several of our lonely parishioners always join us for Christmas dinner, he was really generous and added two pounds of sausages as well.'

'I should think so too,' Gladys Matthews said, glancing around her for a moment. How lucky she was, she thought, to have young company in the house – not just her beloved Eileen, but dear Carrie too who was almost like another daughter. And now Abigail and little Emily Wilson. They had been part of the family for sixteen months and had brought such blessings with them.

'Shall we have tea, or coffee, to go with our ham rolls and mince pies?' Eileen said as she set out the cups and saucers. 'And the sherry has already been opened. Who'd like a glass?'

This had always been the traditional Christmas Eve supper enjoyed at number six, and soon, with everyone opting for a pot of tea to go with the food, with the sherry to come later, the four began to eat. Then Eileen looked at the others.

'Now, I want to talk to you all about something,' she said seriously, and Abigail glanced at her quickly. She'd completely forgotten that Eileen had said she had something important to say.

Gladys Matthews immediately looked up. When her daughter made that sort of comment, it usually meant business.

'It's just that I have finally made up my mind,' Eileen said slowly. 'I'm going to give my notice in at The Royal and volunteer for war work.' She held the gaze of the other three as she went on. 'After all, we must have spoken thousands of words about what we would like to do to help stop this war, if only we could be of some real use. And I've been going over and over it because it's been on my conscience for ages. There's non-stop chatting in the office about where the country's essential needs are so I honestly feel it's time I did something about it.'

Gladys Matthews was the first to speak. 'Well, what exactly would volunteering entail, dear?'

'I don't know yet, it could be anything,' Eileen said. 'But apparently at the moment the greatest need is in the factories because so many men have been called up, and it's proving difficult to find people to replace them.' She paused. 'Anyway, whether or not it's the season of goodwill that's got into my blood, I've definitely decided to do it. I'm not going to sit around any longer. After all, producing insurance policies is not going to help win the war, is it?'

They all thought about this for a minute, then Abigail said quietly, 'I do take your point, Eileen. I mean, when I'm up at Blackwell's – doing the job I *love* – I often think about everyone else putting their lives at risk every day. Men like Mark and thousands more. And I feel ashamed that all I'm doing is packing and unpacking books, making lists, answering queries. And having a crafty read when there's time! So under the circumstances I'm pretty useless, aren't I?'

Carrie broke in. 'Well, that goes for me then, too. I would personally like to give Hitler a black eye – but there's not much chance of being able to do that up at the beautiful Berkeley Hotel.'

Eileen stood up to pour a little more tea into their mugs before going on. 'So, there you are. Straight after Christmas I'm going to enlist at the Council House and see what they think I'd be capable of. It's obvious that I'm going to need training, whatever it happens to be, but I feel ready and willing to put my back into something. *Anything.*'

Abigail looked over. 'Well, I'd be quite happy if my name went forward, too,' she said. 'So bring back all the information you can find, and as long as it would fit in with Emily, I wouldn't mind volunteering my services for war work. Blackwell's will survive without me there,' she added. 'Though Janet will have to find extra help.'

After a moment, Carrie looked at the others solemnly. 'Come on! What about me? You can't expect to keep *me* out of this exciting change of scene, can you?' she said. 'So when you come back with all the fascinating details, Eileen, together with all the forms which are sure to need filling in, make sure you bring some for me to sign as well.' She smiled. 'My father will be very proud of me because he's always saying that we shouldn't leave everything to others. That it's up to us all to pull our weight.'

Abigail broke in, smiling. 'And what will Mark think about his beloved going to war!' she teased. 'You'll have to take great care of that beautiful engagement ring!'

Eileen sat back, clearly thrilled at the reaction from the others. 'Well then, I'll go and find out what's what. And then the three of us should hold ourselves ready to ring in a rather different New Year.' She picked up her glass. 'Come on – let's drink to this – let's drink to us! And what awaits us!'

Gladys Matthews took her own glass to share in the toast, looking at her daughter fondly. Eileen was unstoppable, and if she said she was going to do something, she would do it.

'Well, all I can say is good luck to you all,' Gladys Matthews said. She glanced at Abigail. 'And of course, Abigail, whatever all this turns out to be, you know that you need never worry about Emily. I will always be here to look after her.' She smiled. 'You might even call it my own volunteering for war work!'

Chapter 25

It was to take longer than they might have thought for Eileen, Carrie and Abigail to hope to bring the war to an end all by themselves. As Carrie had suggested, many questions had to be answered first, and they'd each been expected to give their present employers time to find replacements.

Fortunately for the residents of Bristol, the early weeks of 1941, though pestered by constant sirens, did not bring the violent and intense bombing which they continually braced themselves for. But intermittent raids did carry on, accompanied by the deafening and perpetual boom of anti-aircraft guns. And all followed by the everlasting toil of clearing up to ensure the city could carry on as normally as possible. Unbelievably, despite the snow and icy conditions which persisted, many people still managed to get to work, roads were soon cleared for traffic, and some shops – though badly damaged – managed to open for business.

And just as importantly, fire watching went on unabated, and air raid wardens were permanently on duty to make sure that everyone could get to a shelter in time. It was a constant, and ghastly, cat and mouse game, and what also became a continual need was the removal of unexploded incendiary bombs – of which there were almost too many to count, and all within the city boundary. The incendiary bombs were taken to a disposal unit in Ashton Park which became known as the Bomb Cemetery.

For the three girls, their wish to become part of the serious war effort was to be granted straight after Easter when they were to be deployed at a factory just outside the city. The delay in their assignment had been because of their insistence that they be allowed to work together. Eileen had left the officer in charge with no doubt that the war effort would benefit hugely if Eileen Matthews, Carrie Waters and Abigail Wilson worked as a team – whatever it happened to be.

And staring at the three applicants the man had had no alternative but to agree, especially as the factory on the top of his list seemed a highly suitable place to send these three no-nonsense girls. They had attitude, and they were certainly going to need it.

'Please present yourselves here on Tuesday next, the 15th of April, to pick up your uniforms,' he'd said. 'You will be working at the Royal Ordnance Factory just outside Bristol, and you will be given full instruction on your arrival.' He'd glanced at his list. 'A van will pick you up from somewhere convenient, and – um – I see you all live fairly close to Broad Walk so be there each morning at seven o'clock. And you'll be brought back about ten or twelve hours later.' He pursed his lips. 'All according,' he added mysteriously.

'Wonder what he meant by "all according",' Carrie said as they'd gone back home, and Eileen made a face.

'I think we're going to find out soon enough,' she said. 'But – hey you two – we're on our way at last!'

Although no one knew it at the time, the Good Friday Blitz was to be the last really terrifying raid Bristol was to experience. Other, less fearsome assaults by the Luftwaffe did go on, but nothing could compare with the enormity of the 11th and 12th April 1941.

That barrage from the sky came in two waves, resulting in a constant series of desperate cries for help, mixed with frenzied dashes to the shelter, of wardens putting out incendiaries with sand and shovels. And – using hatchets – attempting to dig trapped people out of half-damaged buildings. Those cowering in cellars could look up through their now roofless houses at the flame-lit sky to see bombers circling overhead. And the noise and dust was nothing short of hell itself.

The family living at number six West Road, and their immediate neighbours, remained in the shelter at the bottom of their gardens for the duration of that air raid, emerging safely at 4 a.m. when the all-clear sounded.

And as they all breathed slightly fresher air – though the stench of smoke and cordite made every pair of eyes stream – their overwhelming sense was one of helpless gratitude.

It seemed that, once again, they had defied death.

In the Council House at 10 a.m. the following Tuesday, Eileen, Carrie and Abigail waited dutifully in the line of volunteers all there to receive their uniforms and last instructions.

'Can't wait to see what they've got planned for us to wear,' Eileen said from the corner of her mouth. 'I do hope the colour suits me!'

A woman standing by a large table in the far corner beckoned them over. There was a pile of clothes in front of her. She glanced up, smiling briefly.

'Now – Miss Eileen Matthews, Miss Carrie Waters and Mrs Abigail Wilson? Have I got that right?' And before they could answer, she handed them each a set of clothes. 'I'm afraid it's one size fits all,' she said, 'but I think these should be all right – though yours might be a bit small,' she added, nodding at Eileen.

The uniform consisted of a dark green, heavy duty, linen-type boiler suit, together with short rubber boots, a mask, and a close-fitting hair net.

'This is to protect your hair,' the woman said, picking up one of the nets, 'and you tie it around in a kind of snood, like this,' she added, demonstrating. She half-smiled. 'Not the height of fashion, but it does the job. And I'm sure I don't need to explain how you use the mask. Now then, when this lot of clothes get dirty, you'll be given a fresh set.' She handed the three girls their uniforms and nodded to her right. 'Go over there in the anteroom and slip everything on,' she said, 'just to make sure everything fits.'

Saying nothing, they did as they were told and presently, fully kitted up, they stood and looked at each other. Eileen broke the silence.

'Crikey,' she said, 'I feel like an Egyptian Mummy! And what on earth do we look like!'

'I don't think I would describe this as "comfy", would you?' Carrie said doubtfully. 'It's quite tight, but I don't think I'm going to feel cold when I'm wearing it. And my engagement ring is going to stay safely in its little box at home.'

Abigail nodded. 'I should think so, too. But I can't wait to be given "full instructions" when we get there, can you? I hope I'm going to be up to it, whatever it is.'

'Of course you will be!' Eileen said, starting to clamber out of her uniform. 'Remember, there'll always be the three of us working together, so it shouldn't be a problem. And anyway, we volunteered to do whatever they wanted, didn't we? So there's no going back.' She grinned. 'Come on – you never know, it might even be fun! Let's just call this turn of events part of life's rich pattern!'

When they got back home, Emily and Gladys Matthews were waiting for them in the kitchen.

'We're longing to hear all about it,' Eileen's mother said, but Eileen interrupted.

'We haven't been told anything, Mother, not really,' she said. 'Only that we actually start next Monday, the 21st, and will work a five-day week. Leaving Bristol at seven o'clock, starting at eight o'clock and finishing at five-thirty, so we should be back home by just after six. For the moment, no weekend duties.'

'Well now, why don't I make us some tea,' Gladys Matthews said, moving across to fill the kettle. 'I expect our volunteers are ready for some lunch.' She glanced at the others. 'Emily and I have made some cheese and pickle sandwiches, rather more pickle than cheese I'm afraid,' she added. 'But we get our rations on Saturday, don't we, so we'll be able to stock up a bit then.'

'I hope you haven't wasted any of your cheese on me,' Carrie said at once, 'because my mother will be expecting me home, and—'

Eileen's mother interrupted. 'Of *course* we've made some for you, Carrie,' she scolded. 'What's a few sandwiches between friends! It's only a snack.'

'Oh well – thanks,' Carrie said, 'but then I must be on my way. It's the Mothers' Meeting in the hall this afternoon, and I've promised to help with the tea and cake.'

For the next few minutes they sat enjoying their lunch, and Gladys Matthews said, 'Emily has decided that we're having sausage and mash for our meal later today – and she is *very* good at peeling potatoes. She did all of them by herself! And there are just enough sausages for us to have one and a half each, but they are nice big ones, so no one's going to go hungry.'

Eileen looked at her mother for a moment. Was this the same person who two or three years ago had had so little interest in food – or in anything else – that Eileen had thought one morning she might go in to her mother's bedroom to find she'd slipped away in the night? That she had finally given up on life?

But somehow, a massive corner had been turned, and it was not hard to see the reason. Gladys Matthews was in control once more, not necessarily of all the practical issues, but in control of her feelings. Of her inner self. She had, astonishingly, also seemed able to adjust her health routine, always insisting on using one stick, and sometimes even forgetting to take her tablets. And her appetite had been transformed from that of a little bird into something more normal.

Eileen knew there was one simple answer to this conundrum and it was Emily Wilson. The little girl had rekindled that special fire in Gladys Matthews' heart – the fire which had almost permanently been extinguished. Just look at the two of them now, Eileen mused. So at ease with each other as they giggled at something silly.

'My father loves sausage and mash,' Carrie murmured now, as she bit into her cheese sandwich. 'Especially with onion gravy. Apart from the Sunday roast, it's his favourite dinner.'

'Oh yes – we shall certainly have onion gravy with ours,' Gladys Matthews intervened. 'At least there's no shortage of onions – at the moment.'

Listening to all this, Abigail couldn't help wondering whether Edna was affected by all the rationing. After all, there was always plenty to eat at Coopers, but of course, Edna would now have her own ration book to buy things she didn't grow, so she wouldn't go short of anything.

And it was amazing, Abigail thought, how despite the fact that each person's weekly allowance was hardly generous – four ounces of bacon, two ounces of butter, eight ounces of sugar, two ounces of cheese and one fresh egg (though dried egg was available) plus a pound of jam every two months, and sometimes the occasional shortage of things which were not rationed – no one went hungry. There always seemed just enough to get by, though the dearth of soap was worrying. But Emily didn't go short of sweets – when they were available – because everyone else at number six gave her their tiny ration.

It didn't take long for the five of them to finish their snack then Gladys Matthews said, 'Right. Now I think it's time for us to be told all about your morning. Didn't you say you were to be given uniforms today?'

Eileen finished drinking her tea and stood up. 'Hold your horses, Mother. All is about to be revealed! I think it's time for our fashion parade! You and Emily stay here in the kitchen, and no looking until we make our entrance! I promise that you will never have seen anything like it before!'

As they'd come in earlier, the girls had put their parcel of clothes on the floor by the hallstand, and now, removing their own clothes, they struggled once more into the all-encasing boiler suits before helping each other adjust the hair nets.

'Let's not take the masks in,' Carrie said, 'in case it upsets Emily. But perhaps we should wear the rubber boots – the finishing touch to this beautiful outfit!'

'Come on,' Eileen said briskly, 'let's not keep our public waiting . . .'

They moved forward to open the kitchen door and, arm in arm, the three made their entrance. In a loud and ringing tone Eileen made the announcement.

'Tra-la! May we introduce you to . . . The War Girls!'

For a few moments there was complete silence, then Gladys Matthews said quietly, 'Oh my goodness me.'

Then Emily went over and stared up at her mother. 'I quite like that thing on your head,' she said. 'What's it called?'

'A snood, I believe,' Abigail said. 'It's just to keep our hair clean.'

Gladys Matthews bit her lip. She'd known very well what the Royal Ordnance Factory produced, and had rather naively thought that the volunteers would be doing desk jobs, or some other light tasks. But actually seeing her daughter, and Carrie and Abigail, geared up so specifically for action sent a tremor of fear right through her. What had they done, these three girls, so full of loyal ardour? What had they done in offering themselves for the obvious service which awaited them?

On the following Monday, the three girls got to the top of Broad Walk in good time to be picked up by the van – which was there already waiting for them.

'Hop in, girls!' the driver said, opening the door for them. 'You're my only pick-ups from this area, so make yourselves comfortable in my limousine!' He grinned cheerfully. 'It'll take about half an hour to get there as long as a lone bomber doesn't suddenly pay us a visit and close off one of the roads! But so far so good!'

He glanced in his rear-view mirror at the three young women sitting behind him. Three very *attractive* young women, he thought. Well, good luck to them, that's all he had to say.

The factory, though not that far from Bristol, was fairly isolated, with few other signs of life nearby, and as soon as they arrived the three girls were shown into a small building where they were to get into their uniforms. A man, fully kitted up in similar style, introduced himself.

'I'm Mr Reynolds,' he said, straight-faced, 'I am the general superintendent and there's nothing about this place that I don't know. So, as soon as you're ready, come on out over the road to where it all happens and I'll show you what you've got to do.' He glanced around him for a second and almost managed to smile before adding, 'This luxurious area is where you all take a break – you can bring your own food if you want to, but sandwiches and tea and coffee are delivered each day at twelve o'clock. And hot and cold drinks will be available later.' He turned to go. 'The medical room and the lavatories and the washroom are two minutes away over there outside, so now I'll leave you to get kitted up.'

After he'd gone, Eileen said, 'Well, that was fairly precise.'

'I think all that was the easy bit,' Carrie said, beginning to get into her uniform. 'I can't wait to see what's expected of us and I hope I shall be given full training because I'm only used to thinking about Danish pastries and iced celebration cakes and dealing with members of the public who've come to enjoy a civilised holiday at The Berkeley!' She made a face. 'Do you think we're in for a bit of a shock?'

'I think we probably all are,' Eileen said as, now, they went across the road to the factory – a massive, high-roofed building with what seemed like hundreds of doors, all open – and from which they could hear noises of every description. High-pitched sounds, hissing and humming and banging from working machinery, and human voices all trying to make themselves heard above the din. And as soon as they entered, the smell was so overpowering that Abigail put her hand across her mouth and tried not to heave.

Mr Reynolds came up to them. 'Right then,' he said, raising his voice so that they could hear. 'I've been told you three wish to work together, and that's fine by me because this shop works well with three. So this is to be yours in the production line and in case you hadn't realised it, you are going to be making guns, shells, bullets, grenades and bombs. I'm afraid you'll have to learn everything as you go along, but that's just the way it is. It's the same for everyone and you'll catch on pretty quickly.' He nodded across the room, shouting louder. 'There are fifty workers here at the moment, and everyone is expected to do whatever is necessary when and where it's needed. Now then . . .' He paused and glanced at his file. 'You three will have your own small shop over here, where you'll be filling land mines and shells with TNT.'

For a moment, Abigail felt almost faint at what they were being told. This was a terrible, dreadful business and she had not given a single thought as to what it might mean to be working here. TNT! She knew what that meant – a high explosive material designed to maim and kill! And here she was, about to be shown how to make it fit for purpose!

Mr Reynolds continued undeterred. 'So, take this shell for example. Fill it with TNT up to this level, then insert this tube which contains the detonator. See? Then clean and scrape the shell, right inside, to the exact height. That's the way to do it. When you need more TNT you can get a fresh lot from that cement mixer over there – take one of these cans and fill it from that.' He stood back. 'Just see how everybody else does it and follow suit – and as you'll be working with highly explosive material, I don't need to remind you that great care must be taken at all times.'

Then, he looked at each of them in turn. 'Any questions?'

After he'd gone, the three girls just stared at each other. Eileen said, 'Come on – which one of us is going to make a start?'

'I vote that it's you, Eileen,' Carrie said promptly. Then she smiled, glancing around her. 'Look – everyone seems to be beavering away without much problem . . . perhaps one of them will give us a hand if we get stuck.'

At twelve o'clock they were told to go and take a break, and as they made their way over to the washroom Abigail said, 'D'you think we'll *ever* get used to that dreadful smell? But thank goodness for the snood.'

'Oh, I think that vile fragrance will be with us for a long time yet,' Eileen said cheerfully, 'but I don't think we did too badly this morning, do you? I saw Mr Reynolds watching us with a narrowed gaze, but we weren't told off about anything, were we. I mean, we did get a lot of those shells done – and at least we've survived the first shift without blowing each other up!'

'Oh don't, Eileen!' Abigail said, shuddering. 'I know I'm a country lass, but even I should have thought more deeply about what armaments really meant.'

'What – are you saying that if you had, you would have backed out of our agreement?' Eileen demanded. 'Our triple arrangement?'

'Of *course* not!' Abigail retorted. 'We all agreed from the beginning that the three of us were in this together, whatever it was. But I just wish I wasn't so naive.'

They finished cleaning themselves up briefly in the washroom, which was now crowded with other girls all chattering and jostling for position in the rather limited space. Then they made their way over to the break room and Carrie said, 'Is that coffee I can smell? Lead me to it – I'm desperate!'

Meanwhile, back in the factory, Mr Reynolds took a moment to go over to the shop the three newcomers had been working in to check up how they'd left it and how much they'd done. Everything was in order and ready for the next batch of shells to be filled. He nodded to himself. It was his job to keep a particularly close eye on the uninitiated, and although it had been obvious that none of these three girls had had any experience of this essential war work, they had worked quietly alongside each other and had achieved quite a lot in a short time. He had noticed at once that they enjoyed a close bond with an apparently implicit trust in each other, and this had undoubtedly been an advantage as they'd struggled to get the job done on their first morning. Not saying very much to each other, but just bending over the task as if they meant it.

Mr Reynolds heaved a sigh, hoping that they would turn up again tomorrow and not have been put off by their first experience of working in what he, himself, could only call a hell hole.

Chapter 26

The girls were rather subdued as the van took them home later that day, and the driver was not surprised at that. He'd seen it all before.

'How'd it go then, girls?' he enquired cheerfully.

'Fine, thanks,' Eileen said promptly. 'But I think we're all looking forward to a hot bath and an early night.'

'Yeah. It's not a fun job, is it,' the man said. 'But someone's got to do it.' He glanced briefly over his shoulder. 'Shall I be picking you all up tomorrow at the same time?'

'Of course!' The reply was unanimous.

Presently, the van dropped them off, and after having waved Carrie home, the other two got to number six and Eileen paused before opening the front door. 'I don't think we should say too much about what we were doing, do you, Abigail? I don't want to worry my mother, and Emily certainly doesn't need to know any details.'

Abigail nodded. 'I was thinking about that all the way home,' she said. 'I'm just going to tell Emily that I had to run errands and clear up. Things like that.'

'Good idea,' Eileen said. 'And I don't want to take our uniforms into the house, because that smell clings, doesn't it? So let's leave them in the shed where we keep our garden tools – I've got the key here on my ring.'

Abigail looked relieved at that suggestion. 'Thanks for that, Eileen,' she said. 'As long as we don't forget to take them with us again in the morning.'

They let themselves into the house and went into the kitchen where Mrs Matthews and Emily were busy at the table doing sums. Gladys immediately stood up to greet the girls.

'Well, the volunteers return!' she exclaimed. 'Come in and sit down – the casserole you made for us yesterday, Abigail, is bubbling nicely, and all I've got to do is add the doughboys which Emily has made for us. But first I expect you'd like a cup of tea.'

Emily got down and went over to hug her mother. 'I've learned how to add up four lines now, Mummy – not just two!'

'Yes, she's a very clever girl, aren't you, Emily,' Gladys Matthews said. 'But – we want to know how *you* two got on today,' she added, turning to the others. 'Was it very difficult?'

'No, not really,' Eileen said casually. 'We just had to get on and do as we were told.' She stifled a yawn. 'There were a lot of other girls there as well – they all seem very nice, not that we had much opportunity to talk to them.'

Gladys Matthews said no more, but Eileen knew that her mother wouldn't be content with that explanation. More would have to follow, but now was not the time.

It was quite late before Emily at last agreed to go to bed, and as Abigail tucked her in Emily pulled back, making a face.

'Ugh – I hate the smell of your hair, Mummy! It's horrible! What have you put on it?'

'Oh, it's only from where we were working today,' Abigail said quickly. 'Don't worry. I am going to give it a good wash in a minute, and then it'll smell as lovely as yours.'

Yawning again, Emily said, 'What did you and Eileen and Carrie have to do in that factory today, Mummy? Was it easy? And will you have to do it again tomorrow?'

'Yes, we will, Emily,' Abigail said and, crossing her fingers, she added, 'and it was as easy as pie!'

Later, downstairs, Eileen went along to her mother's room, dreading the explanation which she knew would have to come.

Tapping her mother's door, Eileen went in and Gladys Matthews looked up.

'Come and sit down, dear,' she said. 'You look tired out.'

'I'm not too tired to hear about *your* day, Mother,' Eileen said. 'Have you felt all right?'

'Yes thank you, dear,' Gladys Matthews said. 'Though I didn't have much chance to have forty winks because Emily is unstoppable. We've done pages and pages of sums.'

'But I notice that you did the shopping,' Eileen said.

'Well yes. We went out for a little walk and I did buy us a fresh loaf and a pound of tomatoes, but you and Abigail have organised all our meals for the week so there wasn't much for me to do. And at last I managed to buy some Nuttall's Mintoes – my favourite as you know. They haven't been in for a while, and apparently we're soon going to have to get used to a real shortage of sweets and chocolate – plus cigarettes. But none of us smoke, thank goodness.'

For a long moment neither spoke, then Gladys Matthews said, 'So, tell me what you three have been doing today, Eileen.' She hesitated. 'I imagine it was unpleasant, to say the least.'

Eileen had never been dishonest with her mother, and speaking carefully she said, 'I've never been inside such a huge building before, nor such a noisy one, either. And its purpose is to produce ammunition, bombs, bullets, land mines, everything you could imagine. To kill people. And it was absolutely horrible.'

'But how on earth can the inexperienced be expected to produce the goods?' Gladys Matthews said.

'We were given about five minutes' instruction, then told to get on with it,' Eileen said flatly. 'And don't ask me how it happened, but it became easier as we went along. By the end of the shift we'd actually managed to complete the number of shells and bullets we were given. Trays of them.' She waited before going on. 'And I'm sure the reason we could do it was because the three of us were working there together as a team. It was as if when one of us found something particularly difficult, the other two soon gathered around to help out. It did happen like that, several times,' Eileen said, 'and I'm so glad we were all together.' She smiled. 'We really needed each other.'

'I'm sure Carrie and Abigail feel the same,' Gladys Matthews said. 'And you never know, let's hope that the war girls may find tomorrow a little easier.'

During the following few months, Bristol no longer seemed to be Hitler's main target, but work at the Royal Ordnance Factory went on non-stop, and for Eileen, Carrie and Abigail, their own part in the production of lethal ammunition became relentless and routine.

One day, Eileen said casually, 'My mother did say that all this would become easier – and I suppose she was right. But it's still ghastly, isn't it?'

The others nodded their agreement as they shifted another tray of anti-tank mine fuses. 'I haven't said very much about it to my parents,' Carrie said soberly. 'Of course, they know we're making ammunition, but I've spared them all the details. And I'm relieved that they don't question me about it.' She smiled briefly. 'And as Mark and I haven't seen each other again for ages, he hardly knows *what* I'm up to. But of course, I never know what he's up to, either, although I am getting more letters from him now, thank heaven. But naturally he can't say very much of real interest . . . other than he loves me, of course!'

Abigail looked away for a moment, suddenly longing to feel

Luke's arms around her again. To hear him say he loved her. And perhaps it was her long history of simple country living, and of working on the land, which filled her with depression at what they were doing here. Every time they sent another tray of completed shells or bullets up the production line, she wondered where they would land, which small farms and gardens they would destroy and worse, who they would kill, hurt or terrify.

She turned back to what she'd been doing. It was no good having those thoughts because they had volunteered to be here, and it had one purpose. To bring this terrible war to an end.

Her eyes misted as she suddenly thought of Emily, at home now, enjoying her uncomplicated little life with Eileen's mother. But how different it could have been if they'd had a direct hit during that last raid. If number six had suffered the same fate as number fourteen Redcliffe Way had on that earlier one, Emily would never have known another birthday. Her life would have ended at just four years old.

Abigail felt almost overwhelmed at her own thoughts. Yes, they had been spared in that last blitz, but she knew it was merely random fate which had saved them. What about next time?

Then she was defiant. There was only one way out of this madness, and it was to meet fire with fire. She *must* press on, even though it went against her every instinct.

Thank you, Dada, Abigail thought. There was always her drawing to console her. So tonight, much later, she would find solace in completing one of her greetings cards. Immersing herself in the gentle world of forming and creating something beautiful would help to soothe her conscience and ensure that she'd have a restful night's sleep.

Now, it was twelve o'clock, and as the bell rang for their break all the girls trooped out of the building, making for the wash and rest rooms. Apart from the occasional comment and brief smile they'd exchanged with the other workers, there hadn't been the opportunity to get to know each other. But presently, as they sat at one of the long trestle tables having their sandwiches and coffee, one girl turned to Eileen.

'Wotcha,' she said cheerfully. 'My name's Daisy, and me and my friend Margaret have been watching you three over there on the other corner. We can't make out whether you're related or not – we don't think you're sisters because you're not that much alike to look at, but you could be cousins.' She smiled. 'Hope you don't think I've got a cheek, but you seem very, well, close that we couldn't help wondering.'

The girls immediately smiled back at the speaker, and Eileen said easily 'No, that's OK, Daisy. And we're not related – just good friends, that's all.'

Daisy paused, clearly intrigued about these three. 'Got any family?' she enquired as she poured herself another cup of coffee. 'I've lived in Bristol with me auntie all my life,' she went on chattily, 'and Margaret was brought up in a children's home, weren't you, Maggs?'

Margaret nodded, seeming quite happy at having her life discussed. 'Yeah,' she said, between mouthfuls of sandwich, 'so I had plenty of friends there, but Daisy has been my only real friend.' She giggled. 'She showed me how to nick a bar of chocolate from the confectionery counter as we went home at night, didn't you, Daisy?'

'Hush,' Daisy said, 'don't give away our secrets!' She turned to the others again. 'So, you got family?'

'Yes, we live with our parents,' Carrie began carefully, and Abigail cut in.

'And I have a little girl. Emily. She's four years old.'

That widened the field of interest, and Daisy said, glancing at Abigail's left hand, 'Where's your husband – dudn't he mind you workin' 'ere?'

'We all have our part to play in this war,' Abigail said neatly.

There was a short silence, then Daisy said, 'Margaret and me met at Woolworths where we've worked since leaving school. So what d'you all do? And are you gonna go back there when the war's over?

'Oh, we all work in various offices in town,' Eileen said casually, 'and we'll presumably be going back there. Eventually.'

Just then the bell rang for the end of dinner time, and all the girls got up to return to the factory. And as the three fell into step Eileen said, 'What Daisy said just now has made me think. And I'm wondering if – when I'm no longer needed here – it might be the time to cut off the old ties and do something different.' She made a face. 'The insurance industry is not exactly exciting and won't fall apart if I'm not there.' She paused thoughtfully. 'The war had upset so many plans for so many, will we ever be the same people again? Will there be fewer chances for us, or more? And d'you know, I wouldn't mind going to college and learning something entirely different – I mean, just look at what we've been doing all these months! Did you *ever* think you were capable of it? And if we are, apparently, so successful at this awful business, surely greater, better, opportunities must lie ahead? Once the war is over.' She paused. 'What about you, Carrie? Would you like to change anything in your life?'

Carrie chuckled. 'I don't think so,' she said cheerfully. 'I'm just looking forward to Mark coming home and us getting married . . . and then having children. We both agree that we want at least two and would never mind if two became four!'

They arrived back at the shop and again began the intricate, tedious job of filling shells with TNT. Abigail realised, with some surprise, that she'd almost got used to the stench. And then she thought about what Eileen had said just now. Perhaps it was too early to begin thinking about the future, hers and Emily's, because the end of the war was still a pipe dream. It was enough that they had left Coopers and discovered another world – and what a world! Though this war had never been part of their plan! Yet, so far, and thanks to friends, they had survived, cocooned in kindness, goodwill and good luck.

But of course life would, one day, have to take another turn, Abigail told herself as she weighed and stamped another batch of shells. She and Emily could not go on living at number six for ever – that was obvious – even though it was an arrangement which suited them all. And what about Blackwell's? She'd only worked there part-time, the money, and what she earned at Robertson's, just enough for their needs. But the wage they were receiving here at the armaments factory was absolutely huge by comparison, so she was able to save quite a lot for their future. She had never been this rich.

And what did lie ahead? One thing Abigail was emphatic about was that Emily would be properly educated and not leave school at fourteen. Emily was going to have the benefit of being taught everything there was to know – when the time came. But her school days were not yet. Until then she had the security and kindness of home where she was safe, and untroubled.

Chapter 27

September 1941

One morning, Emily ran downstairs to the kitchen where Mrs Matthews was already making the toast for their breakfast. Emily went straight over to put her arms around Gladys Matthews' waist.

'Mummy is always *so* quiet getting up in the morning,' Emily said. 'I never hear a thing – not even the front door bang when she and Eileen go out.'

'No, well, they do have to leave very early, don't they, so it's kind of them not to disturb us.' Gladys Matthews smiled. She heard every movement in the house, always had done, and knew very well when, at five-forty-five, the two girls got up each day.

'Shall I stir the tea leaves in the pot, Mrs Gladys?' Emily said, and Eileen's mother nodded. Their little girl was growing up so fast and wanted to do everything by herself all the time.

'Yes, thank you, Emily,' Gladys Matthews said. 'And then I think it's ready to pour. There are just the two of us, so the pot won't be too heavy for you.'

'I never find the teapot too heavy,' Emily said as she stirred. 'I asked Mummy the name of her factory and she said it was called the Royal Ordnance Factory, and then I said what does she do there and she said they are making ammunition, which is guns and bullets.' Emily looked across at Eileen's mother. 'Is that what Mummy and Eileen and Carrie have been doing? I thought they were just there to sweep up and keep it all clean.'

Gladys Matthews spread some marmalade onto her toast before replying, then she looked up. She'd always believed that, wherever possible, it was right to give children a direct answer to a direct question, and this child, with her unquenchable curiosity about the world and everything in it, deserved to be told something of the truth. She put down her knife.

'Yes, that is what the factory is there for, Emily,' she began, and Emily stared at her.

'Do you mean that Mummy is making *guns and bullets* to *kill* people with? But that's horrible!'

'But Mummy and Eileen and Carrie are not doing it for that,' Gladys Matthews said. 'That is not the point.'

'Well, why are they doing it, then?' Emily said. 'Mummy would *never* want to kill anybody! And neither would Eileen and Carrie, would they? So, I don't think they should go there! I don't *want* them to go there anymore, Mrs Gladys!'

Eileen's mother put her hand over Emily's before she spoke again, knowing that she must find the right words for this child. 'I do not believe for a single moment that what they are making is meant to hurt or kill anyone, Emily,' she said. 'That is not why they're doing it. But the factories in Germany that are making the bombs they've been dropping on us here in Bristol, must be put out of action as soon as possible so that they can't make any more. Do you see? Our ammunition is to stop the factories from being able to work. And I'm sure the people there will hear the sirens and run into their shelters, like we've had to do.'

Gladys Matthews paused, hoping that her explanation would satisfy Emily. 'And remember, Emily,' she went on, 'Adolf Hitler started this war. Our government tried to stop it, but he wouldn't listen, so the only thing we can do is spoil his plans by destroying the German bombs before they're sent over here to hurt *us*! And that's what Mummy and Eileen and Carrie are doing and we should be very proud of them, Emily. It is people like them who will bring this war to an end.'

Emily, who hadn't touched her breakfast, picked up her toast and took a reluctant bite. 'Are you sure they don't mean to kill people . . . Children and babies and dogs and cats and—'

'Absolutely positive,' Gladys Matthews said. 'Neither of them would wish to kill even a mouse or a spider, would they?'

A few days later as they were in the kitchen together, Emily said to Eileen's mother, 'I've thought up a poem, Mrs Gladys. Would you help me to write it down? I think I can do it by myself, but I might not be able to spell everything because there's one word I don't know how to do properly.'

'Of course I will help you, Emily.'

'I've made it up for Mummy and Eileen and Carrie,' Emily said, 'and I want to read it to them when they come home. And when I've written it out, I want to draw flowers all around the edges of the page, and colour them in so it's pretty,' she added.

Gladys Matthews took down a bottle of orange squash and poured out two glasses. 'This all sounds very interesting, Emily,' she said. 'What have you called your poem?'

'It's called "The War Girls",' Emily announced importantly. 'I remembered what you said the other day about why they're going to that place and that we should be proud.' She sipped from her glass. 'Do you want to hear it?'

'I do, very much.'

Emily cleared her throat and, raising her voice slightly, she began.

'The War Girls, by Emily Grace Wilson.

'Our war girls are so good and brave

'They go to work each day

'They're doing it to *end – this – war*

'So hip, hip, hip hooray!'

Emily looked at Eileen's mother earnestly. 'I'm going to colour "end this war" in red to make it stand out – but does it sound all right to you, Mrs Gladys? Do you think Mummy would like it?'

Gladys Matthews pulled Emily towards her and hugged her tightly. 'She is going to *love* it, Emily,' she said.

December 1941

Gladys Matthews took down all her Christmas cards from the mantelpiece and slowly began to wipe the surface free from dust. Then, one by one, she put them all back, putting Abigail's where it had been before, right there in the centre. Because just to gaze at the beautiful scene depicted – glistening snow covering field and church, the striking red of berries on the holly bush, tiny figures carrying lanterns – yes, a traditional picture repeated many times, but this one had been Abigail's very own creation, as had been the ones she'd given them all last year too. None of them had realised that drawing and painting had been Abigail's lifelong hobby, though as she pointed out, there was not that much time to indulge her interest these days.

Anyway, here we are again, Gladys Matthews thought as she finished what she was doing. *Another Christmas almost upon us.* But what a sad festival for the American bereaved who had just lost their sons, brothers, fathers and in a manner no one could possibly have imagined.

Last week, and out of the blue, Japan's kamikaze pilots had flown over and aimed their machines directly at the American fleet at anchor in Pearl Harbor, destroying all the ships and condemning the unsuspecting sailors to a watery grave. Hundreds and hundreds of them would never see another day.

For most, the terrible news was heard with horror and disbelief, but for Winston Churchill and the allies the awful tragedy came with a small ray of hope. Perhaps now America would add its weight in routing Hitler once and for all.

The catastrophe of Pearl Harbor was naturally the news most spoken about, read about, talked about – but for Gladys Matthews and those living at number six, together with Jonathan Waters and his family at All Saints, Christmas must be celebrated in the usual way. There would still be the carol service and a Christmas tree. There was no other answer. Life just had to go on.

1942 began cold and dry, thankfully not a repeat of last year's ice and snow. And even more thankfully, air raids in Bristol had more or less ceased.

And it was after yet another of Emily's exciting birthday parties that Eileen told Abigail her mother had especially asked to speak to Abigail on her own.

'Don't look so worried,' Eileen teased. 'My mother is not an ogre, as you very well know.'

After a short tap on the door, Abigail went into Mrs Matthews' room. She was sitting in her chair with a book on her lap, the glow from the table lamp beside her casting a strange shadow on the wall beyond. She looked up.

'Come in, Abigail, and sit down,' she said. 'I should think you're just about ready for bed, aren't you, my dear? What a day you've had, organising Emily's party and having to go to work as well.'

There was a short silence, then: 'Eileen said that you wanted to talk to me about something, Mrs Matthews,' Abigail said, and Gladys Matthews smiled.

'Yes, Abigail.' She leaned forward. 'Now, I don't wish to interfere in your life in any way at all, my dear,' she said quietly, 'and of course it's entirely up to you, but your little girl is more than ready to start school. She is now five years old and should really begin her formal education.'

Abigail looked away for a moment, admitting that she had

refused to think too much about this thing she'd been dreading for so long, and Mrs Matthews spoke again.

'From the moment I met you both, it was quite clear that Emily is advanced well beyond her years. Her understanding of speech, her ability to converse without any prompting, is exceptional. And more lately, I have found her quickness to grasp simple sums as remarkable.' Eileen's mother paused. 'All this, of course, is thanks to you, Abigail. From all I have learned about you, you have never failed to give your child your love and total attention, answering every question she has thrown at you with commendable patience – and there will have been many, many questions! As I know to my cost! Emily's wish to know everything is unstoppable. She has been the centre of your world,' Gladys Matthews said. 'And Emily has become the centre of mine too. And she is revelling in it. She is matching us, Abigail, and is becoming a young adult before her time.'

Abigail's eyes were pensive as she listened. Of course it was all too true. Emily had been doted on from the moment of her birth but who else was there more suited than her mother to do that? And who else had there been to do it? No father, no grandparents, no loving aunties and uncles.

Gladys Matthews glanced at Abigail shrewdly. It hadn't taken Eileen's mother long to fully comprehend the possessive tie which held this young mother to her little girl so closely. Mrs Mathews paused before going on.

'Now why don't you think about letting Emily start at the little school up here on the Wells Road – just a few moments' walk away – which would be very convenient. It has a good reputation, and I have known the Head for many years.'

Abigail sighed. The thing she had dreaded most was coming home to roost. She had always known that this moment would arrive, and she'd been deliberately pushing it from her mind. She could not bear to think of Emily being without her mother in a strange place, and among the unkindness of other children.

Gladys Matthews interrupted Abigail's thoughts. 'It's not just Emily's education,' Eileen's mother said. 'It's in her own interest to be with others of her own age. To play and learn to hold her own. It's all very well experiencing the happiness she feels at being with adults all the time, but there is more for her to enjoy. Much more, and she must not be held back.'

'Of course, I understand all you are saying, Mrs Matthews,' Abigail said slowly, 'and you are right. And I admit that I have kept putting the matter of Emily's first school days to the back of my mind. Trying not to think too much about it,' she added.

'That's quite understandable, Abigail,' Mrs Matthews said. 'You have had many other things to think about. Leaving your home without the support of your husband was very brave of you, and you have taken great strides into your future. But you can't do everything at once, none of us can.'

Abigail stood up. 'Thank you for the benefit of your wisdom, Mrs Matthews,' she said. 'And I will speak to Emily and see what her reaction is. But would you let me have the name of the school and the person I should approach?'

'I will certainly do that,' Gladys Matthews said, 'and you and Emily could visit and see what you think about it. Get the feel of the place.' She paused. 'The school year begins in September – as I'm sure you realise – but Emily might even like to start after the Easter holiday. It will be up to you, and to her, what is decided.'

Abigail turned to leave and Mrs Matthews stopped her for a second. 'By the way, Abigail, Emily told me that her birthday card from you was another of your handmade and handpainted ones, and you should be congratulated.' Eileen's mother smiled. 'It's a beautiful little card, one to keep.'

Abigail coloured up at the compliment. 'I do love drawing and painting,' she said. 'I think I explained that it was something my father taught me a long time ago.'

Chapter 28

With the New Year well under way, work at the Royal Ordnance Factory went on as usual, as did the endless clearing of debris in the city's streets and the demolition of houses which were no longer safe to live in.

To their own amazement, Abigail, Eileen and Carrie had become more or less accustomed to the grisly work they were doing each day, helped by the fact that they were doing it together and could chat, now and then, about other things.

'So,' Eileen said one day to Abigail, 'my mother tells me that Emily Grace Wilson seems to like the idea of going to school.'

'Yes, she seems to,' Abigail replied. 'And typical of my daughter, she listened very carefully when I explained what ought to happen but didn't have very much to say until I mentioned that Mrs Matthews thought it was a good idea. That was all it needed, because then she agreed that she'd think about it. Of course, it helped that Mrs Matthews came with us to see the place and we were introduced to the headmaster – Mr Thomas. He was very polite to Emily, shaking her by the hand and saying that he would very much like to have her there.' Abigail smiled. 'It also helped when she was shown the school uniform – royal blue and white, very smart – because she thought it would suit her very well.'

Stopping briefly to wipe her forehead with the back of her hand, Abigail went on. 'But of course, it's only possible because Mrs Matthews has insisted that she is quite capable of taking Emily to and from the school each day.'

'Yes,' Eileen said, 'she's told me all about that. She will take the pushchair to lean on, and after all it's no more than a five-minute walk, is it? And by that time the weather should be fine.' Eileen glanced up. 'My mother is sure that it's going to do her good to get out each day – and I think she's probably right,' Eileen added.

Just then, Mr Reynolds came over. 'Everything all right, girls?' he said.

'Perfectly, thank you, Mr Reynolds,' Eileen said. 'We've nearly finished this tray.'

The superintendent moved away and Eileen said, 'P'raps he doesn't like us talking – but too bad.'

'Anyway,' Abigail went on, 'as you already know, Emily is starting straight after the Easter holidays. But before that we shall go into town to the school shop to buy her uniform. I did point out that there was a little pocket in the skirt for dolly, but my daughter greeted that remark with derision!'

One Friday morning in March, Eileen, Carrie and Abigail were just finishing their last shift before lunch when there was a commotion further up the line, and they heard a young woman screaming for help. Startled, they looked over just as Mr Reynolds ran past them, waving his arms and shouting instructions and pushing a trolley in front of him.

'Out of the way, out of the way!' he yelled, and everyone scattered. Then, with the help of two other men, the superintendent lifted the distraught woman, still screaming, on to the trolley and dashed along the line and out of the building towards the medical centre.

It was terrifying, and Abigail was trembling from head to

foot and Carrie looked close to tears. What on earth could have happened? Eileen put an arm around both of them.

'Hang on, she'll be all right in a minute,' but Eileen's mouth had gone completely dry. After all, every one of the girls took great care – but how could you be sure you'd taken the right sort of care? They all knew they were working with deadly material, and so far nothing too awful had happened, but that young woman was in agony and at the moment seemed to have completely lost her self-control. What had she done – or not done?

They were soon to find out that she'd slipped while holding a can of hot TNT and that it had been thrown all over her face, clinging to her hair and eyelashes and eyebrows.

Now thoroughly shaken, all the girls went to the break room for their sandwiches and coffee.

'That poor girl,' Abigail said as they sat at the table. 'That could have happened to any one of us, couldn't it? I mean, just to lose your footing for a split second and end up with that stuff all over you.' She shuddered. 'I don't feel like anything to eat now . . .'

Daisy, their new friend, sat down alongside them. 'Blimey O'Reilly,' she said. 'Wasn't that ever terrible! I nearly dropped me whole tray of bullets!' She leaned forward, taking a bite of sandwich. 'D'you think she's gonna die?'

'Certainly not,' Eileen said briskly. 'I'm sure she's made of sterner stuff than that.'

Much later, an hour before they were due to clock off, and to cheers from all the others, the victim came back in, doing her best to look nonchalant. Then she returned to her shop and continued with her work as if nothing had happened. But it had taken several hours for the TNT to set before it could be scraped painfully from her skin.

'Poor girl – poor brave girl,' Eileen said as they watched her walk back. 'She won't be sleeping very well tonight.'

In the van going home later, Abigail said, 'Do you think we could go to the cinema tomorrow?' She made a face. 'I don't know about you, but after what happened, I feel like some cheering up. And I would love to take Emily to see *Pinocchio*. I saw in Mrs Matthews' *Evening Post* that it's on at The Embassy.'

Then Eileen said, 'Or the other one that's being shouted about is *Mrs Miniver* with Greer Garson, It's on at The Whiteladies.' She thought for a moment. 'I know! Let's ask my mother to take Emily to the matinee of *Pinocchio* and we three could bunk off later to The Whiteladies!'

Abigail hesitated. 'Are you sure Mrs Matthews would really want to see *Pinocchio*, Eileen?' and Eileen chortled.

'My mother would be in her seventh heaven to sit watching a children's film with Emily Grace Wilson sitting next to her! I'll fix it – leave it all to me!'

Chapter 29

On Monday the 13th April, straight after the Easter break, it was going to be Emily's first day at school. And the night before, Abigail could hardly sleep a wink, going over and over everything and worrying about her little girl having to face a totally new environment by herself. Emily had never been without the company of a caring adult to protect her, and the very worst thing was, Abigail thought now as she plumped up her pillow for the hundredth time, *she* was not going to be there to see Emily through those school gates. Surely that was what every mother wanted, no, expected to do? But this mother would already be at the factory bench, filling and stamping those bombs.

Abigail turned over restlessly, smiling as she thought about yesterday evening, which had been such fun, because they'd played cards, Eileen teaching Emily two new tricks and then, as a little party to celebrate Emily about to be a grown-up schoolgirl, they'd had her favourite fish and chip supper. And as they'd all sat together around the kitchen table – with Carrie there too of course – Mrs Matthews had said, 'Emily and I are really looking forward to Monday, aren't we, Emily?'

Emily had nodded vigorously. 'Yep,' she'd said, as she'd dipped another chip into the salt on her plate, 'and we're going to get up nearly as early as Eileen and Mummy to make sure I'm properly dressed in my uniform. Aren't we, Mrs Gladys?'

Mrs Matthews had nodded. 'Yes, but you are very good at doing it all yourself, because we've been practising, haven't we.'

And remembering that now, Abigail realised that she might actually be feeling a bit jealous of Emily's surrogate mother. But what a terrible thing to admit! Gladys Matthews had been nothing less than a saint from the very moment she had entered their lives.

That Monday was the longest day Abigail could ever remember, and she couldn't wait for their shift to end at the factory so that they could go home. What if Emily had been bullied and didn't want to go back to school tomorrow?

But as soon as Eileen and Abigail entered the house, Emily raced along the hall to greet them.

'Guess what?' she exclaimed. 'I am going to be book monitor!'

Hardly bothering to give the girls a hug, Emily went on, 'Our teacher is called Miss Townsend and the girl sitting at the desk next to me is called Jennifer and she is the milk monitor. And Peter, the little boy sitting behind me, always feeds the goldfish and one of the other boys rings the bell for playtime and going home time.' Emily sighed importantly. 'Miss Townsend said that the school day is always very busy so everyone must help her.'

Relief flooded through Abigail. Why had she worried herself nearly sick all day? Emily was on top of the world, and had been given something to do that was just up her street and a perfect antidote to homesickness.

Presently, after they'd had supper, Abigail drew Emily on to her lap. 'So, how did you feel when you were told you were going to be book monitor? And what exactly do you have to do?'

'I was excited!' Emily said. 'Well, first of all, I've got to make sure all the books are always left neatly stacked on the shelves. And if anybody wants to borrow one to take home, I've got to write their name, and the number of the book, in the book register. Miss

Townsend said books are very precious and we don't want them damaged or lost. And no one must *ever* write in a reading book.'

'And what about Jennifer? Do you like her?' Abigail asked.

Emily nodded. 'Yes. We stayed in the playground together all the time at break when we had our milk and a biscuit, and we sat together in the hall to have our sandwiches at dinner time. She's got a little brother called David, but he's too small to go to school yet. She asked me if I had a brother or a sister and I said I didn't.'

Mrs Matthews broke in. 'When I collected Emily at quarter past three, I don't think she wanted to come home!' Eileen's mother smiled. 'That little school has always had a reputation for being a kind and caring place – quite apart from its high standard of teaching.'

Abigail hugged Emily to her more tightly. 'And what exactly did you do today, Emily? Could you understand it all?'

Emily nodded. 'Well, it was just like Mrs Gladys and I have been doing, sums and writing. And everyone had a turn at reading out, and Miss Townsend asked me to slow down because I was going too fast!'

It was quite late before Emily could be persuaded to go to bed. She was still wound up with the exciting novelty of her day and, tucking her up, Abigail said, 'So I think you enjoyed your first day at school, darling, didn't you. Are you looking forward to going back tomorrow?'

'YES!' Emily shouted at the top of her voice. 'Jennifer asked me if I had a skipping rope and when I said I didn't, she said she would lend me one of hers. Because she's got two. And we're going to do skipping in the playground at break tomorrow.'

Abigail's heart almost burst with happiness. Emily had grown up in one short day. 'Jennifer sounds a very nice little girl,' Abigail said, and Emily nodded, at last appearing to want to settle down.

'I like her,' she said, yawning. 'She's my friend.'

* * *

With America now firmly entrenched in the war, Bristol and the whole nation felt a sense of relief that they were no longer alone in the quest for victory. And one day, some of the factory girls were given the chance to reduce their hours of work, or even to stand down.

So, at the end of June, after working at their bench for nearly eighteen months, Eileen, Abigail and Carrie left the Ordnance Factory for the last time, each silently breathing a sigh of relief that they had come to no harm during their stint of duty.

As he dropped them off for the last time, the van driver poked his head out of the window. 'Well done, girls,' he said. 'You're all still in one piece! But don't count your chickens because you never know, you may have to come back! This war's not over yet, y'know! Personally, I don't think we've heard the last all-clear!'

It was a Friday evening, and as the three walked arm in arm towards number six Eileen said, 'I hope the war *is* over for us, and that we don't have to go back because my nightmare has been about what my mother would do if something awful had happened to me and she'd had to face the rest of her life alone – or even worse, to have to look after *me*!' Eileen shuddered. 'When we volunteered, I don't think we really thought about that aspect of it, did we?'

Carrie agreed. 'No, none of us did,' she said. 'And although my mother and father would still have had each other if I'd copped it, I think the bottom would have dropped out of their world if I was no longer there with them.' She half-smiled. 'And Mark would have shed more than a tear or two I imagine,' she added.

After a moment, Abigail said slowly, 'I believe that we probably did think about it, even if we didn't put it into words. I mean, I don't need to tell you that Emily is always there right in the front of my mind at all times, but . . .' She paused, frowning briefly. 'But because we three were in it together, it somehow made it all right – if that makes any sense – and it honestly didn't occur to me that we wouldn't be going home each night.'

'Well, there you are then. Your optimism was well founded,' Eileen said, 'and I agree with you. It always did feel like safety in numbers, didn't it, or at least safety in the number three!'

When they got back, Mrs Matthews was busy at the stove with the kettle on for a cup of tea as usual, and she looked up as the girls entered.

'Welcome home all of you,' she said. 'Have you *really* finished at that place?'

'Yes, really, Mother,' Eileen said. 'And now, if they'll have me, I suppose I'll soon be going back to The Royal as if nothing unusual had happened in my life! However am I going to cope? Anyway, you can take a back seat again, Mother, and look after yourself instead of us.'

Gladys Matthews interrupted, smiling. 'Now, don't you start bossing me around again, Eileen! Emily and I have been managing perfectly well by ourselves. Haven't we, Emily?'

Emily, who'd gone over to hug her mother, nodded. 'It was easy,' she said. 'I usually peeled the potatoes before I went to school, didn't I, Mrs Gladys, and always wiped up our breakfast dishes.'

'And of course, Eileen, as you and Abigail have been at home weekends to do the cleaning and the laundry and some of the grocery shopping,' Mrs Matthews said, 'it all worked very well in the end, didn't it?'

Dropping a kiss on Emily's head, Abigail glanced at Eileen's mother. 'I have to admit, Mrs Matthews, knowing that our evening meal would be all ready to eat when we got home helped to keep me going, especially as I hadn't done anything towards it,' she said lightly.

Eileen agreed. 'You were always a brilliant cook, Mother, and it's only in the fairly recent past that you haven't done so much of it.'

'You mean, I haven't been allowed to,' Gladys Matthews said. 'But this war has made demands on all of us, and I must say I do enjoy being, well, in charge of things a bit more – and I have to admit that the new tablets the doctor prescribed seem to be working very well this time. And of course,' Eileen's mother added, 'Emily is such a help. She gets herself ready for school each day, and I never have to check whether she'd put on her clean blouse or whether she'd brushed her teeth!'

'Well, my daughter is now five years old,' Abigail reminded everyone, 'and growing very tall. We might even have to buy a longer skirt before the September term begins.'

After they'd drunk their tea, Carrie stood up to go. 'Well, I'll love you and leave you,' she said, 'because my mother will be waiting to spoil me. And I know what she's cooking for our supper tonight,' she added. 'Rabbit! At least there's no shortage of those.'

Emily immediately looked up. 'What? Do you mean a *bunny* rabbit?'

'No, not a bunny,' Carrie said quickly. 'Just a rabbit.'

'So we'll see you tomorrow afternoon, Carrie,' Eileen said, ushering Carrie out of the kitchen. 'We haven't looked around the shops for ages, have we? And we haven't seen very much of Janet lately, either. We really must go and catch up with all the local gossip!'

'Good idea,' Carrie said. 'About two-thirty did you say?'

As Abigail got herself ready to go out the following afternoon, she admitted to a mixture of feelings. Was that it, then? She had volunteered, she had 'done her bit' for the war effort, and now she was redundant. And it had taken more out of her than she cared to admit. The task had been tough. Dirty, smelly, frightening and it was going to take some time to shrug it off and get back to normality. But it would be wonderful to be able to take Emily to school again each morning.

Would Blackwell's be ready to take her on once more? They'd always said they would, but would *she* feel like being among all those books again? Even though she assured herself that yes, of *course* she would, it was going to seem very tame after helping to manufacture bombs and bullets. From that deafening environment of raised voices and machinery and that sense of urgency, to the quiet serenity of a bookshop. How could her two lives be so entirely alien?

But then, she'd done this sort of thing before, hadn't she? By leaving Coopers and coming to Bristol, she'd swapped her life for one completely different, and it had worked. Despite the unbelievable intervention of the war, it had worked.

Just then, Emily pranced into the bedroom, anxious to get going. 'Aren't you ready *yet*, Mummy? Carrie's arrived and we're all waiting for you.'

'Ready,' Abigail said, picking up her bag and following Emily downstairs.

It was a perfect afternoon and, as usual on a Saturday, the city was buzzing with activity although most of the shops had little to show off in their windows. But Parson's, the jewellers, still managed to attract the glance of everyone passing by.

Presently, they all made their way to Robertson's – with Emily running ahead to go in first.

Janet was at the till talking animatedly to a customer who was just leaving, and when the four entered the café she looked up, her face wreathed in smiles.

'Well, what a treat on a busy Saturday afternoon!' she exclaimed, coming around to give Emily a hug. 'Are you ready to do some washing up for me, Emily?'

Emily nodded. 'Yes, but can I have an ice cream first?'

'Tea, shortbreads and ice cream on the house!' Janet said, nodding the order to Pat at the counter.

Then the girls sat down at one of the small tables in the corner and Eileen said, 'Sorry we've seen so little of you lately, Janet, but you know where we've been! Anyway, yesterday was our last shift, our last day – so we're free to come and haunt you and make ourselves a nuisance once again.'

Janet glanced at Abigail. 'So – does that mean my favourite

member of staff is returning to work soon? I've really missed you each afternoon in the shop, Abigail.'

'I don't think there'll be much to stop me,' Abigail replied. 'But we've all just got to catch up on ourselves first. I'll go to Blackwell's next week and see if my job's still there, then I'll come straight back and let you know, Janet.'

Eileen made a face. 'Knowing The Royal, I bet they'll want me at my desk straightaway! No little holiday first, for being a brave girl!'

'Same here,' Carrie said. 'But I have to say that I'm quite looking forward to being back at The Berkeley. Civilisation beckons! And the smell of pastries and other pleasant odours will be a nice change!'

The next day, everyone at number six attended Morning Service at All Saints. Again, the weather was perfect so that after the service, people wandered into the church gardens taking their coffee and biscuits with them.

Carrying their own tray, Eileen led her mother over to the long bench under the Magnolia tree, and they all sat down. Abigail glanced around her.

'The last time we were here, it wasn't quite as peaceful as this, was it,' she said, and Eileen nodded.

'No and poor Emily never got her ride on the roundabout, did you, darling?' she said.

Emily shrugged. 'Well, it didn't matter,' she said airily. 'Anyway, I think it was really meant for very small children.'

They sat there enjoying their coffee and Carrie came out to join them. 'Isn't it a lovely day!' she said. 'Dad was so pleased to see you all there in the front pew.' She sat herself down on the end of the bench for a moment. 'Now, I have some jolly news – Mark has a four-day leave mid-July and Mum and I decided we'd like a little party on the Saturday evening, the 11th. Just for special friends,' Carrie added, winking at Emily. 'When we got engaged there wasn't the time or opportunity for much celebration because Mark was back on duty almost at once, but mid-July he'll be here for four whole days! *Four whole days*! So Mum and I thought – let's have a "do"! And it's time you all met Simon – Simon Hill – who's going to be Mark's best man. He's in the same regiment,' Carrie added.

'Is it to be a full evening dress affair?' Eileen asked. 'Must we turn up looking posh?'

'No!' Carrie said, laughing. 'Just come as you are – but there will be a nice supper. I can promise you that because my mother is used to finding food for everyone at fairly short notice. And of course there will be wine – and a special cocktail for small people!'

'What's a cocktail?' Emily wanted to know.

'It's a little mixture of lovely drinks,' Carrie said. 'Squash, and all sorts of juices, strawberry and blackberry, and with little pieces of fruit floating on the top. You will love it, Emily, and I'll make sure it's nice and sweet.'

'Well, we can bring a contribution to help with the food,' Eileen said. 'Just let us know the sort of supper you have in mind, Carrie, and we'll do our best not to spoil it. But with the rationing and food shortages, it's only fair that we help out.'

'We'll see what my mother has to say about that,' Carrie said, 'but thanks for the offer.' She glanced at her watch. 'I can't stay because there are the coffee things to wash up and put away.'

Emily tugged at her sleeve. 'But when are you and Mark going to get *married*?' she said. 'You've promised that I'm going to be a bridesmaid, and we'll have to look for my dress soon, won't we?'

Carrie made a face. 'It's difficult to make an actual date for the wedding, Emily,' she said, 'because it all depends on what's happening with the war. But it certainly won't be for a while, I'm afraid. It might even have to wait until next summer.'

'Never mind,' Mrs Matthews said, 'that gives us a nice long time to look in the shops for dresses and hats. I'm told that there's very little choice of anything at the moment,' she added.

Carrie stood up to go. 'Well, we're not going to let anything worry us just yet,' she said, 'and Mum has said that if we can't find what we want when the time comes, she will make it all herself. My wedding dress and your bridesmaid's dress as well, Emily! So let's hope there'll be nice material available by that time, but if not, Mum says she has some supplies stored away upstairs where she does her sewing.' Carrie smiled. 'My mother has never wasted a thing and she is a bit of hoarder – so don't worry, Emily, if she can't find material for me, she'll make sure she has something beautiful for my chief bridesmaid!'

As Carrie turned to leave, Gladys Matthews said, 'If the party is likely to go on rather late,' she said, 'would it be better if Emily and I stayed at home?'

'Oh no *please*—' Emily began, and Carrie broke in at once.

'No, Mrs Matthews – it won't be too late for Emily – and besides, we would like you to be there because although we don't expect that there'll be many of us, one of our guests is my godfather – Maurice Stone – and you know Mr Stone, don't you?'

Eileen's mother nodded. 'Well, I hardly *know* him – but I have been to his Art and Sculpture Gallery in Queen's Road many times and have spoken to him once or twice, though not in recent years of course.' She glanced at Abigail. 'Although the Stone Gallery largely exists for special exhibitions by distinguished artists and sculptors, Maurice Stone is a wonderful painter himself. Perhaps you should show him some of your own work, Abigail, because I'm sure he would be impressed. And he is a very nice gentleman to talk to,' Gladys Matthews added.

'Well, there you are, then!' Carrie said. 'And anyway, we want you and Emily to be at the party, Mrs Matthews, because it's for special family and friends, so you cannot get out of it!'

Chapter 30

At six o'clock on Saturday evening two weeks later, the taxi arrived at West Road to take the guests to the vicarage.

'I've never been to a proper grown-up party,' Emily announced proudly as she smoothed down the skirt of her best dress and took her place in the car next to Mrs Matthews.

'And it's been a long time since I have,' Eileen's mother replied. She glanced across at Abigail and Eileen who were holding trays of little canapés they'd made to add to the party feast. 'With all the rationing, I don't know how you two came up with those ideas, but it all looks very tempting.'

'It's mostly thanks to your copy of Mrs Beeton's cookery book,' Abigail said. 'We had to adapt things a bit but they came out all right in the end.'

It was a perfect evening, and when they got to the vicarage the party was already in full swing, with everyone enjoying a glass of wine in the garden. As soon as Carrie saw them, she rushed over with Mark close behind her.

'You're the last to arrive,' Carrie said, 'and don't you look gorgeous, Emily!' Carrie glanced down at the trays the girls were holding. 'Oh, thank you for these,' she said, 'I'll take them straight in to the kitchen. Supper's nearly ready. Mark – will you look after my friends for a minute?'

'That will be my enormous pleasure,' Mark said easily. Not in uniform, he was wearing a dark pinstriped suit, white shirt and blue tie, and he looked down at them all, smiling. 'I can't remember the last time all of us managed to be together,' he said, 'and although I have only seen Emily once before, she has become even more beautiful – and so grown up!' He turned his attention to Eileen's mother. 'I hope you are keeping well, Mrs Matthews,' he said politely.

'I am very well, thank you, Mark,' Gladys replied.

Just then, a man – also formally dressed – came up to them. He was very tall and dark-haired, and he was holding a tray of drinks. Mark glanced at him. 'Oh thanks, Simon. I was just about to go and fetch those.'

Simon grinned. 'Well, I've saved you the bother,' he said pleasantly. 'I realised that you couldn't drag yourself away from this bevy of beauties – and who could blame you.'

'This "bevy of beauties" happens to be Carrie's very best friends,' Mark said, introducing them each by name. Then he turned to Mrs Matthews and the girls. 'And this is Simon Hill, my partner in crime in the regiment who – one day we hope – is going to be my best man.'

Presently, after polite conversation had taken place in the little group, Carrie came back to usher everyone inside. 'Come on, supper's ready,' she said. 'And later on I'll introduce you to the other guests.'

In the dining room, it was a very informal affair as everyone sat down where they liked, and with Emily on one side of her at the table and Gladys Matthews on the other, Abigail couldn't help noticing that Simon Hill had taken the seat next to Eileen and that they were chatting animatedly, their heads close together.

Despite all the shortages, the table was laden. There was cold chicken and fresh salads, and bowls of small new potatoes, with pickles of every description. And somehow or another Joan Waters had managed to make a magnificent pork pie (made with Spam, she told them later) which had pride of place in the middle of all the rest. And as the canapés were being handed around, someone said, 'War? What war? What a wonderful spread, Joan. How have you managed to get all this?'

Joan Waters smiled. 'Well, I spoke nicely to the butcher,' she said, 'but the salads and new potatoes are from the vicarage garden.'

After everyone had eaten enough, which included the pudding of fruit trifle and custard slices, Jonathan stood up, tapping the glass in front of him.

'I have had strict instructions from my daughter that this is not to be a speechy event,' he said, 'but I know you will want to join me in a toast to Carrie and Mark. As most of you know, they were actually engaged some time ago, but unfortunately Mark couldn't stay long enough for a family celebration, so we're having that now.' Jonathan paused before going on. 'A few of you also know that Mark was missing in action for a number of months, and our relief and gratitude that he came home safe and well cannot be overestimated.' Another pause. 'We are living in dangerous times, and this war is not over yet, so we must make the most of every opportunity to be happy and *glad* about something. And my wife and I are very glad indeed, that Mark, one day, is to be our son-in-law.'

There was a unanimous roar of approval at this, and Emily, smiling all over her face, looked up at Eileen's mother. 'I am *glad* – aren't you, Mrs Gladys?' she whispered.

'Very glad indeed,' Gladys Matthews replied.

'So help yourselves to the wine in front of you,' Jonathan said, filling his own glass as he spoke, 'and let us drink to Carrie and Mark – and the hope that their wedding can take place before too long.'

And Emily, leaning forward to reach her cocktail, which she had been gazing at throughout the meal, joined in with the toast.

'Carrie and Mark. God bless them!'

* * *

Presently, all the guests were shown into the sitting room for their coffee, and Carrie immediately came over to where Abigail and Mrs Matthews were standing. Emily was curled up in a corner of the long settee reading the new book Carrie had just given her.

'Here you are,' Carrie said, handing them their coffee. 'All freshly brewed!' She glanced at Eileen's mother. 'Have you managed to speak to Uncle Maurice yet, Mrs Matthews? Look, he's over there talking to Dad. I'll ask him to come over and you can re-introduce yourselves because I know you've had many interesting discussions together when you've visited the gallery.'

Not long after, with Abigail listening politely, Mrs Matthews was talking to the gallery owner. 'I'm very glad that you are still open for business, Mr Stone.' He nodded.

'Yes, thank goodness – we only closed for a week or so – although we've had a few very anxious moments!' He turned to Abigail. 'So, Mrs Wilson, you say that you've moved up from the country to live in Bristol? I trust that the awful raids haven't put you off living here!'

Abigail smiled. 'No. Emily and I love being in Bristol. And we have been most fortunate in living with Mrs Matthews and Eileen – an enormous piece of good luck for us.'

Gladys Matthews spoke up. 'You may be interested to know, Mr Stone,' she said, 'that Mrs Wilson is an artist – and a very good one too. She has produced the most wonderful cards for us all. None of which will ever be thrown away.'

Maurice Stone raised his eyes and looked at Abigail. 'Have you had training in the art world, Mrs Wilson?'

Abigail smiled. 'No, but I might have inherited a little of my father's talent,' she said, 'and he taught me everything I know.' She paused for a second, hesitating. 'As a matter of fact, I have brought some of his work with me this evening. I don't know whether you would be interested in seeing it?'

Abigail felt her heart begin to race. How had she found the courage to actually ask that? But just before they'd left for the party, she'd put the precious packet of drawings into her handbag. Had the moment actually arrived when she might show someone, someone important, how clever Dada had been?

Maurice Stone nodded politely. 'Yes, of course, Mrs Wilson,' he said. 'I am always interested in seeing something new.'

With her hands actually trembling, Abigail took the wax packet from her handbag. Then she opened it and carefully laid out the pictures in three rows side by side on the small table in front of them. She glanced at Maurice Stone.

'Time has passed, of course,' she said, 'because my father did these while in uniform during the Great War, and as you can see, he's dated them all with time and place. He explained that they kept him from going mad because when he was drawing and colouring, he could shut out the noise of battle – if only for a few hours while he was off duty.'

Gladys Matthews stared down, thoughtfully. 'You've never shown us these, Abigail,' she said. 'They are exquisite, aren't they?'

There was silence as Maurice Stone studied each picture carefully. 'These are beautiful scenes, well constructed,' he said slowly. Then after a long moment he added, 'And look at this one!' He leaned in closer. 'There in the corner is what we might at first glance see as a stricken bough on that tree, a dead branch. But look – it has been subtly formed into a cross, a distinct cross. And, that dark smudge there, vaguely discernible on the ground beside it looks like a mound of earth and debris half covering something. I think . . .' Maurice Stone narrowed his eyes. 'I think it could be just part of a tin helmet almost sunk into the ground.' He stood back, clearly moved. 'These are not just pictures, they are war pictures, each one produced at a time when the artist is suffering the hell of battle . . . and the knowledge,' Maurice added, 'that this could be the last thing he ever does.'

Abigail was stunned at his words. She had never noticed that the branch could really be a cross, nor that part of a soldier's uniform might be there. Poor Dada, she thought, poor dear Dada.

Whatever had he gone through all those years ago? But he had left her clues, and she was looking at them now.

Maurice Stone continued to finger the pictures carefully. 'Look at this. Your father must have done all these during the Battle of the Somme, 8th July 1916 . . . 20th July . . . 20th August . . . 1st September . . . 18th October . . . all signed and dated. But nothing after that. Because November saw the end of that particular battle, though nobody won,' he added. 'What a terrible waste of young lives – on both sides.'

Maurice Stone seemed unable to go on for a moment. Then, 'Lovely, these pictures are,' he added. 'The way the darkening clouds outlined above warn of an approaching storm – of evil weather – of tragedy.' He paused. 'This is masterly work,' he added quietly.

And Abigail's heart sang. She'd always known that Dada had been an inspired artist and colourist. And now, someone else, someone with knowledge, had just said so.

Presently it was time to go home, and Abigail went over to where Emily was still on the settee, nearly asleep. 'Come on, we're going now, darling,' Abigail said. 'Is that a good book?'

Emily yawned. 'Yes. I've nearly got to the end.'

With Eileen now having at last joined them, they were just going to the door to wait for the taxi which had been ordered, when Maurice Stone caught up with them.

'Mrs Wilson,' he said, 'would you allow me to show your father's paintings in the gallery? I sometimes have a memorabilia exhibition, and they would be absolutely perfect for that.' He paused. 'I know they would be of enormous interest, not just for their perfection but for their provenance. I found them deeply moving,' he added. Before Abigail could reply, he went on. 'As a matter of fact, I have already planned a memorabilia exhibition in a few weeks' time, and, if you are agreeable, I would include your father's pictures.' He smiled. 'They would have pride of place, and I would show them off in a way which I know would please you, Mrs Wilson. And naturally I would not offer them for sale, because I realise they are very precious to you.'

Abigail was so stunned that she was afraid she might burst into tears. At last, Dada's pictures were going to be seen by others! Because they deserved to be! She knew they'd been right to come to Bristol! She looked up.

'I would be delighted to lend them to you,' she said simply.

'Well, thank you,' Maurice said, 'but I hope you would accept a small fee for the privilege of exhibiting them. They are a remarkable – and touching – piece of history,' he added.

Then, after a moment, 'Might I – dare I – ask if your father made it back home, Mrs Wilson?' Maurice Stone said quietly, and Abigail smiled wistfully.

'He did, thank you, but he had been gassed during his time in France and his lungs never recovered. He was twenty-nine years old when he finally lost his last battle,' Abigail added sadly.

Chapter 31

On the last Saturday in August, Abigail and Emily, together with Mrs Matthews, Eileen and Carrie, took a taxi to Queen's Road to visit the Stone Gallery. It was opening day of the exhibition, and Abigail admitted to feeling nervous. Would Dada's pictures really be as successful as Maurice Stone had thought? And was it because she had loved her father so much that she had put such value on them?

Then she was cross with herself. If Maurice Stone thought they were worth showing in his gallery then there could surely be no doubt that they'd be well received by the public.

Abigail had never been to such a place before, but when they entered the discreet building and were shown into a dimly lit room on the ground floor, she felt a wave of pure excitement flow through her. This was . . . this was a special place, for a special purpose.

When they went in, Maurice Stone came forward to greet them. 'Good morning, ladies,' he said affably, with a special smile for his goddaughter. He looked straight at Abigail. 'I have to tell you that my advertisement for your father's exhibition received more interest than I have had for a very long time, and I expect that there will be small queues every day! But come forward and take a look, Mrs Wilson. I am personally very proud to be showing your father's pictures. They will be exhibited today and the whole of next week.'

With her heart now anxiously beating like a drum, Abigail followed him over to a tall stand right in the centre of the room. And as soon as she saw the pictures, framed and professionally mounted on a dark background, with subtle lighting ahead and around them, she knew she was going to have difficulty in not shedding a tear.

For several minutes, they all just stood there gazing, and Maurice Stone, seeing the expression on her face, said quietly, 'I knew you would be happy at the result, Mrs Wilson. And I am more than happy.'

Staring up, Emily tugged at her mother's arm. 'Are these the ones your dada did, Mummy?'

'Yes, I told you we were coming to see them, didn't I, Emily?'

Emily nodded, still looking up at the pictures. 'They are all very pretty . . . Will you teach me how to do it, Mummy?'

Abigail slipped her arm around Emily's waist. 'Perhaps I will, one day,' she said.

Gladys Matthews spoke. 'They look quite wonderful set up like this, don't they, Abigail? You must feel very proud of your father.'

'I didn't realise we had such talent living under our roof,' Eileen said, nudging Abigail. 'Like father, like daughter.'

Carrie had been silent all this time as she'd studied the pictures and the caption beneath each one. 'They make me want to cry, Abigail,' she said, 'because it is so sad when you think what your father was going through when he did these.' Carrie blew her nose. 'All those young soldiers should have our undying gratitude for what they did on our behalf during that deadly war.'

Maurice Stone nodded. 'My feelings exactly, Carrie,' he said. 'And these pictures are a testament to that time and to the bravery of the artist and his comrades. I doubt I shall ever exhibit such exceptionally touching things again.'

And later in bed that night, with Emily sleeping peacefully beside her, Abigail whispered silently, 'I promised myself that everyone should know how clever and kind and thoughtful you were, Dada, and I've done it. Another of my wildest dreams has come true.'

The rest of 1942 was passing uneventfully for the country and for the three girls who had all resumed their places of employment. But one day when she was alone downstairs in the bookshop, Abigail came to a definite decision. She had been thinking about it – worrying about it – for a long time, because she knew that their present situation could not go on for ever, and that she and Emily must think about leaving number six. There had to come a time when they moved on – and out. Though Emily would certainly not be happy . . .

One of the newer reasons for leaving was that it was obvious that Eileen and Simon Hill had formed quite a relationship since the party in June. They were constantly exchanging letters, and Eileen's rush to pick up the mail each morning spoke volumes. Abigail had teased her about it.

'I think we are going to hear about another engagement one day soon,' she'd said, and Eileen had hushed her up.

'Don't be daft, Abigail. It's not like that . . . but Simon does write interesting letters.'

'I'm sure he does!' Abigail had replied. 'He certainly seems very interested in you!'

And it was true. Abigail had noticed it at the party. Simon had singled Eileen out straightaway, and after supper they'd spent most of the evening outside in the garden, deep in conversation.

But it opened out the worry in Abigail's mind. Surely there would come the day when Eileen would want to be married – if not to Simon, then to someone else – and at least in the beginning they would live together at number six. There would hardly be room for Abigail and Emily to still be there in residence.

But that consideration was little compared to the thing that had begun to give Abigail sleepless nights.

It was that when they moved out would be the time when she would at last somehow find the courage to admit all her deceit to her friends. She could not bear the burden of the lies she had told to go on weighing her down. And moving out would be the time, the only time, when she could break the news. Because when they were told, they would be appalled, Abigail knew it. They would want to know why she hadn't told them before, why she had felt the need to keep her secret for so long . . .

But she would have to find the right moment, the exact little window of opportunity, when she could try to explain. To try to make them understand. But timing was everything, and when *was* the right time? The time when it would upset Emily the least, and Mrs Matthews for that matter. The bond between the two had become as close as that of any blood relatives.

It was the end of the half-term holiday in October and the girls were going to take Emily to Caroline's Cake Shop in Black Boy Hill for afternoon tea (with Gladys Matthews insisting it was to be her treat). They could have gone to Janet's but decided that as this was the last holiday before Christmas, they'd choose something a bit different. Eileen's mother had decided not to go with them, saying that after the dinner they'd just had she couldn't possibly eat another thing until tomorrow.

Much later that evening when Emily had gone to bed and Abigail, Eileen and Carrie were with Gladys Matthews in her room chatting about their outing, Eileen said, 'You must come with us to Caroline's next time, Mother. It is so pleasant there, and her cakes are something different. I don't know how she finds all the ingredients.'

Gladys Matthews smiled. 'Well, I'm glad you enjoyed it.' After a moment's pause, she added, 'Oh – I nearly forgot, Eileen – something came for you after you'd all gone. The second post was late today. It's there on the mantelpiece.'

'Oh?' Eileen said, immediately standing up to pick up the small package. Then she smiled. 'It's from Simon – there's no mistaking his bold handwriting,' she said.

'Well – what is it?' Carrie said. 'Go on, we're all full of curiosity!'

Eileen shrugged nonchalantly. 'Oh, I'll open it later,' she said, but Abigail had seen the warm flush that had swept over Eileen's cheeks. There wasn't much doubt that she was falling in love with the handsome Simon Hill.

'I thought Simon was an extremely nice young man,' Gladys Matthews said casually. 'There was no need for him to have helped us all into the taxi after the party, was there. In fact,' Eileen's mother went on, 'he reminds me quite a lot of Mark, which I suppose isn't surprising seeing that they live and work together. Still, a little masculine charm from a good-looking man is always acceptable.'

Abigail shot a glance at Gladys Matthews. That was quite an unusual comment to come from Eileen's mother, and it proved one thing. She too had really taken to Mark's best man.

It was nine-thirty and Carrie yawned briefly. 'I ought to be going,' she said, and Abigail suddenly realised that this was the moment she knew she'd been waiting for. Clearing her throat, she said, 'Look – I've been meaning to talk to all of you about something important—' But Eileen interrupted.

'Oh goodness me,' she said teasingly, 'what can this be all about?'

Abigail spoke up quickly, trying not to let her words come out in a rush. 'It's that I think the time is coming when Emily and I should move out and find our feet elsewhere,' she said. 'We have been – we are – so comfortable and happy living at number six but we've taken advantage of your kindness for too long. I've been looking in at Clark's, and other agents, to see if there is accommodation which we might find acceptable. There are one or two possibilities but I wanted to talk to you about it before I take any action.'

In the silence that followed, the drop of a pin could be heard. Then

Eileen said, 'What in heaven's name has brought this on, Abigail? Don't you like the food – or is the bed not comfortable enough?'

Gladys Matthews broke in. 'Wait a minute, Eileen,' she said. 'Perhaps Abigail feels the need to break away and live her own life without having to mingle in with ours. We do not own each other,' she added, 'and if Abigail really feels the need to be somewhere else then we must respect that.'

Eileen sat back. 'Well, I don't get it,' she said. 'It has worked so perfectly all this time for all of us. What's changed, Abigail? We need to be told that, surely.'

Abigail steeled herself for the moment she'd been dreading. Her guilt had become too much to bear, and taking a deep breath, she spoke calmly.

'I have told you a great deal about my early life,' she said, 'but not all of it. And now I want you to know everything, because you are the best, the dearest, indeed the only friends I have ever had. And when you know it all you will never want to speak to me again. You will want me out of your house, and that is why I think it better for Emily and me to go soon.'

There was a long pause, then Gladys Matthews said quietly, 'We are listening, Abigail.'

Abigail swallowed before going on. 'Much of what you already know is the truth – Luke *is* Emily's father – and he was the only friend I had. I have never known any other man and never will again. I loved him dearly and will go on doing so for the rest of my days. In my heart and in my soul he is my husband, though not by word, because we never married. We were both very young. I was trapped at Coopers, and I have no idea where Luke is now . . .' Abigail paused. 'He never knew that I was going to have Emily, he and his family had moved away before I could tell him.'

Now the silence in the room was even more painful as, palefaced, Abigail went on. 'It was Luke who always impressed on me to escape from Coopers. He told me to have the courage to live my own life, and that I've managed to do by the saving grace of the friends I never thought I would ever have.' Abigail attempted a brave smile at the group listening. 'But . . . as soon as we arrived in Bristol, I realised what awaited me -- me and Emily. The hateful, dangerous attitude of strangers who judged me as disgusting – because I'd had a child without a wedding ring on my finger. And I also soon realised that, for some men, and for the same reason, I would be "easy" company.'

Abigail's shoulders drooped for a moment. 'My aunt had been right all along. She said I was a disgrace, an evil person, and that Emily was a "bastard child" and that God would never forgive me.' Abigail shuddered, and after a few moments went on, 'But then, I thought there *was* one way out of this. I must pretend to be married. And as if fate had decided it, I found this curtain ring – this pathetic "wedding ring" lying on the toilet floor of Temple Meads.

'Wearing it made me respectable at last.' Abigail bit her lip hard. 'But it also made me a liar and I have hated myself for that. And for deceiving *you*, you of all people, but dishonesty is a terrible trap. Once you've started telling lies, there's no going back. The way out becomes harder and harder . . . I beg you to try and understand, if not to forgive me.'

Abigail did not dare look at Gladys Matthews. Eileen's mother was a lady of high principles, and as a teacher she would have taught her little pupils the difference between right and wrong. That telling lies was wrong.

Carrie was the first to break the painful silence. 'And Emily . . . where was Emily born? I mean, how exactly did you cope alone, Abigail?'

'Emily was born at Coopers with just my aunt there,' Abigail replied slowly. 'No doctor or midwife because my sin had to be kept a secret, from everyone. No one could ever know that an illegitimate child existed at Coopers.'

Carrie moved across to put her arms around Abigail. 'Well, I can only speak for myself, Abigail,' she said softly, 'but I understand your position perfectly. And I will always be your friend, I promise you that.'

Eileen dabbed at her eyes, and blew her nose. 'Carrie has said it all, Abigail. What you have told us changes nothing.'

Gladys Matthews had been deep in thought as she'd listened. Then, before saying anything, she bent to open the bottom drawer of the little table beside her, and took out the small tin which held her spare buttons. Opening it, and with her head bent, she searched for a second or two before holding up something for the others to see.

'I too have a curtain ring very similar to yours, Abigail,' she said quietly, 'and I needed it for the same reason. It fitted my finger perfectly at the time,' she added.

Eileen leaned forward, frowning. 'What do you mean, Mother . . . why did *you* ever need to wear a curtain ring?'

'Because, well, I was young and foolish,' Gladys Matthews said. 'I met my young man at college – though we weren't studying the same course. And we fell in love with each other straightaway.' She paused. 'When these things happen, you just know it, and I was convinced that he was the only one I wanted to be with. But when my parents realised how close we'd become, they were adamant that he was not good enough for me – they were terrible snobs,' she added, 'and didn't approve of his family, insisting that they weren't "like us", that you cannot mix oil with water, and that we must end the relationship at once.'

Gladys Matthews heaved a sigh. 'It was such a long time ago now,' she said, 'but I will never forget it, or how desperate I felt. I could never go against my parents because I was all they had, and they'd given me a good upbringing. I'd wanted for nothing – so long as I toed the family line.'

Abigail, entranced, now, at the unfolding story, touched Gladys Matthews' arm gently. 'So – the curtain ring?' she enquired. 'When did you wear it?'

Eileen's mother closed her eyes for a second. 'I made up my

mind that I would tell my parents there was a special college event which I simply had to attend – it was to be in Hereford and would last a week. They never even queried it,' Gladys said. Then, 'Of course there was nothing of the sort. My young man and I were going to have a holiday together . . . as man and wife. It was to be a farewell to our relationship, because I knew we'd never get married. We were going to a small hotel and he booked our train for first thing on the Saturday morning.'

Carrie spoke up quietly. 'So, you wore your "wedding ring" all the time you were away?' she asked.

Gladys Matthews shook her head. 'No, in the end I never actually put it on, Carrie, because during that night my father had a stroke – from which he never recovered. It was completely out of the blue because he was never ill, but he didn't live to speak another word. And of course my mother was grief-stricken, lost and alone.'

There was complete silence for a few moments. 'So, what could I do?' Gladys went on. 'One thing was certain and that was there was to be no holiday romance for me after all. And I devoted my life to my mother for the next four – and final – years of her life.'

Eileen leaned her head against her mother's shoulder for a moment. 'That is such a sad story, Mother,' she said softly, 'but why have you never told me about it before? Why have you kept it a secret?'

'Because I would have had to admit to the lie I'd been prepared to tell. That I had bought a fake wedding ring – and anyway, I couldn't see what good it would be to tell you, because as it turned out, it didn't matter in the end.'

Still close to her mother, Eileen said, 'Did you ever see him again – the young man that you were so in love with?'

Gladys Matthews smiled. 'Oh yes! Of course I did! Because that young man was your father, Eileen. It just meant that we had to wait a little longer for our dreams to come true, that's all.' She turned to Abigail. 'So you see, Abigail, many of us – perhaps most of us – have told lies of one kind or another. And there are white lies, and black lies. Black lies are those which are meant to hurt, damage or destroy others, but white lies are nothing of the sort. The only person you have hurt by evading the truth as you felt forced to do, is you, yourself, Abigail. You have had to bear the burden alone, all these years, but it is immaterial to the rest of us. We love you, and you and Emily have become an important part of our lives. And what you have told us changes nothing. So – when you feel the time is appropriate, slip that ring from your finger and I will put it here in the tin with mine,' she said gently.

Abigail almost wept with relief at the words she was hearing. 'So – is it all right for us to stay? I mean, you are not ashamed of me?' she asked hesitantly.

'No more ashamed of you than I am of myself,' Gladys Matthews said.

Chapter 32

December 1942, as most of the months of that year had been, was mercifully free from aerial warfare over the city and, as Christmas approached, preparations for the festive season went on as usual. Homes were decorated and fir trees brought in and there was still just enough food in the shops so that everyone could have their Christmas dinner.

To Emily's great delight, school had gone on uninterrupted and on the last day of the term – exactly one week before Christmas Day – Mrs Matthews paused at the gates with other adults exchanging pleasantries about the festive season, and the hope that the New Year would bring good news about the war. Then, all the children came running out excitedly, carrying small presents and bags of sweets they'd been given, and wearing handmade crowns decorated with silver stars. All smiles, Emily ran up to Mrs Matthews.

'Look what I was given from under the Christmas tree, Mrs Gladys!' Emily said, 'You can share all this with me in a minute.'

Gladys Matthews put her arm around Emily's shoulder. 'Thank you, Emily,' she said taking Emily's little canvas satchel, which she'd recently been taking to school, and placing it in the push-chair along with her own handbag and umbrella, and the four apples she'd bought on her way up earlier.

'It's a good thing Mummy bought this pushchair, isn't it, Emily?' Mrs Matthews said as they turned to leave the gate. 'Because just look what it can hold – even if it doesn't hold *you* anymore!'

Emily giggled. 'I would look *very* silly sitting in it now,' she said.

'Of course you would – but see how useful it is for me to hold on to. Now, are you going to keep your crown on or would you like to sit it on the top of all the rest?'

'No, I'll keep it on,' Emily said, 'because that's what everyone else is doing.'

Just then, someone tapped Gladys Matthews on the shoulder.

'Excuse me,' the woman said. 'My name is Helen Andrews and my little girl Jennifer is in the same class as Emily. And I was wondering if I could help you by collecting Emily each afternoon and dropping her off at home.' She smiled. 'I see you need to use a stick which must be quite a nuisance.'

'Oh, that's very kind of you,' Gladys Matthews began, and the woman went on quickly.

'It would be no trouble for me to make sure that Emily got home safely each day . . . you see, I often walk behind you. You live in West Road, don't you, and we live in Tennis Court Road which is just off your end of Broad Walk. So we're just a few minutes away from each other.'

This was an unexpected act of kindness and Gladys Matthews hesitated for a moment. 'I am not related to Emily,' she began, and the woman raised her eyes.

'Oh, I imagined that you must be Emily's grandmother,' she said. 'She certainly loves you very much!'

Gladys Matthews smiled. 'Yes, and I love her very much too – but the fact is she and her mother are staying with us until further notice. As Emily's mother works in the afternoons it is my happy duty to collect her daughter each day.'

Helen Andrews nodded. 'Emily's mother and I haven't actually introduced ourselves,' she said, 'but we smile at each other at the school gates in the mornings.' The woman paused. 'So please do tell her what I have suggested, because I would be very happy to collect her little girl each day.'

By now, Emily and Jennifer had started comparing what they had left in their bag of sweets, and Emily looked up, tugging Gladys Matthews' arm.

'Jennifer is my friend, Mrs Gladys,' she said, 'but she's better at sewing than me, aren't you, Jennifer?'

Jennifer, unable to speak because her mouth was crammed full of Smarties, merely nodded as she continued to practise hopping on one foot.

'I may very well be taking you up on your kind offer, Mrs Andrews,' Gladys Matthews said. 'I will tell Abigail – Abigail Wilson – what you've suggested, so shall we speak again next term when school begins again?'

April 1943

Abigail sat on the edge of the bed, watching Emily get herself ready to go out. It was Saturday, and this was to be a delayed celebration of Emily's sixth birthday because, during the early weeks of January and February, she, and nearly all the class, had picked up a flu-type infection which simply would not go away. So it had been decided that when they were both properly better, Emily and Jennifer would go somewhere, just the two of them, instead of having the usual birthday party.

'Birthday parties and playing games are a bit *babyish*,' Emily had said one day when the subject was being discussed. 'And everyone at school has been talking about the film with Tommy Handley – it's called *Time Flies* and it's on at the Odeon. They say it's really funny.'

'Of *course* parties and playing "oranges and lemons" are babyish,' Eileen had said at once, and Carrie had agreed.

'I think it would be really nice for you to go to the cinema

Emily,' Carrie had said. 'And I'll tell you what . . . I will treat you and Jennifer to afternoon tea at The Berkeley first! How does that sound?'

Now, after putting on her skirt and jumper, Emily started brushing out her hair and Abigail smiled briefly. 'When are you going to let me cut those curls a bit, Emily?' she asked. 'Your hair is getting so long!'

It was true. Emily's shining, dark-bronze ringlets were nearly down to her waist, but Abigail wasn't going to say any more because it was hard not to admire her daughter's appearance. Emily was no longer her little girl, and was unconsciously adopting a more grown-up manner.

Abigail glanced at her watch. 'It's almost time for Mr Andrews to call and take you to The Berkeley,' she said. 'It was kind of him to offer to do that, wasn't it, and to pick you up and bring you home after the pictures.'

Emily paused before answering. 'Mr Andrews is nice,' she said thoughtfully. 'I think he must be a lovely daddy.'

There was a moment's silence before Emily went on. 'Jennifer said her daddy works for the War Office and that's why he's only home at weekends. And she asked me where my daddy worked and I said I didn't know, but that he'd had to go away for a long time and that's why we never see him.'

Emily turned to look straight at her mother. 'But it doesn't matter, does it, Mummy? That we don't see my daddy? Because Mrs Gladys says some things just can't be helped, and that's all there is to it.'

Abigail's stomach dropped as she listened. If only she could tell Emily about her own daddy . . . and how much he would adore her if he was here.

Emily turned back to the mirror to finish brushing her hair. 'It was all right for me to ask little David to come with us as well, wasn't it, Mummy? He looked so envious when he knew what

Jennifer and I were going to do, I just knew I couldn't leave him out. And when I told Carrie, she said there was a lovely little table for three in the corner of the restaurant.'

'It was perfectly all right to include Jennifer's little brother,' Abigail said. 'It was a kind thing to do.'

After seeing Emily off in the Andrews' car, Abigail went back upstairs. At six years old, her daughter had got to the stage where she didn't particularly enjoy tidying up and now, as usual, there were things to put away.

Abigail gazed out of the window, briefly admitting to a sense of depression. And she knew why. It was Emily talking about her daddy. The daddy she had never seen, the daddy who never knew his daughter existed.

Tears filled Abigail's eyes. Luke . . . *Oh Luke. If only I could see you, talk to you, just for an hour. If only I could feel your arms holding me . . , something I dream about all the time . . .*

And if only I could put right the wrong which remains a terrible weight on my conscience. Because in the eyes of the world, Luke, our little daughter is anonymous, she is nobody. She has no birth certificate, no official document, there was no christening. Because my aunt could not bear the shame of an illegitimate child being born under her roof.

But one day . . . one day . . .

Then Abigail put away her hanky and began dusting the dressing table. They had been so *lucky*, she and Emily, lucky to be alive. After all, despite all those bombs falling on Bristol, they had escaped unharmed and there was little talk of future raids to come. The war was being waged much further afield, and local talk now was more about shortages and rationing and the general inconvenience of living in a damaged city.

And Emily? From the first moment that she and Eileen's mother had set eyes on each other, her life seemed so full of hope. And now she was doing well at all her lessons – in fact, just before the Easter holidays, Miss Townsend had spoken to Abigail about Emily's progress. 'Your daughter is very quick to understand and to remember,' Miss Townsend had said, 'and seems to love being challenged. As does Jennifer Andrews who sits next to Emily and who seems to be just as eager to come top in all the tests. The two of them are such good friends – like confident sparring partners competing with each other all the time, which can be a very good thing.'

And the more Abigail thought about it, so many pieces of good luck had fallen their way.

Abigail instinctively glanced over at the holdall containing her precious belongings. After the exhibition had ended, her father's paintings had been returned and they were here, safely with her again. And that should be encouraging her to do some more of her own, shouldn't it?

She stood up, angry at herself for feeling dispirited. Of *course* she was going to do more drawing and colouring. Maybe she'd start again tomorrow.

Chapter 33

For the three war girls, memories of their time at the Royal Ordnance Factory would stay with them for the rest of their lives, but now that they were back at their jobs in the city, it was surprising how soon the comparative monotony of each day filled most of their thoughts. And the fact that the war at home was very quiet added to the feeling that they were now in a kind of backwater.

But for Carrie, her preoccupation was in constantly wondering where Mark was and whether he was safe. Very little news came her way despite the fact that she did receive the occasional letter. But it was obvious that the war was not over yet. And Eileen, too, shared Carrie's anxiety, because she did not hear from Simon as frequently anymore.

As for Gladys Matthews, since September she'd started working at the school just two afternoons a week, Tuesdays and Thursdays, teaching the Infants' class. Emily had been thrilled that Mrs Gladys was going to be there on those days but, as she was very much a junior pupil, she only saw Eileen's mother when they went home together at the end of the day. And it had been generally agreed that if Mrs Matthews found it too much, there'd be no hard feelings should she decide to end the experiment.

It was the last Friday in October, and at the end of the day Eileen, Abigail and Carrie were walking home from the bus stop, arms linked as usual. Eileen turned to the others.

'What shall we do tonight?' she enquired. 'Anyone got any bright ideas?'

'I've got a bright idea,' Abigail said promptly. 'Why don't you two go out by yourselves for once, like you always used to, without me trailing around after you?'

'You do not "trail around after us", Abigail Wilson,' Carrie said. 'It's not like that at all – and never has been.'

'I suppose what I'm really saying,' Abigail went on, 'is that, at the moment, I don't want to spend a Friday evening without Emily. Now that she's at school I don't see so much of her, obviously, and I'm sometimes late home from Janet's . . . But you two are so good about including Emily in as much as you can, and I sometimes feel guilty that sometimes she is in the way and that, between us, we might have been spoiling your fun. The fun you two had together before we came on the scene, I mean.' She glanced up. 'I know that sometimes you used to have supper at The Royal Hotel on a Friday night. Why don't you do that today and leave me to entertain my daughter – and give Mrs Matthews a break! The poor woman must be tired out answering Emily's incessant questions whenever they're together.'

Eileen tucked her arm more firmly into Abigail's. 'You don't need to worry about my mother, Abigail. She hasn't been in such good shape for ages – now that she's a part-time working girl! And I know that she's never happier than when Emily's with her.' Eileen shrugged. 'It's true that Carrie and I used to occasionally do something special on Fridays if we felt like it, but that was a long time ago and we don't even discuss it anymore – do we, Carrie? And certainly not since we discovered Scrabble! Do you realise how competitive we've become, the three of us or should I say the four of us! One of these days I think it may even come to blows!'

Suddenly, glancing up at the others, Abigail said, 'Do you ever think much about the factory?'

'Not more than I can help,' Eileen said stoutly. 'If I do, that vile smell actually seems to fill my nostrils.'

Carrie agreed. 'Yes, it's funny how you can actually recall something as ghastly as that, isn't it?' she said. 'And – although I don't often think back to that time – I did find myself wondering if Daisy and Margaret are still there. Do you think they are?'

'Probably,' Eileen said, 'because I expect they need the money.' She paused. 'I imagine that when Daisy considers they've had enough, they'll both leave.'

Carrie shuddered briefly. 'I will never, ever, forget hearing that poor girl screaming when she was nearly drowned in TNT! I dreamt about it for nights afterwards.'

They arrived at number six and Eileen moved forward to open the door. 'Come on,' she said, 'don't let's be maudlin – it's Friday night!'

Hearing them come in, Emily ran straight up to greet them. Hugging her mother around the waist she said, 'Supper is ready, and I laid the table . . . and are we going to play Scrabble tonight? Because I won last time, didn't I?'

Eileen smiled at the others. 'I think the decision has been made,' she said.

Christmas 1943 was the fifth festive season the world had celebrated since the beginning of the war and, as usual, people were able to buy enough to make sure that there was sufficient food on the table, despite the rationing. It was sometimes a question of 'making do', but for many weeks before Christmas Day everyone had saved a little of their rather meagre supply to ensure there were one or two treats on the table. And, as ever, Christmas trees twinkled in most houses.

Eileen seemed to know which of the places still had any stock of toys and gifts and often in her lunch time she'd gone over to

Bedminster, or up the Gloucester Road, where the smaller shops were, coming back with one or two more things so that Emily had another full stocking to open on Christmas morning and all the adults had something to open as well. And for weeks everyone had saved their sweet ration for Emily. So as they'd sat around the table on the 25th it was possible to push all thoughts of war to the back of the mind. And at Morning Service in church – which everyone at number six apart from Mrs Matthews had attended – Jonathan Waters had invigorated his full congregation with optimism and hope.

'We must give thanks that the country – and certainly our city – has not received any attention from Hitler's bombers all the year,' he'd said. 'And at this time of miracles, we go on hoping and praying for another one. The miracle of peace in the world, and the safe return of our courageous men, wherever they are. And be reassured,' the priest had said, 'right will win the day. Don't doubt it for a single moment.'

Later in the afternoon Carrie had joined them at number six, and they'd all played games and danced the palais glide in the kitchen and had had cold chicken sandwiches afterwards.

And as Abigail had finally tucked her daughter between the sheets, she'd said, 'That was a lovely Christmas Day, wasn't it, Emily? And you've had some nice presents, haven't you? And in exactly one week's time, Emily Grace Wilson is going to be seven years old!'

Emily had nodded happily. 'Yep,' she'd said, 'and I'm having a little party, aren't I, and Jennifer and little David are coming. But . . .' Emily had made a face. 'I wish we didn't have two whole weeks' holiday from school, Mummy, because I *love* school and it'll be a long time before I see all my other friends.'

Abigail hadn't gone downstairs straightaway, but had stayed there, watching Emily until she had fallen asleep – which hadn't been long.

Oh, Luke, if only you were here with us, if only you could see your little girl, so content and so happy. And so beautiful. You would be proud of her, Luke, as I am, because she has been with me all the way on the massive journey we've taken. The journey I promised you I would make. And do you still love me, Luke, as you always said you would? Do you love me as much as I will always love you?

Chapter 34

April 1944

The weather that Saturday was cold and dry – as most of the year had been – but glancing from the bedroom window Abigail could just see a small shaft of sunshine coming through the clouds.

She turned away, wondering what to do next. Emily had been invited to have tea with the Andrews family and wouldn't be home until later, so Abigail had time for herself. But for some reason she didn't feel like doing any of her artwork – sometimes she just had to be in the mood and today she wasn't.

Instead, she would go downstairs, and start preparing the vegetables for tomorrow's Sunday roast. And she'd make a bread and butter pudding if they had enough of everything. She would have the kitchen to herself because Eileen had gone to the local shops for a few things they'd forgotten, and Mrs Matthews was in her sitting room having a rest.

Abigail had only just finished peeling the potatoes when the kitchen door opened and Gladys Matthews appeared. Looking fresh after her little nap, she smiled at Abigail and went over to put the kettle on.

'Ah, I can see what you're doing, Abigail,' Eileen's mother said, 'so

I will make us a cup of tea.' She reached for the cups and saucers. 'Emily looked so pleased to be having tea with Jennifer, didn't she?'

'They do seem to love being together,' Abigail said as she covered the saucepan of peeled potatoes with cold water before starting to scrape the carrots. Then she sat down at the table with Mrs Matthews.

'Isn't it horrible that Carrie and Mark have seen so little of each other?' Abigail said. 'He had those two days off just after Christmas, but since then he's been back on duty and there's not a single mention of any more leave on the horizon. Nor for Simon, either, of course.'

Gladys Matthews smiled quickly. 'No, but the letter writing between him and my daughter goes on unabated! And I notice that she's always wearing that sweet locket he sent her. It was very kind of him.' Then, after a moment, she added, 'And is Janet still busy at the café?'

Abigail nodded. 'Well, let's just say she's always pleased to see me when I get down there each afternoon. Even though I'm not there quite so much because of the extra hours they asked me to do at Blackwell's.'

'Yes, it's lovely for you to be working there again, isn't it?' Eileen's mother said. 'You must have missed it when you were at that other place.'

'Especially as Blackwell's could easily have given my job to someone else,' Abigail said. 'But I slipped into it again so easily it was as if I'd never gone away.'

'I think that my daughter feels exactly the same way at The Royal,' Gladys Matthews said. 'She feels that after the flurry of interest on her return, she's being overworked and taken for granted as usual! But I can't see her sticking there for ever . . . And who knows what my daughter has got up her sleeve for the future.'

The two exchanged smiles, and Abigail said, 'Whatever it is, Eileen will succeed at it. She is always such a tower of strength. I think both Carrie and I relied on her at the factory.'

'If you were to say that to my daughter, she would insist that she was relying on you two,' Gladys Matthews said. 'So it must have been the perfect arrangement.'

Just then, Eileen returned with the shopping.

'Ah good, I see the tea has been made,' she said cheerfully, 'so I hope there's enough in the pot for me because I bring cakes! They're slightly strange things made of marshmallow, with hundreds and thousands on top. We might as well try them. Emily would certainly enjoy them, so we'll keep a couple for her. Oh, I nearly forgot.' Eileen reached into her shopping bag. 'Your *Evening Post*, Mother,' she said, plonking the newspaper in front of Mrs Matthews.

'Thank you, dear, I'll take it into my room where the reading lamp makes it easier for me to see the tiny print,' Eileen's mother said, getting up from her chair.

After she'd gone, Abigail said, 'Doesn't your mother look well, Eileen? She seems to look younger every time I see her.'

Eileen nodded. 'Yes, she's on good form again, thank heaven. And as you must be aware, Abigail, much of that is because of you two. Emily has given back my mother that part of her life which had disappeared. Not to mention her being asked to help out at the school of course – albeit gently. Doing what she always adored. When you said, last year, that you wanted to move out my heart sank.'

Eileen stood up to clear away the tea cups. 'Anyway, thank heaven that little matter has been resolved, I hope, once and for all! You and Emily are part of our household for as long as you want it.'

Just then the kitchen door opened, and Gladys Matthews appeared looking flustered. 'Oh, Abigail,' she said, 'there's something here in the paper which you should know about. Oh dear . . .'

Both girls came forward immediately. This sort of reaction to anything was not like Gladys Matthews.

'What is it, Mother?' Eileen said, taking the newspaper in her hands. 'What is it to do with Abigail?'

'Look at the last page but one,' Gladys Matthews said. 'The column with personal announcements. The one next to Births and Deaths.'

By now, Abigail's heart was racing. What on earth was this all about?

Eileen spread the paper out on the table and she and Abigail both peered at the column in question. And even before she'd finished reading it, Abigail's hand flew to her throat. 'Oh, oh no!'

The announcement was headed: Abigail Wilson.

'Would Abigail Wilson, believed to be living in Bristol and last heard of in 1939, return to her old home address as soon as possible to deal with a matter of major importance.'

After a few seconds of utter disbelief, Abigail stood up. 'Something must have happened,' she said shakily, 'because I never expected to see something like this in . . . in . . . a public newspaper. And it can only mean one thing. Trouble. My aunt must be ill or she must have had an accident.' Abigail put her hand over her mouth. 'I must get down there as soon as I can . . .'

The others could see that the message had really upset Abigail, and Eileen said lightly, 'Oh, I wouldn't worry, Abigail. It'll be something simple and anyway, everything always looks worse when you see it in print. I mean, if there was anything really serious going on – like death or destruction – there would be more formal information from solicitors.' Eileen just stopped herself from asking Abigail why she appeared to care. After all, from everything Abigail had told them, her aunt hadn't given much thought to her niece's finer feelings over the years.

Mrs Matthews intervened gently. 'Of course Abigail is worried, Eileen, and it's obvious that she must get there as soon as it can be arranged.'

Abigail stared at the paper again. 'The wording sounds exactly like my aunt – just enough but giving nothing away. Her miserly instinct. No, it must mean that something really bad has happened

289

and she'll expect us to go back permanently.' Abigail shuddered. 'That is never going to happen. Never!'

'But aren't you jumping the gun?' Eileen persisted. 'You don't know that it's about that, Abigail.'

'No, but I know my aunt. This is not a loving or polite request or an invitation, it's a command. So, I'll obey her, as usual. One last time.' She turned to Eileen.

'I'll go next Saturday. Would you like to come as well, Eileen? I'd like you to see Coopers after all I've said about it. And perhaps Carrie would agree to join us and have a day in the country.'

At nine o'clock the following Saturday morning, Abigail, Eileen and Carrie caught the train from Bristol Temple Meads, later to pick up the branch line, which would take them straight to the village.

It was a pleasant late-April morning and as they sat, looking out of the carriage window at the passing rolling fields, Abigail tried to stem her anxieties. She'd been on edge from the moment she'd read that newspaper, asking herself over and over again whatever was going on. And what was so vital that her aunt wanted her, Abigail, to be there? They'd parted company five whole years ago. And it was supposed to be forever. Her aunt knew that. So why had she gone to the trouble of advertising in a newspaper? The way it had been worded was deliberately evasive, which was just like Edna. 'Come and find out for yourself. I'm not letting on.'

So why not just ignore it? Why go at all? That was another question Abigail had asked herself. But as the train chugged closer and closer to their destination, she knew she was right to go. Because Dada would expect it of her. He would see it as her duty.

Presently, they pulled up at the branch line to find that their next train was already at the station, and almost at once, after the guard's loud whistle, and with a gush of noisy steam, the engine pulled away.

'I didn't say much to Emily about what we were doing,' Abigail said, 'because she would have wanted to come. But anyway, Mrs

Matthews arranging to take her and Jennifer to the museum, and later to have ice creams at Fortes stopped any further comment about our day! Especially as they were going each way by taxi!'

At twelve-thirty the train arrived, and as the girls left the station Abigail said, 'Welcome to our illustrious village. I can't offer you the interesting sights of Bristol, but' – she gestured ahead – 'there's the church over there, next to the school I attended. My sole source of education.'

'I think the school looks nice and very well kept, Abigail,' Carrie said.

'It was certainly very well run,' Abigail replied.

Then, all of a sudden Abigail felt her knees begin to tremble and her throat go dry. She hadn't realised that turning back the pages of her not altogether happy life, and actually being here again, would be so uncomfortable. So strange and painful. Memories that she'd hoped had been blotted out were still there, as clear as ever.

'*Witch's daughter! Don't let her catch you!*'

She swallowed hard. Well, she'd spared Emily from all that and had rescued her daughter from a life of petty and restrictive confinement. And Abigail didn't regret one moment of their uncertainties and difficulties, not even when they'd found themselves in the midst of the Bristol Blitz.

Eileen touched her arm. 'Are you all right, Abigail? You're looking really pale.'

Abigail felt cross at all her introspection, because it didn't help. This unusual day had only just begun and she still had to make her way to Coopers and confront her aunt. 'No, I'm fine, Eileen – I just need a drink and maybe something to eat, that's all. I believe the little café on the corner is quite good – not that I've ever tried it,' Abigail added.

Carrie came over and linked her arm in Abigail's. It didn't take much imagination to understand how Abigail must be feeling after all this time away. 'Yes, I'm ready for something too,' Carrie said. 'I wonder if that café does something on toast?'

Chapter 35

Later, after quite a nice meal of local river salmon and mashed potato, followed by a baked apple each with cream, the girls began walking away from the village. And Abigail said, 'I've been thinking. Would you mind if I leave you two just before we reach Coopers? I know somewhere nice for you to sit and take a rest while I go on to hear the bad news.'

The others immediately agreed, and Carrie said, 'Actually, I was going to suggest it, Abigail. It's obvious that your aunt seeing you with two complete strangers at this particular time, and considering how long you've been apart, wouldn't be appropriate.' Carrie smiled. 'But leave us within hearing distance so that we can arrive to save you if things get tricky!'

'Absolutely,' Eileen said. 'Just warn Aunt Edna about my left hook!'

Abigail smiled. 'Oh, it won't come to blows,' she said. 'But who knows? Whatever it is, I'm ready for it. Ready for *her*, I should say.'

Presently, they arrived at the place where the others could wait. A solid stile separating two small fields, out of sight of Coopers, but no more than a minute's walk away. 'Here you are,' Abigail aid as she mounted the two wide steps and climbed over. 'This quite a comfortable spot to sit – I did it myself many times ˑn I was younger and wanted to be alone.'

'Don't worry about us,' Eileen said. 'You just go and beard the lion.'

With strengthening step, Abigail walked the short distance to Coopers, her gaze taking in every inch of the familiar route. Tall trees and tangled bushes of wild rose and nettle and hawthorn and holly, all vying for space. And now she came to the widening area which led to the front of the cottage. There it was, the home where she and Emily had been born. There was no one about and she stood for a moment just staring, her throat dry, her heart racing. What was she going to find when she went up the short drive?

Coopers had never had a door knocker, and after three short raps with her fist, Abigail was rewarded by the sound of footsteps . . . the cautious opening of the door . . . and then Aunt Edna.

She was dressed in an ankle-length black skirt and loose, long-sleeved cream blouse, but with no sack apron, and her hair was shorter and with no bow. She spoke first.

'Hello, Abigail. I was wondering when you were going to turn up.'

Without thinking, Abigail went forward, placed her hands on her aunt's shoulders and kissed her on the cheek.

'Hello, Aunt. I've been very worried. Worried that you were ill, or that something dreadful had happened. To see that announcement in the paper was upsetting.'

Edna went over to put the kettle on. 'Well, how else could I contact you? I was never given your address.' The statement was straight, but not unfriendly, and Abigail said, 'I'm sorry, but I didn't think you'd be interested in where we were living.'

A pause and then, 'And how is Emily?'

Abigail almost gasped aloud. Her aunt had actually used her great-niece's name. Not 'it'!

'Emily is thriving, Aunt. She is doing well at school and has made lots of friends.' Realising that she was becoming tearful, Abigail went on quickly, 'Emily has gone to the Bristol Museum today with her two very best friends. She was *so* excited, especially as they're having ice creams afterwards and going home in a taxi.' Abigail paused. 'She is growing up so fast, Aunt, getting taller every day. You would not even recognise her now.'

The kettle had come to the boil, and presently, sitting opposite each other at the table, they started to sip their tea. Edna looked up. 'Weren't you affected by the bombing? You got it quite bad, didn't you?'

Abigail nodded slowly. 'We did, but by some miracle we escaped each raid, and Hitler doesn't seem that interested in us anymore.'

Why were they making small talk like this? What Abigail was desperate to know was why she'd been summoned to Coopers after all this time. She shrugged inwardly. At least it was obvious that her aunt was in good health. So the best thing was to let Edna take her time before coming out with it, whatever it was. She would enjoy doing that.

'You are looking very well, Abigail,' Edna said suddenly. 'Better than I imagined you might be after living in the city.'

Surprised again at her aunt's apparent interest, Abigail smiled. 'Thank you, Aunt. We're both fine and I assure you that sufficient food and fresh air are both available in Bristol.'

Moving the teapot over to refill their cups, Edna said, 'And what about work? What have you been doing to support yourselves?'

'I found employment in a bookshop and in a café fairly soon after our arrival,' Abigail replied. 'And my two special friends and I did war work in a factory for more than eighteen months. That was harder, but the pay was very generous, and I managed to save a lot.'

'Where did you meet your "special friends"?' Edna enquired somewhat tartly.

'Oh . . . in a café,' Abigail said, still confused. Had Edna *missed* them, after all? Had she found her young employees not up to standard? Or had she even been lonely without her niece and great-niece? The mystery was deepening!

'And you found accommodation easily?' Edna asked. 'Wasn't it difficult, with the bombing?'

'Ah, but we got to Bristol before all that began,' Abigail reminded her. 'And yes, after a while we found a lovely place to stay. We are still there.'

Edna stood up. 'I expect you'd like a sandwich,' she said. 'I didn't cook anything because I didn't know if and when you'd be arriving – but there's always bread and cheese and eggs . . .'

'No, thank you, Aunt,' Abigail said. 'We had some lunch at the café in the village.'

'Who do you mean by "we"?' Edna said, sitting down again.

'My two best friends made the trip with me today,' Abigail said. 'I would like you to meet them before we go back. They're sitting over on the stile at the moment. But I wanted to speak to you first. And to be told the reason why I'm here today.'

Edna sat back, looking straight at Abigail. 'There are a number of reasons,' she said, 'but the first one is that I want to apologise to you, Abigail.'

It was a good thing that Abigail was sitting down or she might have fallen down!

'*Apologise*, Aunt?' she said. 'But why?'

'Because I was often less than kind to you,' Edna said slowly. 'Inside, I hated myself for being bad tempered and miserable with you, but . . . I must try and explain.'

Edna picked up her almost empty cup and finished the last dregs before going on.

'When our parents – your grandparents – died, Arnold and I were just children. I was eleven and Arnold was nine and the only option for us was to go on doing all the work here by ourselves. We had nowhere else to go and nothing else to do but to keep Coopers going. And we'd had good training! But I'd always thought that Arnold would take over and that one day I would escape and seek my fortune somewhere else. I had a dream, Abigail, a dream about getting to the docks and finding a ship to take me as far away as possible. Anywhere, *anywhere* . . . but somewhere different! Somewhere exciting! I even thought I'd be a missionary and take the good Word to the unenlightened.'

Edna stopped for a moment before going on. 'When Arnold enlisted for the war, I was so cross with him. He was fifteen and when he was invalided out two years afterwards, his health had been ruined. I knew then that he'd never run this place without me. But then he married his girlfriend Sadie, and I thought they might run Coopers together. She was a strong lass.' Edna's eyes clouded briefly as she remembered. 'Within a year you came along, Abigail, and we were all living here together when, unbelievably, Sadie died from an infection. You were a week old.'

'Oh, Aunt,' Abigail murmured. 'It has been so hard for you.'

Edna nodded slowly. 'Yes, and I wasn't surprised when Arnold died when he did. The trenches killed him eventually,' she said.

After a minute, Edna cleared her throat. 'Anyway, years later, when you told me you were expecting, I knew that was it. The end of all my dreams. Because my time was running out. I was no longer young, and now there was another baby to feed and clothe.' Edna looked away for a second. 'But it was wrong of me to be cruel to you, Abigail, and I hope you will forgive me. And I hope God will forgive me too.'

The atmosphere was dense with remorse and there was complete silence before Edna sat back, raising her head.

'Anyway,' she said, 'enough of all that. Because I want to thank you for leading the way. You have given me the courage to do what *you* did. You just walked. You were brave enough to disentangle yourself and your tiny child from all this and have the faith to make your own way, and that is what I've decided to do.' Edna leaned forward. 'Now listen. This is what's going to happen, and it concerns you, Abigail. That's why we need to talk.'

Feeling as if she was going to wake up in a minute from an unbelievable dream, Abigail just sat and listened as her aunt began to explain.

'I realised that if I was ever to follow my dream I must soon make plans.' Edna fixed her gaze into Abigail's widening eyes. 'And the first one was to arrange for Coopers to be entirely run by others. I've employed various lads of course, but one day last year when I suddenly found myself with no help at all, a young couple who'd recently moved to the area knocked on the door, asking for work. The very time when I was struck down with flu,' she added.

Abigail was incredulous. Her aunt had never been ill in her life!

'Anyway,' Edna went on, 'I had no alternative but to try them and they've been more than satisfactory.' She made a face. 'I couldn't get out of bed for three whole days, Abigail and had to leave them to it. And they proved that Coopers can survive very well without me. Anyway, I consulted agents and solicitors in the village who advised me to lease Coopers out to this couple as sitting tenants. They will live here rent-free while carrying it on as a working business and will be paid a salary as well as keeping part of the profits.' Edna paused, clearly excited at her own words. 'But I didn't want to sell Coopers, Abigail. This place has been in the family for too long. Doing this means it will always be there should we want to return one day in the future. The couple – Mr and Mrs Moor – are really happy with everything and we've agreed on a lease, five years to start with, which can be extended if we, and they, wish it.'

Edna sat back, her eyes alight with enthusiasm. 'So – it's important for me to know whether you agree to this arrangement, Abigail.'

Abigail tried to find her voice – which eventually came out as a croak. 'But why does it concern me, Aunt?' she said.

'Because Coopers is half yours, of course,' Edna said, sounding slightly irritated. 'It was left to Arnold and me, and you succeed him. And when this all goes ahead, you will receive your share of the profits and your name will be on all the documents.' She paused. 'And if in years to come we do sell Coopers, the money from the sale would be shared equally between us. This has all been set up properly. All that's needed now is your signature on the Terms of Agreement.'

With her mind reeling at this unbelievable information, Abigail said, 'Aunt, I am so happy that you're taking this step and I think it's the perfect solution. It's nice to think that we will be giving a home and employment to others who will look after Coopers for us, while it still gives us some income.' Abigail leaned over and grasped her aunt's hands which were resting on the table. 'But above all that, Aunt,' Abigail said, 'it will free you up to follow your lifelong dream. And I couldn't be happier for you.' She paused. 'Have you any idea where you might be going?'

Edna smiled. 'Not really, but first I had to find out how *you* faced up to everything, Abigail. From all you've told me today it convinces me that if you managed it, with a small child and during a war – then so can I!'

Abigail felt like jumping up on to the table and doing a jig. All this was like a fairy tale – Aunt Edna seemed to be someone Abigail could barely recognise. Her aunt was ready to fly!

'Now, as I said,' Edna went on, 'the next thing is that you must soon return to sign all the papers. The solicitors' branch office in the village only opens on Tuesdays and Thursdays, and they've said that one of those days later in June would be suitable for them.' Edna pushed her chair back to open a drawer in the table, and she handed Abigail an envelope. 'This is the address and telephone number of Gibbons and Drew, so get in touch soon to make the appointment, Abigail.'

Edna went across to the cupboard and took down a bottle and two glasses which she put on the table. 'Not elderflower cordial today, Abigail. This is my special dandelion wine and it's a good one. Well, we've got something to celebrate, haven't we?' She poured the wine and looked up. 'And thank you for agreeing to this plan. Because if you'd objected, it couldn't go ahead, and I'd have had to stay at Coopers probably until the end of my days.'

They both drank, the strength of the wine immediately going to Abigail's head, and she glanced at Edna. 'If I can manage to stand up after this, Aunt, can I go and fetch my two friends? I'd love you to meet them. And they would love to see Coopers.'

Edna drained her glass and stood up a little shakily. 'Yes of course, Abigail. What did you say their names were?'

Chapter 36

At eight-thirty that evening, the girls arrived back at home to find Emily and Mrs Matthews waiting for them. And as soon as they opened the kitchen door, Emily rushed over and threw herself into her mother's arms.

'Mummy! We've had *such* a lovely day. Will you come with us to the museum next time? You'll never believe what we've seen!'

Mrs Matthews intervened. 'Emily – give Mummy the chance to catch her breath! We'll tell her everything in a minute. But first we'd like to know how she and Eileen and Carrie have got on. They've had a long day too.' Eileen's mother went over to put the kettle on. 'But perhaps a cup of tea would be a good idea.'

Gladys Matthews glanced at each of them in turn, trying to detect any sign of bad news from Coopers, but they all looked as if they'd just had a thoroughly lovely day out.

Abigail disentangled herself from Emily, then everyone sat around the table to have tea and biscuits.

'My worst fears came to nothing, Mrs Matthews,' Abigail said. 'In fact, I found my aunt in the best of health and in the best of spirits. Because she is about to make a huge change to her life. And quite honestly, I am only just beginning to believe it.'

'Yes, and Carrie and I met the lady and found her to be rather pleasant,' Eileen said. 'We were given a glass of her very own dandelion wine' – Eileen rolled her eyes – 'which certainly put a spring in our step as we walked back to the station.'

Emily helped herself to another biscuit. 'So where *did* you go today, Mummy?'

'To Coopers,' Abigail replied. 'Do you remember when we lived at the cottage?'

Emily thought for a second. 'I think so,' she said. 'Where I always collected the eggs? But why didn't I come with you?'

Suddenly, Eileen said, 'I'm hungry! Let's buy fish and chips for supper. Would you like that, Emily?'

'Yes!' Emily exclaimed. 'I'll lay the table. But no vinegar for Mrs Gladys and me.'

Enjoying their milky drinks much later in Gladys Matthews' room, Eileen sat with her mother trying to fill in all the details as to why Abigail had been summoned to Coopers.

'Abigail was quite right about the place, Mother. It's a tiny cottage standing in what looked like a huge amount of land – not that we were shown around, we just sat in the kitchen and made small talk with Aunt Edna.' Eileen paused. 'She seems slightly weird but quite nice and, as Abigail explained, Coopers is about to be run by others so that the old girl can go off and do other things.'

Gladys Matthews nodded. 'That seems fair to me after such a long time running the place. But I'm so relieved that there was nothing worse to hear . . . I've been thinking about it all day.'

'The thing is,' Eileen went on, 'Abigail was amazed that her aunt had bothered to contact her. Because if she hadn't, Abigail would never have known what was going on, nor that she had to be part of this arrangement *nor* that she was in line to receive substantial money! It has come as a complete shock, and she was going over and over it all coming home on the train, trying to make sense of it.'

'But what a wonderful end to the story,' Gladys Matthews said. 'Despite everything, old, hard feelings have disappeared and there's some financial security for Abigail and Emily. And they both deserve this, Eileen. What courage Abigail showed in doing what she did, and as a single mother, entirely alone.'

Eileen squeezed her mother's hand. 'And what luck they had in coming here, Mother – in meeting you, I mean. Because Emily wouldn't have blossomed as she has without your influence in her life.'

Gladys Matthews shrugged off the compliment. 'No, what luck that Emily fell out of her pushchair and that you and Carrie were there to pick her up! Lucky for them and lucky for me too,' Gladys Matthews added.

Eileen stood up, yawning. 'Gosh, I'm quite tired after all the excitement! And Abigail must be shattered – it's been a lot for her to take in. And she still has to return to the village to sign all the papers. She's already decided that she'll go on Thursday the 22nd of June – the solicitors specified June, and they're only there on Tuesdays and Thursdays. So she'll get the day off from Blackwell's, and Emily will have to miss school for once because Abigail wants her to go as well. As she said, once this is all sealed and settled, it could be a long time before either of them go to the village again.'

Eileen picked up their empty mugs. 'And you did say that you three had a lovely time today too, Mother? Emily certainly seemed to have enjoyed it – plus the ice creams!'

'They were so happy and good, the pair of them,' Gladys Matthews said. 'I've promised that we'll do it all again.' She smiled. 'And to conclude the event with Emily's favourite supper made the day!'

Eileen went over to the door. 'Oh, talking of food – don't

forget that we've all been invited to the vicarage for afternoon tea tomorrow. That includes you, Mother – so you will come, won't you?'

'I see no reason why not,' Gladys Matthews said. 'Though I have no idea where I'm getting all my appetite from!'

Chapter 37

22nd June 1944

It was one of the finest days in what had been a cool and unsettled month, and Abigail and Emily were standing on the platform at Temple Meads, waiting for their eight o'clock train.

'Do you remember being here before, Emily?' Abigail said.

Emily nodded. 'I think so,' she said. 'I remember all the noise and all the people.'

Abigail had decided that there was no need to take Emily to Coopers because Edna had offered to buy them all lunch at the café before going on to Gibbons and Drew together, so she would meet her great-niece then.

Suddenly, with a huge roar, their approaching train hissed its way into the station, eventually pulling up for them to get in. And as they found a carriage, Emily clambered on to the seat looking up at Abigail. 'I do *remember* this train!' she exclaimed.

Abigail smiled to herself, wondering just how much Emily did remember of her little past.

It was midday when they arrived at the village station and, as usual, Abigail felt her heart rate gather. Even though being here the other day with Eileen and Carrie had softened her feelings of anxiety, those feelings persisted. Not just about her school days, but about all the years without Dada, all the years when Edna had been so cruel. How had she survived that time? Abigail asked herself. It had been a long nightmare and although she'd managed to wake up and break out, the memories still lingered. And they wouldn't ever go. She was sure of it. Childhood memories must be like that, she thought. Indelible and unforgettable despite all the good things which may follow.

And added to all that, today was market day, the familiar sights and sounds of the street traders shouting their wares hitting Abigail hard. It was as if it was yesterday. Was that Edna screeching from the trap? *Fresh vegetables, new laid eggs, honey . . . best you can buy!* But Edna would not be doing that today. She had a more important appointment with the solicitors.

They crossed the road, Abigail holding Emily's hand tightly, and Emily said, 'What's going on over there, Mummy? There are crowds of people.'

'Yes, because it's market day. There are all sorts of things to buy, things to eat and some little craft stalls that sell homemade things, jewellery and purses and soft toys.'

'Oh – can we go there after we've had lunch?' Emily asked eagerly. 'I've never been to a market before.'

'If you like, later on,' Abigail said. 'But we're going to meet Aunt Edna at the café first, aren't we, like I told you. You said you thought you remembered Aunt Edna.'

'I *think* I do,' Emily said.

'And then we've got to go that office for me to sign things and after that we'll look around the market. All right?'

'All right,' Emily said, then, 'Where's the café?'

'Over there, look,' Abigail said, pointing. 'And we're just about to pass the school I went to, where I learned everything that you are learning at yours, Emily. And see, the children are just coming out into the playground because it's dinner time.'

'Yes, it'll be dinner time at ours now, as well,' Emily said, glancing back over her shoulder to keep looking as they went past. 'Did you like it at your school, Mummy?'

'Some of the time,' Abigail replied. 'Here's the café. And I expect Aunt Edna will be here waiting for us.' Abigail felt a warm rush of pleasure at her own words because she was going to love reintroducing her daughter to her aunt. And judging by recent events, Edna would surely be pleased to meet 'it' again.

The place was always crowded on market day, but as soon as they entered they saw Edna sitting at a table in the far corner. She immediately stood up and waved.

'Oh hello,' she said as they came towards her. 'Glad you made it. Was the train crowded?' She pulled out two chairs for them, then sat opposite and stared at Emily.

And for a moment, not a word was spoken. 'So, this is . . . this is Emily,' Edna said slowly, 'and she is a replica of you, Abigail – apart from the dark ringlets.'

Abigail nodded slowly. 'Yes, this is my daughter, Aunt. Do you remember Aunt Edna, Emily?'

Emily, straight-faced, murmured, 'I think I do.' Then, holding out her hand, she said gravely, 'How do you do?'.

Abigail smiled inwardly. Emily would have heard Mrs Matthews say that on a number of occasions. Edna took Emily's hand gently.

'I am very well, thank you,' she said. Then, briskly, 'Shall I order us some lunch? What would you like, Emily?'

Still finding it hard to grasp this situation – and above all her aunt's newfound attitude – Abigail hoped Emily would ask for something simple – like bread or cheese.

'I would like some chips, please,' Emily said.

After they'd eaten their lunch, it was time to leave for the two-thirty appointment. And as they stood up, Edna said, 'You are wearing a very pretty dress, Emily, but I seem to remember that you used to carry a little doll around in your pocket.'

Abigail felt yet another pang of astonishment! Fancy her aunt remembering that!

'Oh, I don't do *that* anymore,' Emily said. 'It would be very childish. Though I still have dolly but Mummy had to make her a new outfit because the other one had worn out.'

They left the café and began to walk slowly along the High Street towards the solicitors' office. Emily tugged her mother's arm.

'Can I go to the market now, Mummy? I've got some of my pocket money here in my purse, and I would like to buy Mrs Gladys a little present.'

'Good idea,' Abigail said at once. 'I shouldn't think the appointment will be a very long one, and afterwards I will come and find you, Emily. Don't wander off – just stay around the stalls.'

'Apparently,' Edna said, 'there's sometimes a Punch and Judy show when the kids come out at three-fifteen. Quite a new innovation for the village but I'm told they love it.'

Abigail raised her eyes. There'd been nothing as exciting as a Punch and Judy show in her day.

As hoped, the meeting was a fairly short one, with the solicitor going over everything while his secretary placed all the relevant papers on the desk for Abigail and Edna to countersign each document.

'I think Miss Edna Wilson has come to a very sensible decision,' Mr Gibbons declared. 'Now she can be relieved of all the responsibility she's had over the years, and the new tenants are a very respectable, hardworking couple.' He smiled broadly. 'And I'm sure you will agree – Miss Abigail Wilson – that the financial arrangements are more than acceptable.' He leaned back in his chair. 'So there you are. Life seems quite full of good things doesn't it,' he said. 'And with the enormous success of the D-Day landings a couple of weeks ago, at last we've got the Huns on the run. Praise be to Almighty God! The month of June has been crowned with glory!'

They left the office, and standing outside for a second, Edna said, 'I expect you'd rather get the next train home rather than come to Coopers for a cup of tea?'

'I think so, Aunt,' Abigail said, 'because I don't want to be too late arriving in Bristol.' Abigail put her hands on her aunt's shoulders and kissed her very briefly on the cheek. 'You have my address now, Aunt,' she said, 'so will you promise to let me know where you are and how you are getting on? Because I am going to be very, very interested in knowing where you are and how your plans work out.'

For the first time in her life, Edna returned her niece's kiss. 'I promise, Abigail,' she said. 'We mustn't lose touch a second time.'

'Shall we look for Emily for you to say goodbye?' Abigail said, and Edna hesitated.

'No, there's not really time because I want to speak to Mr and Mrs Moor as soon as they get back from the market.' Edna smiled. 'They can't wait to move into Coopers.'

Finally, the two parted company and Abigail made her way over to the large area where all the stalls were. The Punch and Judy booth at the far side was just being set up, and she could see Emily already sitting cross-legged with lines of other children, all waiting for the performance to begin.

Seeing her mother approach, Emily stood up quickly. 'Oh – can I stay and watch this before we leave? Please, Mummy!' Then frowning, she asked, 'Where's Aunt Edna?'

'She had to go back to Coopers,' Abigail said. 'And of course, you can stay and watch. There's a bit of time before our train. But look, I'd like to go for a little walk, so I'll come back for you perhaps in half an hour? Don't move from here. Promise?'

'Promise,' Emily said. Well satisfied with this arrangement, Emily sat down again just as Mr Punch threw back his curtain. And with her heart full of contentment at the way life seemed to be turning out, Abigail began to walk slowly along the street, recapturing all the moments she'd gone this way before. Yes, there were huge gaps in her life and nothing could change that but, as Mrs Matthews had said more than once, what can't be helped, can't be helped and that's all there is to it.

The afternoon sun was warm on her face as Abigail strolled along, her gaze taking in all the familiar twists and turns of the country road. And then there it was. Mulberry Court. Perhaps the reason she was treading this path today although she hadn't meant to. And if Emily hadn't wanted to see the Punch and Judy show they'd have been on their way to the station by now.

Abigail didn't increase her step, she just walked slowly, thoughtfully, towards the beautiful building. The wide frontage was still hosted by those magnificent trees and the two stone pillars still supported the elegant gate. The posh family who'd owned it before the Jordans used to hold summer garden parties, and Abigail had often wondered what it must be like to be served tea on that immaculate lawn by uniformed maids.

Now she was here, and for a few moments time stood still. A long time ago this had been Luke's home and Abigail had never forgotten – how could she ever forget – the times she had spent there with him, just the two of them.

Her thoughts making her feel dizzy with longing, Abigail turned to walk away when suddenly she heard, 'Hello? Did you want something?'

The voice. *That* voice! It couldn't be anyone else, but, 'No – sorry, I was just stopping to look . . . to admire the roses.' Her voice trailed off because she was sounding silly.

'Wait. Don't go.'

Then suddenly, completing her dream, Luke Jordan opened the gate and slowly, carefully, came over to join her. He was looking down at her with an expression of such utter disbelief that any moment Abigail knew she was going to faint.

But Abigail had never fainted. 'Luke?' she whispered in disbelief. 'Luke?'

No, surely not, because this wasn't the Luke she'd held in her heart and in her memory for so long. He had grown into a tall, dark-haired man with an elegant turn of head, just like she had always imagined he would become, but he looked so much older than he was. Older and more tired, the rings beneath those black eyes making him appear drawn.

And worst of all, he was supporting himself on two crutches.

Coming forward awkwardly, he put one crutch under his arm then opened the gate for Abigail to come in. And without another word, they went together towards the wide bench outside the entrance door and sat down, Abigail afraid to get too close in case she hurt him in some way.

'Abigail.' He smiled crookedly. 'So, you have obviously been allowed out for the afternoon.'

She nodded. 'Oh yes, and for many other afternoons as well. I promised you I'd escape, didn't I, Luke?'

For a moment it didn't seem as if he was able to speak. 'And . . . has life been good to you, Abigail? I mean, are you happy?' He hesitated. 'Are you still living down there?'

'No. I haven't lived with my aunt for a long time.'

He leaned forward, obviously mystified. 'So, what happened?'

She waited before answering. 'It's a very long story, Luke – far too long to go into now. But, yes – life did change, dramatically. And I am happy, most of the time.'

He nodded. 'So where are you living now?'

'In Bristol,' Abigail replied. 'I've been there for the last five years.'

Now he was thoroughly taken aback. 'What? Do you mean you were there while the city was being *bombed*?'

'Yes. But as you can see, I came to no harm. And I have been blessed by having met good friends. Luke – do you remember you telling me that I would have friends one day? And you were right. I think my friends were sent straight from God.'

He looked away. 'Of course you would find friends, Abigail. Because you are the kind of friend others would want to be with.'

Abigail was suddenly tired of this. She'd often wondered what she and Luke would have to say to each other if they ever met again, and now it was all about her!

She touched his arm hesitantly. 'What have you done to yourself, Luke?' she said quietly, glancing at the crutches.

That half-smile again. 'I didn't actually do anything,' he said quietly, 'other than not spot the ME109 on my tail. I was too busy congratulating myself on having shot down two of their Junkers.'

At last, and without hesitation Abigail clutched his arm, realisation hitting her like a blow. 'You were in the RAF, Luke. Flying . . . flying aeroplanes in combat?'

'Yep,' he said casually. 'And although none of us had had much training I was actually getting better at it. In the beginning we were shown the rudiments plus a short time to practise, then it was, "Off you go, chaps".' He couldn't help smiling. 'Suddenly, we novices found ourselves in the middle of a war and although we were mostly terrified, the bond which immediately formed between us gave us strength – and a certain amount of youthful courage.'

Abigail knew all about the strength gained by having close comrades.

He waited a long moment and Abigail didn't interrupt. All she wanted to do was to put her arms right around him and hold him close.

'The very worst part of the whole thing was waiting for everyone to return after a mission,' he went on. 'Waiting to learn we'd lost another friend.'

There was a lump in Abigail's throat as she listened. She could understand his words, remembering those dog fights they'd all witnessed in the skies above Bristol. Had Luke been part of that?

'So – you were shot down?' she whispered, hating to hear herself say that. 'You . . . crashed?'

'Well, sort of,' he said. 'I jumped out because my plane was on fire. My parachute did open, and I floated to the ground but part of me, unfortunately, was in flames. At least I came down well into our side of the Channel, so I was picked up a few hours later. And spent the rest of my call-up in hospital,' he added.

Abigail felt overcome at hearing what Luke had gone through. So young, so brave – as all his friends had been – trying to protect those at home. She leaned against his shoulder, and he automatically rested his head on hers.

After a moment's silence Abigail asked, 'Are you here at Mulberry Court for respite?' Her voice was muffled.

'Yes, my parents eventually bought the place the year after the war started. They're still mostly in London but this is a wonderful bolthole for them from time to time. And just the place for me now, to have some peace to recover.' He moved in to her a little more closely. 'There's a housekeeper here to look after me and she is sure to remain, because Mulberry Court will always be our summer holiday home – and for long weekends.'

Abigail was suddenly desperate to know more about his injuries. 'So – how badly were you hurt, Luke?' she asked quietly. 'How long do they think it will take for you to make a full recovery?'

He looked grim. 'Oh, they never tell you anything exact. And to be fair, burn injuries always take a very long time.' He shifted his legs, making a face. 'But with a bit of luck I expect to be working in our Bristol office – perhaps by this time next year.' He glanced down at Abigail. 'I did go into Law – as I thought I might – and although my degree course was cut short when I was called up, I've managed to recover some of that time, and when I begin running the Bristol office of my father's firm I should be reasonably fit and, hopefully, reasonably competent,' he added.

Abigail could bear it no longer, because it was now or never. He was obviously not married – and neither was she! And they were here, together again! This was her moment!

She buried her face into his neck, and after several seconds, she asked softly, 'Do you remember us promising that we'd be true to each other for the rest of our lives, Luke? Well, I have never stopped loving you, never stopped thinking about you, never stopped wanting you. And if you still feel the same about me, if you do, Luke, please say you'll marry me. Please say you will.' She paused in the heat-filled seconds. 'We have both come through turmoil and I have so much to tell you – so could today be the happy ending I have dreamed about every night of my life?'

Not waiting for him to reply, and swallowing hard, Abigail went on quickly. 'The most terrible part was not knowing anything about you or where you were studying. I mean, by chance I found out that you'd all left Mulberry Court, but that was all. You seemed to have disappeared without a trace and . . .'

Now he pulled her in towards him. 'But I *wrote* to you, Abigail! A long, long letter, giving you the address of my London digs which I was going to be living in and promising to keep in regular touch.' For a moment he looked aghast. 'Are you saying that you didn't get that letter? Or did your aunt destroy it before you were even aware of it?' he said.

Abigail shook her head briefly. 'The postman seldom has any reason to visit Coopers,' she said, 'and difficult though my aunt can be, I don't think she would destroy anything addressed to me.'

'Well, I just don't understand it,' Luke said, 'and I can't imagine what you must have thought of me in not contacting you! Surely you knew I would never cut off our relationship like that, Abigail! After all we'd said to each other, promised each other . . . did you really think me that cold and uncaring?' He raised an eyebrow briefly. 'Though I did wonder why I never had a reply to that letter,' he added.

Gazing up at him as he spoke, Abigail felt a rush of love and longing run through her. Of course there'd had to be an explanation of his silence, and he'd just given it to her. With her arm around his waist, she leaned against him.

'It was all a long time ago, Luke, wasn't it?' she said softly. 'None of that matters anymore. All that matters is that we could be together again, for ever this time, and whatever happens in the future, I promise to take care of you for the rest of my days.'

Now the silence between them was so painful, Abigail thought she really was going to pass out. Her senses were swimming, distant sounds from the village were fading and she could feel her body sag against his.

'My dearest Abigail,' he said softly. 'I have kept my promise. I have never loved anyone else but you. Have never even thought I would.'

In the silence that followed she caught her breath, looking up.

'Darling Abigail,' he murmured. 'What man living would not wish to hear those words from a beautiful, kind and loving woman?' He held her away, looking into her eyes. 'But I'm sorry I cannot marry you,' he said quietly. 'This war has changed me and I am not the same person you once knew. So, although it tortures me to say it, I cannot marry you, that is how it is I'm afraid. How it has to be.'

Abigail was horrified. What did he mean? Why couldn't he marry her?

'Of course the war has changed you, Luke!' she said. 'It has changed us all! But we are not going to let that ruin the rest of our entire lives, are we? There is still so much to do, to achieve, to live for, and doing it together will make it all happen! Whatever lies ahead will be easy – if we're in it together!'

'No. Look at me, Abigail,' he said earnestly. 'I will never marry – and I cannot marry you – because I was so severely burned it's very unlikely that I would ever be able to give you what we both would want. Children. The chance to bring a child into the world, a child as lovely as you must be for someone else to do.'

With relief flooding her senses, Abigail stood up. 'Wait here,' she said. 'Don't move before I come back. I'll only be a few minutes.'

With winged feet and her heart on fire, Abigail raced down the path and he stared after her, frowning.

'What is it? Where are you going?'

But she was already through the gate and running along the road and around the corner, past the school towards the market.

At first glance, it looked as if the performance was over because children were now milling around the stalls again. Almost at once she could see Emily coming towards her, smiles all over her face.

'Emily – come with me,' Abigail said breathlessly, taking her daughter's hand. 'There's someone I want you to meet.'

Trotting obediently alongside her mother, Emily looked up. 'Why? Who is it, Mummy?'

'Tell you in a minute.'

Then they were walking back up the path of Mulberry Court towards the bench where Luke was still sitting. And seeing them, he stood up shakily, grasping one of his crutches and staring at Emily. After a long moment, he said huskily, 'Yours?'

Abigail smiled up at him and paused before answering.

'Ours,' she replied.

For what seemed like an eternity they just stood and gazed at each other until, like the sun coming out from behind a cloud, realisation crept over Luke's handsome features. And swiftly, he encircled Abigail's waist and pulled her in to him.

But Abigail turned and looked down at Emily. 'This is your daddy, Emily,' she said softly. 'We both knew he had to go away for a long time, didn't we? Well, he's here now. He's here with us again.'

Emily gazed up at Luke. '*My* daddy. My very own daddy?'

'Your very own daddy.'

Then with a beatific smile on her lips, Emily stepped forward and held out her hand.

'How do you do?' she said.

Epilogue

On Tuesday the 8th of May 1945, VE Day – Victory in Europe Day – was celebrated by the many millions who had been praying for it for six long years. It was a bank holiday, and everyone made the most of it, dancing and singing in the streets. Complete strangers hugging each other in relief and gratitude. Standing at the balcony of Buckingham Palace, the King and Queen and the two Princesses, together with the Prime Minister Winston Churchill stood and waved, returning time after time to respond to the demands of the thousands below. And everywhere in the country people remained glued to the wireless, drinking in all the sounds and excitement of victory.

Later, after the dropping of the first atomic bombs in early August, the war with Japan ended and finally, World War Two reached its terrible conclusion.

Number Six West Road, Knowle, Bristol
2nd April 1946

Dear Aunt Edna,
I am really hoping that you are still living at the last address you gave me. I haven't heard from you for a while.
I also hope that, wherever you are, Aunt, you will

be able to join us at All Saints Church, Knowle here in Bristol, where I am to marry Emily's father – Luke Jordan. Did you know anything of the Jordan family who lived at Mulberry Court in the village? Well, the wedding will be the week after Easter, on Saturday the 27th of April, and the day after, Sunday the 28th, Emily Grace is to be christened.

Please say that you are free to be with us that weekend, Aunt. I really would like you there because it will somehow mean Dada is there with me as well. And of course, I want you to meet Luke – and he has said that he is looking forward to meeting you, too.

As you can see, I am still at the same address, but after we are married Luke and Emily and I will be living at a house in St Stephen's Road – which is also in this area so I will still always be close to my best friends.

Please let me know soon, Aunt. And if you can be there I will arrange accommodation for you for that weekend.

With my love,

Abigail

On a fine morning on the 27th of April, Abigail in her white bridal gown, accompanied by Emily holding her hand and with her bridesmaids Carrie, Eileen and Janet walking behind, made her way slowly down the aisle of All Saints to reach Luke, who was waiting for her at the front. He was without his crutches.

Reverend Jonathan Waters greeted the bride and her little supporter with his usual generous smile, and at the appropriate moment in the ceremony announced himself as the one giving the bride to her groom.

In pride of place in the front pew on the left, Gladys Matthews, almost overwhelmed with happiness, sat next to Edna Wilson while the opposite front pew had been quite properly reserved for Luke's parents. They had never been as happy in their lives

– after having once thought their son had been killed in the war, now they had 'a beautiful daughter-in-law and the sweetest granddaughter anyone could wish for.'

Next morning, with the church almost full to witness the event, Emily Grace was christened, with her five godmothers Edna Wilson, Gladys Matthews, Eileen Matthews, Carrie Waters and Janet Robertson in close and loving attendance. Standing alongside in full military uniform were the two godfathers – Mark Anderson and Simon Hill.

After Jonathan Waters pronounced solemnly, 'Emily Grace – I baptise you in the name of the Father and of the Son and of the Holy Ghost,' the longed-for words which Abigail had thought she would never hear, Emily spoke up, to the amazed surprise of everyone present.

'Thank you. Thank you very much,' she said.

On the 26th October that same year, Carrie and Mark, and Eileen and Simon, were married in a double-wedding ceremony at All Saints, with Abigail as Matron of Honour and Emily as chief bridesmaid.

At all three nuptials that year, Joan Waters had been in charge of the catering, and despite the ever more stringent food rationing, the tables at each event had groaned with the wedding feasts.

Finally, after the double-wedding breakfast was over, Emily Grace started to help clear the tables in the church hall and she looked up at Mrs Matthews who'd just finished washing up another tray of wine glasses. 'I'm very *glad* that we were both given the piece of wedding cake with the most icing on it, aren't you, Mrs Gladys?' Emily said.

Eileen's mother smiled broadly. 'Very *glad* indeed, Emily,' she said.

As Joan Waters stored away the remaining piece of the one-tier cake, to be eaten she hoped at a future christening, she glanced fondly at those two and shook her head. The gracious lady and the bright little girl were chattering away non-stop. Joan could not imagine what those two always found to giggle so much about.

Acknowledgements

All details concerning the air raids and their effect on the city were taken from Bristol historian Reece Winstone's fascinating book *Bristol in the 1940's*. Should there be any minor discrepancies they are, of course, entirely mine.

Dear Reader,

We hope you enjoyed reading this book. If you did, we'd be so appreciative if you left a review. It really helps us and the author to bring more books like this to you.

Here at HQ Digital we are dedicated to publishing fiction that will keep you turning the pages into the early hours. Don't want to miss a thing? To find out more about our books, promotions, discover exclusive content and enter competitions you can keep in touch in the following ways:

JOIN OUR COMMUNITY:

Sign up to our new email newsletter: hyperurl.co/hqnewsletter

Read our new blog www.hqstories.co.uk

🐦 https://twitter.com/HQStories

📘 www.facebook.com/HQStories

BUDDING WRITER?

We're also looking for authors to join the HQ Digital family!
Find out more here:

https://www.hqstories.co.uk/want-to-write-for-us/

Thanks for reading, from the HQ Digital team

If you enjoyed The War Girls,
then why not try another fascinating
historical novel from HQ Digital?

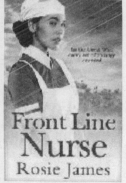

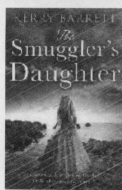